JACK SLATER
FALSE FLAG

A **JASON TRAPP** THRILLER

FALSE FLAG

JASON TRAPP - BOOK 2

JACK SLATER

1

L abor Camp 15
  Yoduk, North Korea
  January 12th, 1981

THE BODY SWUNG FROM A NOOSE, the slow creaking of the rope competing with the cawing of carrion birds. They had picked the flesh off his bones, starting the moment he was dead. They took his eyes first. Soft, defenseless. There was little left of them now except a bloody hole. A pit, where life used to be.

The little boy stared at the corpse with no visible emotion. He was used to death. At just seven years old he had seen more of it than most people would in their entire lives. He watched as a crow landed on the man's frozen shoulder and began pecking at his pitted cheeks. The bird tore off a lump of frozen flesh no bigger than a thumbnail.

The boy crouched. His belly was distended with hunger. Although he did not know it, at that very moment television commercials in America were collecting donations for the child victims of an Ethiopian famine. Those children looked very much like him. Except their hunger was an accident. His was man-made. The regime had condemned his family to death. And death would take every one of them. Not fast. But with agonizing slowness, with hunger clawing at their minds every day until the darkness embraced them.

But if the boy could just catch that crow he could eat for a week.

He would have to tear the flesh from its bones and swallow it raw. He didn't dare light a fire. The smoke would attract other prisoners—bigger, more violent men, and they would take everything he had. Even women would tear the food from his fingers without a second thought.

Camp 15 was no place for kindness. It was kill, or be killed. Eat when you got the chance, or starve to death.

The boy didn't know what the man's crime had been. Probably nothing. In Camp 15, life was cheap. It was the place where the North Korean regime sent its political prisoners. Not just those who dared to criticize the state, but two generations of their family as well. The Supreme Leader had decreed that every trace of disloyalty needed to be wiped from the face of the earth.

In the distance, a gunshot echoed around the mountainous hills that surrounded the concentration camp. It was a common sound. Perhaps an execution, but more likely a guard having fun. There was little to do up here in the mountains. No television. No radio. Just endless work for the prisoners, and cruelty to occupy those who guarded them.

The sound of the gunshot startled the crow, and it leapt into the air, beating its wings furiously until it was little more than a dark speck in the frozen sky. The boy let out a little whimper of defeat.

A tear leaped from his right eye. It froze almost instantly as it met the bitter chill of the North Korean winter. He leapt up and beat the air with frustration. For a few seconds, he had been able to forget the hunger gnawing at his belly. But now it was back, and the realization that there would be no food today redoubled the pain.

"Why am I here?" he whimpered. "What did I do?"

Guards competed with each other in this place to demonstrate their brutality. The boy was no stranger to their attentions. His body was marked with bruises that never healed, due to the lack of nutrition in his diet. His back was carved with thick, deep ridges—the result of a whipping when he was just four years old. His crime was stealing a crust of bread.

Now a new sound filled the mountain pass.

The boy's mind filtered out the usual cries of pain and despair and hopelessness, the daily rhythm of violence and hunger that filled the enormous camp. Even gunshots barely registered in his brain anymore.

But this was different. It was the sound of machinery. Trucks. Most likely, it heralded the arrival of new prisoners.

Fresh meat.

The boy took off running, moving as fast as his emaciated frame would allow. He darted through alleyways between the tightly packed wooden huts in which the prisoners lived. Shortcuts that no guards knew of, but the children of the camp did. They were places to hide, places to catch a moment's peace. Places to store stolen food and valuables.

The arrival of new prisoners meant that the boy had a brief opportunity. They would be cityfolk, most likely. The security forces tended to ignore ordinary peasants, thinking them little more than animals—no more capable of independent thought than a mule or an ox. But city people were different. They had wealth, of a kind. Not money, or gold, but something far, far more valuable in a place like Camp 15.

Food.

Perhaps real, white rice, of a kind that the boy could barely remember having eaten. He couldn't recall much about life before his imprisonment. After all, he was only seven, and he had lived in this place for years, fed on a thin gruel of grain porridge, day after day, year after year. The only protein in his diet was the occasional maggot, wood louse or cockroach.

And if not food, then maybe the new arrivals would have cigarettes, or something else that he could steal and barter. Like all the children who survived in this place, at just seven years old the boy was an accomplished pickpocket. He knew how to move without being noticed, not just between the wooden huts of the camp, but also within crowds.

He exited the row of huts he had been running through and slowed. He didn't dare be seen by a guard. They would ask him where he was going, why he wasn't working, and he didn't have a good answer. They would beat him. Again. And not just him, but his mother too. She was pregnant.

The whore.

The thought of his mother filled the little boy with rage. How could she be pregnant? They had too little food as it was. He hated her. Hated the little boy or girl growing inside her, too, for stealing what was rightfully his. He was the man of the family now that his father was dead. What right did she have to take food from his mouth?

No. The little boy resolved that whatever he managed to steal today, he would not share it.

It wasn't always like that, a thought at the back of his mind reminded him. *You shared. Your mother is only looking out for you.*

But then the red mist of anger descended on the boy's vision. It was his mother's fault he was in this place at all. She was the criminal, but *he* was the one getting punished.

Several trucks rolled to a halt ahead of him, a Jeep at the front of the small procession. They were painted in army green. Soldiers packed the first of the trucks, and terrified, frozen prisoners the last three.

"Get out!" a guard screamed.

His bayonet was fixed to his rifle. The boy knew what was about to happen. He had seen this story play out dozens of times over his short life.

The prisoners shuffled out of the truck, and the boy dropped to his knees, pretending to be searching the ground for insects. Lifting frozen stones and searching fruitlessly underneath. All the prisoners did this. It was the only way they had to survive. Even rats couldn't live long in a place like this.

The women could sell their bodies for food. It wasn't a choice, but the guards didn't want to screw dying women, so they fed the whores better than most. The little boy was condemned to die. So they didn't bother with him.

"Traitors, step out of the trucks and form lines!" a guard shouted, through an antiquated wooden megaphone. It was painted red, and daubed with patriotic slogans. As all eyes turned to the speaker the boy made his move, stealing between the new arrivals, fingers brushing against pockets and bags as he moved unseen.

"Boy," a cold voice said from above him. "What is your name?"

The little boy froze.

Surely the voice wasn't speaking to him? He had been so careful. The guards never saw him. But this man had. The boy knew it. And he knew it was over. There was no stealing in Camp 15. At least, not officially. Thieves lost their hands. Without their hands, they could not work. If they did not work, they didn't even receive the meager rations the other prisoners did. They were condemned to waste away.

So the little boy was dead already. He kept his gaze fixed on the ground.

"I asked your name," the cold voice repeated. "Answer me."

The boy looked up. The man's face looking down at him was hard and pitted from a case of childhood chickenpox. He was dressed in an olive green army uniform, his shoulders decorated with four parallel red lines, and two silver stars. The boy didn't know what that meant, but he knew the man was powerful. He was well fed. His shoulders were broad, his eyes a cold black.

"I am Kim Youp-Min, sir."

"You were stealing, Kim."

The boy, Kim, nodded. His head felt heavy, his limbs slow. He knew better than to lie to the army officer. A quick death would be better. Perhaps a bullet from the pistol at the man's hip. Or hanging, like the man swinging in the wind. Anything was better than the cell.

Kim had seen it. It was little more than a few feet high, with freezing water up to waist height. There was no food. Once they went in, a prisoner would stand until exhaustion overcame her, then topple into the water. The mind will not let its host drown without a fight. And so the prisoner stands again. And exhaustion overcomes her again. And she drowns. And she stands, and so it goes. It is a horrible way to die.

"Yes. I was hungry."

"You were good at it," the voice said, sounding almost impressed, Kim thought. "How long have you been in this place?"

Kim shrugged. He couldn't tear his eyes away from the darkness in the man's eyes. "I don't know. Most of my life."

"And you are still alive," the officer said. "You must be good at stealing."

Kim did not reply to that loaded question. He looked up at the officer with untrusting eyes. In his world, adults were to be feared, not loved. Yet in a way, his silence was a form of defiance.

"Do you have a family, Kim?"

The boy nodded. "A mother," he said.

"Do you love her?"

Kim shrugged. *Did he?*

Honestly, he did not know. Perhaps there had been a time when he did. Before the camp. Before the cruelty, and the hunger, and the whippings and the death. But Kim could barely remember the world outside the barbed-wire topped fences that surrounded Camp 15. Those memories he did have were so faint they might not even have been real.

The uniformed man smiled coldly, as if he understood more about Kim's response than perhaps the boy even did himself. He lowered himself, resting one knee on the hard-packed ground.

"Are you hungry, Kim?"

The young boy nodded warily.

He was always hungry. With his belly distended from lack of food, the hunger pains never left. They never dulled. The brain screamed an incessant warning that he was on a path toward an early grave. Not that the young boy understood the mechanics of his peril. There was no schooling in Camp 15, and even if there were, he was too young.

"What would you give not to be?" the man asked, fixing dark eyes on Kim's own. "I can make it so that you are never hungry again. So you're never cold again. Give you everything you have ever wanted."

The boy studied the nameless officer for a long time, the wind whistling in the background, carrying the sounds of trudging, wailing prisoners. He knew they would learn to be quiet soon enough. Even when inflicting their beatings, the guards didn't like their charges to make a sound.

But this man was different. His shoulders were broad, unlike even the best-fed of the sentries. His skin had a life to it unlike anyone in this camp. He clearly did not know hunger, or suffering. And that was something the boy had yearned for his entire life.

Was it a trap? Was this man going to kill him? And if that

was his plan — was it so bad? It would put an end to his hunger. To his pain.

He nodded. "Anything. I'll do anything."

The officer stood up and snapped his fingers at the nearest guard. "You," he spat with cold derision. "Bring the boy's mother to me."

The guard took off at a run, his worn boots slapping against the frozen ground. Kim watched him until he disappeared past the first row of wooden huts. Dozens of pairs of eyes were trained on him, though they pretended not to be.

Even the guards were curious.

This went against everything Kim knew. The best, the only, way to stay safe in this place was to remain unnoticed. To blend into the background. And yet now he had made himself the center of attention. All for a pack of stolen cigarettes, or a crust of bread.

Moments later the guard returned with a colleague, both dragging Kim's mother by her greasy, tangled hair. Strangely, Kim felt nothing for her. No worry. No fear. He had an opportunity to get out of this place—whether a quick death, or with this strange army officer.

And whatever the man asked, he would give it.

"Kneel," the officer ordered coldly.

Kim's mother did as she was told. Her eyes were dull in her gaunt face, yet a tear leaked from an exhausted eye. She had given everything for her child, and to simply survive, but what mother could live knowing that her offspring was in such peril?

The officer turned to Kim. He pulled a revolver from a holster on his waist, spun the cylinder and removed all but two of the bullets. He motioned at another soldier, who wore a similar uniform to his own. Kim didn't know the man's rank, but he knew that he, too, was well fed.

Strong.

"If you do something for me, boy, I will take you with me. You will have everything I promised."

"What do you want?" the boy whispered. He thought he knew. His stomach clenched, and for the first time in his young life, he didn't know whether it was from hunger or fear.

The officer ignored him. He extended his arm, aiming the weapon at the sad broken woman in front of him, broken by fear and hunger and pain. She wept silently, but knew better than to beg.

And he fired.

Two sounds split the mountainous landscape. The report of the weapon, and a scream. Kim's mother fell to the ground, blood spouting from her shoulder. It gushed, thick and dark, and soaked the frozen ground.

Kim froze.

His limbs were ice, and not just from the biting winter wind. His mother's wails cut through the sound of prison life like a knife. They tore at his ears, made him want to scream with frustration.

"Shut up!" he yelled. "Just shut up!"

His mother fell silent, shocked out of her pain by the venom in the little boy's voice. Next to him, the army officer smiled coldly. "Good," he said.

And then he handed the little boy the revolver, with one bullet left. The mother's eyes locked onto her son's. Tears streamed down her cheeks, carving rivulets through weeks of accumulated filth.

The officer gestured at Kim's mother coldly. "Now it's your turn," he said.

Kim knew that the offer was simple. If he pulled the trigger he would leave this awful place today. If not, he would die. Perhaps not today, or even tomorrow—but death was inevitable. The world beyond the barbed wire fences which surrounded Camp 15 was a mystery to him. But Kim knew it could not be worse than this.

The smartly dressed, well-fed army officer was offering him a way out.

Still, his finger trembled where it grazed the trigger. The weapon felt heavier than it had any right to—not simply because the boy was weak from lack of food, but due to the weight a decision of this magnitude would have on any grown man's soul, let alone a boy of seven. There would be no turning back.

"Do it," the officer growled, gesturing at one of his men for the soldier's pistol. He leveled the weapon at Kim's forehead. And then, with devastating slowness, he moved his aim to Kim's mother. "Or I will."

A single gunshot rolled across the mountainous terrain, and an emaciated body slumped against the ground.

2

J ason Trapp sat in a dark, empty booth of the bar at the Peninsula Hotel, swirling a glass of expensive scotch. Neat, just the way he liked it. The scotch was a Glenrothes 1985, and came in at almost seventy dollars for just two fingers of amber liquid. But it wasn't his money, and he needed to play the part.

He wouldn't lose any sleep over it.

Trapp was in Hong Kong, and he was there to kill a man. With any luck, things would go smoothly, and it would be the last time he would ever spill blood in the service of his country. But he was experienced enough an operator to know that things rarely went to plan.

Still, this target was personal. And once the man's name was crossed off Trapp's own personal list, it would close a very painful chapter in his life. So on this one, Jason decided, he could take a little bit of rough. Especially if the Agency was going to put him up in a place like this.

A woman appeared at the end of the booth. She was tall, with golden brown skin, and looked to have Japanese ancestry.

Her name was Eliza Ikeda, and she was his contact while he was in town.

"You're late," he said, finishing the dregs and motioning toward the bartender for another. "What are you drinking?"

"Had to lose a tail." The woman smiled. "Looks like you're enjoying your vacation."

Trapp grinned. She wasn't afraid to give it back to him. He liked that. He worked with too many operatives these days who were, put politely, factory settings. Dull. By the book. Everything Trapp wasn't.

But he sensed Ikeda was different.

"Wouldn't you?" he said, gesturing at the expensive wood-paneled bar. "In this place?"

"I take your point."

The bartender appeared promptly, and Ikeda ordered a gin and tonic, two cubes of ice and a twist of pink grapefruit. Not what Trapp would have chosen, but it was humid as all hell outside, and this was Hong Kong. The British had ruled here for a hundred years and more—and they had left their mark. Trapp ordered another Glenrothes and put both drinks on his tab.

"Mind telling me why I'm here?" she asked, eyebrow arched. "And what was so damn important I got pulled off all my cases to come meet a man in a bar?"

"I apologize for that," Trapp replied. "But I need some help, and I need it kept off the books. This is the kind of operation you were never involved with, understood?"

Ikeda nodded slowly. She glanced around the bar, making sure that no one could overhear the conversation. Trapp had scanned the place himself, and a device inside an expensive leather attaché case was jamming any listening devices in the immediate vicinity. He didn't think there would be any, but it paid to be certain.

"I figured that much," she replied, taking a sip of her drink.

Trapp withdrew a single sheet of paper from his briefcase and slid it across the polished mahogany table. Ikeda took it from him and glanced at it briefly.

"Do you recognize him?"

She shook her head. "Should I?"

"His name is Emmanuel Alstyne. Until five months ago, he was a silent partner in Atlas Defense Systems."

"What happened five months ago?" Ikeda quickly asked. And then the light of understanding blossomed in her eyes. "Oh."

"You know the drill, so I won't bore you with the 'if you tell anyone this, I'll have to kill you' routine. Mr. Alstyne was involved in an attempted coup against the United States. I've been tracking his whereabouts for months. I'm here to eliminate him. And I need your help to do it."

Ikeda nodded, a pained expression appearing on her face. Trapp knew that she would never breathe a word of what she learned in this meeting. He had read her file. She was a conscientious, intelligent agent who had aced every personnel evaluation since she joined the Agency seven years before. She was half-Japanese, half-American by birth—and she was a patriot.

"Then we have a problem," she said.

"What?"

"We can't do it in Hong Kong."

Trapp paused a beat before replying. He knew everything she was about to say but wanted to gauge her reaction regardless. It would tell him a lot about the kind of operative she was. Trapp liked to know who he was working alongside. So far, his impression of Ikeda was positive. She hadn't blinked at his revelation that he was here to kill Alstyne. Whether or not the idea offended her on the inside, she didn't let it show.

"Why not?"

"The Chinese *tolerate* our presence here. They let us, the Brits, the French, and a dozen other agencies operate without too much interference. But they do it on the basis of an under-standing that we won't kill anyone. It's win-win. They get to watch what we're doing"—she grinned—"when we don't ditch our tails, of course. And we get to operate with a freedom that we simply can't on the mainland."

"We could take him alive?"

"That's out, too. Unless you get my station chief authoriza-tion from the White House, we can't do much but watch your guy. If we blow things up in Hong Kong, we lose our foothold in this part of the world, and that's a non-starter. Our allies would raise hell."

Trapp knew that if he dialed the phone, President Nash would sign an executive order authorizing the elimination of Emmanuel Alstyne within minutes. The man been involved in a conspiracy to kill Nash himself—and take down American democracy with him. It wasn't just Trapp for whom this was personal. It was the president, too.

But he didn't reveal that particular piece of information.

"What about Macau?"

Ikeda looked up, her eyes glinting with interest. "Now that," she said, "is a different proposition entirely. Macau is the Wild West. As long as we don't get caught red-handed, anyone's fair game."

"Good," Trapp said. "Alstyne will be there in two days. He's booked into a suite at the Ritz-Carlton Hotel."

"Okay. What do you need from me?"

"A couple of spotters. Surveillance equipment. Weapons. But there's a catch."

Ikeda's eyebrow crinkled. "There always is. What is it this time?"

"Alstyne is carrying a flash drive." Trapp leaned across the table, resting his elbows and fixing Ikeda's eyes with a gaze of deadly seriousness. "The contents of that drive cannot be allowed to fall into Chinese hands."

"What have the Chinese got to do with it?"

Trapp grimaced. "You know I said there was a catch?"

Ikeda nodded.

"There's another one. The MSS are sitting on him. He's in Hong Kong to negotiate a deal with them. Information for protection."

The MSS was the Ministry for State Security—the Chinese equivalent of the Soviet KGB. They were a feared, secretive organization. Just in the past few years they had rolled up most of the CIA's human intelligence assets within China after penetrating a cyber dead drop system. The breach had set the Agency back in the region by years, perhaps decades—and had left dozens of good assets either dead or incarcerated.

Ikeda leaned back in her padded leather seat, gripped the gin and tonic tightly and drained it in one gulp. "State security," she groaned. "Great. You holding back anything else that might ruin my day?"

"The seventh floor wants this done quietly. We've got to make it look like an accident. And we need to switch the flash drive. I brought an exact replica."

Ikeda did not look convinced by Trapp's plan. Admittedly, he didn't have much of one. "You don't think they'll notice?"

Trapp grinned. "Of course they will. They'll suspect it was us—but they won't know for sure."

"Until they inspect the drive. Then the game's up."

"That's where you're wrong. The drive is encrypted. That's the only reason the Chinese are negotiating with our friend Emmanuel and not simply strong-arming him. They'll never break the encryption algorithm protecting it—at least, not without a hundred years of brute forcing it with their most powerful supercomputer. From what the boys down in the Directorate of Science and Technology tell me, if the activation sequence isn't managed correctly, the drive will wipe itself. So the Chinese can't go with the torture route, either. At least, not until it's their only option."

Ikeda smiled. "So that's why they're letting him go to Macau. Warming him up, getting on his good side."

Trapp nodded grimly. "You got it. I want to go in under my current cover as a businessman. Bump into him at the craps tables. Maybe invite him for a drink. He'll be dying for talk from back home. The next bit—" He shrugged. "I guess I'll have to figure that out later."

Ikeda rubbed her temples for a second, with her eyes closed. Then she looked up, meeting Trapp's inquisitive gaze. "You mind if I speak plainly?"

"Be my guest. I've got a thick skin."

"Good. Because honestly, I think you're out of your depth."

Damn, Trapp thought.

The girl had balls. That was for sure. Ikeda didn't have to have looked at his file—not that one existed outside of Langley's deepest sub-basement levels—to know that he was one of the CIA's prized assets. You didn't get the kind of carte blanche that Trapp had on this mission without being friendly with some very powerful people. And yet the CIA officer hadn't blinked before delivering her coolly worded insult.

Ikeda raised her finger before continuing. "Don't get me wrong. I'm sure you have a significant amount more expertise in the field than I do, in some much nastier places than Hong Kong. But you don't know Asia. And you sure as shit don't know State Security. Those guys don't mess around. They'll have your boy locked down tighter than an asshole in a prison shower. You won't get within 50 feet of him. Even with that nice new suit of yours."

Trapp couldn't help but notice the way Ikeda was looking at him. He was in good shape, and he knew it. The suit didn't hurt. It was Italian, made with Trapp's precise measurements by a high-end bespoke tailor in Milan. It had set the Agency back several thousand dollars—Trapp didn't have to have seen the receipt to know that for a fact.

The other detail that had not escaped Trapp's attention was quite how attractive Ikeda was. It wasn't her lithe, healthy frame or her exotic features. It was something less obvious from a passing glance, but significantly more alluring. Her confidence. The way she carried herself. Even her build, which was powerful yet still most assuredly feminine.

"I'm glad you noticed. So what do you suggest?"

"Let me go in."

Trapp shook his head. "I can't authorize that. You said it yourself, State Security won't mess around with this guy. He is quite literally holding the keys to the castle—designs for almost every American military project Atlas has worked on in years."

"Jesus," Ikeda breathed. "Isn't that—"

"All of them?" Trapp nodded. "More or less. The ones worth a damn, anyway. So now you know why I'm here. And why the Chinese will do anything to keep this guy alive. I can't let you go in. It has to be me."

"Bullshit," Ikeda said, fishing an ice cube from the bottom of her empty glass. Trapp beckoned for another couple of drinks.

"I'm the best option, and you know it," she continued, crunching on the ice. "So why don't you humor me for a second?"

Trapp admired Ikeda's fire. She knew what she wanted and she wasn't afraid to go after it. And she certainly wasn't afraid of putting herself in danger.

"Okay then, I'll bite," he replied. "What's your plan?"

"I'll go in alone. Dressed like an escort. Tell the muscle at the door that I'm *on the room*. It's not unusual for whales in Macau. Which I'm figuring your boy is."

"Three commas," Trapp agreed. "That we know of."

"I'm figuring you were thinking of going chemical? Something undetectable?"

Trapp nodded. "I brought something I've used before."

"Good. I'll tell him I want a drink. Slip a sedative into it. Then when he's passed out, I'll inject him, switch the drive, and walk out of there without anyone suspecting a thing."

Trapp leaned back, considering Ikeda's plan. He had to admit, it was a good one—certainly better than his wing and a prayer option. And Eliza was no naïve girl. She was a well-trained field CIA officer with years of experience under her belt, and clearly had a deep understanding of the melting pot region that was the Far East.

As he contemplated, the bartender arrived with the two drinks he'd ordered, set them out on napkins, and disappeared with their empties.

Trapp picked up his new glass of scotch. He raised it to Ikeda and clinked it against hers.

"Okay then. We do it your way."

3

Trapp lay on the thick, luxurious four-poster bed in his suite at the Peninsula Hotel, drinking in the delicious cool of the air-conditioning and attempting to get to grips with his jet lag. It was about four in the afternoon this far east, which meant it wasn't yet dawn back home. Outside the wall-to-ceiling glass windows the bright lights of the skyscrapers that bristled from Hong Kong Bay rose through a light fog, and the iridescent waters of the bay itself glimmered against the warm sun occasionally breaking through the clouds.

Trapp was, of course, accustomed to long-distance travel. It was one of the benefits—and drawbacks—of his line of work. The CIA, legally speaking, is not permitted to operate within the borders of the United States, so most of his career had been spent far from home. Of course, several months before, when VP Robert Jenkins had waged a war of terror against America and her president in an attempt to install himself into the Oval Office, Trapp had been forced to take up arms to save his country.

Although in truth, six months earlier he hadn't just been retired from the Agency—he'd technically been dead.

Trapp had only returned from the grave out of necessity, not any great desire to resume his career with the CIA. Even now he wasn't an employee of the federal government. He was operating in a gray zone—and a darker shade than ever before. He was a contractor, paid with black budget funds into an offshore bank account, working on a program that was authorized by President Nash himself—but if discovered, would be denied to the man's dying breath.

It was the way Trapp liked it.

And before very long the last of his debts to his murky past would be paid, and his time with the Agency would finally be over. He didn't know what he would do afterward. Maybe spend some time working in Joshua Price's bar back in Boston. Trapp was a partner in it now. A silent one out of necessity, for Price wouldn't accept his money any other way. But maybe he'd enjoy a second life front of house, after a first act that was shrouded in shadow.

The daydream was an alluring one, a pleasant distraction from the looming operation.

Hong Kong in August was a cauldron of heat, into the nineties in the shade and hotter in the sun. Spending just a few minutes on the streets outside, craning his neck up at the vast glass skyscrapers which dotted the skyline was enough to leave his T-shirt soaked with sweat. The humidity here was a killer. It was a heavy blanket that drained the strength from Trapp's exhausted mind and sapped the energy from his limbs.

He tipped his head back and sighed. All he wanted to do was climb in between the sheets, drift away, and not have to think about his mission for the next twelve hours.

But he knew he could not. Not just because if he succumbed to the clutches of sleep now, he might as well dash his body clock against the wall, but because he needed to feel out Eliza Ikeda.

He had read the basics in her file, but Ikeda was an NOC, so her jacket was thin to the point of pointlessness. In Agency parlance, NOC meant 'No Official Cover.' Just like Trapp himself, Ikeda was an illegal. She didn't have a diplomatic passport, or a job at the embassy. If she was caught in the act by the Chinese Ministry of State Security, she would be imprisoned or killed—and tortured for information either way.

That meant Ikeda was an enigma. And Jason Trapp didn't like working with operatives he couldn't trust.

His cell phone buzzed on the bed next to him. Trapp briefly considered ignoring it, but forced his eyes open to the silk canopy of the four-poster overhead and reached for the device. The number was blocked.

He brought the black rectangle to his ear. "Who is it?"

"Eliza," came the simple answer. "I'm outside."

"Why?"

"Did you bring swimming trunks?"

Trapp's face creased at the question. *What the hell is she talking about?*

"What do I need them for?"

"Come downstairs and I'll show you."

ELIZA IKEDA LEANED against her matte black Triumph Bonneville T120 motorcycle and watched as Trapp strode confidently out from the Peninsula Hotel. The hotel was by Kowloon Bay, so salt was heavy in the thick air, and the raucous cry of diving seagulls competed with the thundering of waves crashing against the shore.

Trapp was wearing dark jeans, black boots, Ray-Ban sunglasses and a thin, cream linen jacket over a white T-shirt.

Ikeda couldn't help but cast an interested eye over the man. A light stubble covered his cheeks, but the outfit had a little of James Dean about it, even if the muscular frame underneath made it plainly obvious he was no movie star. His bulk was effective, not for show.

She lifted her arm and waved Trapp over, studying him as he moved. He had a predator's grace which reminded Ikeda of the wraithlike quality his eyes had possessed the previous night. She filed away the note. That was why she was here, after all: to observe, and to learn exactly who she would be working with.

Eliza Ikeda had not survived as a CIA operative for as long as she had without being careful. Though the Hong Kong posting wasn't as overtly dangerous as the CIA's outposts in war-torn countries like Afghanistan or Iraq, the Far East had its own hazards.

Ikeda operated across the entire continent of Asia, using the cover of her successful trade consulting business, along with exquisite command of half a dozen languages, to slip through border security in countries from Cambodia to China.

Most of those countries paid little more than lip service to the concept of human rights—if they observed them at all. Jason Trapp owed nothing to Eliza, nor she to him—so while she intended to complete this mission to the best of her ability, she was equally interested in surviving the end of it.

"Nice ride," Trapp grunted as he came to a stop in front of Eliza.

He glanced appreciatively at the motorcycle, his eyes drinking in every last detail, from the matte black finish to the chrome exhaust pipe, which started at the rider's knee and caressed the engine as it fed its way to the rear.

"My pride and joy." Ikeda grinned. "Fancy a ride?"

Trapp shrugged. "Depends where you're taking me."

As his shoulders rolled, the white T-shirt pulled back just

an inch, revealing a thin white scar that circled the front of his tanned neck. Again she stored the detail for future examination but did not react to it, as Trapp quickly reached up and tucked it away.

"Here," she said, tossing a British racing green helmet at Trapp's chest. He caught it without flinching. "Wear your sunglasses, there's no visor."

Trapp rolled his eyes at her coy manner, pressed the helmet down on his head, and gestured at her to get on the bike. Before she did, she handed him a small canvas rucksack to carry.

Ikeda did as she was bid, climbing onto the motorcycle and pinning her long, leather-clad legs to either side of the bike. She clipped her own helmet, a matching matte black, to her chin and waited for Trapp to join her. He did so, latching his powerful arms loosely around her slender torso, his thighs pressed close against her own. At five foot ten, Eliza could normally stand toe to toe with most men without looking out of place. But Trapp had five inches and at least a hundred pounds on her. She fit into him like a hand into a glove.

Cool it, cowgirl, she thought.

"Hold on." She grinned, turning back to Trapp and squashing that particular thought from her mind.

The Triumph's powerful engine growled beneath the entwined operatives and belched a cloud of black smoke as Eliza kicked away the stand. The smell of motor oil and gasoline hung briefly in the humid air before Ikeda put the bike into gear and turned into traffic.

Red Toyota taxicabs flashed past on either side as the warm wind whipped at the strands of Ikeda's long black hair that had managed to escape the confines of the helmet, and she weaved through traffic with the supreme skill of a graduate of the CIA's training facility in Langley, Virginia, known as the Farm.

The destination Ikeda had in mind was only six miles away, though midweek, approaching rush hour in Hong Kong's notoriously crowded streets, even that short distance might take an hour. On the bike, it would be far quicker than that. Less than two minutes after picking Trapp up, the Triumph roared through the tunnel cut into the bedrock beneath Kowloon Bay, dark yellow lighting melding into a solid line overhead.

Shortly after that the lush green racing fields of Hong Kong Jockey Club filled Ikeda's vision to her left, and she sensed Trapp shifting his position in order to take a look. The air hung heavy, smelling of fish and salt and smog blown in from mainland China. And then they were in the hills, and the smoke was gone, her nostrils tickled instead by the fresh scent of thick vegetation. The bike climbed up the jagged road cut into the mountain and then roared down toward Deep Water Bay.

Ikeda slowed as she neared her destination, the Triumph's powerful engine growling beneath her in aggressive, throaty roars as gasoline exploded inside its cylinder. She tucked the bike into a narrow parking space next to an idling taxi and killed the engine. After the short, loud journey, Ikeda's ears were ringing, but she felt alive in the newfound silence.

"So where are we?" Trapp asked as he stepped off the bike.

He took the helmet off his head and ran his fingers through his dark hair. Ikeda wasn't certain how old he was—he looked mid-30s, though his eyes seemed older than that. Nevertheless, his hair was thick and healthy, accented well by the occasional gray.

"The real Hong Kong," she said with a smile. "Kowloon is Disneyland. I prefer it out here."

"Okay then," Trapp replied. "*Why* are we here?"

He removed his linen jacket and slung it jauntily over one shoulder, the canvas rucksack over the other. His gaze was piercing, Ikeda thought. It was as though he could read her every thought. She wondered what he saw when he looked at her.

"I want to find out what you're made of," she replied slowly. "Come on."

Ikeda led Trapp down to the shoreline, then angled left, hugging a thin, rocky path that hugged the bay to an isolated spot she had discovered several months before, stopping dead once she arrived.

Trapp threw her a quizzical yet still patient look, crinkling his eye as he spoke. "What now?"

"Now," Ikeda said, a smile tickling her high cheekbones, "we swim."

She grabbed the rucksack from Trapp, unzipped it, and tossed him a pair of trunks. "I guessed the size," she said. "But they should fit."

"Seriously," Trapp groaned, looking at the light blue floral trunks, decorated with yellow orchids. "This is all they had?"

Ikeda grinned back. "You've been to Asia before, right?"

Trapp nodded.

"And how many six foot three, two-hundred pound linebackers have you seen walking around? Those are all they had. And besides"—she winked—"I think they'll look good."

"Point taken." Trapp nodded, still looking grumpy.

Reaching again, she pulled out a full-body swimsuit, and two pairs of goggles, tossing him one, and began to shrug off her leather riding pants.

Trapp glanced around the rocky cove in search of somewhere to change.

"Oh, don't be a prude," Ikeda laughed. "Just don't look."

A minute or so later, Trapp was clad in a white T-shirt and the floral trunks. His jeans were folded neatly and stacked next to his boots. Ikeda stood opposite him, wearing only a dark blue swimsuit that revealed long, tanned legs—legs she was distinctly proud of.

"Take it off," she said. "Trust me. I only brought one towel, and the humidity at this time of year is nearly 100%. That T-shirt gets wet, it'll be dripping all night. And I'm taking you to dinner after we've worked up an appetite."

Trapp's eyes flashed at Ikeda as he stood opposite her, making her think of a jaguar prowling the Amazon rainforest. She sensed he felt uncomfortable and wondered why. He had an enviable frame—not an ounce of fat anywhere on his body.

So why the hesitation?

The moment only lasted a couple of seconds before Trapp shrugged off the white garment. He turned quickly, folding it and bending down to place it by his boots. Ikeda got a glance at his entire, unclothed upper body—and the sight stole her breath.

The CIA operative's back was marked with deep, thin wounds—long ago healed, but still red and ridged like mountain ranges seen from space. As he turned back, Ikeda saw the scar around his neck for the first time. It marked him like a hangman's noose.

What the hell happened to you, Jason?

Ikeda did not vocalize her question. She turned to face the lapping waters of Deep Water Bay, tied her hair in a quick ponytail, and looped the goggles over her head, hoping Trapp hadn't caught her staring. He clearly had a story—a long and painful one—but it wasn't her place to ask.

"Race you to the other side," she said without turning back, before diving gracefully into the water. Her olive skin briefly glowed gold in the setting afternoon sun, and then the waves claimed her.

Ikeda set a fast yet steady pace. The swim was just shy of a mile, as the crow flies, but she lengthened it by looping around the unimaginatively named Round Island. Her lithe arms propelled her through the water with the grace of a dolphin, working in a steady rhythm with her muscular legs. Every couple of minutes she stopped briefly to scan the waves for oncoming boat traffic, since they were near the Royal Hong

Kong Yacht Club, but it was a weekday and the few sailors out were easy enough to avoid. Trapp did not say a word, but kept pace alongside her.

Eliza lived for this. After her time with the Secret Service she might easily have become a competitive open water swimmer if the Agency hadn't recruited her. It wasn't just the familiar taste of the saltwater, or the feeling of freedom she got when cradled by the sea, or even the challenge of submitting herself to one of the world's last great dangers that drove her on —it was the competition. And it wasn't often she found a worthy opponent.

Jason Trapp certainly qualified.

Ikeda drove herself to race pace—a mile through choppy water in under seventeen minutes. By the time the other side of Deep Water Bay came into view, her lungs were screaming for oxygen. But Trapp stuck to her side like a limpet.

With a hundred yards to go, he began to pull away. Ikeda pushed herself on desperately, unwilling to lose to this newcomer from Langley. But as they dragged their exhausted bodies onto the opposite shore, she had to admit defeat.

"You're quick," she panted. "Ever compete?"

Trapp spat a mouthful of salt water into the ocean and leaned against the rock, smooth from millions of years of the sea's relentless assault. He shook his head and grinned. "I just don't like losing."

"Me neither." Ikeda grimaced. "But we're not done yet. Last one to the bike buys dinner."

IN THE END, Trapp bought. Ikeda wondered whether he had let her win but decided against it. He said he didn't like to lose, and Jason Trapp did not strike her as the kind of man who lied.

They were in a relaxed beach bar looking out into Deep

Water Bay as the sun set and darkness settled across the hilly area of Hong Kong. The bar was mostly empty, since it was a Wednesday night, and they had chosen a quiet corner on the wooden decking that lay closest to the water. Strands of acoustic guitar music floated out into the night's blackness from the speakers overhead.

Lights twinkled from the hillsides. It was a wealthy area, and though much of it was too inhospitable to build upon, in spots expensive glass-fronted apartments looked out onto the ocean.

"I guess *you* do," Trapp said.

"Do what?"

"Compete," he replied. "You're good."

Ikeda took the compliment without reacting, and although she couldn't put her finger on precisely why, it pleased her. She knew it was the truth. She was a damn fine swimmer. Then again, besides her work for the Agency and the occasional consulting gig she took to maintain her cover, it was pretty much all she did.

"I've lived around the ocean all my life," she replied. "Japan, then Hawaii, Los Angeles and now here. I'm working my way through the Ocean's Seven, though not as fast as I would like."

Trapp's eyebrow kinked. "Ocean's Seven?"

Ikeda grinned. "Sorry—I forget not everyone's as geeky about it as me. They are the seven hardest open water swims. Everything from the English Channel, which has been done more than a thousand times, to the North Channel in New Zealand, which is still waiting for its ninth."

Trapp grinned. "So what you're saying is today was a cakewalk?"

Ikeda raised an ice-cold bottle of beer to her lips. One was fine, she figured, since they wouldn't be heading back into town for a couple of hours. "More or less," she said. "I wanted to see how you'd handle it."

"Did I pass?"

"So far."

It was the truth. Trapp had impressed Ikeda. At the age of thirty-three, she'd spent five years in the Secret Service running down counterfeiting cases, mostly in the Los Angeles area, before being recruited into the CIA in whose clutches she'd spent the last five. In that time, she'd worked with a lot of good operatives—but also some bad ones.

Since 9/11, the Agency had recruited from a very specific pool: US special forces.

And while many of those men, because they were usually men, were undoubtedly the best at what they did, for them every problem was a nail—and they were the hammer. There were exceptions, of course, like Ikeda herself—and, it seemed, Jason Trapp.

She wasn't sure what it was about him that she liked so much. He had a dry, laconic style—a man who chose his words carefully, but had a good sense of humor nevertheless. It wasn't even that he was one of the few men she'd met who could keep pace with her in the water. He just seemed...

Reliable.

Ikeda got the sense that if she found herself in danger in the upcoming mission, Trapp would put his body on the line to spring her from it. Perhaps she did not need to be quite so worried after all.

4

Two weeks earlier

COLONEL KIM YOUP-MIN sat in a black Mercedes Sprinter van about two miles from the State Research Center of Virology and Biotechnology in Koltsovo Siberia, otherwise known as the Vector Institute. He was a short man, standing at little more than five foot six inches tall, with a gaunt face and deep, sunken eyes. His hunted appearance and limited height were the result of years of malnutrition in early childhood. Stunting at that age is irreversible.

Kim had once hated looking at himself in the mirror. But he had come to first tolerate and then appreciate his unique appearance, seeing a strength in the way it inspired fear in those around him.

The colonel was on the ground in Siberia because this mission was too important to delegate to his men. The events of the past few months had presented an unmissable opportunity for his organization, but also significant challenges—his timeline had been moved up.

The turmoil in America following Bloody Monday had led to sweeping changes in the military and intelligence communities. President Nash had decreed that America would never be found vulnerable again. He had dedicated unprecedented amounts of money and resources to protecting the homeland. Appointed new directors and streamlined decision-making processes. After years of decline,

But over the previous few months there had been a window of opportunity, and Kim had seized it. The Americans had taken their eye off the ball. Several targets had come into play —one of which Kim was now about to acquire. The man he was in Siberia to meet was on that short list. And although Boris didn't know it yet, the chubby scientist was essential to Kim's plan.

Kim's encrypted radio crackled. "Colonel, Savrasov has made contact."

"Copy. Keep me updated. If he deviates from the route we gave him, take him immediately. No harm must come to him, understood? Even if it costs the lives of you or your men."

"Yes sir."

Kim set his radio on the dash of the Sprinter van. It was a Japanese unit—a fact that caused the colonel a significant amount of distaste. He hated the Japanese almost as much as he hated the Americans. But the truth was that his own country did not produce technology of this quality, not any more. North Korea had been humbled by the hated Americans and their South Korean lapdogs. That was what he was here to change.

Boris Savrasov was a senior research scientist at the Vector Institute. Now well into his fifties with a growing bald patch and a potbelly that protruded from his belt, he had first been assigned to the Siberian bioweapons facility shortly after grad-

uating Moscow University in 1987. It was a bad time to become a
Soviet research scientist.

For the five decades that preceded the fall of the Berlin wall,
the job was a prestigious one. It came with a car, a larger than
average government-provided apartment, and a good pension.
But just as Savrasov embarked on his career at Vector, the
Soviet Union was buckling under the pressures of Ronald
Reagan's arms race. Before he reached his thirties, the Soviet
empire was gone, and a humbled, bankrupt Russia shuffled
into her place on the world stage. In the years that followed,
salaries were paid late or never at all. To make ends meet,
Savrasov and his colleagues freelanced on the side—selling
their expertise, or equipment from the facility itself. Some of
the women even sold their bodies to the army regiment that
guarded the isolated research facility deep in the midst of the
thick, dark Siberian forest.

Those were hard days for Boris Savrasov. He came home to
a wife who despised him. Their life together was nothing like
he had promised. Their daughter went to school hungry, in
ragged clothes, and came home to a dark and freezing
apartment.

Kim had done his research. He knew the utility bills had
remained unpaid. He'd seen the divorce papers. He knew he
had his man.

The radio crackled. "Target acquired, Colonel."

"Bring him to me."

In a matter of minutes, Boris Savrasov climbed into the
back of Kim's van, followed by one of the colonel's men. The
scientist was clutching a metallic briefcase, a little thicker than
his ordinary model. He had been carrying a replica for months
in preparation for this day. Security was accustomed to it. They
hadn't blinked an eye as Savrasov stepped out of the Vector
research center and into the cold of the Siberian winter.

The sliding doors slammed shut, momentarily leaving the

two men in darkness before the lights blinked back on in the rear compartment. Kim stared at the plump scientist with cold disdain. Boris might be essential to his plan, but that didn't mean that Kim liked dealing with men who would sell out their country for money.

"Mr. Savrasov," he said. "I trust everything went to plan?"

The scientist nodded quickly, anxiously, his cheeks wobbling as his head bobbed up and down. He glanced backward nervously, looking at Kim's man, who was holding a Type 66 pistol, a North Korean copy of the Russian Makarov. The weapon wasn't pointed at Savrasov, but the message was clear.

"Is that completely necessary?" he asked. "I brought what you wanted."

Kim understood the man's Russian. The language had still been taught in North Korean military academies when he was a young man, since at that time the USSR still provided significant amounts of weapons, cash and oil to its communist brethren. After the fall of the Berlin wall, all that had changed.

The language was falling out of favor now. But Kim found it useful. Many of the world's foremost mercenaries and criminals hailed from the former Eastern Bloc. And the North Korean colonel did plenty of business with men of their ilk.

"How much did you manage to smuggle out?"

Savrasov looked back at Kim, the fear in his eyes blending with the condescension so beloved by intelligent men. "Enough to kill the world a hundred times over."

"How much?" Kim repeated, his tone hard, black eyes glinting.

"50 milliliters of culture," Savrasov replied, his voice harsh with that irritation so peculiar to experts in their own field when faced with a layperson. "But it doesn't matter. A single drop is enough. That's the beauty of a bioweapon. It grows itself. Replicates dozens of times a day."

Kim nodded, satisfied. "Good."

Savrasov clutched the metal briefcase. It was a futile gesture. If Kim wanted to take the case from him, he would. This deep into the forest, no one would hear a gunshot. They could bury his body, cover it with a thin layer of snow, and no one would find it for months. Perhaps years. Maybe ever.

"And my money?"

The superiority in Savrasov's eyes disappeared now, replaced by a gnawing hunger. The briefcase in his arms was his meal ticket. The million dollars that Kim had transferred into a numbered Cayman Island bank account was only a token of good faith. In this part of Russia, it was enough to live like a king for the rest of the scientist's natural life. But as Kim knew, Savrasov was done with Russia. He wanted beaches, exotic foreign women and expensive imported liquor.

The colonel withdrew a small, ruggedized laptop from a case by his feet. He powered it on and navigated to the webpage of a small private bank based in Geneva. The account held four million dollars in untraceable cash. In a country like North Korea, it was an unimaginable amount of money. And yet it was Kim's. To do with as he pleased.

"My friend, I am afraid I am going to have to change the terms of our deal," he said softly.

Boris's eyes widened. First came shock, then rage. He was being cheated! And then the fear returned. Kim watched as the man's chest, briefly puffed with anger, shrank, as his shoulders hunched over.

"You promised..." he whimpered. "I did exactly as you asked."

Kim spread his arms wide. A cold smile flickered on his gaunt face. He could taste the man's fear. It was like an elixir to him. Sweeter than the most expensive liquor.

"And I will give you everything you deserve, Mr. Savrasov. In fact"—he spun the laptop around and showed the scientist the open webpage—"let me demonstrate how serious I am."

Kim tapped the return key on his laptop keyboard, and the transaction initiated. He studied the scientist's pasty, sweating face as the man's eyes tracked the screen, line by line. Saw the flash of recognition in Savrasov's eyes as he noticed his own bank account. Then joy and naked greed at once when he registered the amount.

"But that was the deal?" he said, looking up uncomprehendingly. "Five million dollars, in return for the modified virus. I don't understand."

"I will double it, Boris." Kim smiled.

He molded his face into as pleasant an expression as he could manage. He needed the man's fear—he knew there was no more potent motivator—but he needed to appeal to his greed as well.

"Double it?" the scientist stammered.

Kim nodded. "Another five million. A fresh identity, and a brand-new face. Everything you need to disappear in luxury for the rest of your life. But I need you to come with me. I only need you for a couple of weeks. Maybe a month. After that, the money is yours, and you will never see me again."

"Where?"

Kim smiled, shutting the laptop lid. He had his man. And his plan was falling into place.

"Home."

5

P*resent day*

PRESIDENT CHARLES NASH fingered the thin brown manila envelope as he gazed out onto the South Lawn of the White House. He was dressed casually, in a faded plaid shirt he'd had ever since his college days, and a pair of gray jogging pants. It was an outfit his wife had hated. Perhaps that's why he wore it now.

Nash knew exactly what was inside the envelope—and yet he could not bring himself to open it. It had arrived a week ago, and it had sat on the mahogany coffee table in the White House Residence all that time. He absently wondered why the cleaning staff hadn't at least put it to one side. At least there, it would be out of sight, and out of mind.

It was as though they knew what was inside it. Just a short document—the negotiations were amicable enough. Both parties were hurting, but only one wanted to carry on fighting.

Me.

The White House butler, Rupert Everett, knocked discreetly and entered the living room. "Sir, you have a visitor."

Nash knew exactly who the mysterious visitor was, and why he was receiving him in the residence rather than the Oval Office. He coughed quietly, pushing the darker thoughts out of his mind. "Send him in, Everett."

Mike Mitchell was the director of the Central Intelligence Agency's Special Activities Center. The SAC is what most people think of when they picture the CIA. In reality, most of the Agency's work is carried out through intelligence gathering and analysis. Though the Agency has thousands of analysts and officers, most of their day-to-day work does not involve kicking down doors and assassinating either cartel kingpins or weapons smugglers.

The Special Activities Center, by contrast, does exactly that.

It grew out of the famed World War II clandestine unit known as Office of Strategic Services, and cut its teeth in Korea in the 1950s. Since 9/11, the threats to America's national security had only come thicker and faster—and the SAC was at the heart of keeping the country safe.

"Mr. President," Mitchell said. "It's good to see you."

Nash turned, set the envelope back down on the coffee table with no small sense of relief at the distraction from his own problems, and shook Mitchell's hand. He gestured at the sofa. "Sit. Can Rupert get you anything to drink?"

Mitchell shook his head, and Nash dismissed the butler.

Nash settled back into the opposite sofa, a pale baby blue piece of furniture that was exquisitely comfortable. He took a second to clear his thoughts. Ordinarily, the First Lady would have picked out the furniture. But not in his marriage. In fact, she had never even visited the place, and in all likelihood never would. The White House Residence felt comically large for one man. Five luxuriously appointed bedrooms, three reception rooms, and only a single inhabitant.

"Mike, thanks for coming," Nash finally said, aware of a growing tension in the silence. "You get over here okay?"

Mitchell nodded. "Came through the tunnel from Treasury," he said. "And drove over in a car without government plates."

Nash nodded, pleased. It was no doubt a bit of a dog-and-pony routine—there was no reason to think anyone was tailing the director, but the two men knew a secret that under a dozen individuals in the entire government were privy to: that just six months before, the vice president, Robert Jenkins, had launched a coup that had very nearly succeeded. It would have, in fact, without the actions of one man: Jason Trapp.

The chaotic events had ended with Trapp eliminating the vice president after the man signed a confession that now resided in the president's own private safe. It was a secret that— if it got out—would not just bring down his administration, but perhaps the very concept of American democracy itself.

Charles Nash had authorized the execution of his own vice president.

It had been necessary—and yet at the same time it was the act of a dictator. Nash grimaced at the thought. There was a reason Mitchell was here alone—a reason that even the director of the Central Intelligence Agency wasn't read in on this operation.

They were tying up loose ends.

"Good," Nash replied. "Where are we on Hong Kong?"

Mitchell unclipped a thin black attaché case and slid a glossy photo over to the president. "This is Emmanuel Alstyne," he said. "Fifty-three years old, worth about eight hundred million dollars, according to his IRS filings."

Nash raised an eyebrow. "What's he really worth?"

"Just shy of four billion dollars, as far as we can make out. We got his name from the vice president—"

Mitchell caught himself just in time, as the president's eyes flashed black with anger. This was far from the first meeting the two men had shared together over the past six months. Nash had made himself very clear: Robert Jenkins was not to be referred to by his former title. He was a traitor who had caused the deaths of thousands of innocent Americans — and he didn't deserve the respect of the office he had betrayed.

"Apologies, Mr. President," Mitchell said. "Jenkins gave us his name when he confessed. As you know, he was the head of the snake—he controlled everything. But we've been hunting various minor players in his conspiracy for the last six months. Emmanuel Alstyne is the last one left. He financed the whole thing. On Bloody Monday, he had short positions against half the NASDAQ, and made almost a billion dollars in just twenty-four hours. I guess he was relying on a future Jenkins SEC not to investigate too hard."

Nash had read his briefing book. "You're sure he's the last one?"

Mitchell nodded. "Positive."

Nash paused, running his fingers through his hair as he thought. He didn't enjoy these meetings with Mitchell. Not because he disliked the man—Mike Mitchell was the very definition of an American hero. He worked from the shadows and would never receive public recognition for his vital role in keeping America safe. No, Nash was uncomfortable with the untrammeled power placed in his hands.

The power of life and death.

But for this individual, Nash knew, there could be only one fate. He hadn't just known about Jenkins' conspiracy—he'd profited from it. The very thought turned the president's stomach. "And you're watching him?"

Mitchell nodded. "That's correct, sir."

"This file Alstyne took with him when he fled. What's on it?"

Mitchell grimaced.

Nash wished he could thank the man. He looked tired, his ordinarily close-cropped brown hair now lank, as if he hadn't had the time to get it cut. His face was creased with exhaustion, and he had the kind of impenetrable 5 o'clock shadow that only comes out during periods of stress. Nash knew that Mitchell would have shaved before meeting him—it was the kind of man he was. But it didn't matter.

"Everything, sir," Mitchell replied. "It's a gold mine. Alstyne was a major shareholder in Atlas Defense Systems, and he was on the board. We believe he downloaded blueprints for every hardware and software program Atlas was working on before he fled to China."

"And now Chinese state security is sitting on him," Nash growled. "He's trying to cut a deal."

"Precisely, Mr. President. We believe he intends to trade the contents of that file to the Chinese state in exchange for their protection."

"That can't be allowed to happen."

"No, sir," Mitchell said. "If the Chinese get that information, it'll be like Aldrich Ames on speed. They'll get the blueprints for the F-22, the F-35, our next generation drones, aircraft carriers and battle tanks. They'll learn how to hack our satellites. It will herald a generational shift in their capabilities."

Nash fixed Mitchell with a glowering stare. "The Chinese must suspect we'll try and take him out. They would do the same."

"We don't believe they know precisely what Alstyne has. We think he'll try and trade the information over a number of years in order to ensure his security."

"So we have time?"

Mitchell shook his head. "Not much. Dr. Greaves managed

to penetrate the Chinese Ministry of State Security several days ago. They are planning on offering him permanent asylum in three days' time, after he returns from a short trip to Macau. We have to assume that's in return for something big."

"Then you can't let him return to China. What's your plan?"

Mitchell grinned. "Simple, sir. Jason Trapp."

6

Trapp performed some light background research on Macau on the privately arranged boat over from Hong Kong. The Chinese territory was classed as a Special Administrative Region, just like Hong Kong, and had been ruled by the Portuguese for a hundred and fifty years until it was handed back to Chinese rule just before the turn of the millennium.

As Trapp stepped off the chartered boat, he chewed the air instead of breathing it. It was heavy, and crackled with the electricity of an oncoming thunderstorm. He had just barely avoided being drenched several times over the past few days in Hong Kong and figured his luck might be running out. Already, his once neatly pressed white shirt was beginning to crinkle under the humidity.

He opened a secure messaging app on his phone and typed a short message:

Have arrived. Will meet you as planned.

Trapp had some time to kill. According to his credit card statements, which had been obtained by the NSA and passed to analysts back at Langley, Emmanuel Alstyne was booked onto a private helicopter transfer from Hong Kong later that evening. Only the best for a man who had done more than any other to attempt to destroy American democracy.

The thought sickened Trapp. His fist clenched around the handle of a small carry-on luggage case, knuckles white with tension. He consciously forced himself to relax as a tumult of emotion raged through his mind, reflecting the dark, roiling clouds forming overhead.

Alstyne was the last remaining player in the conspiracy that had almost launched a successful coup in America. He was the last man living who had played any role in the death of Ryan Price—Trapp's partner, and the best friend he had ever had. Theirs had been a deep bond, even by the standards of the special operations community, which tended to foster incredibly close working relationships. Not surprising, when men shared foxholes in the most dangerous hotspots and war zones the world has to offer.

But the connection Trapp had shared with Price was different. When Trapp first joined the US military, he was on a one-way ticket to the grave, and he didn't much care how he got there. The bottle, a pill, or a bullet were all much the same to him then. The only question was which one would get him first.

The term 'broken home' didn't come close to describing the horrors of Trapp's childhood. The thin scar around his neck, once red but now faded white with the passage of time, was far from the only physical manifestation of the beatings which had been inflicted by those who were supposed to protect and care for him.

Though he was pushed toward the army by a friendly judge who didn't want to see a young boy's life unfairly squandered in prison, it was Trapp's meeting with Price that had truly saved his life. The two men served together for years. Saved each other's lives. Went through special forces selection together and were even recruited by the Agency just two years apart.

And then that solitary human connection was snatched away from Trapp in the course of just one night, on a mission that never mattered, for ends that he would never fully understand. Price's death had almost returned Trapp back to that vicious spiral, until just months before the events of Bloody Monday offered him a chance at redemption.

No, not redemption. *Revenge.*

That was the thought that had driven Jason Trapp to this very moment. He was so close now. He could not fail. And so he pushed the memories deep within. He could deal with them later, but now he needed to focus.

Trapp's phone buzzed with a reply, startling him back to the present:

Understood. Surveillance assets in place.

The car from the Ritz Carlton was waiting for him once he had cleared passport control. Since Trapp's boat had traveled directly from Hong Kong to Macau—both Chinese-controlled territories—his false identity was given only a cursory examination. He was just another American businessman spending the weekend gambling. His expensive suit made him invisible in a place like this. Every year, Macau took in five times as much gambling revenue as Las Vegas. The place made Sin City look like a sleepy Florida retirement village.

Not long later, Trapp arrived at plush five-star hotel. His suite was booked on the floor above Alstyne's, and had an adjoining door to the suite containing Ikeda's surveillance team. He didn't accept the bellhop's offer of assistance with his meager luggage, but tipped the man anyway, in case he needed him later.

The hallway leading to his suite was carpeted in a rich cream material, patterned with startling blue floral spirals. The sight of such luxury almost tempted one of Trapp's thick eyebrows into rising, and he wasn't a man who took much interest in interior design.

Ikeda was waiting inside the suite when he stepped through the door. He raised his eyebrow at her presence.

"Don't remember telling reception to give you a key."

She grinned. "I didn't ask."

"So what are we looking at?" Trapp said, setting his case against the wall and working the knots out of his neck and back. Traveling was never comfortable—even when it was just a short hop in a million-dollar pleasure yacht.

"State Security's advance team is already here. Two men. Looks like they're trying to keep this one under the radar."

"What's your setup?"

"I've got three guys. Two shooters and an ops specialist next door running comms. Bringing any more people in on this might raise some eyebrows."

"No, your way is better," Trapp agreed. "Have you got eyes on Alstyne's room?"

Ikeda nodded. Her jet-black hair shimmered in the hotel suite's calm mood lighting, and Trapp was reminded—not for the first time—of quite how attractive she was. Pretty, but in a deadly way—and no doubt pretty deadly, too.

He wondered whether he could handle a woman like that, and concluded he'd like to give it a shot. He thought back to their race through the warm waters of Deep Water Bay, and the graceful sight of Ikeda's athletic body cutting through the saltwater.

"Couldn't get a camera feed from inside his suite. Too much risk of his guards doing a sweep. But we are hooked into the hotel's security system, and I've got one of our own devices in the hallway as backup."

"Good," Trapp said.

He had to hand it to Ikeda. She was a damn good operative. Every base seemed to be covered. But then, as Trapp's favorite saying went, everyone has a plan until they get punched in the mouth. And Trapp never felt confident before a mission. In a perverse way, he almost enjoyed the nerves that gripped his stomach in the hours before battle. They reminded him that he was alive—and that his life was a precious thing.

"Are you ready?" he asked, studying her Asian features for any hint of nerves. He wondered if he was doing the right thing. It wasn't too late to rethink the plan. He could still do this himself.

Ikeda stood to leave and walked toward the door. She shrugged and shot Trapp a cheeky wink as she did turned the handle. "I guess you'll have to wait and see..."

7

The electronic lock to his suite snicked, and within an instant, Trapp had sprung to his feet and leveled his Beretta 9 mm at the entrance way.

Eliza Ikeda stepped through and kinked her eyebrow, turning slightly to close the door behind her. "You sure know how to greet a girl..."

Trapp relaxed, lowering his weapon and shoving it between his waistband and his back. He studied the female operative for a few seconds, his brain almost unable to process the change in her appearance.

The Eliza Ikeda standing in front of him now wasn't just attractive. She was *stunning*.

"Cat got your tongue?" she asked.

A glimmer of amusement in her eye told Trapp that she knew exactly what effect her appearance was having on him. He ground his teeth together with irritation. He wasn't exactly playing it cool. And what was worse was that Ikeda clearly knew exactly what was running through his mind.

Jesus, Trapp. Pull it together.

"I'm sorry," he said. "About the nearly shooting you thing. Old habit. I'm working on it."

"I'm glad." She grinned. "Blue on blue is a one-way ticket to endless paperwork. So—how do I look?"

She twirled, and Trapp's eyes nearly broke free of his skull. She was dressed in a black cocktail dress made of shimmering silk, which broke several inches short of her knees. The material wasn't tight around her body, but it didn't need to be. The way it hung complimented her figure, the expensive material dancing and glittering in the light when she so much as breathed.

The material wasn't cut low at her chest, but rather fell in two waves that crossed at her breast, hiding all but the barest hint of a restrained yet lacy silk bra, yet revealing enough that the effect was obviously intentional.

She didn't look like an escort, less still the coarser description of 'hooker.' Her hair had been washed and conditioned and shone. Ikeda looked more red carpet than red light. A slim leather purse completed the look, adding a layer of elegance to the overall ensemble.

Trapp whistled quietly. He figured she knew how good she looked—and knew how he felt about it. There was no point trying to hide it. "You're wasted in the Agency, you know that?"

"How's that?"

"You'd make millions on the catwalk," he said simply. He wanted to add more, perhaps embellishing with a description of her long legs or her perfectly toned body. But he knew better than to take this beyond flirting. Soon enough he would be done with the CIA—and no matter how appealing, Eliza Ikeda was the kind of complication he definitely did not need in his life.

Ikeda grimaced and faked a retch as she walked toward him and tossed her purse onto the bed. "Gross. Believe me, I'm not a green salad and straight vodka kind of gal."

"I don't doubt it. Run me through the plan one last time," Trapp said, quickly refocusing his mind.

He trusted Ikeda. She seemed not just competent, but driven, and Trapp had worked with enough operatives through his long career to be able to identify the good ones by smell, let alone sight. But he also knew that they were on enemy soil, and that surviving this operation would require meticulous attention to detail.

"State security has two men watching the door at all times, and three in the suite next to Alstyne's," Ikeda replied with a challenging stare. "The whole floor is closed off, and only the Chinese and Alstyne have access to it."

Trapp gestured for her to continue.

"One of my team will call his suite, and tell him there's a girl on the way, courtesy of management. From everything we know about Emmanuel Alstyne, he won't be able to resist. You have the nerve agent?"

Trapp nodded. "Langley couriered it over this morning, in the diplomatic pouch. It'll send him to sleep, and he'll never wake up. Not without the antidote, and except for the dose in my fridge, there isn't one for thousands of miles."

Ikeda grimaced. "About that... is it intravenous?"

"Yep."

She went white. "I hate needles."

"You're telling me you're comfortable swimming twenty miles through Arctic water, or going toe to toe with Chinese state security—but you don't like *needles?*" Trapp exclaimed in disbelief.

Ikeda shot him a sharp, challenging glare.

Trapp raised his hands in surrender.

"Good," she replied, more softly this time. "You'll need to do the injection."

Trapp diplomatically agreed, and decided to return to safer ground. "Surveillance confirms he's still wearing the USB drive on a chain around his neck. We've made an exact copy. All you need to do is drug him, switch the drive for the fake, make it look like you both partied a little too hard, and walk out of there. We'll be out of Macau before the Chinese know he's dead."

"That easy, huh?"

Trapp knew better than that. He'd rarely been on a mission that had gone to plan. And when he'd realized that he wouldn't be working alone on this one, he'd twisted Mitchell's arm into securing some more unconventional assistance.

"It never is." He walked over to the wall safe inside a cream-painted cupboard with a sliding door, punched in a code, and retrieved a thin printed piece of paper. He walked back to Ikeda and handed it to her. "If we get separated, or if things go sideways for any reason, there's a Los Angeles class nuclear submarine sitting a couple of miles off the coast. It'll surface at four a.m. at those coordinates, and then again twenty-four hours after that. Head there, and the navy will get you out."

It was Ikeda's turn to whistle. She spoke in an affected Southern accent. "Well, hell, mister secret agent man. Seems you got some *real* clout with the boys upstairs."

Trapp fixed her with a serious stare. "You know the stakes we're playing for on this one. The Chinese won't mess around, so nor can we."

"I get it. Let's hope it doesn't come to that."

"On that, we agree."

JUST AN HOUR later the operation was underway. Trapp had drawn the curtains to his suite, blocking out the blinking lights of Macau, which stood out against the onrushing gloom, and administered the antidote to the nerve agent—a necessary step due to the means of delivery. Ikeda nearly passed out when she saw the needle.

She had painted her lips an alluring shade of red, courtesy of a tube of lipstick formulated in a lab at Langley. The makeup contained a deadly toxin. The second Ikeda brushed her lips against Emmanuel Alstyne's face, the man would be dead—he just wouldn't know it. Within minutes, he would start to feel drowsy. Within an hour, he would slip from sleep into a coma from which he would never wake.

He would be dead by morning.

The nerve agent would leave no trace in Alstyne's system, and if everything went to plan the CIA team would wipe every trace of their presence from the Ritz-Carlton's computers. Ikeda had added a wide-brimmed black hat to her outfit which would hide her face from any cameras the Chinese themselves had set up.

The female operative would no doubt be frisked and searched before entering Alstyne's suite, but her purse contained a small hidden compartment which hid the replacement USB drive.

And so, at that very second, she was in an elevator rising to Alstyne's floor.

Trapp paced in the control room the CIA surveillance team had set up. His Beretta was tucked under his waistband, and he had several additional magazines distributed in his denim pockets. He wore an 'I Love Macau' baseball cap reversed on his head—just in case he needed to make a quick exit—which he twisted absent-mindedly, first forward and then back, as he returned to the surveillance equipment. Ikeda's silhouette was just barely visible in the grainy footage delivered by the elevator's camera.

"The shooters?" he asked the surveillance tech for at least the third time. The man, to his credit, replied without a hint of irritation. "In rooms next to the stairwell, above and below

Alstyne's floor. If something goes wrong, they'll be there in under twenty seconds."

"If the shit hits the fan, they shoot to kill, understood?"

The technician nodded and communicated the message to the CIA special operators.

Trapp knew that if anything went wrong, Ikeda would likely be dead long before the cavalry arrived. His heart was racing a mile a minute in his chest. He ground his teeth together, wondering why the hell he had agreed to her plan. He hated endangering other operatives. Maybe he should have done this his way after all.

He wished he could contact Ikeda and call the whole damn thing off, but they had decided against giving her an earpiece. He figured the MSS grunts were probably just muscle—but they couldn't be sure. If Alstyne's babysitters were even halfway competent they might notice the communications unit and blow the mission before it even began.

So all Trapp could do was wait. He watched on the fuzzy camera as the elevator's doors slowly opened, and Eliza Ikeda stepped out.

8

Ikeda's palms were slick with sweat as she entered the hallway. She barely noticed the calm mood music playing through the ceiling-mounted speakers as she wedged her purse between her upper arm and her torso, then wiped them against her forearms to avoid marking her dress.

You can do this, she assured herself.

The truth was, Ikeda had never killed a man. She had run drills of course, hundreds of times, both during her initial training back at the Farm, then on refresher courses all around the world. But while those had honed her skills, that was all in theory. The American government had taken the soft, pliable clay of her body and fired it into a deadly weapon.

But could she kill a man? Was she truly prepared to turn that theory into practice?

She *thought* she was. She agreed with the operation's goals, had no moral qualms with what had to be done. Emmanuel Alstyne was a traitor. That much was clear. He had proved himself willing to sell out his country for little more than a life of creature comforts, and Chinese protection from the long arm of American justice.

She was that arm.

But extending it, that was a whole other question.

"Hey, who the hell are you?" a man said in thickly accented Mandarin, starting toward her and leaving his post by the door to Alstyne's suite. He had the features of an ethnic Han Chinese, but Ikeda sensed from his voice that he was from the provinces, perhaps Xinjiang, not far from the Mongolian border. His cheeks were puffy from overindulging, so she nicknamed him Chubby. The second agent didn't move, but his eyes flickered in Ikeda's direction, giving the CIA operative the distinct impression he was checking her out.

Chubby had the telltale bulge of a slimline pistol just beneath his left shoulder. He made no move to go for his weapon, no doubt seeing a pretty woman and instantly discounting her as a threat. The Chinese were nothing if not chauvinistic, Ikeda thought tartly. Sure, she was a woman—but she knew she would be able to lay him on his ass without a second thought.

"I'm a present," Ikeda said in perfect Mandarin. "For the American."

"Fuck off," Chubby grunted, gesturing toward the bank of elevators Ikeda had just exited. "You're not supposed to be here."

Ikeda placed her hands on her hips, resting most of her weight on one leg, and spoke in a voice that screamed attitude. "I didn't ask you. Management sent me. Ask the American."

Chubby traded a glance with his partner. "How do you know about him?"

Ikeda knew that she didn't look her true age—thirty-three. Her keen exercise regime meant she barely had an ounce of fat anywhere on her body. In this dress, with this makeup, she looked a decade younger, and she played up to it. She rolled her eyes and let out a long, grumpy sigh. "I told you. Management sent me. And I don't get paid if I don't screw him."

The light finally dawned in Chubby's dark, recessed eyes. "You're a whore."

Internally, Ikeda recoiled at the use of the word. But somehow it had disarmed Chubby's suspicions. He still seemed conflicted, a dark wave of confusion crossing his face as though wondering why the Ritz-Carlton Hotel would have sent his charge a prostitute. But then again, this was Macau—it was the Wild West of Asia, like Vegas back in the sixties. They were babysitting an American billionaire. It wouldn't seem that out of character.

She nodded. "You got it," she said, leaning into her bitchy persona. "Now be a good little boy and ask the man if he wants me."

Chubby grimaced, but probably figured it was above his pay grade to stand in her way. And after all, she was only a woman.

"Search her," he grunted.

Ikeda walked toward the door of Alstyne's suite. The second Chinese bodyguard, the one called Xi, pushed her roughly against the wall. "Hands above your head," he said.

She complied, placing her palms against the wall and grinding her teeth together as the creep's touch lingered altogether too long on her body. He swept his rough fingers from the bottom of her ankles to the top of her head—even though there was no way she could have concealed any form of weapon inside her cocktail dress. His breath was hot and rancid and danced over her shoulder into her nostrils. He was a pig.

He grabbed the purse next, flicking the gold clasp open and cursorily scanning its contents. Ikeda held her breath, but seconds later learned she needn't have. Xi wasn't just a pig, he was a fool.

"She's clean," Xi said, covering Ikeda in a thin wisp of spittle as he spoke. She concealed her distaste.

Chubby knocked on the door, and Alstyne answered within

seconds. Judging by the bright gleam in his eyes he was extremely interested in the proposition of spending an evening in the presence of a woman as attractive as Eliza Ikeda.

"Let her in," Alstyne said.

He was a chubby man, draped in a pair of crumpled navy blue suit pants and an untucked shirt open several buttons too deep. A wisp of gray chest hair escaped the crisp white fabric, and then she saw it—the chain around his neck. Proof that Trapp's intelligence was correct—and that Emmanuel Alstyne deserved his fate.

Ikeda shot the American traitor a seductive stare from her slate gray eyes as she closed the last few yards to the door. Before she stepped through, she stroked the line of Xi's hairless jaw with one outstretched finger.

"Good boy." She grinned. Before the night was out, his principal would be dead, and she would be gone. The pervert's career in the Ministry of State Security would be as good as dead.

"Well you're a sight for sore eyes," Alstyne leered as the door swung closed behind her, sealing the pair of them into his opulent suite. The gentle sound of blues music played from the overhead speakers. If Ikeda wasn't very much mistaken, the artist was John Lee Hooker. She smiled at the coincidence.

"How so?" Ikeda replied seductively.

She felt isolated now she was alone in the suite with an unknown man. She knew Trapp was watching the door—but he couldn't listen in. It would've been too dangerous to drill a line into Alstyne's suite with the Chinese surveillance team just next door. But she squashed the sensation. Reframed the fear, just like she did on a long open water swim. She wasn't alone; she just didn't need anyone except herself.

Alstyne didn't answer her question. In fact, an almost jealous look crossed his face. He jerked his thumb at the closed door. "What was that all about?"

Ikeda bent down, ensuring the folds of silk on the front of her dress briefly parted as she did so to reveal the skin underneath, and set her purse down on a nearby coffee table. "Oh, him?" she replied. "He got a bit handsy patting me down."

"I'll have him fired." Alstyne glowered. "I'm sorry."

Ikeda straightened and took a pace toward the American. Her heart was racing, and she wondered whether he could tell how nervous she was. Could he see it in her eyes? Smell it, somehow?

She reached out and stroked the side of Alstyne's torso. She leaned in close and whispered into his ear. "I'm just going to freshen up. Why don't you get us something to drink?"

Alstyne nodded furiously, and Ikeda had no doubt that if she glanced downward she would catch sight of a most unwelcome bulge. But she didn't. She stayed precisely where she was, her hot breath tickling the billionaire's ear. Slowly, deliberately, she turned her face so that her left cheek grazed his and kissed him gently on the lips. Her tongue flickered out, and his mouth opened greedily, unleashing a snake.

Ikeda pulled away.

Her eyes roved hungrily over Alstyne's lips, but not out of attraction. The man disgusted her. Not because of his sexual appetites, but the things he was prepared to do to sell out his own country. Had been, anyway. Because although he didn't know it yet, he was already dead. His lip was smudged red. The nerve agent formulated into the lipstick was even now crossing the skin barrier.

"I'll be right back," she whispered, leaving the dead man panting.

Ikeda almost stumbled to the bathroom, closing the sliding door and locking it behind her. Her heart thundered in her chest. She felt as though her ribs might explode at any second, and briefly rested her forehead against the wall for support. She was unsteady on her feet as she crossed the distance to the basin. She twisted the faucet, then gripped the porcelain with both hands as water hissed out, swirling and eddying before it plunged into the drain.

You just killed him.

An overwhelming, irrational desire to get rid of the evidence overcame her. There was more risk of discovery in changing her appearance than sticking to the plan, but her lips crawled from the thick sensation of the impregnated makeup. She grabbed a tissue from the box in front of the mirror in front of her and dragged it furiously across the skin until her lips were clean. She tossed it into the toilet bowl then took another and washed her face until every last trace of the nerve agent— and her lipstick—was gone.

"Are you okay in there?" Alstyne called.

Ikeda took a deep breath, steadied herself as much as possible, and replied, her voice low and seductive, "I'll be out in a second."

She steadied herself in the mirror, her steely gray eyes seeming almost to tear up before she blinked them away. She exhaled deeply. She had done what she came to do. Emmanuel Alstyne deserved to die, and now it was only a matter of time.

But she wasn't out of the woods yet. She still had a role to play. She quickly flushed the toilet, and the red-stained tissue paper swirled away, taking with it all evidence of her crime. A second later she turned off the faucet and returned to the suite. Alstyne was holding two champagne glasses, the bottle sitting on the dresser behind him. Bubbles danced in the pale amber liquid, as Ikeda gratefully accepted the offered flute—she'd never needed a drink more in her life.

"What happened to your lipstick?"

"I wiped it off," she replied. "Didn't want to make a mess of your lovely white shirt."

A look of childish petulance crossed Alstyne's face. "I liked it," he grumbled.

Ikeda took a sip of her champagne, knowing without examining the bottle that it was more expensive than anything she'd ever tasted. Half the glass was gone before she knew it, and she had to consciously force herself to pump the brakes. She wasn't out of the woods yet.

"I'll put it back on." She smiled. "Whatever you want, baby."

The word sickened her. But as her eyes roved across Alstyne's face, Ikeda got the sense she wouldn't be talking with him much longer. He frowned, a haze seeming to cross his gaze, then stumbled. The champagne glass slipped from his grip and went flying, and Ikeda moved faster than most people would think possible, catching it seconds before it hit the lush floral carpeting. It probably wouldn't have made a sound, but she knew she couldn't take the risk.

"How'd you do that?" Alstyne slurred.

Ikeda set both glasses onto the floor. She straightened and looked at the traitor with exaggerated concern. "Do what, baby? Hey—are you okay?"

"I don't... I don't feel so good," he mumbled, confusion crumpling his features.

"Why don't you lie down?" Ikeda replied softly. "I'll get some help."

Alstyne nodded and stumbled backward, collapsing onto the bed. "Help," he repeated, his eyes closing. Within seconds, he drifted into an incoherent sleep.

Ikeda stared at him for a short while, a mixture of revulsion at what she'd done fighting with a detached professional satisfaction at the nerve agent's fearsome efficiency. But the paralysis didn't last long. She sprang into action. She knew that she had to get out of here while Alstyne still looked unconscious— and not dead.

Otherwise things would get very messy, very fast.

She found the control unit for the overhead speakers and cranked up the volume until the room was almost reverberating. She wondered what Chubby and Xi would be thinking on the other side of that door. Next, she opened the minibar and removed a large bottle of Grey Goose vodka. She opened the cap and spilled a little onto Alstyne's upper body—just enough that he would stink of alcohol if anyone checked.

Ikeda went to the bathroom and emptied half of the vodka and most of the champagne down the drain, and then returned each bottle to the suite. She spent a few seconds adding to the effect, filling shot glasses with just the merest hint of vodka so it looked as though they had been knocked back.

Finally, she removed the chain from around Alstyne's neck and reached for her purse to make the switch. As she did, several things happened at once. First the lights went out, leaving the lavish suite bathed only in the glow of Macau's vibrant skyline. The hum of the air conditioner and the minibar died in unison, leaving a chilling silence in their wake. Ikeda was alone, with only Alstyne's increasingly labored breath for company. She froze, every sense on high alert, tendrils of anxiety winding like searching vines into her brain. And then she heard a sound that sent ice through her veins.

The distinct sound of suppressed gunfire. Right outside the door to the suite.

9

Deep in the bowels of the Macau Ritz-Carlton's service areas, far from the glitz of the two thousand dollar per night suites and two-hundred-dollar afternoon teas complete with English scones, or *foie gras* on muesli toast, a small explosive charge packed with Semtex plastic explosive and topped with a radio-controlled detonator was attached to the main electricity junction box that fed the hotel.

A separate, secondary charge was attached to the backup generator, a half-ton hunk of metal painted firetruck red, angled far enough away from the large tanks of diesel to ensure there was no chance of the hotel going up in flames before the sprinklers kicked in.

Six men stood ready in a hotel room located on the floor below Alstyne's suite, by sheer coincidence the same floor on which a CIA asset attached to the Special Operations Group was waiting in support of Eliza Ikeda's mission. The men wore black paramilitary gear complete with Kevlar helmets, ballistic plate-carriers and steel-toed leather boots. Though they were emblazoned with no unit markings, they resembled SWAT team members.

None of this, however, could have been seen by the naked eye. The men waited in complete darkness. Even the blinking light of the coffee maker had been taped over to avoid ruining their night vision.

Each man was equipped with night vision scopes that turned night into day, with one eye left attuned to the darkness at all times. The goggles were not of at standard American that soldiers were familiar with. They were a cheap Chinese model, supplied to certain People's Liberation Army units and sold all over the world. In short, they were untraceable.

"Ready the charge," the leader said.

He spoke in a clipped Asian dialect. His men would obey his command absolutely. No questions. No hesitation. That was the way they had been trained. They were the best of the best at this kind of work. Not because millions of dollars was spent on their training, for it was not, nor because they were equipped with the best weaponry, which they were not, but because they were utterly ruthless. Each man was a killer. Each man had been plucked from a place of violence, cruelty and destitution like no other and offered a way out.

They had become fervent converts to their new faith, because they had tasted the alternative. And they understood that what had been given to them could also be taken.

"Both charges read green, Captain," his subordinate replied.

The officer checked his wristwatch one last time. He issued the order crisply.

"Detonate."

This far up they could neither hear nor feel the impact of the explosions far beneath their feet. Outside, the lights flickered, then died. It was as though the entire building sighed in unison, as hundreds of televisions, thousands of lightbulbs, entire floors of catering equipment and minibars died in sync.

The men waited for five long seconds to ensure all the lights were out. The only sounds they heard were a symphony of their own ragged breaths, raucous in the darkness as the adrenaline pumped into their systems, anticipation building for the violence that would soon be upon them.

The captain spoke softly. "You know your roles. We must take the American alive. It is time."

They stormed out of the hotel room, moving in pairs, both robotic and graceful in the darkness. To them the world was green and light. The first thing they saw was completely unexpected. A man emerged from a hotel room several doors down. He was armed with a pistol.

But they were ready for him.

Suppressed rifle fire lit the dark hallway, tongues of flame burning the shadows away. A corpse danced and fell.

THE SECOND THE lights in the hotel suite died, Trapp's stomach clenched. He spun on his heel, sprinted to the drawn curtains and swept them open. The streetlights of Macau twinkled below him, and the iridescent blue of the Ritz-Carlton's riverine swimming pool glowed at the base of the structure.

The blackout isn't citywide, he realized, adrenaline dumping into his system and super-charging his brain. Ikeda's life might well be on the line, her survival resting on the decisions he made in the next few seconds.

"What the hell's going on?" he growled at the CIA technician, who was frantically checking his equipment. The man tapped his keyboard several times to no end. Trapp could only just make out his silhouette in the darkness.

"I don't know," the man replied.

Trapp forced himself to concentrate. It had been perhaps six seconds since the power died. By now, the hotel's backup generators should have fired up, and emergency lighting should be blinking on across the building.

None of that was happening.

This could just be a coincidence, a localized power fault that happened to affect the very hotel Trapp was operating in. If so the Ministry of State Security grunts upstairs were probably equally confused, even now contacting their handlers for instructions.

But Jason Trapp did not believe in coincidences. Not when they occurred during a mission whose successful completion was vital to America's national security.

Behind Trapp the technician's surveillance monitors began booting up. The light caught Trapp's attention, but he quickly lost interest. The equipment was fed by an uninterruptible power supply that had just kicked in.

And that was exactly what should have happened in the Ritz-Carlton. When guests were paying thousands of dollars a night to live in luxury, they didn't appreciate the lights going out. Which meant this could not be an accident. And even if it was, Trapp would rather beg forgiveness than ask permission. The rules of engagement from Washington had been clear: try not to start a war. But definitely kill Alstyne and return with the stolen secrets.

No matter the cost.

None of this makes sense, Trapp thought. Several more seconds ticked by as he forced himself to stop, to think. To consider the situation from first principles. He knew that he himself had not killed the lights. There was no reason for Chinese state security to have done so either.

Which meant that either this was an accident, or there was only one other rational piece that could complete this puzzle.

A third player had entered the game.

Trapp strode back toward the technician, grabbed an encrypted Motorola from the table, and spoke curtly into it. "Bravo One, Bravo Two, this is Hangman. Close on Ikeda. You are weapons free."

THIS IS NOT GOOD.

That might have been the understatement of the year, Ikeda thought. She was swallowed up by darkness, the only lighting in Alstyne's luxurious hotel suite coming from the billboards and casinos of the Macau strip.

She was unarmed. But she still had a job to do. She yanked the chain from around Alstyne's neck, fumbling with her purse in the darkness as she searched for the minute lever that opened the hidden compartment, and switched the real for the fake.

Ikeda looked around desperately, searching for a hiding spot large enough to conceal her. Adrenaline flooded her system, making it difficult to think, difficult even to function. But that was where all those years of training paid off. She breathed deeply, squashed her fear, and forced herself to think through the panic that was clenching her mind.

Outside, she heard a *thump.* Rationally, she knew it could only be one of Chubby or Xi dropping to the ground, a bullet through his forehead. None of it made sense. Trapp wouldn't have started firing unless something had gone horribly wrong —and as far as she could tell, until this very moment, nothing had.

At least, not in here.

So who's shooting?

"Crap," she whispered, growing paralyzed with indecision. Her fingers felt numb as she locked the purse's hidden compartment. There was a sound at the door. Someone was opening it. She was out of time.

As the door began to swing open, Ikeda dropped the purse. As it bounced off the floor, she kicked it as hard as she could toward the bed. It skidded underneath the bedframe. She knelt, grabbed one of the champagne glasses she had placed at the foot of the bed a few minutes before, and sank to the floor.

And that was when it struck her. She was still holding the necklace, the fake USB drive. She hadn't had time to replace it around Alstyne's neck. Her stomach clenched with fear.

"Don't move!" she heard.

Ikeda's mind translated the words without any effort. Her father was American, her mother Japanese, she'd lived in Hong Kong for years, did business all across Asia, and had majored in Asian Languages at UCLA in Southern California. She spoke English, Japanese, Mandarin, passable French and a little Cantonese, amongst several others.

But the language she heard in that moment made no sense at all.

Korean.

Ikeda let out a little whimper. But cold calculation had replaced fear in her mind. She knew she could neither flee nor fight. Not in that moment. She had no weapon, and there were an unknown number of assailants at the door. If she was going to survive the next few seconds she needed complete and utter clarity. There was no time for terror. She slipped instead back into the role she'd played for Alstyne.

"Who is it?" she said in a soft, tremulous voice, speaking in fluent Mandarin. "What do you want?"

Several men flooded into the room. In the darkness they were merely silhouettes, monsters in the gloom, like a child's nightmare. The sound of their boots would ordinarily have been heavy but was instead swallowed up by the thick carpeting.

"Where is he?" a man asked, still in Korean.

"What's going on?" Ikeda whimpered. "Why did the lights go out?"

Her mind was racing. There was something else going on here. It wasn't just that these armed men were speaking

Korean. The very words sounded strange. Almost old-fashioned.

And then it hit her. They weren't from the south. They were from *North Korea*.

A hand closed on Ikeda's shoulder, roughly yanking her up. A flashlight clicked on, bathing her in light, and she squinted, her eyes dazzled by the sudden flash. A man glowered at her, though still dazzled by the flashlight's beam, it was hard to make out his features. Still, Ikeda sensed that he was in command.

Ikeda's eyes flashed to her left. Another of the men was kneeling on the bed, shaking Alstyne. He was completely unresponsive.

"He's not breathing, Captain," the Korean said.

The slap came out of nowhere, but it almost knocked Ikeda over. Her mind stopped functioning for a few seconds.

"What's wrong with him?" the leader asked her in thickly accented Mandarin, his fingers biting viciously into her shoulder.

"I don't know," Ikeda whimpered. "We were having fun. He drank too much... who are you people?"

She hung from the man's grip, attempting to present herself as unthreateningly as possible. She knew that these men would not leave this hotel room without killing her. Whatever they had come for, they could leave no witnesses to their crime. But if she could just make them believe she was exactly what she looked like—an escort—maybe she would buy herself a fraction of a second to act. It might mean the difference between life and death.

And then she saw the flash of white in the man's eyes as he looked down, the flashlight tracking his gaze. It stopped at the necklace clutched in her fingers. He grabbed it from her, his nails scratching her palms. And then he spun and pushed Ikeda toward one of his men.

"We don't have time for this," the leader growled in Korean. "Take both of them."

In the hallway outside Ikeda heard the sound of gunfire. Still suppressed, so it crackled rather than barked. Someone let out a bloodcurdling scream.. She intentionally tripped and tumbled to the floor, knowing she had at most two seconds to make a decision.

There were four men in the suite with her. One was occupied hoisting Alstyne onto his shoulder. Two had started toward the door, including the leader, as they reacted to this new threat.

The only weapon in Ikeda's hand was the champagne glass. She crunched it against the floor, leaving only the sharp stiletto-like point of the shattered stem, coiled her body, and sprang toward the man who was coming for her, plastic cuffs in his hand.

10

The two Mi-17 helicopters swept low over the mountainous terrain of Sichuan Province. Over twelve thousand such aircraft had been built, and many were operated by the People's Liberation Army Air Force, so a sighting would arouse no great suspicion. The choppers were flying low enough that neither military nor civilian radar could spot them, at least not for long enough to distinguish them from a flock of birds. This far into the cavernous Chinese interior, most radar facilities were far from state-of-the-art.

Colonel Kim was attired in air force dress blues, complete with the single gold star on his epaulets that marked him out as a brigadier general in the Chinese military, and wore a pistol on his right hip. Besides the two pilots, five Unit 61 commandos occupied the helicopter's cabin with him. Unlike their leader, they wore Kevlar helmets, ballistic vests and the dark blue pattern digital camouflage fatigues issued to Chinese special forces. They cradled their weapons against their foreheads as though they were praying.

They were not, of course. At least to no god other than their Supreme Leader. And given that the colonel held the power of life and death over all of them at all times, that might as well be Kim himself. As he surveyed his men, the thought gave him great satisfaction.

"We're two minutes out, Colonel," the pilot reported.

Kim nodded in the darkness of the helicopter's cabin. All interior and exterior lights were running dark, in order to minimize their chances of being discovered. Before long, the whole world would learn what had happened here. But these last few minutes of secrecy were vital.

"Make the call," he grunted into a mic attached to his protective headphones.

Though he could not hear it over the roar of the helicopter's engines, Kim knew that the pilot was at this very moment following his orders to contact the communications officer at the Xishang Satellite Control Center. He sensed the subtle change in the whine of the engines as the two aircraft began their final descent toward the facility. As the change in momentum pushed him back against his jump seat, Kim allowed a smile of satisfaction to crawl across his scarred face. Tonight's events would remake the world. And he was responsible for all of it.

The two helicopters touched down in unison, and Kim's heavily-armed men spilled out of the aircraft. The rotors did not slow, nor would they do so until this mission was complete.

Kim's leather-soled dress shoes clipped against the helipad's asphalt as he followed them, suspecting that the sound was audible to him alone.

"What is the meaning of this?" an irate young officer shouted, his eyes screwed tight against the gale.

His shirt was untucked as he ran toward the two helicopters, and it billowed in the downwash from their rotors. He looked up at the last second, and his face blanched. "My apologies, General. I was not informed of your visit. Is this an inspection?"

"If it were an inspection," Kim spat, assuming an air of supreme confidence, "you would have failed, Captain."

The officer, his face pale, shirt now hastily tucked into the uniform pants, adopted a rigid posture, his eyes straight forward. He knew better than to argue with a man so much his senior. That was what Kim was counting on. "Yes, sir."

"If you follow my orders to the letter," Kim snarled, "I will not write your dereliction of duty into my report."

The captain, Kim knew from reading the surveillance reports his men had compiled on the Xishang facility, was in command of the facility's small security detachment. Twice in the previous year his superiors had written him up for inattention to his work. He bobbed his head nervously up and down, seemingly unwilling to trust his faculties of speech.

"The General Staff has been made aware of a threat to this facility. My men and I are to secure it until reinforcements arrive."

"A threat?" the officer croaked. "Why wasn't I informed?"

Kim cut the man's whimpers off with a snarl, baring his teeth and letting the jagged scar across his cheek do the talking. "Now you have been. Gather your men. All of them, and bring them here. The scientists, too. And Captain?"

The man nodded, his legs shaking so hard Kim wondered idly whether they might give way.

"Move fast. Don't give me *another* opportunity to doubt your competence."

TRAPP SPRINTED through the darkened hallway. The only illumination was a dim green emergency sign over the entrance to the stairwell, but otherwise the hotel was black. There were no windows to the hallway, no emergency lighting, so Trapp clicked a flashlight on as he ran.

The illumination flared like the rising sun, but not in time to avoid a collision with a terrified-looking hotel guest, who he shoulder-barged into the wall. Trapp barely felt the impact, his mind consumed by anger at himself for putting Ikeda into this position. He should have situated himself closer, not two floors away. But the time for recrimination would come. Right now he needed to focus on getting Ikeda out of this mess.

Alive.

Trapp didn't stop to apologize. He burst into the stairwell and hissed into the encrypted radio in his other hand as he moved. He wished he'd had the time to get set up with an earpiece, but there hadn't been time. "Bravo One, Bravo Two, report."

He took the stairs two at a time, then three, not slowing until the entire flight disappeared in his rearview. The radio in his left hand crackled, and he instinctively lowered the volume and pressed it to his ear.

"Hangman, this is Bravo One," the man whispered. "I'm exiting the stairwell. I think Bravo Two's down. I've got at least two shooters, heavily armed—"

Trapp didn't need the broadcast to hear what happened next. The sound of suppressed gunfire echoed through the silent stairwell, and as he took the last few steps down to Alstyne's floor he saw Bravo One's bullet-ridden body slump backward into the darkened space.

Immediately Trapp killed the flashlight and froze, sliding the device into the pocket of his jeans and noiselessly placing the radio on the floor. He needed both hands, and the only remaining CIA operative on-site was the surveillance technician in the suite he had just vacated. With the power out, so were the cameras, rendering the man less than useless. In place of the radio Trapp retrieved the Beretta from his waistband and ensured he had a chambered round.

He cursed.

What the hell was going on? Whoever the shooters were, they were packing some serious heat. Somehow they'd known exactly where Alstyne was and what he was carrying, and they weren't worried about using force to acquire it. Trapp's mind raced as he tried to work out who he was up against. The Russians? The Iranians?

It had to be a nation state, and one that didn't have a problem pulling the tail of the Chinese tiger. That was a very short list. But even so, Trapp didn't have time to examine all its possible permutations.

He moved silently, taking the last few concrete steps heel-toe in order to deaden the sound of his footsteps. He didn't so much walk as prowl, entirely at home in the darkness. Making it to Bravo One's body, he knelt, pistol steady as he crouched, every sense on high alert. With his left hand, he checked the man's pulse.

Dead.

Trapp's fingers came away sticky with hot blood. He grimaced, but forced the sorrow from his mind. The operator's body was half-in, half-out of the entrance to the stairwell, blocking the door half-open. That was good. Trapp was six foot three and two hundred pounds of lean muscle, but he figured there was just enough space to make it through without arousing attention.

He paused, listening. He knew from Bravo One's dying words that there were at least two shooters, but sensed there were many more than that. The volume of fire that had cut the former CIA operator to bits had been intense. Trapp knew that if he burst through the stairwell's exit, he might well suffer the same fate.

Quiet voices echoed from the hallway beyond. He stopped breathing, straining his ears in an attempt to listen in. He spoke a little Mandarin, but not much. But one thing became instantly clear—whatever language these killers were speaking, it wasn't one of the Chinese dialects. That meant the state security goons must already be dead.

But if they were, and the newcomers weren't Chinese—then who the hell were they?

Trapp pressed his body against the stairwell's bare concrete wall, extending the side of his face almost like an antenna as he strained to listen in to the conversation. He couldn't understand a word of the unfamiliar language, but he immediately understood what was going on.

The new players were coordinating something. But what it was—or whether that something involved him, Trapp had no idea...

11

A s Eliza Ikeda uncoiled, driving all of her not inconsiderable muscular power through the balls of her feet to spring into the air, she looked more like a comic book character than a flesh and blood human being.

Dark shapes moved like wraiths in the inky blackness all around her, but she only had eyes for the man standing five feet in front of her. She closed the distance in the blink of an eye, grabbing the back of his neck and driving the sharpened point of the shattered champagne flute through the man's carotid artery—the pipe that supplies blood to the brain.

The second the conduit was cut, hot liquid spurted out, painting Eliza's face and soaking her shimmering silk dress. She kept moving as the man fell to the ground like a cut puppet, spasmodically jerking as the life drained from his body. She crouched, going for the pistol holstered at his hip rather than the rifle slung around his shoulders. She knew she didn't have time to free it from the canvas strap.

The second the weapon was in her hands, she spun toward the man hoisting Emmanuel Alstyne into a fireman's carry and fired three rounds into center mass. The operator grunted, and then slumped forward against the bed.

"Get that fucking bitch," someone screamed.

Ikeda turned to face the source of the voice, the muzzle of the pistol searching unerringly for its next target. But before she got the chance to the press the trigger, something thick and heavy and *metal* collided with the back of her skull.

The world flashed white, and then it was her turn to drop to the ground.

THE *SOMETHING* TRAPP had been puzzling over immediately became clear.

An explosive charge detonated in the hallway, the vibrations reaching Trapp's feet a moment later as the thirteenth floor of the Macau Ritz-Carlton rumbled and groaned beneath him. The shockwave was limited, which Trapp quickly figured meant the explosion was probably a breaching charge. The new assailants were targeting the three additional MSS babysitters in the suites next to Alstyne's own.

What the hell is going on? he thought. One of the most expensive hotels in the world had been turned into a war zone. Both the Chinese and the CIA teams had taken casualties, and neither had any idea who the third player was.

But he didn't ponder the question for long. Barely a second had passed since the charge detonated. This might be the only chance he would get. The assailants would be focused on their Chinese targets, and he might be able to take them in the rear.

Trapp pressed his boot against the half-open door, stepping over Bravo One's already cooling body. He whispered a brief prayer as he passed over the man. There was nothing more he could do for the dead operator.

But Ikeda was still alive.

He pushed against the door, moving it just an inch at a time, holding his breath as he waited for a hailstorm of bullets to crack against the hardened fireproof entrance.

But none came.

At least, none aimed at Jason Trapp. A deluge of suppressed rifle fire crackled in the hallway, and Trapp listen to the shouted commands of men in combat—in a language so different, and yet so alike the sounds he had known all his life.

He was right. The new guys were focused on taking out the Chinese—and that meant he had an opportunity. He moved fast, slipping through the half-open doorway like a thief in the night, his pistol aimed high and steady. It wasn't suppressed, but this situation had gone a long way past deniable. Unless Trapp was very much mistaken and the Chinese government cracked down, this would be front page news across the globe by the next morning.

The hallway was empty, but it was lit by two streams of thin light, more like moonlight than anything electrical. Each emanated from a doorway. The farthest away, Trapp figured, was the one in which the sounds of an intense battle were currently taking place. Flashes of gunfire lit the hallway.

That meant the first doorway must be Alstyne's suite. Ikeda would be inside. He just hoped she was still alive. It was about twenty yards away, but Trapp had no idea what lay between him and his target. His eyes strained in the gloom, but it was no use. He couldn't use his flashlight for fear of drawing down a stinging stream of bullets.

Slowly, the gunfire in the farthest hotel suite began to peter out. Trapp gritted his teeth, knowing he was all out of time.

Screw it.

He charged forward, sprinting toward the doorway to Alstyne's suite. And that's when everything went to hell.

Two men emerged from either suite, rifles nestled into their shoulders, but muzzles pointing loosely toward the ground.

Trapp did the math in his head. There was no way he could take all of them out, not before one of them got off a shot. And he wasn't wearing any body armor, whereas from what little he could see, the new guys were.

"Freeze!" Trapp yelled. "You move, you die."

The four men looked up in sync, though pretty much all that Trapp could see of their faces was the whites of their eyes. They would make as good a target as any. One man began bringing his rifle to bear, and Trapp fired a single round. The bullet pinged into the plaster of the wall beside his head.

He quickly got the point. One of his comrades started shouting at Trapp, the melodious Asian language sounding harsh in his throat. But Trapp had no idea what the hell he was saying. It was a stalemate.

The problem was—what the hell was he supposed to do now? The odds were still stacked against him. Trapp knew that the second he started shooting for real, all hell would break loose. This temporary truce would fall apart, and even if he managed to take one or two of the shooters down, the rest of them would quickly pump his body full of lead.

"Any of you motherfuckers speak English?" he growled.

The four sets of white eyes stared back at him uncomprehendingly. Trapp swore. "Didn't think so."

And then the rug was pulled out from beneath Trapp's feet for about the third time that day. A voice spoke in English from inside the nearest open hotel suite. The speaker was from an Asian country, just like these shooters, but Trapp had no idea which. The English sounded strangely old-fashioned, like a fifties film.

"The girl," it said. "Is she yours?"

Trapp's veins froze like the River Moscow in winter. These men had Ikeda, and that was bad. Very bad. They were killers, that much was sure, and her life meant nothing to them.

Trapp thought fast. Only one move sprang to mind. It was a

bad one, yet it was all he had. "What girl? I'm here for the American. Give him to me, and we all get out of this alive."

"I don't have time to play games," the clipped voice said. "I have a gun to her head. If you try anything, I will put a bullet in her brain."

Trapp knew he was screwed. He couldn't let Ikeda die. It just wasn't the way he was made. Ever since he had failed his mother, allowing her to die at the hands of his own father, this very situation had been his blind spot. His weakness. The voice had him in check, and Trapp couldn't foresee a single move that would get them out of it.

"Hey—you okay in there?" he called out.

"She is unconscious," the voice said from inside the suite.

"How the hell do I know she's even still alive?"

"You don't. It is a leap of faith. You either jump, or my men will kill you both."

Trapp ground his teeth together. The odds were clear—and they were stacked in his opponent's favor. There were at least five of them, and only one of him. The math simply did not stack up. Whether he liked it or not, he would be forced to play this man's game. At least until he could figure out a way to change the equation.

"Here is how this situation will unfold," the voice instructed. "My men and I are going to leave quietly. You are going to enter this hotel suite and stay there until we are gone. If you do exactly as I say, none of us have to die."

"Why the hell would I agree to that?" Trapp growled.

"Simple," the voice replied. "You do what I say, or the bitch dies."

12

The next few moments played out like a twisted ballet recital. Six men, weapons drawn, circled each other in the darkness, each knowing a single misstep might cost him his life. The shooters moved to a soundtrack of ragged breaths and hushed footsteps, swallowed up by the thick carpeting underfoot. Trapp's boot knocked a bullet casing against the wall, and for a second every man froze, weapons trembling in the gloom.

Trapp wondered whether this was how he would go out, his body riddled by weapons far superior to his own. He was all too aware that his pistol was a poor cousin to the battlefield weapons these shooters carried. In the darkness, it was hard to make out the precise models, though Trapp noticed a cylindrical magazine slung underneath the barrel.

The weapon was unusual. Perhaps of Russian design, and not used by any major country's armed forces—at least none Trapp's adrenaline-suffused mind could think of. But he couldn't focus on the detail. He had to concentrate on not getting himself killed. And the calculus was simple. In the time it would take him to squeeze off a single round, they could fire a dozen. He simply could not afford to turn this into a pissing contest, since it was most assuredly one he would lose.

The moment passed.

Trust was, if not regained, then at least not shattered. The dance resumed. The man Trapp had been talking to, the one he took to be the leader, stepped out of Alstyne's hotel suite cradling Ikeda's body like it weighed nothing. She was slumped in a ragdoll fashion, head lolling against her chest. Trapp's heart stopped pumping, and then a wave of adrenaline dumped into his system, corralling his rational brain and unleashing a primal urge to protect one of his own.

But it was the Makarov pistol held tight against her temple that stopped Trapp from flinging his body into action right then and there. The man opposite him was a pro. That much was obvious. One wrong move and a lead round would split her head like a watermelon hitting asphalt.

So he froze. He was between a rock and a hard place, and he was all out of explosives with which to blow the rock apart.

"Stay right where you are," the man said, his accented English cutting through the darkness and sticking in Trapp's ribs. He glanced backward and grunted a harsh command to his subordinate. The second man emerged from the hotel suite, Emmanuel Alstyne's still body carried like a sack of laundry over his shoulder.

"Leave the girl with me," Trapp said, his back flush against the hallway wall. It was a crappy tactical position. And he had no leverage. Both men knew it, which made the conversation that followed inevitable.

"I can't do that. And you know it."

The man carrying Ikeda jerked his head back into Alstyne's now empty hotel suite. "Get in."

Trapp didn't move. "What will you do with her?"

"Get in the room," the man said, enunciating every word without ever answering his question. "Or she dies."

"Maybe I put a bullet in your head first. Take you out with me."

The man holding Ikeda shrugged — at least, that's what Trapp figured he was trying to do. The girl's weight made it difficult. "Be my guest. But you'll sign her death warrant if you do. My men have orders to kill her first."

Trapp clenched his free hand into a fist. He tried not to show his frustration, but it was palpable, leaking out of him like oil from a stricken tanker. He choked out the words. "Then what?"

"I have the man I came for. If you do exactly as I tell you, I'll leave your girl in the elevator and send her down to the lobby. Give the pigs who run this place a hell of a shock."

Trapp knew it was a lie. He could see it in the man's eyes—even through the gloom that filled the hallway. He wore a predatory look. Trapp knew that he intended to take Ikeda with him.

It's what he would've done.

And yet he had no other choice. If he tried anything stupid, then he would be as good as signing her death certificate. And that was a risk he couldn't take. As long as Ikeda was alive, then Trapp would find her—even if it took him to the very ends of the earth itself.

"I'll do it."

THE SECOND THE door swung closed behind Trapp, he dropped to the ground and belly crawled into the depths of the enormous hotel suite, fearing that at any second a spray of lead would chase him through the door.

It never came. But the captain's accented voice called out after him.

"My men have rigged explosives to the outside of this door. If you step through, you will die."

"Why are you telling me this?" Trapp growled. "Why not just let me blow myself up?"

"What is it you Americans say?" the man gloated. "I prefer to give you a sporting chance. Good luck, Mr. American. When the Chinese get their hands on you, I think you'll need it."

Trapp didn't dignify the prick with a response. His body hummed with anger, vibrating like an over-strung guitar. Mostly he was angry at himself. He had been outplayed, outmaneuvered, and he was trapped in a luxurious prison, waiting for a one-way ticket to the basement under State Security's headquarters in Beijing.

He ground the frustration into mincemeat and pushed it away. He could deal with it later. Right now he needed to focus on getting himself out of this mess. He was the only chance Ikeda had, and every second he was stuck in here was a second in which the unknown kidnapper was getting away.

His eyes were by now accustomed to the gloom, and picked out most of the details he remembered from the images of Alstyne's suite in his briefing packs. The bed, the coffee table, the private bar.

But Trapp was almost certain the Ritz-Carlton advertising materials didn't mention the last item he saw. A body, lying face down on the floor, with what looked like a vicious shard of glass sticking out from a deep cut in his neck, glinting like a stalactite growing from rust red rock.

Atta girl, he thought with grim satisfaction. Trapp had known from the second he met her that Eliza Ikeda was a different class of operative. He hadn't needed proof of it—but here it was nonetheless. She had been in an impossible situation, and she'd done what she could to tip the scale in her favor.

Still, it wasn't enough.

Trapp remembered the flashlight he still had in the pocket of his denim jeans. He retrieved it, flicked it on, and played the beam over the dead body. Like the others, the shooter was East Asian, and wore all-black fatigues. The blood from his neck had drained fast, and the carpet beneath his corpse was stained red. Trapp's eyes were drawn inexorably to the wound in his neck. With the aid of the flashlight, he saw that Ikeda's improvised weapon had been what looked suspiciously like a champagne flute.

"Jesus," he whispered. "What a way to go."

He took a step toward the body, nestled his flashlight between his teeth, and crouched down. That was when he felt it: the faintest tingling at the base of his spine. An iron tang on his tongue. In short—the unmistakable feeling that something was wrong with this picture.

It was too easy.

Trapp shone the flashlight across the corpse. The beam glistened against the setting blood, but that wasn't what Trapp was looking for. In truth, he had no idea what that was, but he'd know it when he saw it. Something about this didn't make sense.

Unless...

Gently, Trapp began to lift the body, moving it only a fraction of an inch at a time. He pressed his head against the ground, guided by the beam of the flashlight.

And then he saw it.

"Ah, hell."

His opponent had lied. There were no explosives on the other side of the door. They were in the room all along. And they were about to detonate.

13

For one long second, Trapp froze, staring down at the explosive package with something akin to shock. His legs felt nailed to the floor, and thoughts crawled in his mind at the glacial pace of cement in a mixer.

Trapp let out a deep, ragged breath, expelling all his fear with it. He instantly catalogued his options. They were not good. His opponent had played him, and he'd fallen for the man's trick hook, line and sinker. The explosive device was simple: a rectangular block of plastic explosive, wrapped in mylar film and equipped with a simple anti-tamper radio-controlled detonation switch. Trapp's experienced eye played over the sight. He only had matter of seconds to make his decision.

Crap.

The unknown operative would have expected that the dead body would attract Trapp's attention. Like a fly to an electric trap, he'd allowed himself to be drawn in. Before long, an unseen thumb would hover over the detonation switch, before punching down, and Trapp's fate would be sealed in a wall of flame.

Trapp had neither the experience nor the time to attempt to disarm the device. Which meant only two options remained: either to get as far away from the bomb as he could, or get *it* as far away from him as physically possible. He quickly discounted the first option. For all he knew, there might still be a second charge waiting for him on the other side of the hotel suite's door, or else he might run into a barrage of gunfire.

Trapp sucked in a deep breath and prayed. He would only get one shot at this.

He sprang into action, picking the block of plastic explosive up with one hand. He didn't recognize either the manufacturer or the language scrawled on the wrapper, but it weighed about as much as its American counterparts—about a pound.

Enough explosive power to reduce the hotel suite, and anything inside it, to blood and dust. The only upside, as far as Trapp could tell, was that it was a makeshift device. Whoever had set the trap up hadn't had the time—or the deadly ingredients to hand—to pack the plastique with ball bearings.

It meant he had a chance.

A slim one, but a chance nonetheless.

"Here goes nothing," he muttered, levering his arm back and aiming for the depths of the bathroom at the opposite side of the suite. His bicep contracted, forearm surged forward, and the package of death sailed through the black air in a perfect arc.

Trapp didn't wait around to watch it.

He spun on his heel and scrambled backward, dragging the thick goose down mattress off the top of the bed. He grunted as he did so. It felt like attempting to shift the body of an obese shut-in.

Every sinew strained, threatening to tear loose from bone, and just as Trapp was ready to collapse from exhaustion it moved an inch, and then another, and then another. He dived beneath it, sliding his body between the slats of the bed and the thick mattress, and pressed his palms against his ears. For a brief time, he felt slightly foolish as he stared up into blackness, feeling the thick weight of the mattress pressing down against his face. He began to count.

One.

Two.

Three never came. A geyser of flame filled the suite, and the explosive shockwave flipped Trapp over, pummeling his lungs, his ribs, his eardrums. A wave of heat followed, singeing without burning. Behind closed eyelids, Trapp's vision surged white.

And then it receded. But Trapp just lay there, gasping for breath, his entire body vibrating from the shock. His ears rang, but it was a far-off sound, like a class bell heard through the hissing of waves breaking against a rocky shore.

Trapp opened his eyes. Gingerly at first, half-expecting a second wave of flame to follow the first. He was facing down now instead of up, his right cheek pressed against the bed's wooden slats. He tasted iron where his incisors had sliced through a section of gum and grimaced, expelling a thick, stringy mixture of blood and saliva that lingered on his lips like a bungee cord before kissing the floor.

And then he saw it underneath the bed. Eliza Ikeda's parting gift: her purse. Whether it contained Alstyne's drive or the dummy, Trapp did not know, but he flung his fingers at it as though fearing some other entity might swoop in and pluck it from his grasp. They reached it, and he opened it with numbed fingers, depressing the hidden lever and closing them tight around the silver drive.

How it had found its way under the bed, Trapp didn't know. The simplest explanation was that it had simply been carried there by the force of the blast wave. But he did not believe that for a second. He knew that Ikeda had left it there for him to find.

And he had.

Now it was time to repay the favor. Trapp vowed that wherever the unknown players had taken Ikeda, he would find her. And if they so much as harmed a hair on her head, he wouldn't stop until he killed them all.

THE EXPLOSION HAD THROWN a chunk of the heavy porcelain basin out of the bathroom and straight through the suite's door. Tiny shards of ceramic lay strewn around the bottom of the destroyed door like a field of fresh-fallen snow.

Trapp snapped into action. He knew every second he lingered, Ikeda's kidnappers were getting farther away. It had probably only been two minutes since they'd taken her, but that might as well be a lifetime. Their operation had been well-planned—they would no doubt even now be entering a getaway vehicle and screaming out of a basement parking lot, tires leaving black kisses on the concrete.

Trapp found his flashlight, which was miraculously in the center of the room, its beam still alight. He entered the destroyed bathroom at a run, his boots splashing into a deep puddle of liquid, since a powerful jet of water was spewing from a damaged pipe. The mirror was already destroyed, and he removed a shard of reflective glass from the wall, ignoring the thin line of blood that glistened on his fingers as its sharp teeth bit into his flesh.

He went for the door to the suite, crouching down in front of it and thrusting the mirrored shard through. He pressed his eye against the hole, straining to see any sign of an explosive device on the outside of the door. But he got nothing. The angle was bad, and the hallway outside was pitch black.

Trapp chewed his lip. He reached for the flashlight and shone its beam at the far wall.

Better.

It wasn't much of an improvement, but it was enough. He could just make out the outside of the suite's door in the right-angled reflection. He saw the chrome knob, and the decorative wooden paneling.

But no bomb. It was a trick all along.

Trapp breathed a sigh of relief. He sprang to his feet, pushing his weary body on for one last effort. He pulled the door open, and was half out before he stopped dead, desire battling with duty in his brain. He wanted to go after Ikeda immediately, but there was no guarantee she was even still alive.

The unknown operators might have put a bullet in her brain the second the door to the hotel suite shut closed behind Trapp.

He didn't think it was likely, but it was possible. If it had been him, he would've clung on to Ikeda. With Alstyne unconscious, and possibly out of the picture, she would be their only lead. But either way, the second he left this room, that was it. Local police would swarm the area. And as soon as they realized who—and what—they had lost, the MSS would close a dragnet around the entire city.

"Fuck."

Trapp needed a lead, and the only man who could give him one was lying in the center of the room, his sightless eyes forever turned to the ceiling. He spun back to the dead man. The man's corpse was peppered by debris. The shooter's helmet and Kevlar ballistic vest had protected the torso and head, but his legs had been shattered by the explosion.

Trapp quickly searched the body but found little more than an assortment of weapons and ammunition that could be purchased from any black-market arms dealer this side of the Pacific. He snapped a couple of pictures of the man's face, but it was charred from the blast, coated with dust and smeared with blood. Even the whiz kid, Dr. Timothy Greaves, would struggle to get anything from it.

The commando's vest was secured with two clips to either side. He undid them and searched the man's uniform. He found nothing. No rank insignia, no unit tags. No clue as to where these men had come from, or where they had gone. They had just appeared, like the monsters in a child's bedtime story, and disappeared into the darkness just as easily.

The dead operator had a knife in a sheath strapped to his left thigh, and Trapp removed it, using the sharp blade to slit the man's black, dust-coated T-shirt open from belly to collar. He was looking for manufacturer's tags, anything to hint as to where these killers had appeared from, because everything else was coming up empty.

He found something else entirely.

A tattoo of a five-pointed star, inked onto the olive skin around the man's left nipple, the points of the star intertwined in barbed wire. The illustration was faded and uneven, like a prison tat, and Trapp had no idea what it meant.

But he intended to find out.

14

Barely a minute later, Trapp grunted as he shouldered his way into the suite the CIA team had turned into an operations center. He had the body of a dead Agency operative over one shoulder, and looked up to see a Glock pointed at the spot dead between his eyes.

The barrel was trembling.

"Put that down before you hurt someone," he growled.

The CIA technician almost collapsed with relief as he realized that he wasn't about to die. "What the hell happened out there?" he asked. "It sounded like a war zone."

It was the exact question that Trapp had been asking himself—and since he hadn't come up with an answer, he didn't bother trying. Instead, as he reverently set the man's body down against the bed, he fired back another question. "You got any incendiaries?"

The technician stared back at him blankly. "Incendiaries?" he repeated. "What for?"

"What the hell do you think?" Trapp said harshly.

The man nodded quickly. "In the bathroom, with the rest of the weapons."

"Good," Trapp grunted. "Go get the other body. If you're not back in the next three minutes, I'm leaving without you."

"Leaving…"

The technician looked at Trapp's black expression, and clearly thought better of finishing his sentence. He nodded and ran headlong from the room. Trapp watched him go, absently analyzing his slight frame and wondering if he'd even be able to carry the body of the other dead Agency operative.

Trapp moved quickly, hating himself for what he was about to do, but knew it had to be done regardless. The weapons and equipment were ghosts—mostly purchased on the civilian market with cash, serial numbers filed off. They were dead ends, and he left them where they were. Just another false lead to slow the Chinese down.

He entered the bathroom and opened a green crate containing an Agency special: a rectangular incendiary device about the size of a shoebox. It contained a couple of pounds of thermite, as well as a significant quantity of a napalm-like substance. The combination of the two chemicals would render flesh from bone, and turn anything they touched into unrecognizable char.

Returning to the main suite, he piled all of the technician's computer equipment next to the body of the operator. He only left a satellite phone on the trestle table. He set a thirty-second timer on the incendiary, but didn't yet arm it.

As the technician returned, his arms lashed around the second dead operative's torso, droplets of sweat running down his face and his breath ragged and uneven, Trapp helped the man gently lower the body to the ground, next to his fallen comrade.

"What are you—oh," the technician said, his voice finishing in an upward hiccough of surprise.

Trapp gave the technician a push. "Go," he growled. "I'll finish cleaning up here. Follow your extraction protocol, get to the safe house, and don't even fucking blink until someone comes to get you. Understood?"

The man gulped and nodded. He gave Trapp one last, almost longing look, and then spun on his heel and exited the room.

Trapp picked up the satellite phone and punched in a number from memory, spoke two codewords, then waited for the call to connect.

THE SCIENTISTS WERE LINED up in a row in the main control room of the Xishang Satellite Control Center. Most lived onsite, in spartan barracks, and many were dressed in casual clothes, off-duty this late in the evening. Their cell phones had been collected and were now piled up in a trashcan, as one of Kim's men doused them in gasoline.

"Which one of you is Dr. Chu?" Kim asked, his grating voice provoking a shiver of fear that trembled down the line of five men and three women. His only answer was a whimper of terror.

Kim grimaced.

"That was not an answer," he said calmly, though his finger grazed the sidearm holstered at his hip. Eight pairs of eyes followed his every move, dancing between Kim's terrifying complexion and the stolid, expressionless faces of the commandos who flanked him on either side.

"Please," one of the men whimpered. Kim's nose wrinkled as he noticed a stain of dark urine on the man's khaki pants. "What do you want from us?"

"If Dr. Chu does not step forward immediately," Kim growled, "my men will be forced to execute you one by one."

A short, spectacle-wearing scientist dressed in a white lab coat broke free of the crowd and aimed an accusing finger at one of his colleagues, his outstretched arm shaking as he pointed at the woman Kim presumed was Dr. Chu.

"Do whatever he says," the sniveling man said, "and maybe we'll get out of this alive."

Kim smiled. At least, that was what he tried to do. On his gaunt, scarred face, it was more of a sneer. "Listen to your friend," he said.

In truth the man's cowardice disgusted him. Kim hadn't risen to command North Korea's feared Unit 61 without an inordinate reserve of bravery. The things he had seen and done and lived through would have broken most lesser men. The life he had lived fashioned him from raw clay before firing him and then chipping away at his weaknesses until all that was left was power, cruelty and resolve.

Kim stepped forward, stroking Dr. Chu on the chin. "Now, doctor," he said, leading her to a control console, "I need you to activate your weapon."

Dr. Chu was not much shorter than Colonel Kim himself. She had an oval face and dark brown eyes. Commendably, even though she had to be terrified, when she spoke, her voice was level. "Why?"

Kim pressed his hands against her shoulders and pushed her down into a computer chair. "No questions," he said, sliding a sheet of paper out from inside the breast pocket of his uniform jacket, unfolding it and handing it to her. "If you do as I say, you and your friends will survive."

He left the flipside of that statement unspoken. Dr. Chu was an intelligent woman, with an undergraduate degree from MIT, and a PhD from the Beijing University of Technology. She would work it out.

She accepted the sheet of paper with trembling fingers and brought it close to her face as she studied it. "These coordinates..." she whispered. "Do you know what they are?"

Kim nodded curtly. He didn't approve of women questioning his decisions. But she seemed pliable enough, so he resisted the intense urge to deliver a backhand slap. "I do."

"What do you want me to do with them?"

"Target them."

"Which ones?"

Kim was tiring of this. He pressed his fingers against Dr. Chu's shoulders and gripped hard enough to draw tears from the woman's eyes. "All of them," he snarled.

Dr. Chu was a brave woman. She drew on one last reserve of strength, though it might well have risked her life. "If you do this, you'll start a war…"

Kim leaned toward her, seeing his own reflection in her eyes, the jagged scar on his cheek, the hunger in his expression plain for all to see.

"That," he said, "is what I am counting on."

Two of his commandos stepped out of the nearest building, carrying a squat green box that was hinged around the middle and about the size of a small suitcase. Kim clenched his fist, a wave of fierce joy overcoming him. Despite themselves, several of the scientists turned to see what had caught his attention. Mostly, they looked blank—not comprehending the gravity of the device his men had acquired.

But one of them moaned, the sound low and deep and broken.

Kim grinned. "Ah, Dr. Chan," he chuckled coldly. "You thought I didn't know about Project Songbird?"

The squat, graying scientist did not reply—in fact, he could not speak. His chin collapsed against his chest. He had none of the delightful Dr. Chu's resolve. It was a shame, Kim reflected. But then again, he did not need the man.

"No, Doctor," the colonel snarled, "you should be proud. Your invention will help me destroy a nation."

～

TRAPP PACED the length of the suite's long glass window as the scrambler connected his call to Langley.

"Kyle, it's Trapp."

"Jason, we lost contact. What the hell's going on down there?"

"It went to shit," Trapp replied simply. "The two shooters are dead, Ikeda's been taken, and I'm on my own."

Kyle Partey breathed in sharply, the air whistling between his teeth. "God. You're saying the Chinese have her?"

Trapp shook his head, though Kyle couldn't see him. He was wound up like a flywheel, alive with nervous energy. "Not the Chinese," he grunted. "Someone else. Professionals; they clearly knew who Alstyne was and what he was carrying."

"Shit. What's the status of your mission?"

"I think Alstyne got tagged. If he's not dead already, it won't be long."

"And the drive?"

"I've got it. Maybe."

"I don't like the sound of that *maybe*," Kyle replied. "You know what's at stake here, Trapp. We can't let that drive fall into Chinese hands."

Trapp gritted his teeth. "Kyle, next time you want to question me, do it in person. I know the threat we're dealing with. Besides, if I'm holding the dummy, then it's not the Chinese who have the real drive. It's whoever sent these new guys. And if someone's gone after us, we need to find out who they are. I thought there was no way of cracking into those files without Alstyne's passcodes? We should be safe, right?"

It was Kyle's turn to prevaricate. "Maybe."

"What the hell does maybe mean?" Trapp growled. "Can they hack it, or not?"

"*We* can't. So probably not. But that's not a guarantee."

Trapp gazed down at Macau. Lights glistened off the skyscrapers and reflected down onto the shimmering waters of the perfectly still bay. There was a black at the bottom of the Ritz-Carlton where the swimming pools had glowed earlier that evening. Thin lines of red and white lights snaked around the structure in neat blocks.

Trapp linked his smart phone with the satellite connection. "I'm sending you some photos. Ikeda killed one of the tangos, and they left his body behind. It was rigged to blow, but I got there in time. There's a tattoo. I don't recognize it, but your guys might have better luck."

"Got it. Hangman—I need you to get that drive back to Langley like yesterday. We need to know if the real one got taken. If it did, then we are in a whole world of shit. I'm tasking the *Cheyenne* to pick you up."

Trapp barely listened to the voice on the other end of the phone. "What's our satellite coverage like over Macau?"

"What—?"

"Kyle, get your head in the game. I've got an operative in the wind. We need to get her back."

Kyle's voice was softer, more conciliatory now. It was as though he was attempting to calm Trapp down. "Jason. This is bigger than Eliza. She knew the risks when she signed up. You can't go after her. There are greater priorities at stake."

"Says a man who's never been in the field," Trapp spat back. "We need to get her back. This is our only shot."

Maybe he was being irrational, but he couldn't help it. And besides, he'd spoken the truth when he said the new guys were the greater threat. Trapp knew in his gut that the USB drive now on a chain around his own neck was the real one. With Alstyne dead, and his files most likely in Trapp's possession, they needed to know who had attacked them—and *why*.

He decided to take a less adversarial path to convincing Kyle. "You're right. There's more at stake here than just Ikeda's life. Someone knew about what we were doing here. We've got a leak, and we need to plug it. I need you to trace every vehicle that left the hotel in the last ten minutes. Anything bigger than a fucking tricycle. You got that?"

"Jason..."

Trapp froze. The phone at his ear beeped twice, but he was too entranced by the unusual sight unfolding in the skies above to notice. He thought they were fireworks at first. It wouldn't be unusual for a party town like Macau.

But the lights were too high up. They grazed the very atmosphere itself, like shooting stars streaking through the night sky, or overexposed airplane taillights at an impossible height. First one, then two, then half a dozen. First they were streaks of light pulsing in the darkness, and then they shattered into an orgy of sparks.

"Kyle," Trapp said, pulling his attention away from the spectacle in the skies. "Are you still there?"

But the line was dead. And Trapp didn't need to be an astrophysicist to figure out why. The lights in the heavens were too high to be fireworks or planes. They were satellites. American satellites.

And they were burning.

15

"Get me up to speed, General," Nash said, speaking loud over the dull rumble of Air Force One's powerful jet engines. "What the hell is going on out there?"

The world's most famous jet was returning him to DC from the opening of a semiconductor factory in the Midwest–an event that was supposed to herald America's bright new industrial future –and just as importantly, get Nash's domestic agenda back on track, after months of economic gridlock that had followed the terrorist attacks following his inauguration that January. The day had started on an optimistic note, for once. It was ending on one that was anything but.

"Yes sir," came the clipped terms of General Jack Myers, chairman of the Joint Chiefs of Staff. He was being beamed in from a wood-paneled conference room somewhere deep in the bowels of the Pentagon. His complexion was ashen, and an aide to his right was quite literally holding his head in his hands.

"About fifteen minutes ago, we suffered a massive attack on our satellite surveillance and communication capabilities over the Pacific and most of Asia. As of this moment, the United

States military is completely blind across the entire region," Myers said.

Nash's stomach clenched as though a two hundred pound prizefighter was winding up to land a jab at it. His mouth felt suddenly dry. "Who is capable of this? Terrorists?"

Myers shook his head solemnly. "No, Mr. President. To our best knowledge this is exclusively a nation state capability."

"Stop playing games with me, Jack," Nash muttered. "*Which* nation state? Are you telling me that the United States is at war?"

"We don't know, sir," Myers admitted. "Several countries in the region have the capability to take down one satellite. Maybe two. That includes the Indians, the Japanese, the Russians and maybe the South Koreans."

Nash could almost smell the elephant in the room. The one country that Myers hadn't mentioned. "You're saying it's the Chinese," he stated.

Myers closed his eyes for a second, then nodded curtly. "Yes, Mr. President. China is the only country in the region capable of downing all of our satellites at once."

"Jesus Christ," Nash whispered.

He leaned back in the conference room chair. He wished he could tilt it backward, to get some distance from this unfolding disaster, but it was bolted to the floor of the cabin. He ran through the scenario in his mind. Out of nowhere, China had unleashed a sucker punch at the United States. But why? Was it a prelude to all-out war?

"This doesn't make sense," Nash said. "I saw Premier Wang at the G7 last month. I sensed no indication he was planning anything like this."

Which only meant, Nash realized, that either there was against all odds an innocent explanation for all this–or he had been played for a fool.

One of Myers' aides pushed a piece of paper toward his

boss. The general scanned it briefly before replying. "Mr. President, my people are telling me that we lost 90% of our ballistic missile distant early warning capability in this wave of attacks. They are recommending–"

"English, General," Nash growled. He didn't need his people talking in riddles right now. He needed actionable information, transmitted in plain English.

"Yes sir. With the exception of the radar installations on Guam and Hawaii, we are currently blindfolded. The Chinese could launch their missiles, and we'd have just minutes to respond."

"What kind of missiles, Jack?"

"The nuclear kind, sir."

Nash blinked. Had he heard that right? "Say that again?"

Myers' expression was grave. He leaned forward, elbows on the mahogany table in front of him, fingers clasped together. "Mr. President, it is my belief that we are currently in a state of war with the People's Republic of China. The navy currently has three *Ohio* class ballistic missile submarines within range of China's nuclear launch sites: the *Nebraska*, the *Louisiana* and the *USS West Virginia*. If you give the order now, we can have missiles in the air inside five minutes."

Nash knew the armament carried by the *Ohio* class submarines. They weren't cruise missiles. They were nuclear. The chairman of the Joint Chiefs of Staff was proposing that he launch a thermonuclear attack on China.

"Damnit, Jack. You're talking about a first strike. A *nuclear* first strike. The American people would never forgive us."

Myers shook his head. "I disagree, Mr. President. The Chinese struck first. This is a proportionate response, targeting only China's nuclear weapons program. We have to act, and we have to act now–before it's too late."

Nash thought fast. He felt the sweat beading on his temple, felt the weight of his advisors' stares beating down on his shoulders, and he heard the drumbeat of war. After almost six months in the job, Charles Nash was no ingénue. He knew that the term 'leader of the free world' was a crock of shit. The American public thought that their president was God–and in some ways, he was.

Nash had the power to reach out from his office and order the death or destruction of any person or place on the planet.

But most of the time, their elected president knew, he was a glorified firefighter. And that was the situation at the present moment. Only he wasn't fighting to save a factory, or even a national park. His job was to stop the whole world from going up in flames.

"Jack, I can't start a nuclear war to prevent one."

"Mr. President –"

Nash slammed his palm down on the conference room table. "That's my final decision, Jack," he growled, cutting off the general's protestations in their infancy. "Before the satellites went down, was there any indication the Chinese were planning anything? Troop movements, anything like that?"

Myers shook his head. "No, sir."

Nash let out a deep sigh. There was something else going on here, he was sure of it. The Chinese had too much to lose by starting a war. Their economy was on the rocks, and a shooting war with the world's only remaining superpower wasn't exactly his idea of a stimulus package.

Nash glanced left, the way his chief of staff, Emma Martinez, was sitting. "What about State? Have there been any political developments I haven't been briefed on?"

Martinez shook her head. "I'll confirm with the State Department, sir, but I haven't seen anything of note."

Nash addressed Myers directly. "Jack–have we got any eyes in the region? Any satellites that didn't get taken out?"

"No sir. The air force can re-task assets, but moving orbits takes time. And getting new birds in the air will take weeks, maybe months."

"What else have you got?"

"The *Nimitz* battle group is a few hundred miles off the Chinese coast. We can get surveillance drones in the air immediately–but that only gives us minimal coverage."

Nash flicked his fingers irritably. "Get them flying, Jack."

"Yes sir. Additionally the *USS Reagan* and her escorts are currently refitting at Pearl Harbor. The navy wants to get them out onto the ocean where they can't be hit."

Nash ran his fingers through his hair, exhaling deeply as he took in the import of that statement. Would the Chinese really be so brash as to try and repeat the attack on Pearl Harbor? He could picture it now: thick oil shimmering black on the water, sailors swimming for their lives as fire rained down from above.

Only this time, the danger wouldn't come from propeller planes. The US Navy would be hit by laser-guided missiles fired from planes capable of traveling above Mach 3. The death and destruction would be on a completely different scale. The vision was humbling. It could not be allowed to happen.

"Do it, Jack. Report back to me the second you hear something."

General Myers saluted and signed off. Nash turned to his chief of staff, recalling a conversation he'd had a couple of days before with Mike Mitchell, and spoke in a hushed voice for her ears only. "Emma, get Deputy Director Mitchell on the line. It's urgent."

President Charles Nash knew something that not even America's most senior generals were briefed on. At this very moment, a man named Jason Trapp was on the ground in China, conducting a mission that was of paramount importance to America's national security.

Trapp was an operative like no other: deadly, effective, and entirely off the books. Perhaps he could acquire the intelligence that his country so desperately required.

America was on the brink of World War III, and her generals were urging their President to strike first and to strike fast. But Nash had not ascended to his current position by allowing himself to be bullied into action. He had no intention of dragging the United States into a war with the second most powerful country on the planet unless all available intelligence suggested that was the only course of action.

The US military was blind. But Jason Trapp wasn't–and he was his President's ace in the hole.

NASH HAD NOT LONG RETIRED to his private suite on board Air Force One when Emma Martinez thrust her head around the cabin door with an urgent, taut expression on her face. The presidential plane was essentially a flying communications suite. Nash could ask the onboard switchboard to place a call to anyone on the planet and have them on the phone within seconds. He could also command the full might of America's armed forces from this very chair. It was a double-edged sword. There were times, like right this very second, when all he needed was a moment to think.

But he wasn't going to get it. Nash was used to the frenetic pace by now; it came with the job.

"You've got him?" he asked.

"He's waiting on line two, sir," she said, withdrawing her frame from the doorway.

The President shook his head and gestured for her to join him. "I need you in the room on this one, Emma."

She entered the office, and Nash leaned forward, jabbing a button on the Cisco-branded secure telephone that sat on the right-hand side of his desk. "Mitchell?"

"Mr. President. I'm here."

"Are you read in on the recent development in the Pacific?"

"That's affirmative, sir."

"I need to know: is this connected to the operation in Macau?"

Mitchell paused before answering. "Who's in the room with you, Mr. President?"

"Just me and Martinez," Nash growled. "Answer the damn question already. I want to know if there's any possibility *we* started this fight."

"Apologies, sir. At the moment our best guess is that we–we don't *think so*."

"You're not exactly filling me with confidence, Mike," Nash muttered, chewing the inside of his lip. "What the hell does that mean?"

"Shortly before the antisatellite attack, Trapp checked in. The operation was a mess. A third player took out the Chinese, left most of Trapp's team dead, and took one of our people with them."

Nash struggled to process what his CIA deputy director was telling him. Hell, there was a lot about the last few hours that didn't make sense. The Chinese–out of nowhere–had unleashed a devastating attack on America's surveillance and communications capabilities in the most strategically signifi-cant region on the planet. And yet, as far as anyone could tell, they weren't making any move to follow it up. If they had intended to start a war, it was a hell of a funny way of going about it.

"What about Alstyne?" Nash asked. "Is he—" He paused, wondering whether to go with a euphemism in front of Martinez. He decided against it. "Did we take him out?"

"We believe so, Mr. President. And we may have recovered the information he was attempting to sell. We're trying to confirm that now."

Nash rubbed his temples, frustration rising in him like a rocket launch, and burning with the same intensity. He listed his current problems on his fingers, even though Mitchell couldn't see him. "Mike, I've got two carrier battle groups heading for the Chinese coast. I've got half a dozen F-35 fighter jets watching over my plane in case the Chinese launch their nukes. I've got the Joint Chiefs hassling me to open up the nuclear football and throw a few plays. So what I need from you right now is a little more substantial than 'may have.' I need certainty, and I need it fast, otherwise this country will be at war with China. You understand?"

Mitchell's tone was more sober when he replied, as though he truly appreciated the import of what the president had just said to him. "I understand the gravity of the situation, Mr. President. My team will do everything we can to get you the information you need. But..."

Nash's nails bit into his fleshy palm. He didn't want to hear any 'buts' right now. "But *what?*"

"Trapp's a lone wolf, sir. If he follows the extraction plan, he'll be on a navy sub in about six hours. But I'm not counting on it."

16

Trapp exited the Ritz-Carlton on foot, knowing that as he moved the combination napalm/thermite incendiary device would have detonated in the hotel suite far above his head.

Even now, white-hot flames would be burning at temperatures approaching four thousand degrees. By the time the flame burned itself out, there would be little left of the pyre of equipment and bodies. Nothing would be left for the authorities to pick over, magpie-like, in their search for the truth–and for Trapp himself.

A muscle on his clenched jaw flickered as images of the flickering inferno invaded his mind. He spared a prayer for the two dead CIA operatives and promised himself that their sacrifice would not have been in vain. Trapp did not yet know who the third party was, how they had known about Alstyne, or what they were planning.

But he intended to find out.

As he stepped out of the hotel's darkened lobby, sparing a glance back at the now gaunt black structure, he saw emergency lights reflected against the windows, and a flare of light in a window high above. The fire grew in intensity with every passing second. Trapp quickened his step, knowing that he needed to get out of the area before the Chinese authorities worked out what the hell had just happened.

Macau was, technically, a Special Administrative Region with its own government, albeit one that reported to the Politburo in Beijing. Right now, the local police might not even know the true details of what had occurred inside the luxury hotel. The chaos would have disrupted communications, and the bulk of the fighting had taken place on an otherwise empty floor, with no witnesses.

But Trapp wasn't kidding himself. He knew that the Ministry of State Security was no laughing matter. They would have people on the ground, and those people would be headed straight for the Ritz-Carlton.

And straight for him.

Trapp's mind spun as he tried to work out what the hell to do next. His link with Langley had been severed by the loss of the satellites in the skies above. He briefly considered finding an Internet café and contacting his handlers using the portal dedicated for that purpose, but discounted the option immediately. Just a couple of years before, the MSS had penetrated a system the Agency used to communicate with its Chinese sources. The CIA's entire network of Chinese spies was quickly rolled up, and many executed.

Given the importance of the thumb drive that now hung from his neck, its chain circling the eponymous scar that had lent the operative his call sign, Trapp knew he couldn't risk attempting to make contact. In China, he was the outsider. If the MSS realized they were looking for a Caucasian male, they wouldn't play by American rules. They would shut the entire city down and arrest Americans, Canadians, Europeans, in fact anyone without even a hint of a tan until they got their man. He couldn't give them so much as a single clue to his location.

He was on his own.

Hotel employees were attempting to corral the Ritz-Carlton's guests in an empty lot just opposite the dark structure. A short, yet nevertheless powerful firefighter collided with Trapp as he rushed toward the hotel, a length of hose coiled around his shoulder. Alarms finally began to blare behind him.

"I'm sorry," he muttered. The man didn't stop.

That was good, Trapp thought. He was invisible. He took advantage of the momentary confusion, aware that every second he lingered, more emergency personnel were arriving on scene. The second the firefighters reported on the blaze burning in the suite the CIA had coordinated their operation from, or the bullets and bodies strewn two floors below, the tone of Trapp's evening would change – and it would change fast.

He had no intention of rotting away in a Chinese jail. Not with so much on the line.

Trapp glanced around, checking no one was watching. His eyes fell upon irritated businessmen and vacationers, cell phones pressed to their ears as they no doubt attempted to book different accommodation. He was clear. He propelled his body at a chain-link fence that bordered the parking lot, swinging his legs up and hooking his feet at the top. He crouched there for a second, and then dropped down into a building site that faced the hotel. Above the emergency sirens, he could hear the dull roar of traffic from the four-lane highway not far from where he stood. His first order of business was to put that road between him and the cops.

Then he could figure out what to do next.

~

TRAPP ENTERED the Venetian and paid cash for a dark blue windbreaker in the hotel store. He replaced his baseball cap and quickly cleaned himself up in the nearest bathroom. A guest looked at him quizzically, no doubt noticing the dark hue of the water disappearing down the basin as he washed his hands, cleansing them of the thick layer of blood and grime he had acquired in the Ritz-Carlton. But the man asked no questions, and Trapp was in no mood to provide any answers. Just like Vegas, what happened in Macau stayed in Macau. It was his job to prove he was the exception to that rule.

He splashed a few droplets of water on his face and briefly closed his eyes. In the darkness, he saw Ikeda's slate-gray eyes looking back at him, her expression accusing.

Why did you abandon me? it asked.

Trapp gripped the basin tight. The chain around his neck hung low, swinging in and out of his peripheral vision—a constant reminder of the gravity of the situation he found himself in. He was at a crossroads. He knew what he wanted to do: drive off after Ikeda and do whatever it took to find her.

But he also knew that right now, that was a fool's errand. He had no idea where she was, nor who had taken her, what they wanted or where they were going. But there was one person who might. Kyle Partey.

Trapp had sent the young CIA analyst the photographs of the dead soldier before his communications went down. It was the only lead he had—and without the Agency's help, he knew Ikeda was as good as dead.

Following his extraction plan went against Trapp's every instinct. He knew that every moment he tarried was another in which Ikeda was only being taken further away. It was entirely plausible that doing so might cost him so much time it would also cost her life.

But he also knew he didn't have any other choice. Macau was about to be a very dangerous place for a CIA operative to be. Standing at six foot three, with his powerful frame and tanned, weathered—yet still recognizably Caucasian—

complexion, there was no way he would be able to operate in secrecy in this town. He stood half a foot taller than most of the local population, and a full foot above some.

More importantly, without intel there was nothing Trapp could do for her.

No. He only had one option: to get out now, while he still had a chance.

THE CITY WAS CRAWLING with cops. The officers of the Public Security Police Force, still known by its colonial Portuguese name as the *Corpo de Policia de Seguranca Publica de Macau*, wore light blue short-sleeve shirts, navy blue baseball caps and had radios clipped to their left breasts. Unlike most American police, they didn't wear ballistic vests.

But they were most certainly armed.

Trapp was in the grips of a dilemma. Though the Agency, and specifically the Deputy Director of the Special Activities Division, Mike Mitchell, had considered this particular operation of such preeminent importance to America's national security to allow the stationing of a Los Angeles class nuclear attack submarine off the coast of China, no one had expected it to go this far sideways.

By the time Trapp made it across town on a rented electric scooter, the city was in lockdown. Everywhere he looked he saw another officer of the CPSP, and the thought filled him with dread. He was still armed, though a magazine down, but he had no desire to be forced into killing a police officer.

The guys in blue shirts were just beat cops—they wouldn't know who they were hunting, or why. If there was no other option, Trapp would fire the lethal shot. He had done it before, and would no doubt do it again.

But he hoped it wouldn't come to it.

His destination was the Macau Ferry Port, the same location from which he had entered the city that very morning. There was a small boatyard attached to the commercial harbor, designed for wealthy, yacht-owning gamblers to leave their vessels while they delighted in the luxuries the city of Macau had to offer. And there was a boat waiting for him there.

Baseball cap pulled down low over his face, Trapp scanned the yard. Sailboat masts swayed as the yachts beneath them bobbed gently on the slightly choppy surface of the bay, and motorboats swayed at their moorings, the ropes that held them fast groaning as they moved. But Trapp's attention wasn't taken by the boats.

It was on the cops that were swarming the whole area. Blue-shirted men with flashlights were walking up and down the closely-packed piers, gruffly interviewing the owners of the boats that were occupied and carefully searching the ones that weren't.

Trapp's stomach sank. Unless he went full James Bond, there was no way he was making it to the small boat that the Agency's local stringers had left at bay 47. And with several coast guard cutters prowling ominously in the waters beyond, Trapp knew that unless a nearby US Navy carrier group stepped in to provide aerial support, any attempt to make for the open ocean would be doomed before it began.

A nearby police cruiser chirruped, and Trapp thrust his hands into his pockets, swiftly losing himself in the dark of night. He needed to find another route out of Dodge.

And as his wraithlike gaze surveyed the inky seas, he decided he might just have found one.

17

I keda awoke into blackness, and a sharp, aching headache that throbbed like the thundering of war drums.

Where am I?

Her befuddled, damaged brain struggled to answer the question she posed it. She couldn't remember where she was, or even how she had gotten there. She tried to move, but couldn't. It was as though she was paralyzed, trapped in blackness, with no control over her limbs or even her mind. Panic surged within her. Was she dead? Was this what life was like in the beyond?—just nothingness, forever.

If so, Ikeda knew that she would surely go mad. Her thoughts raced as she searched for an explanation of what was happening to her.

None of this makes sense.

The ground swayed underneath her, and a wave of nausea rose in her stomach. At any moment she thought she might vomit, but something stopped her. She forced the desire back, clenching her jaw tight.

Okay. Back to the beginning, she thought. *What happened? How did I end up here?*

With all her senses on fire, Ikeda could sense the weight of individual beads of sweat on her forehead, and something else —an alien presence that she couldn't yet make out. A thought occurred to her: If she was dead, would she really be able to sweat?

She thought not.

The idea both comforted her and helped her to tame the swell of fear that rose inside her, helped her to remember that the sensation of her heart thundering in her chest like a herd of runaway horses, hooves beating against the ground in a furious rhythm was just that—a sensation. A physical reaction to the cocktail of chemicals her brain was pumping into her bloodstream.

She mastered it, reining back on her terror, breathing deeply to force her brain to regain control of the body it rode.

And as her fear faded, her mind's clarity increased. Ikeda was not yet firing on all cylinders, but she was returning to baseline. She focused on what she could control: her senses. She did not yet dare to move, as her anxious, fractious mind presented her with a million scenarios, each more terrifying than the last.

She could be unconscious, on the edge of a cliff, and one wrong move could send her plunging to her death.

It wasn't likely, of course, but neither did it seem a risk worth taking. Ikeda forced her mind's attention back to her body, using a meditation technique she'd learned as a child in Japan. She focused all of her attention on her toes, wiggled them, and felt an entirely disproportionate level of pride at her tiny success. Next she attempted to roll her ankles.

But this time she was out of luck. The joints seemed stuck fast, as though they were glued to, to...

To whatever it was she was lying on. Which Ikeda thought with frustration, she still did not know.

Okay, forget the ankles. Keep going.

Ikeda did exactly as she instructed herself, repeating the technique until she had performed it the length and breadth of her body. When she was done, one simple truth was immediately apparent: she was tied up. Wherever she was, and whatever had happened to her, she was a prisoner.

The realization dumped a surge of adrenaline into her brain. In a fraction of a second she went from numbed and groggy to entirely alive, her breath ragged in her lungs, and her limbs straining at her bonds.

She quickly realized that the alien object she had sensed on her face was a blindfold. Now she could feel the plastic ties cutting off the circulation at her wrists and ankles, and the rigid surface of whatever she was lashed to sending the muscles in her back into spasm.

The panic returned, and Ikeda forced herself to master it. Quicker this time, since she had been through the process already. Fear wasn't helpful. Fear was weakness, and weakness would get her killed. She remembered what had happened now. The men storming Alstyne's suite. Killing one and...and then the blackness that had taken her.

Eliza Ikeda had never felt more abandoned. Forgotten by her country.

On her own.

And then a memory returned to her. The first day of training at the Farm. Her instructor had said something that had stuck with her for years. When the words left his lips, many of the trainees had blanched. Most of those never made it to the field: either the instructors washed them out, or they chose to transfer to a more sedate career in one of the Agency's analysis teams.

"When you leave this place, you are on your own. If you screw up, best case you'll do ten years in some shithole foreign jail before they send your body back in a spy transfer. I say your body, because you'll technically be alive, but your mind will be long gone."

At this, the trainee next to Ikeda had almost pissed himself.

"*Worst case,*" the instructor had continued, "*we'll never know what happened to you. You'll get your star on the wall at Langley, and no one will ever know your name. So ask yourself this: are you ready? Because there's no shame in walking out of that door and never coming back. But if you stay, know this: when you're out in the field, no one's coming to save you. It's up to you. You think you can handle that?*"

Ikeda had.

She still did. And now she heard voices beyond the kind of blackness that surrounded her. The growl of an engine—low and throaty, some kind of goods vehicle. A truck, probably.

A man spoke, again in that strangely accented Korean. "He's dead."

"Fuck," another swore. This voice reminded her of the leader of the unknown assailants. "And the drive?"

"It looks real, but..."

"But what?"

"Without the American's codes, it's as good as useless. We might be able to crack it, but not in the time we have."

"Has the colonel checked in?"

"No, sir."

"Then we better hope he was successful. Otherwise this fuck-up will be very bad for us. It might still be."

Ikeda frowned, then quickly relaxed her facial muscles. The last thing she needed right now was to attract any attention. The best thing she could do was stay out of sight and out of mind, acquiring as much intelligence as she could while they thought she was asleep. But her honeymoon didn't last long.

"Tokko, how far are we from the safe house?"

"Ten miles, sir."

"As soon as we get there, wake the bitch up. It's time to find out who sent her."

THE IMAGE that caught Trapp's attention was the sight of dozens of multi-million-dollar motor yachts bobbing on the waves about a mile down the coast. A memory from earlier that day flashed into his mind: a sign announcing that it was Macau Yacht Week.

It gave him an idea.

To get to his submarine pick-up, Trapp needed to be about five miles off the coast of Macau. This close to mainland China the seas were heavily trafficked: in fact, in the distance Trapp saw the dim outline of a container ship steam past every couple of minutes, navigation lights gleaming bow and aft. The navy wouldn't risk a billion-dollar submarine colliding with a Chinese merchant ship, especially in China's territorial waters–no matter how vital the mission. This would have to be a case of Mohammed going to the mountain and not the other way round.

He just had to figure out how to get there.

Even for an athlete of Eliza Ikeda's open water prowess, a five-mile swim in the tiger shark-infested waters off the tip of Macau in the dead of night would have been a dicey prospect. And as fit as he was, Trapp knew he couldn't hold a candle to the elite CIA operative.

Taking the exfiltration boat left at the yard was out. Swimming to the exfil point was *most definitely* out.

But Trapp was pretty sure he could make the swim to one of the yachts anchored offshore. If he was lucky, and he maneuvered without any navigation lights, he might be able to make it to the pickup point. And since the clock was ticking on Ikeda's survival, Trapp figured he didn't have any other choice.

"The hell with it," he muttered.

He started jogging toward the dock hosting Yacht Week. It was hard to miss. As he picked up the pace, a wave of fireworks crackled in the night sky, painting the darkness in shades of green and red and gold. Trapp figured that the super-rich were no more subtle in Asia than they were back home. He didn't know what it was about money that made people feel the need to advertise it.

Jason Trapp was a man born in the shadows, and he liked it that way. Still, the thought of stealing some rich asshole's boat filled him with a certain sense of satisfaction. Though he had no desire to live the high life, it couldn't hurt to taste it once in a while.

18

Macau Yacht Week looked like something out of Great Gatsby. The boats closest to the dockside convention center were enormous, at least a hundred and fifty feet in length and Trapp shuddered to think what they would cost.

A mission deep in his past had sent Trapp to Monaco, the small principality on the southern coast of France, and he'd killed a man on a thirty million dollar yacht half the size of the gleaming, no doubt hand-polished boats lined up on the other side of the fence from where he currently stood.

Trapp subtly but thoroughly cased the joint, seemingly buried in a Sunseeker yacht brochure he'd swiped from a stand out front, but his eyes really drinking in every last detail.

Access to the dock was regulated by numerous uniformed guards, and security was being taken very seriously. Trapp supposed that made sense. The kind of high net worth individuals the yacht manufacturers were wooing at this event did not like to mix with ordinary people. He wasn't exactly 'ordinary', but on the other hand he was intending to borrow one of their boat without permission, payment, or guarantee they would get it back, so he couldn't exactly blame them.

Still, Trapp didn't need to make it onto one of the super yachts. Stealing one of those would be a little *too* obvious, and even if he made it on board, there was no way he had the skills to pilot a boat that size.

No, he needed something smaller. Something in the five-million-dollar range would suffice—there was no need to let his ambitions sink too low, after all...

The waterside path that circled the convention center was thronged with high-end bars, each of which was thrumming with beautiful women, all attired in expensive cocktail dresses and swirling matching sugary drinks. Trapp briefly considered sweet-talking one into a tour of their yacht, but quickly discounted the idea. There was no telling which of these ladies actually had access to the kind of boat he was looking for, and which were merely aspiring to the comfort of such a life.

Even if he could somehow make the distinction, his watch warned him he had a little less than six hours before tonight's exfiltration window would snap shut—whether or not he was safely ensconced within the black submarine slipping into the warm waters of the South China Sea. Trapp knew he wasn't an unattractive man, but he didn't have time to waste striking out in an attempted seduction.

And finally, there was the prospect of inflicting the inevitable trauma that would occur when he revealed himself to be not only a liar, but a thief. No, there had to be a better way.

Trapp walked slowly down the coastline path as he searched for it. He didn't speak much Mandarin, but as it happened, he didn't need to. The man who finally attracted his attention was speaking English, clearly in an attempt to convince the two startlingly tall European women opposite him to join him in bed.

"It'll be fun, I promise," he slurred. He gave each girl a leering wink, which swept away any of Trapp's remaining illusions as to his intentions regarding the two women. "I'll take you out to my boat, we'll have a few drinks. See where the night takes us..."

The two girls looked at each other, communicating silently. Damn, they really were something—both perfect tens, and even without their heels, they would have stood a head taller than most of the locals.

With them, it wasn't even a contest.

But Trapp's gaze was focused on the man, not the two girls —much as he would have liked to linger on their assets a little longer. The man's hair was jet black, though he must have been in his early sixties, and he wore a cheap suit paired with a twenty-thousand-dollar Rolex on his left wrist. The combination was incongruous, and Trapp's eyebrow kinked upward as he pondered it.

But the explanation quickly became clear. A Communist Party pin, blood red and studded with yellow stars, was nestled on his lapel. By itself, it didn't mean anything. China was a nation of one and a half billion souls, nestled among which were almost eighty million party members—and you didn't get far in either the business or political world here without paying at least lip service to the little red book. Or whatever it was the propaganda people were peddling these days.

But Trapp's instincts told him there was something else at play here, and he intended to use it.

"What kind of boat?" they asked in unison.

"It's a seventy-six footer. Do you know what that means?"

"Um, I'm not sure..."

The girls were playing hard to get, but Trapp had run across their type before. They were playing a game, one that would end up satisfying a wealthy old man and leaving the pair of them considerably better off than they were the day before.

They weren't exactly garden variety hookers, but they weren't considering spending a night on their backs for charity, either.

"I don't know." The first girl smiled, flicking her blond head back coquettishly. "What do you think, Anna—shall we do it?"

Trapp made his move. He transferred his pistol from the small of his back, stepped forward, in between the two women and the man in the suit. When he spoke, he affected a British accent. It was a paper-thin disguise, but there was no sense telegraphing his employer more than he already had. "Not tonight, ladies. I need to have a chat with your friend."

The look of shock on their twin faces as another predator attempted to steal their prey was almost priceless. Though they sounded northern European, perhaps Scandinavian, Trapp detected a little 'Valley girl' in their joint tone of horror. "Who the hell are you?"

"Yeah," the Chinese man slurred. "Who the hell –?"

Using his body to shield what he was doing from the two onlookers, Trapp closed the distance between him and the man with the lapel pin. He painted a look of violence on his face and placed his arm on the man's shoulder, pressing the barrel of his pistol against the man's stomach in an unmistakable warning.

"What are you doing?" the man whispered, retaining enough presence of mind not to scream for help. "Do you know who I am?"

"I'm hoping to find out," Trapp growled. "Let's get rid of these two ladies. We need to talk."

Hiding the weapon beneath his windbreaker but keeping it tight against the man's torso, Trapp wheeled around. He kept his arm looped across the man's shoulder to prevent him making a break for it.

"Better luck next time, ladies." He grinned. "I'm sure you won't need it."

The two women slipped away, wearing an identical expression of disgust on their faces.

Trapp turned back to his newest acquisition. "What's your name?"

The drunk Chinese man was quickly sobering up, apoplectic rage replacing his earlier shock. He was clearly a man of importance—at least in his own mind—and reached for the same line he'd previously used, no doubt on numerous occasions.

"Do you know who I am?" he spluttered. "They'll hang you for this. I'll be there to watch."

Trapp doubted it, but knew that the MSS really did still execute dissidents by hanging from time to time. The scar around his neck itched just thinking about it. He needed his new acquaintance to appreciate the full gravity of his situation, and it needed to happen fast.

He leaned in, maintaining his British accent when he spoke but layering it with gruffness, and an implicit threat of violence if he was disobeyed. "Let me run you through what I need from you. If you do exactly as I say, I will let you live. If not, then I make no promises. You understand?"

The man nodded, his expression now laced with the appropriate level of fear. Trapp had no intention of killing him, unless he did something stupid, but he didn't need to know that.

"What's your name?" Trapp asked, falling into an easy step with the man, arm slung across his shoulder as though they were old friends.

"Liu. *Secretary* Liu."

Trapp grinned. "Nice to make it official," he said. "Secretary of what?"

Liu gritted his teeth, and spoke in a low growl. "The Party."

Trapp's eyebrows danced with surprise. "When you say Party..?"

Liu's expression vibrated from abject fear to supercilious satisfaction, and then back again. He clearly thought he had gained the upper hand with his declaration, but Trapp merely held his breath, waiting for secretary Liu to confirm that he had in fact just hit the jackpot.

The man stopped his chest out and preened as he spoke. "Secretary of the Shenzhen Communist Party. Which means you, my friend, are about to enter a whole world of hell."

19

Mike Mitchell strode into sub-basement 3A, his tie loose around his neck and his fists clenching and releasing in an almost manic fashion. He had at least two operatives dead, one confirmed captured, and one whose status was unknown. This was the part of the job that Mitchell hated. Years before, he had been among the Agency's most deadly assassins, filling much the same role as Jason Trapp did today.

But those days had long ago passed in the rearview mirror. Now his days were swallowed up with endless meetings, trips to the oversight committees on the Hill—and occasional interludes of sleepless nights and nail-bitten worry when the shit hit the fan.

Tonight would be one of those nights.

During his long and successful career in the field, Mitchell had always slept like a baby. Back then, his life was in far more peril but it was at least in his hands. If he screwed up, then it was only him who would pay the ultimate price.

These days he was responsible for the safety and well-being

of operatives undertaking some of the Agency's most dangerous missions. And so he rarely slept, especially not for long.

"Where are we?"

Two familiar faces turned toward him, lit by the blue glow of their computer screens. The first was Kyle Partey, a young black analyst who dressed like a college professor, at least twenty years before his time. Mitchell trusted the man implicitly. He had recruited him from the Agency's Middle East analysis desk and knew him to be one of the finest minds on the CIA's payroll.

The second was Dr. Timothy Greaves. Until six months earlier he had been the chief research scientist at the National Security Agency. Back then, his hair was dyed blue, but he'd since added a streak of red. Presently, he was seconded to the CIA, and more specifically to the tightly knit team Mitchell had set up in the wake of the attempted coup a few months earlier.

The team had no official name, and its very existence was only known to a precious few. Mitchell had created it in the image of the Mossad's "Wrath of God" operation—the mission to exact revenge for the attacks on Israeli athletes at the 1972 Olympics.

Kyle barely stopped typing as he spoke. Streams of data scrolled past on his screen, and his eyes flickered incessantly as he interpreted it.

"That's unclear, boss," he said in his faintly upper-class accent. "Right now nothing seems to make sense."

"Take it from the top."

He nodded, tapping a keyboard shortcut and changing the display on the largest curved monitor in front of him. "Okay. Shortly before the region went dark, Hangman sent me a series of photos."

Mitchell leaned forward, his forehead creased. The photos were arranged in a patchwork fashion, with an image of a man dead center, lying on the ground with his shirt stripped open, and a shard of glass emanating from his throat. "So who is he?"

Kyle shrugged. "That's the million-dollar question. I've run his face through every facial recognition database I can think of, and they are all coming up empty."

Mitchell tapped the screen, his finger bouncing off the dark shadow on the man's left breast. "What's that—a tattoo?"

"Way ahead of you, boss," Kyle replied. Mitchell thought he noticed a glimmer of intrigue in the man's dark brown eyes, as though he knew something that Mitchell didn't. His fingers danced across the keyboard, and a high-resolution close-up of the tattoo appeared on the monitor.

Mitchell frowned. "A star in chains? The hell is that?"

Kyle shook his head quickly. "No, not chains–barbed wire."

"And that's supposed to mean something to me?"

Kyle gave his boss one single, definitive shake of the head. "No. I didn't have a clue either. But I ran the variables through the computer: the star, the barbed wire, the fact that the tattoo looks homemade, as though it was done in a prison. And I got a hit. If I'm right, these guys weren't Chinese."

"So who the hell were they?"

Kyle grimaced, baring his teeth in an expression that Mitchell presumed was supposed to convey his unease at the paucity of his conclusion. "Honestly, it's little more than an urban myth."

"Kyle..."

"They might be North Korean. From a special forces group called Unit 61."

~

SECRETARY LIU'S YACHT, Trapp learned, was at anchor about half a mile outside of the mouth of the harbor. The boat wasn't large enough to hold a full-time crew, which as far as he was concerned was another tick in the jackpot column.

"There are two ways this can go," Trapp muttered quietly as they made their way down the pier, their footsteps echoing off the wooden decking, and the light floating structure slightly sinking in response to their combined weight. "Either you play it cool, get me off this damn island and onto your boat, or I'll put a bullet in the back of your head. I'll take my chances after that. They won't be great, but they'll be better than yours."

Liu nodded sullenly, but didn't speak. His scuffed black oxford shoes dragged as he walked, and the dark water lapped gently just inches from his feet. The air was thick, muggy with salt and heat.

"And pick those up," Trapp growled, noticing the man's posture and gesturing at his feet. He needed this to look natural, like two friends returning to their boat, or a pair of businessmen sealing a deal on the water. If anything went wrong, it would only take one errant gunshot or call on the radio and the game was up. Sound traveled a long way over water, and radio waves even further.

"You won't get away with this," Liu protested. "But I'm a powerful man. If you surrender to me now, I'll negotiate a light sentence for whatever you have done. I give you my word."

"Secretary Liu, I understand exactly how powerful you are. It's what I'm counting on." Trapp grinned. "You are going to get us past those two men up there," he said, gesturing at two armed officers from the Macau Police Department, "and onto your yacht. In a few hours, I'll be nothing but a distant memory. How does that sound?"

Trapp gave the Party official one last prod with the barrel of the pistol hidden in his windbreaker before shoving it in his waistband. The threat lingered, however, and Trapp was certain that Liu had received the message loud and clear.

"Halt!"

The two policemen were cradling Heckler and Koch MP5 submachine guns and were dressed slightly differently than the beat cops Trapp had sidestepped earlier–they came equipped with steel-toed boots and military-style helmets. He figured they were from a different unit, and that probably came with additional training.

Which wasn't good.

Liu glanced at Trapp, a shadow of a frown dancing across his face, as though he was making a difficult decision. The shadow cleared, and Trapp hoped he'd made the right one. Though he'd briefly paused, he resumed his forward motion, striding confidently toward the two policemen.

Trapp held his breath and followed alongside, fingers grazing his hidden pistol. There was a lot riding on the next few seconds, and his reading of Liu's character. Corrupt, venal and greedy secretary Liu might be, but to make it to the highest echelons of a branch of the Chinese Communist Party as important as Shenzhen meant that he probably wasn't a man to be trifled with. Though most Americans had never heard of it, Shenzhen was a city of over twelve million people—fifty percent larger than New York City itself.

And he'd made it to the top.

Secretary Liu had most probably sent men to their deaths on more than one occasion. Trapp just hoped he wasn't about to join that illustrious list.

"I said halt!" the same officer growled, raising his weapon more for show than anything else. His toes remained where they were, at ten and two, and Trapp figured he took the oncoming Liu for a drunk.

"Get out of my way," Liu snarled. His chest was puffed out, just as it had been when he first informed Trapp who he was. Despite himself, Trapp was impressed by the man's confidence. For such an unremarkable little man, he certainly didn't seem cowed by the two policemen in front of him.

They glanced at each other uncertainly. "Sir—I don't know who you are, but this whole area is off limits."

Liu came to a stop just a few inches in front of the police officer on the left, the one who had spoken. Though shorter than either of the Macau cops, he seemed to loom larger every second as the confidence grew within him.

"Not to me," he asserted confidently.

Trapp watched the scene play out with hawk-eyed fascination. A long career in clandestine operations had taught him a fundamental truth about human nature. Most men, and women for that matter, are extremely simple. They respond to a short list of motivations: fear, greed and power.

Many times Trapp himself had impersonated a senior officer, a CEO or even a doctor, and used the implicit imbalance of power to get his own way. Even in free Western countries like the United States or England, most people would not question someone above them in their chain of command. It was a truth that held in companies, just as it did in military organizations—and apparently, it worked with the Macau Police Department too.

That was exactly what Liu was doing.

"Do you know who I am?" Liu asked, balancing on his toes and prodding the officer in the chest.

That line again.

But it worked. The two policemen glanced at each other nervously, the one on the right backing away slightly as though to indicate he had no desire to get involved in this conversation. The one on the left grimaced. "Sir, it doesn't matter. My orders are clear."

"And what about your loyalty to the Party?" Liu said, his voice low and cold.

Trapp watched intently. Macau wasn't mainland China, but just like on Hong Kong, ever since the city returned to Chinese control in 1999, the Party elites had exerted their control over the once separate province. In theory the city governed itself, but in practice it was anything but independent.

"The Party –?" the officer whispered.

"I am the general secretary of the Shenzhen Communist Party," Liu said, "and right now I see two men impeding my business. Should I report that to your superiors?"

Two heads turned inward. The men communicated silently. And then, like low-level bureaucrats across the world, they decided that this was way above their pay grade. And Trapp found his way out of Dodge—and not just a way out, but a path guaranteed by the might of the Chinese Communist Party itself.

20

The tender used to ferry guests to and from Liu's yacht was big enough to carry six passengers. It had a dark, rubberized exterior, a choice of material Trapp presumed was intended to ensure the boat was light enough to be winched aboard the yacht, and was finished with a varnished hardwood decking.

In short, it was the kind of boat Trapp himself would like to own, if he ever retired and found himself a nice cabin by the sea. Just forty-eight hours before, he'd allowed himself to picture that life, after meeting the irrepressible Eliza Ikeda for the first time. It was far from the first of several such fantasies, of allowing himself to wallow in what could be, and Trapp knew it was a sign that he was losing his edge.

Very few operatives could push themselves past all natural limits and remain there for year after bloody year without eventually causing their instincts to dull and their bodies to fail. Several months before, he'd had keyhole surgery on the rotor cuff issue that had bugged him for so long. For the first time in years, he could manipulate the joint without pain and apply its full range of motion without restraint. But it was only the first in a long line of physical complaints that, after almost two decades in the service of his country, were making themselves impossible to ignore.

Concentrate, old man, he chided himself.

Trapp leaned back, a warm breeze tousling his close-cropped dark hair as the small boat cut through the water. Now they were out of sight of land he didn't bother hiding the pistol, though he kept it in his lap. Not directly intimidating, but a reminder of the deadly threat he posed.

"Not too fast," he chided Liu. "I don't want to attract any prying eyes."

His prisoner grimaced but eased back on the throttle. "What are you expecting to get out of this?" he asked. "I'm an important man. People will realize I'm missing."

"Not until the morning." Trapp smiled. "And by then I'll be long gone. And you, my friend, can forget that any of this ever happened."

The tender chugged through the water, the low, throaty roar of its engine suggesting to Trapp that if he needed to, they could open up the throttle and outpace most pursuers. Of course, if it came to that, then he was as good as dead already. You could only outrun the law for so long. Eventually the gas would run out.

Under the cover of darkness he removed the only remaining spare magazine for his pistol from his pocket, looped the chain of the USB drive around it several times, and made sure it was stuck fast. If the Chinese figured out his ruse, he intended to toss the device overboard, ideally without them noticing. They were a couple of hundred yards out into the South China Sea, and the ocean floor beneath them sloped away sharply. If he tossed the drive the chances were a million to one that it would ever be found. Better still if no one knew what he'd done.

Liu shook his head. "You're crazy."

The bubbling white wash behind the outboard engine faded as the boat slowed and began a lazy arc in the water. Trapp jerked the muzzle of his weapon at the plush yacht emerging from the blackness about twenty yards away, navigation lights twinkling at the bow and stern.

He whistled. "Who'd you have to blow to get one of these?"

Liu's face crinkled. "Blow?"

"Forget it. It's a saying. How did you afford a boat like this on a public servant's salary?"

Trapp knew that for most of the past decade the Chinese government had engaged on a relentless crackdown on corruption. Bureaucratic exploitation was rife across much of developing Asia, and bribery was needed to get almost anything done. He also knew that the Agency estimated the Chinese president had a personal fortune that ran into the billions of dollars, even as he accused those below him in the pyramid of corruption to cover his own tracks. Just like back home, the politicians were the biggest crooks of all.

Go figure.

Liu pointed toward a coiled length of rope instead of replying. "Tie us up," he said.

Trapp sprang into action, leaping onto the decking at the stern of the yacht and lashing the two boats together. The tender now seemed positively Lilliputian by contrast with its older and significantly more luxurious, brother. The two men winched the smaller boat aboard, and once the job was done, Liu turned to Trapp. "What now?"

Trapp gestured for him to climb the small set of stairs that led up to the body of the boat ahead of him. Though he was a keen swimmer, he didn't have much experience fighting on ships. Or boats. Whatever. It was the Navy's job to get pissy about the technicalities. Trapp had cut his teeth in Delta, the army's premier special forces unit, but most of the wet work was left to the SEALs. Still, he didn't expect Liu to pose much of a challenge. If the MSS came after him, of course, he might be forced to rethink his position.

"Now," Trapp said, "you rest."

He didn't have any plastic cuff ties on him, but there was no shortage of rope on board the opulent yacht. Trapp quickly and efficiently lashed the senior Communist Party official to a chair in one of the sleeping cabins, wondering the whole while if he was about to cause an international diplomatic incident. It wouldn't be the first time he'd stumbled into a nest of hornets on a mission, but China would definitely be the biggest country whose nose he had put out of joint.

Still, that was a matter for the State Department to lose sleep over, since Trapp definitely wouldn't.

With his prisoner properly secured Trapp entered the small but highly advanced bridge. The yacht was anchored close enough to the shore that the boat rose and fell as the seeds of waves grew beneath them, and he could have been forgiven for imagining that all was right with the world.

The control panel in front of him gleamed with chrome and high-definition LCD monitors. He didn't know precisely what he was doing, but he had picked up enough about these high-end yachts in the brochures on offer at the show to know that they were designed to be fairly idiot proof. The millionaire businessmen who purchased these extravagant boats wanted to be able to sit up in the captain's chair and feel the grumble of the engines beneath them without having to complete a doctoral dissertation first.

Trapp punched a couple of buttons and the system blinked into life. All he needed to do was enter the memorized exfiltration coordinates into the GPS navigation system, and the yacht would do most of the work. But as he looked at the glowing screen on the console in front of him, Trapp's stomach fell straight through the floor.

A GPS unit took pride of place in the center of the console.

The map view was familiar: focused on the Zhujiang River Estuary, with Macau and Hong Kong at opposite ends of the river's mouth. But where the icon for the yacht should be, it wasn't.

Instead, it was pulsing on the screen, dancing from spot to spot, as though its tiny electronic brain was stuck in an endless loop. Trapp frowned, then squinted as he tried to make sense of the Chinese language information on the screen in front of him. All he could understand were the numbers–and they were not good.

His eyes crossed the figure 1/24, and he instantly realized what it meant. The GPS unit on this boat was only able to connect with one of the twenty-four Global Positioning Satellites in orbit over the planet at any time.

And that was bad. Very, very bad.

Trapp knew that for an accurate reading, the system needed at least three available satellites, and preferably a whole lot more. Whatever had happened in the skies above, it had wiped out the GPS coverage above the Asia-Pacific. The satellites orbited the planet, so coverage would be reestablished at some point–but how long that would take, Trapp had no idea.

Jesus, how could he have been so stupid?

His mind raced as he tried to figure out a solution to his problem. He ground his teeth and returned to the man tied up below decks. Liu's head was resting on his chest when he stormed through the cabin door, but jerked upward sharply.

"How do you navigate this thing?" Trapp grunted.

"*I* don't," Liu replied with a supercilious sneer. "My *pilot* has the night off."

Trapp bit down on a wave of frustration that threatened to boil over. He wanted to smash the butt of his pistol into the smarmy, corrupt communist's mouth, but knew he couldn't. He needed his help.

"You know how this thing works?" he asked.

Liu shrugged, though his movement was hindered by the ropes lashing him to the chair.

"Do you, or don't you?" Trapp said, a note of danger accenting his voice. "I'd advise you to answer me very carefully, Mr. Secretary. I'm in no mood to be toyed with."

Liu's eyes widened, and his breathing once again grew ragged. He nodded quickly. "Yes."

"Why do you have a pilot?" Trapp asked.

No answer.

Trapp let out a short, sharp laugh. "You nearly crashed, didn't you?"

Again, no answer, but the reddening of Liu's cheeks was all the confirmation that Trapp needed.

"Just my luck," he muttered, chewing his lip as he figured out what the hell to do. "I'll be right back."

He spun on his heel and went to the yacht's small galley, where he found a kitchen knife. When he returned, Liu flinched, staring at the knife in his hand with terrified eyes.

"I'm not going to kill you, dummy," Trapp muttered, sidling behind the diminutive Chinese bureaucrat and cutting him free of the knots he'd tied just moments before. "Upstairs, now."

Liu didn't seem entirely convinced of Trapp's intentions. He walked slowly, with all the enthusiasm of a dead man, scuffed shoes dragging against the boat's decking. Jason guessed he was probably worrying that he intended to stab him, then throw his body overboard for the sharks to finish off. In fact, that couldn't have been further from the truth—but Trapp was happy to indulge the man's worst fears. They entered the bridge together.

"Are there any maps on this boat?" Trapp asked. "Real ones. Paper."

Liu turned and stared at him quizzically. "Why? Just use –"

"If the GPS was working, we wouldn't be having this conversation," Trapp growled. "I need a real to goodness map, Mr.

Secretary, otherwise my day is about to get even worse. And trust me when I say that won't be in your best interests."

Liu's face crinkled up as he considered Trapp's question. He did a sort of pirouette in the small bridge, his eyes flickering over the many small cabinets. And then he stopped dead, turning to face his captor. "What about BeiDou?"

"What?"

Liu grimaced, and Trapp could almost hear him thinking *dumb American*. He–mostly–kept his irritation out of his voice when he spoke. "It's like... China's version of global positioning. Did you try it?"

"Mister Secretary," Trapp muttered, "until about a second ago, I didn't know it existed."

Liu crouched and retrieved a small black device from a cabinet beneath the main console. He powered it on and handed it to Trapp. "It's new," he said. "The government mandated all boats above a certain size had to carry one only last year. So you got lucky."

"Apparently," Trapp said. He cast his prisoner an appraising look. Why had the man helped him? And how far was he willing to go to save his own hide?

"We need to have a conversation," he said.

Liu nodded cautiously, as though not wanting to risk speaking.

"Do you know who I am?" Trapp asked.

The Chinese man winced. "A criminal?"

Trapp shook his head. "Try again."

Liu's eyes flashed with recognition. He opened his mouth to speak, then caught himself, his expression tightening with concern. Trapp grinned and gestured at him to continue. Liu spoke slowly, hesitantly. "A... spy?"

"Bingo," Trapp grunted. "Now, I have no particular desire to kill you."

At this, Liu blanched, his eyes bugging half-out of his head. "Good to hear," he choked.

Trapp leaned forward, his expression grim. The pistol was an unspoken warning, but no quieter for it. "But I will. Believe me when I tell you that."

Liu fell silent. Though a moment before he had been on the verge of panic, he visibly exerted his will to calm himself. "I do. So what is it that you want?"

Trapp was reminded that the very fact that Liu had risen to his position meant he must be a canny political operator. Though he was clearly terrified, he knew better than to let the emotion overpower him. "What's best for both of us."

"Which is?"

"Your silence."

Liu returned Trapp's steady gaze without speaking. The experienced operative knew the game—the Party boss wouldn't reveal his hand until he saw the flop was to his advantage. "Go on..."

"How do you think your people will react when they learn you helped me?"

"Who says they will?" Liu said, his tone laced with outrage that built as he continued. "And it's not like I had a choice!"

Trapp shrugged slowly. "You were very convincing at the pier..."

"At gunpoint!" Liu shouted, slamming his hand down on the yacht's control console.

The CIA man made the pistol disappear beneath his clothing. He painted an innocent look on his face. "What gun?"

Liu pulled up his fists, teeth grinding together audibly, and mastered his rage. "What then?" he spat.

"I knock you out. Bruise you up a bit. Maybe split that lip of yours. And when your people find you, you tell them you don't remember a damn thing."

Not for the first time since his ordeal began, Liu visibly trembled. "Why would I agree?"

Trapp spun, gesturing at the beautiful boat, and more broadly out to the sparkling Chinese coast. "Because, my friend, the alternative is losing all of this. How do you think your bosses will react if they found you helped a Western spy escape the country?"

"Not well."

"Maybe they would prefer to sweep the whole thing under the carpet?" Trapp asked, his tone the picture of reasonableness. "Forget it ever happened."

"They might..." Liu admitted.

"Then what's it going to be, Mr. Secretary? Tell the truth and lose all your perks, or stick to a little lie?"

There was a long pause before Liu replied. He spoke quietly, in a tone that was more embarrassed than anything else. Perhaps the plain facts of his corruption had never before been stated out loud. "I'll do what you want."

A smile broke on Trapp's face like a tropical sunrise. He wasn't exactly looking forward to brutalizing the old man, but it was better than killing him. And ultimately, it was his own choice. "Then you know the drill. Get back down below."

21

Trapp glanced at the mariner's watch on his left wrist for the hundredth time. Just under twenty minutes remained until his scheduled pickup time with the USS Cheyenne, and he was unable to relax. He scanned the distance in a bid to release his tension. Lights glistened on the Chinese mainland, twinkling in all manner of colors like the Christmas lights in Times Square. A ribbon of car headlights outlined the coastal road, and Trapp's wraithlike eyes were drawn to it like moths to a lamp. The unbroken chain of cars seemed never ending.

Though he had traveled to Asia many times over the course of his career, the scale of the continent never failed to amaze him. China alone had almost one and a half billion citizens, and the country, while undoubtedly the largest, was just one of half a dozen such budding superpowers in this region.

One and a half billion souls, Trapp thought, turning the very concept of that amount of people over in his mind. It was almost impossible to imagine. China had a population five times larger than that of the United States, and an economy that was a roaring tiger, not a wheezing donkey.

He shook his head silently in the darkness.

The yacht was several miles off the coast, waves lapping lazily against its hull as it drifted without navigation lights. If he hadn't been aware that a nuclear submarine was lurking somewhere in the depths of the ocean beneath him, cutting through the saltwater like a killer whale, Trapp would have thought he had died and gone to heaven. A cool sea breeze kissed his face, ruffling his dark hair and providing some respite from the overpowering, muggy heat.

Every now and again a low thud rumbled the yacht's hull, reminding Trapp of the real monsters that lurked in the deep. He reassured himself that the sounds were most likely the unfortunate result of a flying fish colliding with the unexpected presence of his boat, but an older fear haunted him. The waters off the coast of Macau, he knew, harbored tiger sharks. They weren't the deadliest, nor the meanest of the many species of man-killing sharks...

But then again, they wouldn't need to be.

It would only take a single adventurous—or even merely confused–predator to take the first bite, and once his blood began to pool in the water the waves would become a frothing feeding frenzy. In a matter of minutes, there wouldn't be enough left of Jason Trapp to send home in a box.

Trapp's gaze shifted out to sea and fell upon an enormous container ship several miles in the distance. It was little more than an outline in the darkness, a ghost passing through the night, bracketed by the navigation lights that warned the unwitting of its presence.

"Snap out of it," he chided himself softly.

He turned and strode back into the yacht's small bridge, checking the Chinese satellite navigation system to ensure that he was in the correct location. Just like the other ten times he had checked, he found he was. The tide was low, the waves almost non-existent, and while there was a light breeze, it wasn't enough to push the heavy motoryacht off course.

The radio on the yacht's dashboard crackled, and an unintelligible stream of Mandarin erupted from the unit's speaker, a woman's voice in a clipped military tone. The words seemed to blend into one another without so much as a pause for breath. Trapp's command of the language was rusty. He'd picked up the basics on the Farm, but that was almost a decade ago, now —and even back then it would have been charitable to describe him as proficient. The CIA's instructors certainly hadn't.

He thought he had caught a couple of the words regardless. Something about a boat. An *unidentified* boat.

Trapp checked his watch. Nineteen minutes, thirty seconds. *Damnit.*

Time seemed to be moving slower now, as it always did in these situations. Trapp often wondered if there was a cruel god up there, tipping the scales and testing his resolve, making the seconds crawl as enemies closed in all around him.

He considered his options. There were few good ones, and pitfalls on every side. There were only two constants: first, that he could not allow himself to be captured, even if it came at the cost of his own life. And second, the USB drive could not be allowed to fall into Chinese hands.

The radio sounded again, and this time the woman's voice was even more insistent. A crawling sense of dread enclosed Trapp's stomach. He had no doubt that someone out there had identified a boat where a boat was not supposed to be.

His boat.

And that spelled trouble.

Reflexively Trapp checked his pistol. Even as he did it, he knew the action was fruitless. If a Chinese coast guard cutter emerged out of the darkness, it would be equipped with a fifty caliber machine gun on its bow, a weapon capable of cutting not just his body but the entire yacht in half with consummate ease. There would be no shooting his way out of this one.

Not this time.

He needed a better option and needed it fast. He paced the small hardwood deck, chewing his cheek. He didn't have long before a team of Navy SEALs would emerge from the inky blackness of the South China Sea, submachine guns at the ready, prepared to go to battle with any foe on his behalf, and die in the process if necessary.

But that salvation was twenty minutes away, and he might not have that long. He needed an edge of his own, a way to tip the scales. It came to him in a flash of insight.

Radar.

Trapp remembered the brochure, remembered that yachts of this class were sold with a navigation radar. He grabbed his flashlight, masking the beam in order to minimize any unwanted light emissions, and scanned the yacht's control console.

He thanked his lucky stars once again that these million-dollar boats were built as toys for rich boys. They were user-friendly to a fault. Much of the console was taken up by a single touchscreen which blinked into life the second his fingertips grazed it, illuminating the inside of the yacht's luxuriously appointed cabin. Trapp grimaced. In the darkness, it was like a *come and get me* sign.

He flipped through the screens until he found the one he was looking for. A two-dimensional map of the area, bracketed on one side by a representation of the coast. Ghostly icons at the very edge of the radar's range blinked in and out of existence, and contacts in the center, larger or smaller depending on the strength of the radar signal received in return, were given an icon commensurate with their size.

In the distance, far beyond even Trapp's excellent night vision, the sea was alive with vessels. Large container ships drifting on set trade routes could be linked like constellations and scattered all around them were smaller craft: pleasure yachts and fishing boats.

Most of the boats moved sedately, in set patterns, or with no particular intention at all.

All but one.

A single icon zipped across the screen at a frightening speed on a vector that would bring it directly to the yacht that Trapp was currently standing on. According to the scale at the bottom of the screen, Trapp estimated that the boat was several nautical miles away—but it was closing fast.

He glanced up through the glass windshield that protected the yacht's small bridge and oriented himself, tracking his eyes through the darkness until he settled on the unknown vessel's chosen route. It wasn't hard to pick the oncoming boat out of the blackness that had settled on the ocean like a thick winter blanket. It dwarfed his own yacht, an illuminated bridge sitting at least fifteen feet off the surface of the water. Beyond that, it was impossible to make out any details. Then again, he didn't need to be able to read the number stenciled on the side of the cutter's hull to know that, in about seven minutes, he was going to be in a whole world of hell.

"Fuck," Trapp growled.

The word neatly summed up his current predicament. Put simply, he was screwed. The Sunseeker yacht's engines were frighteningly powerful, capable of propelling the boat at speeds of over thirty knots. He had no doubt that no matter how fast the boat chasing him was, he would at least push it to its limits if it came to a drag race.

But there was one problem with that option. Well, actually there were a number of problems with it, but Trapp's mind focused on one in particular. If he moved from this very spot, then the SEALs on the USS Cheyenne would emerge from the depths of the ocean only to find their prize was long gone.

The Sunseeker's engines were built for speed, not fuel economy, and Trapp had no doubt that even if he *could* outrun his pursuers, they would guzzle through his limited fuel supplies long before the larger boat ran dry. Running wasn't an option.

Trapp slammed his fist down on the yacht's navigation console, chewing his lip with frustration. He was boxed in.

Unless...

Perhaps there was a way out of this, after all. He would be putting his life in the hands of the man upstairs, but he had done so dozens of times before, and a Hail Mary play had never failed him on those occasions.

You can only push your luck so far...

Trapp ignored the warning. His subconscious was correct, of course, but in an entirely meaningless fashion. He only had two choices: wait for the Chinese to apprehend him, or do something that they would not expect.

And since he had made a career out of always choosing that latter option, Trapp decided that right now was no time to change the habits of a lifetime.

He pushed a button on the console in front of him, and the yacht's powerful engines thrummed into life, coughing huskily before they settled down into a rhythmic throb. He brought the yacht around so that its bow faced into the dark of the ocean and glanced at the radar console to ensure that the path ahead was clear.

Plotting a route through the maelstrom of coastal sea traffic felt like playing an 80s arcade game—one wrong move, and the expensive yacht would collide with a steel-hulled container ship many thousands of times its size. The larger ship probably wouldn't even register the impact, but the luxury yacht certainly would. Trapp had taken a liking to the sullen Communist Party official trussed up below decks and had no great desire to send the man to an initially fiery, then very wet demise.

Still, the mission was more important than one man's life—and that held true whether that life was Trapp's own or Secretary Liu's. It was a risk the experienced operative was willing to take if it meant getting the job done.

Trapp set the yacht on his chosen course, crossing his fingers one last time as the powerful engines turned the saltwater below his feet into white spray, sending the yacht surging forward through the ocean. He thought about going below decks to wish Liu luck but decided against it. He turned to leave the cabin and was almost away before he stopped. He turned back, drew his side arm in one swift movement, and fired several rounds into the communications console. The small LCD screen on the front died instantly, a bullet hole cracking the glass. A singed smell filled the humid air, and satisfied the system was out of operation, Trapp left, snatching a small waterproof bag from a neatly organized shelf as he did so.

"Sorry, buddy," he muttered, imagining the apoplectic expression on Liu's face when the crooked communist discovered the damage to his yacht.

If he lasted that long

The Chinese GPS unit in his other hand looked waterproof —at least, Trapp hoped that was the case. With the American satellites seemingly out of action, his only chance of making the pickup destination in the right place at the right time rested —ironically enough—in China's hands. He entered the coordinates for the rendezvous destination into the device and watched as the icons indicating his own position and that of his destination began to diverge.

It was time to go. At thirty knots, it wouldn't take long for the yacht to outpace the range of the mode of transport he was planning on taking. And the success or failure of the next few minutes would rest entirely on timing.

As the yacht's engines growled, the hull of the luxurious boat cutting through the water with the relentless grace of a marine predator, Trapp jogged slowly to the back of the boat, checking once again that the flash drive was still prepared to take a one-way trip to the depths of the ocean in case he was indeed captured.

When he was certain, Trapp put the GPS device to one side and checked his pistol. He had one spare magazine and half a dozen rounds remaining in the one currently loaded. It wasn't enough to put up much of a fight.

He threw one last, lingering glance over his shoulder, noting with shock that the onrushing coast guard cutter had halved the distance between their two vessels already.

This is going to be tight.

Standing on the rear deck of the Sunseeker, Trapp quickly began to undress. He removed his boots, pants and jacket, and tossed each item off the yacht in quick succession. He briefly wondered what the SEALs would think when a half-naked man emerged from the waves and asked them for a ride down to the Cheyenne.

And then he decided he didn't care. If he'd made it that far, then it probably meant he was getting out of this mess alive.

He tossed the flash drive into the waterproof bag along with his spare magazine, but kept hold of the pistol itself, along with the Chinese GPS unit. He sealed the bag, looped its strap over his shoulder, then turned to complete his final task.

A sleek, powerful-looking JetSki sat on the yacht's rear deck. Trapp quickly unlatched it from its moorings, grunting as he heaved the heavy toy across the deck, scratching the wooden surface in the process. The toy was finished with a shiny black coating, which Trapp hoped would fade into the night. He was pretty certain that it would ride too low over the water to be visible on the radar, but couldn't be certain until he put it to the test.

With one last heave, he pushed the JetSki off the Sunseeker at a right angle to the yacht's current trajectory, watching as it crashed into the ocean, briefly submerging beneath the yacht's powerful wash before, with agonizing slowness, it righted itself. Then, without further ado, Trapp dived into the sea after it, clutching the pistol in one hand and the GPS unit in the other. Each was as vital to his survival as the other, and he couldn't afford to lose his grip on either.

The roiling sea swallowed Trapp whole, the saltwater rushing up his nose and stinging his eyes. For a second, in the darkness, he wondered if this was what it was like to be dead. Beneath the surface of the water all was silent. He couldn't even hear his own heartbeat, or the roar of blood in his ears.

And then the madness returned. The top of his head broke the surface of the waves, and Trapp gasped in a deep breath. All around, waves towered over him like snow-capped mountains, blocking out his view of the line of cars on the coast road, reminding him that in this environment he was nothing more than an untested stranger.

Briefly, panic filled his veins, ice against the warm embrace of the tropical ocean.

The Sunseeker's wash tossed his body about like a ragdoll, submerging his head once more, starving him of breath. And then for a second time, Trapp burst through, sucked in a mouthful of precious oxygen and began to swim. The JetSki was already barely visible in the darkness, and though Trapp's brain was screaming, protesting the lack of oxygen in his blood, he shut out the ancient terror of drowning, windmilled his arms and cut a path toward his salvation.

Minutes later he hoisted himself out of the water, collapsed onto the JetSki's padded leather seat and sucked mouthfuls of oxygen into his straining lungs. Rivulets of water ran down his bare skin, and salt stung his eyes. A sense of exhaustion bore down on him like a tidal wave, threatening to unseat him entirely. It was all he could do to clutch on to his tiny vessel for long enough to recover.

Get moving.

The voice inside his head growled a warning, as it had done so many times before. Trapp knew that he wasn't out of danger yet. There was no guarantee that the cutter had fallen for his bait.

If the larger vessel gave chase, rather than following the enticing, lit-up prize of the Sunseeker, then Trapp knew what he had to do. He would be forced to ditch the flash drive, then set a course for the shore. He couldn't risk leading the SEALs into a trap.

Slowly, fighting against muscles that had almost given in to exhaustion, Trapp brought the GPS unit to his face, praying that it still functioned. Thankfully, it did. A thin sheen of salt blurred the screen, but Trapp wiped it off. He was already almost a mile away from the rendezvous point.

Glancing at his watch, he realized he had only nine minutes left.

And then he realized he had a far bigger problem to contend with. The Sunseeker's glistening lights were already far into the distance, chased by a searchlight from the powerful cutter which was quickly making up ground. Already he could barely make out the sound of the two boats' engines over the lapping of the waves against the JetSki's hull.

But the cutter wasn't the problem.

Another boat was emerging from the darkness. Trapp squinted, attempting to make out the source of the sound: higher-pitched, and harder-working as it chewed through the water. More Jack Russell than the thunderous, pedigree growl of the larger vessel's engines.

Could it just be a coincidence? He struck that option down immediately.

Only one explanation made sense. The cutter had–somehow–detected the smaller radar signature of the JetSki and detailed another vessel to come check things out. Trapp respected the skill of the radar operator, if not the results of his tenacity.

This had just turned into a race.

The problem was, at top speed, the JetSki could cover a mile in a minute–and the rendezvous point was only sixty seconds away. Trapp realized that he would have to lead his pursuers on a merry chase for the next few minutes, or he would bring all hell down on his extraction team.

"Okay then," he growled, revving the JetSki's engine. "Let's see what you got."

22

E liza Ikeda awoke from the darkness a second time. As before, confusion reigned in her mind. The world was black, and her stomach churning. But this time the fog didn't last. A piercing cold brought her back to her senses with a start.

She was naked.

Eliza choked air into her lungs as her chest rose and fell in ragged gasps, her body on the edge of panic. Why was she naked? Where the hell was she?

Although the cold had kickstarted her mind, pouring fuel on the pyre, lighting a match and sparking her gray matter into action, she still had no idea what was happening to her. In the darkness her brain struggled to make any sense of the multitude of contradictory sensory signals it was receiving.

Open your eyes.

She did as the insistent voice inside her head commanded and prised her eyelids open. They were sticky with sleep and resisted her efforts, groaning in protest like a long-stuck door. But although her vision returned, it wasn't very revealing. The room she was in was cloaked in darkness. Eliza moved her head from side to side, searching for a frame of reference, or any clue as to how she had ended up in this predicament.

She was in a warehouse. Crates loomed out of the darkness like Soviet statues, big and blocky, stretching twenty feet upward on their racks. The only light emanated from small windows cut high overhead into the walls of the structure. From far off in the distance she heard the dull whirring of machinery.

A wave of nausea grew in Eliza's gut and gave her no time to prepare. A hot puddle of vomit coursed up her throat, the stomach acid burning its tender flesh, and she shifted her mouth to the side just in time for it to spray out onto the floor and not her own body. Her stomach heaved, as though physically trying to expel the last remnants of whatever chemical the North Koreans had dosed her with to put her to sleep. Tears stung her eyes and fell freely onto her bare skin, hot then cold.

Exhausted, she collapsed, her chin slumping against her chest. The nausea faded, not disappearing entirely, but prowling in the background like a monster in the darkness. She accepted the momentary respite gratefully and used it to regain control of her breath.

In, one, two; out, three, four.

In, one, two; out, three, four.

The trick worked. The panic hiding out in the far recesses of her mind subsided, allowing her brain to refocus on the situation at hand. She was naked, in a freezing cold room, imprisoned in a darkness so complete it barely allowed her to make out her own frame. But she was alive, and she could think. Puzzle out what had happened to her and settle on a plan that would get her out of this mess.

Experimentally, she attempted to move her fingers. She wiggled them and felt the digits respond in the darkness. Next, she tried to move her right hand, raising it in the air—but was unsuccessful. The movement started, then almost instantly stopped dead with the force of an iron door slamming shut.

The fear that Eliza had been biting down on returned in full force. She was bound by the wrists, and she now realized, also by her ankles. Someone had stripped her naked and tied her to a chair. Overhead an HVAC unit rumbled, pumping out a cold that bit at her exposed skin, causing goosebumps to rise like mountains in the darkness.

Was she hurt?

She considered the question, her mind probing her body to arrive at an answer. She attempted to move, first digit by digit, then limb by limb, and detected no pain other than that dull throbbing emanating from her skull where she had been hit. So she was okay. Or at least as okay as anyone knocked out by the butt of a pistol had any right to feel.

She puzzled over her options.

Like a captured soldier, Eliza knew that she only had one duty: to escape. But right now she did not see how that was possible. She was bound tight to a chair, in what was presumably a locked warehouse. And though her eyes were finally acclimatizing to the gloom, she could make out no tools that she could use to break free of her binds.

She cast her senses further into the inky gloom. Her eyes were useless: capable only of picking out objects in her immediate vicinity and tricking her into seeing threats where there were none. Instead, she stilled her own breath and listened.

At first she heard nothing useful. The world was confined to a cone comprised of little more than her own body: the groaning of her stomach, the thundering of her heart, the rushing blood in her eardrums. But she waited, calming her awareness of her body's instinctive processes, forcing her consciousness to recede.

Slowly, the cone of her awareness grew. By painstaking inches, at first, then yards, then expanding at pace, like a bat soaring through the night sky. She took in the whir of the HVAC unit, the rustling of scurrying rodents, the dull thundering of her own heartbeat. She listened, and her mind created a mental map of her surroundings.

Though her eyes deceived her into believing the darkness might stretch out forever, her ears told Eliza the truth. The warehouse was small, probably no larger than a couple of thousand square feet. She sensed no cavernous emptiness around her; the whir of the HVAC motor bounced back too quickly from the hard structures all around rather than being lost to infinity. Her nose fought the acrid tag of vomit and picked out musky undertones: sweet scents and savory ones; the telltale sign of food.

Ikeda's stomach writhed as she realized that not only was she starving, but she was like a man dying of thirst in the middle of the ocean. There was food all around her, but she had no way of accessing it. It was the cruelest form of torture.

You hope, she reminded herself caustically. Whatever the Koreans wanted, they certainly hadn't forgotten about her. She had no doubt that they would be back, searching for answers. And with Alstyne most certainly dead, the only person left to answer them was her.

A sound penetrated the darkness, deep and sonorous, and all-encompassing. Eliza flinched, her restraints biting into her wrists as she pulled against them. Reassured that it didn't pose an immediate threat, she puzzled over what the hell it was— and any clue it might provide.

A train? Was she near a set of tracks?

No.

A ship's horn.

Having grown up on the seafaring island nation of Japan, and then finished her schooling on Hawaii's Big Island, Eliza Ikeda was no stranger to the sounds of the ocean. And without a doubt, she knew, that was where she was. Not on a ship, but a warehouse near the waterfront.

And that could mean only two things: either the Koreans intended to kill her and dispose of her body at sea.

Or...

A chill ran down Ikeda's spine, standing out even against the cool of the air-conditioning, which had caused the temperature in the warehouse to plummet to what felt like no more than ten degrees.

If they were hiding out in a warehouse by the sea, and if her assumption about their country of origin was correct, the logical conclusion was that her kidnappers intended to take her back to North Korea with them.

And if they succeeded, she knew without a doubt that she would never return. Nobody did, not from the Hermit Kingdom.

Especially not an American spy.

Eliza's teeth began to chatter. She closed her eyes and offered up a silent prayer, hoping that someone up there was listening. This wasn't just *a* nightmare, this was *her* nightmare. She had been raised an only child, not because her parents hadn't wanted siblings for her, but because of the disappearance of her mother when Eliza was just a young girl. And like any child struggling to understand why her family wasn't like all the others, Eliza had asked her father why she didn't have a mommy.

"Go to bed," he'd replied, fingers clutched around the mouth of a dark brown bottle.

That bottle, and thousands like it, were a fixture of Eliza's childhood. They contained beer, at first. Then whiskey—initially expensive, then cheaper by the year, as the taste ceased to matter, forgotten in favor of the fiery liquid's numbing embrace.

"Where's Mommy?" Eliza had insisted, hands on her hips, face

contorted not with sadness, but anger. Even back then, she was a headstrong child.

"She's gone," *her dad had growled.* "And she ain't never coming back."

Eliza crossed her arms. "What do you mean gone? Gone where?"

The bottle sailed through the air, another victim of a drunk's irrepressible rage. Frothy liquid danced from its lips as it cartwheeled, then collided with the kitchen wall. Her father sprang to his feet, his expression black as the memories he was drowning assailed him once more.

His arm shot out, finger pointing almost in accusation. "Bed, now!"

"No! Not until you tell me."

Eliza didn't stomp her foot, but she may as well have. Her father blinked, then crumpled as a wave of guilt overcame him. He was barely holding it together, she knew that even then. He collapsed into the chair, fingers searching automatically for the bottle, now lying in shards against the wall. "They took her," *he whispered.*

"Who?"

"The North Koreans."

Now Eliza blinked. She hadn't dared to ask her father about what happened to her mom again, not after that night. But even growing up on a US army base in Japan, surrounded by American children and taught in American schools, Eliza had heard the rumors, the tales told by children on the playground.

Tales of Japanese women stolen in the night and spirited across the sea, never to be seen again. Taken to North Korea for God knows what purpose. Perhaps that was why Ikeda had learned Korean in the first place. Even in Japan, a close neighbor—and for centuries the fiercest rival of the Korean people—few spoke the language.

But she did.

And Eliza had also learned the truth in those tales. About the hundreds of Japanese women, just like her mother, stolen to order by the North Korean state. Taken to serve as wives for their elite, to teach Japanese in their espionage schools, and perhaps merely as a twisted act of revenge for the centuries of Japanese pillage of the Korean Peninsula.

Whether that was truly her mother's fate, neither Eliza nor her father would ever know. Like hundreds of others, plucked from the beaches and towns that dotted Japan's western shore, she became a ghost—never to be heard from again.

And although Eliza had no clear memories of her mom, just a composite constructed from fragments of her father's insensible ramblings as he plunged ever deeper into the depths of the bottle, and the photo books hidden away so that her face couldn't trouble him, Akira Ikeda had left her daughter with the gift of the Korean language.

A language whose sibilant tones now drifted into the warehouse.

Eliza froze in the darkness, holding her breath—more out of instinct than any other reason. The words were indistinct, but they were getting closer, accompanied by the scraping of boots against concrete, and the screech of a poorly oiled hinge being wrenched open. It was difficult to make out which direction the voices were coming from, but as the door opened, Eliza realized it was from behind her. She silently cursed her restraints as she attempted to crane her neck left, then right. It was as though her body was locked into a straitjacket.

"—the colonel will never know. Why not have some fun?"

There was a crash, as though someone was being slammed up against a wall, and a second voice spoke, its tone low and harsh. "He knows everything, you fool. If you think one fuck is worth risking your life for, be my guest."

A wave of nausea rose in Eliza's stomach once more, and this time she knew it wasn't a result of the knock her head had sustained. The men were talking about her. Talking about *abusing* her.

Eliza Ikeda had never felt so alone—or so vulnerable. Secured to the chair beneath her, she knew she had no prospect of escape, no way to fight back. Whatever these men planned for her, she would be no more than an unwilling passenger. She had no way of evening the odds.

At least, not *physically.*

The first voice spoke again. "What makes this bitch so different? She's just some Chinese whore. Or..." His tone changed, and Eliza painted a picture in her head of a sly expression crawling across his face. "Is it that you want her for yourself?"

"Jung, I have a wife," the second voice replied with disgust. "And you know why. We let the American die—"

"So what?" the first voice interjected. "We have the drive. Let's put a bullet through the girl's skull and get the hell out of here. The longer we wait the more likely the Chinese find us. And if they do, we're dead men."

"We have the drive," the second man conceded. "But it's encrypted. Without the American, it's useless to us. Are you volunteering to tell the colonel we failed him?"

There was a pause. "No."

"I didn't think so. The bitch is our only hope of surviving this. So we had better get some answers from her, hadn't we?"

"What if she doesn't know anything?"

The first man was silent for a long time. When he spoke, his voice was low and angry, with such malevolent menace that Eliza couldn't help but fear for her life. "Then we're fucked."

There was another pause, and Eliza pictured the two men staring each other down. And then the scraping of boots against concrete resumed, and they closed on with every step. She gripped the arms of the chair beneath her tightly, her entire body shivering, no longer from the cold. A flashlight clicked on, and its beam played out across the scraped, oil-stained concrete floor. It kicked up for a second, revealing crate after crate of foodstuffs, packaged and ready for export.

Eliza realized she was right. She was near the docks. If she managed to free herself, there would be a thousand routes she could take without getting caught.

If she managed to free herself...

Her head snapped left, and it was only a second later she realized that she had been slapped—hard.

She groaned in pain, her ears ringing, tears stinging her eyes. The action physically rocked the chair off its legs as Eliza was forced to one side, and the movement wrenched her wrists in their restraints, burning the tender skin underneath.

The flashlight jumped upward, its beam pointed directly at Eliza's eyes.

"Tell me your name," the man said.

Her brain groaned from the repeated assaults it had sustained over the past few hours. Adrenaline flooded into her system, but as her mind recovered, it was like attempting to run through quicksand. The harder she worked, the further she sank.

She opened her mouth to reply, but her lips moved wordlessly.

Another hit, and her face screamed with pain. Even through it, Eliza knew that something was wrong; her subconscious screamed a warning. What was it?

English, she realized. *He's speaking in English.*

It was a trap. The man was attempting to bait her into revealing her true identity. He clearly suspected she was more than the escort she'd presented herself as.

"Who are you?" she replied in flawless Mandarin, purposefully sagging forward against her restraints. "I don't speak English."

Tears and saliva and snot streamed down Eliza's face. Though she could not see herself, she knew she must look a pitiful sight. It was perfectly fine with her. She didn't expect it would slow this psychopath down but maybe, just maybe, it would give him pause for thought.

"Tell me the truth," her interrogator growled, still speaking heavily accented English. "We know who you are."

"Please," she whimpered in reply, "please don't do this to me. I promise, if you let me go I won't say anything. To anyone, I swear it..."

Eliza allowed herself to cry. Cunning mixed with gut-clenching fear, and the tears that fell from her eyes were more real than she dared admit. The beam of the flashlight still hovered over her eyes, blinding her.

The interrogator paused, allowing the silence to stretch out. "Who are you?"

Eliza realized that this time, he had spoken in Mandarin. She counted it as a victory.

"Why are you doing this to me?" she cried. "I don't know who that man is, I promise. I went where I was told."

Another slap. Eliza's head rocked back once more, and this time the ringing in her ears did not stop so quickly. Nausea cramped her stomach, and it took all of her resolve to bite back on a wave of vomit.

"You're lying."

"I swear it, I'm not. Please, just let me go."

As her lips moved, Eliza's mind worked furiously. She didn't expect her deception to convince these men. Whoever they were, they were hardened killers, that much was clear, and would be as relentless as hunting hounds. It would take more than a woman crying to throw them off the scent. Besides, she had killed one of their own.

No, Ikeda knew that even if they decided she was innocent of the first crime, that she was merely a bystander in the wrong place at the wrong time, they would not let her go. Not after what she had done. Either they would put a bullet in her brain and dump her in the sea, or torture her to death and leave her right here.

She didn't allow herself to consider the third option: that these men might use her before they killed her.

There was only one way she was getting out of this. She needed to buy herself enough time and space to survive, so that when an opportunity to escape presented itself, she was both strong enough—and alive enough—to seize it.

And the only way to ensure both of those outcomes was to allow her interrogators to believe that she might just know something.

Another hit, fast and powerful, impacted her stomach. It drove the wind from her lungs, made her retch with pain, sending saliva flying from her mouth and sliding down her chin. Eliza gasped desperately for air, but it was no use.

"OK," she whimpered, false tears mixing with real ones in her desire to convince her captors she was telling the truth. "The American, he paid me, that's all. To steal a USB drive."

A chair scraped against the concrete floor, and the leader of the men, the man known as Jung, settled across from her, a gleam in his eyes. "Who are you?"

"An escort."

Jung sneered. "A whore."

Eliza set her chin with determination, as though insulted, as though she had to live with that kind of insult every day.

There was a kernel of truth to it.

Though she was no prostitute, the world of espionage was a man's game—or so they liked to insist. Many operatives, particularly from the old school, believed that a man could do any job a woman could, only better. They looked down on the 'skirts' as evidence of political correctness gone mad. Ikeda knew better, of course. Her assassination of Emmanuel Alstyne just that evening had proved beyond a shadow of a doubt that there were places that a woman could go that her male counterparts could not.

She could do things that the men simply couldn't.

And so her performance wasn't merely an act. Ikeda's voice came out low and hard. "An escort," she spat, eyes flashing red.

"I don't believe you," Jung replied. He snapped his fingers, and barked a command, and the second commando left the room. He returned a second later dragging the body of Alstyne himself—stiff and cold, and quite obviously dead.

Jung smiled, as though he had her in check. His upper lip curled, and he spat the words, "He died three hours ago, you lying bitch. Do you expect me to believe that was merely a coincidence?"

Ikeda looked away, guilt written on her face. She'd known it would come to this, of course. And she also knew the next few seconds would demand the performance of a lifetime—and more than a shred of the truth.

"I—," she stammered.

"You what?"

Tears flowed down Ikeda's cheeks, carving a path through the blood and landing dark red on her tanned, naked body. "I didn't know," she whimpered, her voice a low, pained moan. "He said..."

Jung leaned forward. "He said what?"

"He lied!" Ikeda howled, in faux anguish laced with real emotion. Alstyne was her first kill. He deserved it, but she was no psychopath. She should have been flown directly to an Agency shrink after completing the operation, for a debrief to check her mental state.

That, of course, would not now happen.

Ikeda stumbled over the rest of her confession, the speech pained and halting. "He said it would just put him to sleep. So I could search the room, and get out without him noticing. He said the American would wake up with a hangover, and I'd be long gone."

Jung turned to his comrade, a sneer stretched across his face. He muttered two words in Korean. Ikeda had to strain to hear them. "*Useful idiot.*"

"Please," Ikeda whimpered, hoping she'd sold her story. "Just let me go. I'll tell you everything I know. And no-one will find out about you. I promise."

"Oh," Jung said, turning back to face her with contempt in his voice. "I know. You're coming with us, bitch. I'll find out if you're telling the truth. One way or another..."

23

The matte-black miniature submersible cut through the inky waters of the South China Sea, invisible both to the naked eye and, this close to shore, to even the most advanced sonar systems operated by the People's Liberation Army's Navy.

Lieutenant Mitchell 'Nero' Quinn sat in the flooded compartment of the SEAL Delivery Vehicle, as the minisub was officially—and unimaginatively—named. In his platoon, they called it the Pig.

The Pig was, like her namesake, fat, slow and ugly. But it afforded Quinn and his men a greatly increased time on station, supplying them with oxygen and minimizing the loss of vital bodily fluids to the ocean: an inevitable, inescapable natural law that ordinarily constrained naval special warfare. The SDV, built to carry six men and their equipment into battle, was the US Navy thumbing Mother Nature in the eye.

Naval special operators were generally considered to be a breed apart—but even among the Navy SEALs, members of the SEAL Delivery Vehicle Team One, or SDVT-1, were known to be hard nuts to crack.

You would have to be, since climbing into one of the cramped, windowless minisubs was like entering the black hole of Calcutta. With a range of fifteen nautical miles, the Pig could carry SEALs on missions that lasted as long as eight hours.

Nero hoped that would not be the case tonight. It was supposed to be an easy job—a pickup of a nameless CIA asset. In Lieutenant Quinn's opinion, however, there was no such thing as an easy mission, especially when the job entailed operating inside the maritime borders of the world's only other superpower: China.

He wouldn't rest easy until he was back on the USS Cheyenne and making twenty knots back out to open water.

The silence didn't help the lieutenant's nerves. The Pig was battery operated, and even inside the submersible itself only a faint vibration from the electric motor was detectable—and only if Nero was concentrating extra hard. Add to that the fact that the re-breathing devices the SEALs wore rendered their breathing almost silent, and Nero often thought the SDV resembled nothing better than a sunk coffin.

A low red light filled the flooded rear compartment of the Pig, just enough for Nero to make out the remaining two members of his fighting team, who sat opposite him displaying no visible emotion behind their facemasks.

Like Nero himself they were equipped with fins, a dark wetsuit, a diving knife strapped to their left thigh, and a modified version of the venerable M4 A1 carbine, known as the Close Quarter Battle Receiver, or CQBR. The weapon was compact, designed to combine the stopping power of an assault rifle with the condensed form factor of a submachine gun. It was the perfect weapon for the confined environment of the SDV, and in the hands of his highly trained Navy SEALs, it was lethal.

Nero brought his wrist to his face, fighting against the familiar tug of the water resistance to check the time. The watch face cast off a luminous green glow, so it was protected by a plastic covering which he flicked off. Only a few minutes remained until the designated rendezvous time.

A pilot and navigator sat at the bow of the Pig, facing forward unlike the three members of Nero's fighting team. They were hunched over the controls, studying dimly lit screens to make sure they remained on course.

Nero was aware that the Cheyenne had lost contact with the navy's network of satellites some hours before, but GPS was useless underwater anyway. Every SEAL was an expert navigator—but none more so than the man navigating the Pig: Chief Petty Officer Dan Dunn, known in the platoon as 'Double-D,' a nod to the unfortunate choice of names his parents had chosen, and not the impressive circumference of his muscular chest.

The lieutenant twisted and tapped Double-D on his shoulder. The special operator turned to face his CO, and Nero flashed the man a hand signal to indicate that it was time to begin surfacing the Pig. Double-D nodded in confirmation, relayed the information to the pilot, and then shot Nero a thumbs-up.

Even were it not for the fact that each of the SEALs was breathing from a tube that rendered it impossible to talk, it was equally impossible for radio waves to traverse through water. As a result, communication in the submersible was limited to the complex sequence of hand signals that Nero and his men had long ago mastered. It was good practice for warfare on the surface, too. As such, Nero's team was a finely tuned machine, and one that had gone into battle together dozens of times.

The sub began to rise slowly through the waters of the South China Sea, and Nero followed its progress on an illuminated diving meter on the ceiling of the SDV. Ten minutes before the designated rendezvous time the Pig breached the surface of the ocean with little fanfare. The pilot sent up a thin periscope, spinning it three hundred and sixty degrees, then shot Nero and the two members of the fighting team the A-OK sign.

Both the pilot and navigator were fully qualified members of Nero's team in their own right, but on this mission they were slated to stay in the sub in case the fighting team needed to make a quick getaway. Nero checked that his two shooters were ready to go, then released the retractable ceiling on the rear compartment. His two men slid out, and he followed them.

Once on the surface, Nero undid his rebreather and allowed it to hang loosely around his neck. He would need it on the return journey, so out of habit he double-checked it was secure.

It was.

His two men had already assumed firing positions crouched on top of the Pig, carbines scanning the horizon for targets. But the ocean was empty, bar the blinking navigation lights of faraway container ships busily crossing the waterways in search of China's rapacious ports. The heat of the thick, polluted air off the Chinese coast pressed down on him immediately, palpable even through the sleek wetsuit that covered every inch of his body.

"How we looking?" he hissed.

"Clean as a whistle, Nero," came the drawled reply from Petty Officer Tim 'Homer' DiMaggio, whose eye was glued to a thermal night vision scope, slowly scanning the sea in a full rotation. "I don't see nothing."

"You don't see *anything*," corrected the third member of his team, a squat, powerful Latino named Santiago 'Santa' Reyes. Like the lieutenant himself—but unlike many enlisted SEALs —Santa was book smart as well as street smart, and the petty officer loved playing up to his reputation.

"Cut it out, guys," Nero added, hiding a smile at his men's

irreverent humor–a feature of special forces teams the world over. "Save it until we're back on the Cheyenne."

"You got it, boss. So where's our boy?" Homer asked.

Lieutenant Quinn shrugged and glanced down at his still-open watch face. Nine minutes remained until the designated rendezvous time. His instructions were to remain on the surface for ten minutes past the allotted hour, and then to retreat to the safety of the ocean's depths, ready to try it all over again in a few hours' time.

"Your guess is as good as mine."

Nero hoped the package he was expecting would be delivered tonight. If it wasn't, then he and his men would be right back in the Pig tomorrow night. He didn't know who—or what —was so damn important that it had his men out here, risking discovery, capture, or even death. But ultimately, he didn't care.

This was what he lived for. Leading these SEALs was the best job he'd ever had.

"Hold up lieutenant, scratch that," Homer said, his voice immediately assuming a cool, businesslike tone that immediately grabbed Nero's full attention. "I've got a vessel, no—two of them, heading south fast. Looks like a chase."

"Shit," Nero muttered. "You think that's our guy?"

"If it is," Homer added, typically economical with his vocabulary, "then he's fucked."

Nero moved low over the bobbing SDV, riding the movement of the waves like a born sailor. His carbine was slung around his neck, but he kept one arm pressed against it, to avoid creating any unwanted sound. Reaching Homer, he stretched out his hand. "Let me see."

He took the scope off his subordinate and brought it to his eye. The world lit up in varying shades of white and gray. Through the scope, the chase was as clear as day. It was impossible to make out the class of either boat through the blurry grayscale painting, but Nero knew immediately that the pursuing vessel was military.

"Shit," he growled for the second time. "This isn't good."

"Hell no it ain't," Homer murmured.

Nero catalogued his options. His orders were to remain at the rendezvous point, not go on a wild goose chase—though beyond that, the rules of engagement were practically nonexistent.

His job was to successfully expedite the retrieval of an Agency asset, no matter what the consequences—even if that meant creating an international incident. The SOCOM colonel who'd issued his instructions had been crystal clear on that point.

The problem was, the Pig was built to go low and slow. It had neither the range nor the speed to join the chase quickly disappearing in the distance. Nero chewed his lip. It wasn't in his makeup to simply give up, but he didn't know what else to do.

Reyes' slightly accented Hispanic voice called out, low over the slapping of the waves. "You hear that, boss?"

"Hear what?"

Reyes held a finger to his lips. Nero followed the man's instructions, stilling his breath and listening. At first, he heard only the waves lapping against the black hull of the miniature submersible, the dull roar of waves crashing against the cliffs many miles in the distance, and the occasional screech of a seabird overhead.

But then he heard it. A high-pitched whine, like that of the mosquito, combined with another sound, like a hand slapping against their flesh.

Or...

"Dude, is that a JetSki?" Homer mumbled.

Nero brought his carbine to his shoulder, scanning the surface of the waves for any sign of a target, his ears slightly cocked as he attempted to home in on the source of the noise. The lieutenant's forehead wrinkled. The idea of a JetSki this far out to sea, this late at night made no sense at all. Not unless some vacationer was very, very lost.

If that was the case, and the unlucky soul came across a squad of Navy SEALs, bristling with high-powered weapons, they were about to be in for the surprise of their lives.

But somehow, Nero didn't think that was the case.

"Stay sharp," he ordered. "Homer, get on the scope and tell me what you see."

"Way ahead of you, boss."

The three men fell silent, swaying up and down as the Pig was buffeted by a set of increasingly large waves. Neither Nero nor Reyes' barrel so much as shifted an inch, however. Both men were exquisitely attuned to operating in the aquatic environment they now found themselves in.

"Got it," Homer drawled with satisfaction. "One contact, coming south, southeast."

"JetSki?" Nero asked urgently, pivoting toward the direction Homer had indicated. Without the scope, it was harder to make out the contact, but Nero's left eye was perfectly accustomed to the darkness, after spending several hours in the gloom of the Pig before breaching the surface of the ocean, and he saw the glint of a light, low over the surface of the water.

"Naw," Homer replied. "Bigger. And heading straight for us."

The sound of another engine was audible now—a growl, not a whine. In the darkness, it carried easily over the waves, displacing the high-pitched whine that Nero had heard earlier.

"I don't like this," Nero said, stating the obvious. "Can you see what we're up against?"

"Nope."

Nero ground his teeth. "Great."

What the hell was he supposed to do? Was the oncoming

contact the asset he'd been ordered to retrieve? Or was the operative's cover already blown—and if so, was the onrushing vessel on its way to roll up him and his men?

Nero had no great desire to spend the next ten years languishing in a Chinese military prison. He had no doubt that his team would be tried as spies, leading to a fate that he didn't even want to contemplate.

"What's the plan, boss?" Reyes said.

Nero grimaced in the darkness, glad his men couldn't see how torn he was. He desperately wanted to give the order to retreat into the Pig, and thereafter to sink into the safety of the inky waves, but he knew he could not give that command. He was here to do a job, and he was damn well going to do it.

He shook his head, punching his thigh with frustration. "Hold tight," he ordered. "If something looks at you funny, take the shot—but you better be damn sure it's not a friendly before you do."

"Got it," Reyes replied.

Nero knew that the compact Latino was the best shot—and the steadiest personality—under his command. It was the reason he'd picked the man for tonight's mission. Reyes would not let him down.

The lieutenant just hoped that he could say the same about himself. Night after night, he agonized about failing these men in battle. It was why he pushed himself so hard to be the best— so that he had the right to *lead* the best. Because that's what Reyes and Homer were—along with the rest of the SEALs under Nero's command.

Not just the best operators he'd met—but the best damn people he'd ever known.

"They're about a click out, and closing fast," Homer added.

Nero could see the boat more clearly now, or at least, the searchlight on the front of it. As the vessel cut through the waves, bouncing against the surface of the ocean, it jerked up and down, occasionally seeming to shine directly in the lieutenant's eyes. He squinted, training the optical sight on the top of his carbine onto the oncoming vessel. He was missing something, he was sure of it.

Jackpot.

The light was probing the darkness, jerking left and right, as though searching for something. Which meant...

His eyes widened. "Gentlemen, stay frosty. I think our boy's on a JetSki like we thought. And he's got company."

Reyes and Homer signaled their understanding. Nero focused his hearing, searching for the whine he'd heard before. It was more difficult to make out now, over the deeper growl of the chasing boat. And then he caught it.

It was close. Damn close.

And then it died.

A voice called out the darkness, low and urgent. "Don't shoot! I'm American."

Nero spun, searching for the source of the voice. And then he saw it–a naked man, sitting atop a pitch black JetSki that was now silently cutting through the waves under its own momentum alone.

By the time it had closed to within twenty yards of the Pig, Nero realized that the man wasn't, in fact, naked–though it was close enough. He trained his weapon on the powerfully built man, who responded by pointedly keeping his hands on the controls.

"Half a click," Homer muttered, referencing the chasing boat. "We don't got long."

"We don't have—" started Reyes before cutting himself off, thinking better of doling out a grammar lesson in the middle of what might soon descend into a firefight.

"Authenticate," Nero growled, keeping his weapon aimed directly at the unknown guest's head. Chances were ninety-nine in a hundred that he was the man they were here to pick up, but neither Nero nor his men had made it this far by taking chances.

The man reeled off a short alphanumeric sequence, one that Nero immediately recognized. He beckoned the man over.

"You're a sight for sore eyes," the man said as he clambered aboard the Pig, casting an anxious glance over his shoulder at his pursuers.

Nero couldn't help but grin at the man's strange appearance. He understood the thought process that had led the man to shedding his garments—a sensible desire to avoid sodden clothes pulling him into the depths of the ocean—but even so, it made for an amusing sight.

"You can tell me about it later," he said. "Looks like you brought company."

"I'm Jason, by the way," the visitor said, pulling a pistol from the elastic waistband of his underpants with an apologetic smile.

"I'll shake your hand later," Nero replied in a clipped tone of voice that betrayed his anxiety over the pursuing boat. "Homer, get Jason squared away."

"On it, boss," the Southerner drawled, scampering over toward the CIA operative.

Nero put all thoughts of their guest out of his mind. The first part of his objective was secured: he had the package. But the navy didn't give out prizes for coming second, and nor did they approve of only completing half of the mission. He didn't intend to let that happen.

He crouched down next to Reyes, who was staring down the optical sight on the barrel of his carbine. He spoke low, so as not to distract the man. "How's it looking?"

"It slowed down. Looks like four men aboard, with a fifty cal."

"Crap." Nero spun, held out his hand and barked, "Homer, scope."

DiMaggio broke away from equipping their guest with a rebreather, and talking him through what he could expect when the Pig disappeared beneath the surface of the waves, and handed Quinn the night vision scope.

Nero pressed it to his eyes, following the direction of Reyes' barrel. He saw the boat easily now, causing a surge of adrenaline to flood into his veins. The hairs on the back of his neck would've stood straight up if they weren't already soaking wet and sticky with salt.

Reyes was right. The boat had slowed, and was playing its searchlight left and right, searching for its lost target. The men aboard were searching a section of ocean several hundred yards from where the Pig was currently floating, but Nero knew that it wouldn't take long before they were discovered.

"How long you need, Homer?" he growled urgently.

"Sixty seconds, boss," the man replied.

Nero clamped his hand down on Reyes' shoulder. "You got a shot, Santa?"

"Yessir."

Lieutenant Mitchell Quinn grimaced. The last thing he wanted to do was order the execution of four men that evening. Judging by the class of the boat he could see through the scope, they were police or coast guard, not fully fledged military. They probably had no idea who they were hunting, or why.

But he would do it if he had to. The mission came first. The mission always came first. He gritted his teeth, and gave the order. "The second they look at you funny, light 'em up."

"You got it, boss," Reyes said, his tone cold and emotionless, belying his ordinarily sunny personality.

Nero crouched on the surface of the Pig, pressed his eye to his scope, and took aim. Reyes might be the best shot in his platoon, but the lieutenant was no slouch either. And if there was killing to be done, then he wasn't about to wash his hands of it.

"Thirty seconds," Homer updated.

The boat's engine grumbled as it shifted position, circling. Nero wondered what the men aboard were thinking. Would they open fire? Or would they die, eyes wide with shock as the searchlight played over the Pig, revealing highly trained men with weapons aimed directly at their skulls?

The searchlight moved agonizingly slowly, shifting left, then right, searching the empty ocean for any sign of Jason's JetSki. It was only fifty yards away now.

Then forty.

Nero counted in his head, holding his breath as he prepared to pull the trigger.

Thirty.

Twenty.

It would be a slaughter.

And then Homer hissed, "Good to go, boss."

Nero breathed a sigh of relief but left his eye trained on the barrel. He clipped his rebreather into place, then his face mask. It made aiming considerably more difficult, but the boat was now so close he couldn't miss.

He tapped Reyes on the shoulder and jerked his thumb back, then pointed his index finger into the water, giving the man the command to dive.

Behind him, he heard splashes as Homer and Jason entered the Pig's flooded rear compartment, then another as Reyes joined them. Mere seconds later, with Nero crouched on top of the SDV, it began to sink below the surface of the waves. And all the while, the searchlight crept closer and closer.

Finally, the lieutenant's barrel disappeared below the inky-black surface of the ocean. He looked up as the glow illuminated the water above him.

But the Chinese were too late.

The SEALs were already gone.

24

The US Navy helicopter flew low over the South China Sea, its rotor blades cutting through the hazy mist that lay over the surface of the ocean as it waited for a landing spot on the deck of the USS Nimitz, a one hundred thousand ton aircraft carrier currently located a few hundred nautical miles off the coast of China. The blades forced air downward, where it beat against the surface of the choppy waves, creating a crop circle that would disappear the second they were given permission to land.

Trapp gazed out of the MH-60 Knighthawk that had fetched him from the USS Cheyenne, his eyes taking in the grandeur of a US carrier strike group in its full pomp. The vessel's escorts stretched out into the horizon, arrayed in a ragged circle around the enormous vessel they were sworn to protect. Helicopters buzzed like gnats in all directions, ferrying supplies to and fro between the various ships, packages slung in great cargo nets held beneath the belly of the aircraft.

His current ride had been in a holding pattern for several minutes. That wasn't too great a problem, since the helicopter had refueled on the deck of a navy destroyer sent to meet it halfway—evidence of the importance the brass had placed on his successful retrieval.

He only wished he was arriving with better news.

High overhead, thunder crackled as F-18 fighter jets circled in a lazy pattern over the carrier as they flew their combat air patrol. Trapp couldn't make the gray aircraft out against the steel of a sky that threatened to burst at any second, but their afterburners made it plain that they were watching.

"We'll get you down in the next few minutes, sir," a member of the flight crew informed him, the man's head swallowed by his large flight helmet, his eyes covered with a black visor that made him resemble an enormous insect.

Trapp nodded his thanks. He wondered how these men and women kept themselves sane out here, surrounded by hundreds of miles of empty ocean, mostly bedding down in so-called 'hot racks,' where bunks were assigned to as many as three sailors, who rotated in and out of the cramped space in their cabins according to ever-changing work rotas.

He knew that he would never be able to cope.

Jason Trapp was a lone wolf, a man who positively required his freedom. And yet as far as the eye could see, thousands of sailors toiled to keep their country safe, just as he did. He silently paid his thanks.

As he did, his subconscious picked up on a change in the tempo of operations down on the aircraft carrier's flight deck. Two jets, which had been circling as they prepared to land, suddenly lifted their noses and rocketed almost vertically into the clouds. The noise of the engines was deafening even over the rotor noise currently pummeling Trapp's eardrums.

"What's going on, Chief?" Trapp asked.

Having spent years in the US Army, then Delta, and finally the Central Intelligence Agency's Special Operations Group, Trapp had little experience of naval operations. Though he was a relatively strong swimmer, as he had demonstrated when racing Eliza Ikeda in the sea of Hong Kong a couple of days earlier, he was certainly no expert in naval special warfare. That was the domain of the squids: the Navy SEALs.

Still, Trapp had spent more of his life in the clutches of military and paramilitary organizations than he had before he joined the green machine. He knew on an instinctive level that something was wrong. There was no prickling at the back of his neck, no throbbing of his jaw, just a heightened sense of alert. His eyes flickered as they scanned the horizon, and his hand searched instinctively for a pistol that wasn't there.

He caught the action, feeling somewhat foolish. If there was a threat, perhaps a Chinese sub lurking beneath the dark blue waves, then what the hell was he going to do about it—fire a few rounds from a pea shooter? That was about as likely to work as taking down a charging rhinoceros with a BB gun.

The helicopter banked sharply, and Trapp felt his stomach drop out from underneath him. His fingers clutched against his canvas seat restraints,.

"Inbound threat, sir," the chief replied. "We've been ordered to clear the area."

Trapp's forehead wrinkled. "Why?"

"So the escorts have a clear field of fire," the man replied quickly, too focused on the consoles in front of him to meet his gaze this time.

Trapp got the message. The navy chief's voice was taut with tension. The last thing the man needed was a passenger getting in his ear at a time like this. He shut up and leaned back in his seat, crossing his hands over his arms in a brace position, just in case.

Whatever was going on, it didn't sound good. Could the Chinese really be so brazen as to attack an American aircraft carrier in international waters? He didn't think so, but then again, he had been wrong about a lot over the past twenty-four hours.

The helicopter turned sharply to the left, banking so low over the frothing seas beneath it that a spray of salt water caught Trapp directly in the mouth. He watched out of the helicopter's open sides as all of the rotor craft in the area did the same thing. They fled in the same direction, like a flock of geese migrating south for winter.

Trapp didn't have to wait long to learn precisely what the threat was. A low rumble built over the waves, breaking into an open roar the closer it got. Two new fighter jets, painted dark with glistening, tinted canopies broke free of the low-hanging clouds overhead and screamed past the USS Nimitz, their red-hot jet turbines painting a streak of color on his vision.

Trapp froze. *Those weren't American jets.*

Two flights of navy fighter planes screamed past, in what seemed to the naked eye like close pursuit, but was in reality seconds behind. Trapp ignored the roller coaster motions of the helicopter beneath him, his eyes tracking the high-speed chase unfolding in the skies above. Below, cannons and missile batteries on the Nimitz and her escorts zeroed in on the Chinese planes, guided by the high-powered fire control radars on the Arleigh Burke destroyers somewhere in the distance, but did not open fire.

Yet.

He wondered what the hell was going on in the heads of those American pilots, and the gunners by the waterline. Dollars to doughnuts, this was nothing more than a Chinese dick-measuring contest. A fighter jet buzzing an aircraft carrier wasn't exactly an everyday occurrence, but nor was it unheard of. The Soviets had done it regularly throughout the Cold War.

The problem was, the Nimitz cost a billion dollars to build, and that was back in 1975. In today's money, it was worth more than Trapp could make in several million lifetimes. On board were thousands of sailors, and thousands more crewed the dozen escort ships that surrounded the enormous floating flight deck.

The United States of America was not technically at war. But her eyes in the skies overhead had been destroyed, and she didn't know why. For all America's leaders knew, this was the moment at which Red China had decided to assert her superiority over the Asia-Pacific once more. And what better way than by destroying that most potent symbol of American imperialism—an aircraft carrier?

Trapp had no doubt that at this very moment in the Combat Information Center somewhere in the bowels of the Nimitz, an admiral was crapping his pants over the prospect of accidentally starting World War III.

All it would take was one wrong move, misinterpreted action, or itchy trigger finger, and those two Chinese pilots would be barbecued inside their rides. Or worse, they might fire on the Nimitz.

If they did, it would be tantamount to a declaration of war.

Trapp watched the scene above play out with numbed fascination, his neck snapping left and right as he followed the delicate yet equally jaw-dropping ballet. The fighter jets—on both sides—were built to destroy their targets without ever setting eyes upon them.

Yet just like their forebears in World War II, Korea and 'Nam, the aircraft were equally adept at dogfighting. As the planes screamed around the carrier group, flying so low over the ocean that the water was whipped into steam from the engine backwash, he realized that what he was watching was the equal of any hand-to-hand combat he'd ever found himself embroiled in. It was like a knife fight, both sides endlessly tussling for advantage in altitude and airspeed before ever attempting to strike the killing blow.

He wished he was tied into the pilots' radios. It would be an illuminating insight into his own mind when under stress.

Except where Trapp was a lone wolf, the navy pilots hunted in packs.

And yet neither side opened fire.

Trapp recognized this for what it was: a Chinese show of force. They were warning America of the consequences of getting too close. He breathed a sigh of relief.

Only for his stomach to drop out from underneath him.

The two Chinese jets spun on one wing, leaving a thin contrail behind them which quickly disappeared into nothing. They turned on a dime, reversing a course that was taking them out into empty ocean, and slingshotting back toward the carrier group.

And toward the small group of navy helicopters that was attempting to escape the scene. Most of them, including the MH-60 currently carrying Trapp, were in one large group, and far away from the danger zone.

All except one—a Super Stallion heavy lift chopper that was flying erratically and emitting a thick stream of dark black smoke. Under ordinary circumstances, it would have received a priority routing toward the carrier's flight deck.

But these were not ordinary circumstances.

"Oh, shit," the crew chief grunted on an open mic. "That ain't good."

Their engines blasting them forward at hundreds of miles an hour, the two Chinese jets had already closed half the distance that separated them from the Nimitz.

They were on the Super Stallion in seconds, still kissing the surface of the ocean. As they attempted to evade this new found threat, the heavy helicopter jinked in the wrong direction. And collided with one of the Chinese J-20 jets.

Both aircraft tumbled into the South China Sea. An enormous geyser of water exploded up where the fighter jet impacted, and the chopper, now shorn of its main rotor, spun manically before going down hard, without a doubt killing everyone on board. The frames of both aircraft quickly disappeared beneath the hissing ocean.

Trapp's gut clenched with shock.

But the drama was far from over.

The second Chinese jet reacted instinctively, pulling a hard left and attempting to gain altitude fast. But the maneuver pushed it on a direct course over the Nimitz—and somewhere in the bowels of the enormous naval vessel, a crewman reacted on instinct.

A radar-guided point defense machine gun chattered into life and spewed out a horrendous rate of fire. The jet disintegrated in midair, chewed up by dozens of rounds of heavy caliber ammunition.

And as Trapp was still blinking in horror, a second jet disappeared beneath the waves.

MIDAFTERNOON in the South China Sea was five in the morning in Washington. President Nash was roused from an unsettled sleep that was punctuated by dreams of flames scouring the night sky by the hushed yet unmistakably urgent tones of an aide who had shaken him awake. He listened to the young man, yet heard not his words, but the drumbeat of war.

Nash threw on a pair of jogging pants, a navy polo shirt decorated with the presidential seal, and a plain windbreaker, all found lying on the back of an armchair where he had deposited them the night before. Right now, he decided, speed was the better part of valor.

He entered the situation room barely five minutes after waking, still picking the sleep from his eyes. None of his administration's senior personnel were present. He expected that right this very moment, his national security adviser, the Joint Chiefs of Staff, and a variety of critical national security staffers were being awoken by men in black sedans. Yet even in their absence, the situation room was alive with a sense of focused activity.

"What happened?" Nash asked the room at large.

He cast his mind back to the first of the presidential debates, when the moderator had challenged the two candidates as to who would be more prepared to receive the phone call in the middle of the night. The president had, of course, confidently put his best foot forward, seizing the question and making it his own. Charles Nash had, after all, seen active military service, having been deployed to the Persian Gulf for the first Gulf War.

"Once a Marine, always a Marine," he had said, confidently grasping the lectern in front of him and promising the American people he would keep them safe. He'd spoken the truth. The Corps had made Nash who he was, shaped him from raw clay and hardened him into a leader.

And yet what was also unmistakably certain was that there was no training for being woken in the White House residence and led to the basement of the West Wing in the middle of the night. Of seeing the determined faces of the duty watch team as they sacrificed sleep to keep their fellow citizens safe.

The duty officer was a young air force captain attired in dress blues, with a stenciled name tag on his left breast that read: 'J. Clay.'

"Mr. President, approximately twelve minutes ago the USS Nimitz was buzzed by two fifth-generation J-20 Chinese fighter jets. We're still getting a full picture of the situation, but it is my understanding that both of those jets were lost, along with one of our own—a CH-53 Super Stallion chopper."

Nash blinked. Had he truly heard that correctly? "Say that again, Captain?"

A pained expression crossed Captain Clay's face as he confirmed the news. "I'm sorry sir, there's no mistake. There was a midair collision, following which the Nimitz's air defense system took out the second Chinese jet. We're still trying to piece together what happened."

"Were there any survivors?"

Clay glanced over at another staff member, a female air force sergeant. She shook her head subtly.

"No chutes, sir," he said.

"How did they get that close?" the president asked, shoving his trembling hands into the pockets of his windbreaker in a vain effort to hide his reaction. Judging by the looks on the faces of the watch officers around him, each was as worried as he felt. It hadn't escaped Nash's attention that if Chinese intercontinental ballistic missiles were launching at this very second, then the White House would shortly be ground zero of an irradiated wasteland. But surely that couldn't happen.

Could it?

"Sir, the J-20 is roughly analogous to our F-22 stealth fighter program. In fact, we believe they stole some of the blueprints from Lockheed Martin about ten years ago. What that means is that the J-20 has an extremely low radar signature –"

Nash cut him off. "You're telling me we couldn't see them?"

Clay shook his head. "No sir. They flew low over the ocean, probably at an altitude of below a hundred feet until they were within twenty miles of the Nimitz. That's when we picked them up."

"What now, Captain?" Nash asked.

"I'm sorry, sir?"

"What's China's next move?"

Clay looked uncomfortable. "Mr. President, that's way above my pay grade."

"Son," Nash growled, "I'm asking you a question. Don't make me ask twice."

The young air force captain nodded. "Yes sir. We used to war game situations like this back at the Academy. The

Russkies buzzed us frequently during the Cold War—still do, in fact. Under the current rules of engagement, the Nimitz would have been authorized to take the Chinese down immediately after detection."

Nash pictured the fresh-faced, now dead crew of the navy helicopter. "So why did that not happen?"

Clay cleared his throat uncomfortably. "Because, Mr. President, that's how you start a war."

The President sank back into a chair halfway down the table that sat in the center of the situation room. He couldn't remember ever feeling this alone. He knew that the fate of his nation, perhaps even the entire world, depended on the decisions he would take in the coming hours and days.

And yet the ramifications of that thought were terrifying. He was operating in a perfect storm of incomplete information and multiplying threats, with the certain knowledge that any mistake would end not just in two Chinese fighter jets kissing the surface of the ocean, but the planet's two most powerful nations entering another world war, except this time with thousands of nuclear warheads on either side.

Worst of all, he couldn't see a way of stopping it.

25

Colonel Kim was running on fumes.

His return from Sichuan province had taken almost 36 hours, and involved the crossing of nine borders: a long, tense, extremely low altitude helicopter flight into Myanmar to avoid Chinese military radar, then a road transfer to an airfield 50 miles into the cover of the jungle, to confuse any surveillance.

A propeller plane took him and his men, now dressed in civilian clothes and using a cover of a group of South Korean businessman, from Myanmar to Vietnam, where they boarded a jet that took them to Vladivostok, with a refueling stop in Japan.

In the air, Kim had seen the bright lights advertising the roaring South Korean economy as his plane flew through the night, a vivid contrast to the darkness that enveloped the country north of the demilitarized zone.

The sight sickened him. It was a country of traitors, lapdogs of the hated Americans, and yet in the new, global economy, South Korea had triumphed, as his own country fell ever further behind. It had to change.

He would *make it* change.

And now Kim was home, out of the adopted cheap suit and into a fresh set of combat fatigues sandwiched between a white T-shirt, and polished black boots.

Home was a medium-sized military encampment in the mountains about 80 miles east of Pyongyang, near a small city called Yangdok. The camp housed several thousand men, women, and children, all of whom were under Kim's command. He had grown up here. And now it was his: a meteoric rise in a country as stifled by petty bureaucracy as the Democratic People's Republic of Korea, and yet one which by now Kim considered was little more than his by right.

"Colonel," a female aide said, snapping to attention and saluting as Kim strode into his headquarters. "Welcome home."

"Update," Kim replied, not looking up from a small tablet that had been handed him the second he walked through the camp gates.

He scrolled through a list of news headlines, some written in English, most in Mandarin. All discussed the sudden and mysterious destruction of the vast array of satellites that covered the Asia-Pacific region, most of which were American, and speculated as to a cause. Kim noted with approval that none of the commenters were correct. Though since his plan had been executed flawlessly, he hadn't expected anything to the contrary.

"The destruction was total, Colonel. The Chinese anti-satellite technology worked perfectly. Our scientists tell us that American surveillance coverage across the region has been degraded by at least 90%, perhaps more. The blame is already falling on China. Congratulations."

Kim looked up, ignoring the compliment. He studied the woman. She was dressed in green military fatigues, with no rank insignia. Her hair was severely cropped, but she might be pretty, if she was cleaned up. "Does Pyongyang suspect anything?"

The aide struggled to hide a proud smile as she replied, "No, sir."

"Good," Kim replied without displaying any emotion. "And Macau?"

"Captain Jung made contact yesterday evening, Colonel," the woman replied, the smile dying on her face.

Kim ground his teeth. "And—?"

"They met resistance."

"They were *expected* to meet resistance," Kim growled, irritation spiking behind his fearsome visage. "And they were expected to overcome it. What happened?"

"Our team dealt with the Chinese operatives, Colonel. A third party interfered with our operation. But our men took a prisoner, a woman. They are interrogating her now."

Kim hurled the tablet across the room. It smashed against the far wall, shattering into fragments in an instant. He snarled with rage as his face contorted in a rictus of anger. The woman had served him for a long time, and knew his capacity for blind fury. Yet even she flinched.

"Who were they?"

"Who—?"

"This third party," Kim snarled. "Americans?"

The woman half-shook, half-nodded her head, trapped in a paralysis of indecision. "Perhaps. We don't know."

Kim stood in the center of the small office, all activity now dead as his people hunched over computers, unwilling to become the next target of his fury. He would brook no further failures. If Captain Jung did not return with the information he so desperately required, then he would punish the man severely.

"What of the Russian?" he asked, voice low and dangerous.

The woman gulped, her complexion going pale, though

whether it was at the mention of the activity taking place in Building 12 or a reaction to Kim's brief outburst of rage, he didn't know.

"His work is proceeding well," she said, trembling with fear. "Take me to him."

~

THE ARMY JEEP sped through the encampment. The top was open, and Kim sat in the passenger seat, the humid wind caressing his closely cropped head. His back ached from the long journey back to Camp 61, and the vibration from the old vehicle's engine wasn't helping. His knee juddered up and down restlessly as he considered his options.

If the Macau mission was a failure, it wasn't an outright disaster. Kim had only learned of Emmanuel Alstyne's existence a few weeks before, from a mole inside the Chinese Ministry of State Security. The man's information would have been a useful resource for the battle that was to come.

But not a vital one.

Still, the involvement of this third party unsettled the colonel. Kim did not like surprises, especially when it came to the hated Americans. And in his bones, Kim suspected that they were indeed involved. It was how they operated: even thousands of miles from their own backyard, they couldn't help but stick their noses in places they were not wanted. This fuck-up wore their stink.

"We're here, Colonel."

Kim didn't look up as he brooded over what action to take. Should he order Captain Jung to bring the prisoner to him? It was a risk, but perhaps he needed to look her in the eyes. His men had failed already. Could he trust them a second time?

"Colonel?"

Kim's gaze snapped upward. He found himself sitting in

front of a large concrete building, deliberately dilapidated, at least from the outside. It was rectangular, some eighty yards in length and thirty in width, and topped with rusting corrugated iron, streaks of which had stained the gray walls below.

He ignored the crisp salute from a sentry who stood just inside the keypad-operated door and turned toward his aide. "Take me to him."

He followed the woman through the sterile hallways. The building's interior was modern and pristine, and reminded Kim of a hospital. A little ahead, a gaunt prisoner from the nearby labor camp mopped the vinyl floor, his exhausted movements slow and jerky, his posture slouched, eyes focused on the floor in front of him. He didn't seem to notice the two new additions to his environment.

As they passed him, the ammonia stench of bleach reached Kim's nostrils. He wrinkled them slightly, but did not look to the right. As far as he was concerned, the prisoner's life meant nothing. It was owned by the state, and in Camp 61, the state was Colonel Kim.

The mop sloshed from its bucket, and an eruption of bleach-tinged suds spattered Kim's boots.

Kim stopped.

The prisoner froze, hands trembling around the mop's thin pole, the wood polished smooth and glossy through years of hard work. His legs shivered beneath him, threatening to give way.

The colonel finally turned his neck to look at the terrified prisoner. Then he glanced down at his feet, grimacing as he saw the rivulets of filthy water running off the polished surface of his boots.

The prisoner said nothing. A thin stream of urine ran down his left leg, pooling on the floor, and mixing with the water from the bucket.

"Clean them," Kim hissed.

The prisoner dropped to the vinyl floor, his emaciated body barely making a sound as it hit the deck. He whimpered wordlessly, pulling the stained labor camp top from his shoulders. As the man bunched it in his fingers, preparing to use it to clean Kim's boots, the colonel's eyes fell on the man's skeletal frame, dispassionately studying the stark lines of the ribs that studded his torso.

"Not with that," Kim growled with disgust. He clicked his fingers, turning to the aide who stood silently behind him, eyes watching everything but saying nothing. "Give me a cloth."

She handed him a handkerchief, and he dropped it to the man cowering on his knees beneath him. The prisoner threw himself into the task, polishing Kim's boots with the tears that flowed from his own eyes. The colonel watched the man with revulsion.

He had lived in a place like this, once. His own life subject to the whims of others. But he had never been broken, not like this pitiful specimen before him. He'd risen up. He'd found a way to not just survive, but thrive. And yet the experience had given him no compassion, no sympathy for the plight of those less fortunate. Childhood fear had hardened into adult rage.

A few minutes later, his aide showed him through an anonymous doorway, and Kim found himself standing in a messy office, adjacent to a sealed biohazard laboratory. His eyes picked out a balding man, head in his hands, slumped in an office chair a few yards away amid towering piles of papers.

"Dr. Savrasov," Kim crooned. "So good to see you."

The scientist spun around, eyes narrowing immediately with fear, the chair falling away behind him as he stood up. Kim studied the man. His beard was stained with foam from an American-style frothed coffee, and his face was haggard from exhaustion. Kim had ordered that the doctor be given everything he needed to complete his work. He wrinkled his nose as he saw that this apparently included the provision of a capsule coffee machine, which now sat upon Savrasov's desk, accompanied by a stack of brown-stained cups.

The Russian scientist nodded quickly.

"Are you ready for your demonstration?"

A pained expression crossed the fat man's face. It was a look of grim indecision; horror battling with self-preservation. "I—" he stammered, "I don't think it is necessary."

Kim leaned in, ever so slightly, so that his nose was only a few inches from the Russian's face. He didn't say anything, just stared into the man's terrified, tiny eyes. And then he flicked the small catch that fastened his pistol's holster. The sound echoed around the room like an actual gunshot, causing the scientist to flinch.

"And I decided that it is," Kim whispered. "So I will ask you again: are you ready? Or will you force me to find somebody else?"

The threat lingered in the silent room. Savrasov shook his head violently, his face so pale, skin so wet with droplets of sweat that Kim wondered if he was about to vomit.

"No," he whimpered. "No, I'll do it."

Kim remained entirely steady for a long second, unmoving, reminding the Russian exactly where the power lay in this arrangement. And then he straightened himself and smiled, gesturing for Savrasov to continue. "Good. After you."

THE ROOM WAS stark and contained no decoration, nor in fact any contents other than eight camp beds, topped with plastic-coated mattresses, and screwed into the concrete floor. Attached to each of the cots was a small length of chain and a single cuff.

Each was empty.

Kim and his aide stood with Savrasov and several white-coated lab assistants in an adjacent observation room. A length of wall had been cut from between the two rooms and replaced with an impenetrable sheet of toughened glass, to allow for easy monitoring.

Kim stood directly in front of it, his nose almost grazing the windowpane. He closed his eyes briefly, contemplating how far he had come, and how much he had sacrificed to get here. And then he turned to the Russian.

"This is your show, Dr. Savrasov," he smiled. "Send them in."

The Russian gulped, his mouth opening and closing wordlessly as he contemplated the horror of what Kim was asking him to do. In fact, Kim thought, he wasn't asking—he was ordering, but he enjoyed watching the man twist in the wind regardless.

"Do it," Savrasov whispered.

His assistant nodded and spoke into a small microphone that lay on top of the metal worktop. For a heartbeat, nothing happened, and then Kim heard a distant, electronic buzz. Shortly after, a door set into the far side of the room containing the hospital beds opened. A soldier entered wearing army fatigues, a flimsy white infection mask on his face, and a rifle slung over his shoulder.

Behind him trudged two men and two women, both of an Asian complexion. They wore filthy prison rags, but looked well fed. After them followed four Caucasians, again separated equally by sex, and several more armed soldiers. The Westerners wore their own clothes, which were dirty, but not inculcated by year after year of filth. Their posture too, was subtly different: though clearly terrified, they still wore the subtle arrogance of the recently free.

Kim watched as all eight were directed to a camp bed, and chained efficiently to its frame. The soldiers worked without showing a hint of emotion. They were trained to treat enemies of the state as no more human than rats.

"How long will it take?" he asked.

"The incubation period is five days," Savrasov replied. He faced Kim, but his eyes seemed to be looking a hundred yards past the colonel, as though his mind was disassociating itself from the consequences of his actions. "As you know, my work in Russia revolved around modifying contagious microorganisms to attack only carriers of a chosen gene sequence. *Any* gene sequence." His voice grew in confidence as he focused on his area of expertise. "In theory, I could create a weapon that might infect millions, but only kill a single, chosen individual. Anyone. Even you."

Kim's voice was cold. "I trust you have not."

Savrasov's eyes flickered back to life, and he shook his head quickly as he realized the implication of what he had just said. "Of course not. I did exactly as you asked. Only carriers of the CJXR gene will succumb to the impact of the virus. Everyone else will transmit the virus without suffering harmful effects."

"And the mortality rate?"

Savrasov trembled as he spoke. "Eighty percent."

Kim smiled coldly, his thin lips showing no hint of humor, but a wealth of satisfaction. "You have done well, Dr. Savrasov. Very well. Once you have completed the delivery mechanism, you will have everything I promised."

It was, of course, a lie. But there was no sense in telling the good doctor that. Not yet.

He turned back to the glass window, and watched the unwitting prisoners. Specifically, his eyes fell on the four Caucasians. They were all American, though they did not need to be. It was their race that Kim was concerned with, not the nationality in their passports. They had been kidnapped from a remote hiking tour on Hokkaido, Japan's northern island. They might be missed, but the disappearance would no doubt be chalked up to an accident, rather than a result of human interference.

The four test subjects didn't *need* to be American. But it pleased Kim anyway.

"Release the virus, Doctor."

Kim wondered whether he would need to repeat his instruction. After all, by pressing the button, the Russian would directly be condemning four innocent individuals to a horrifying death. But gratifyingly, Savrasov did not hesitate.

As the colonel watched, a thin mist hissed from vents built into the ceiling of the sealed experimentation room. Like insects provoked within a glass cage, the eight captives threw themselves into a frenzy, cuffs biting into their limbs as they tore against the chains until blood dripped onto the floor.

But just like insects, their efforts were fruitless.

26

Trapp stood on the deck of the USS Nimitz, catching the occasional curious glance as passing sailors noticed his civilian attire. He barely noticed them. His head was still spinning from the events of the past few hours, sharing more in common with the choppy South China Sea than the stationary steel flight deck of the huge aircraft carrier.

A salt breeze licked at his hair, which was flat and greasy from the combined effects of high-intensity combat and taking an unexpected dip in the ocean on his way out of China. Exhaustion tugged at his limbs, and the lids of his eyes, but he barely noticed it. Trapp was used to pushing his body right up to its limits, and then past them.

This was no different.

He watched with his hands clamped over his ears, half-wishing he had hearing protection, half relishing the almost physical pain as a fighter jet rocketed along the flight deck, dragged by the steam catapult, and tumbled off the end of the aircraft carrier, dipping slightly before its powerful engines rocketed it into the sky.

Trapp wondered where the jet was heading.

The pace of flight operations on the Nimitz had noticeably increased since the two Chinese jets hit the surface of the ocean. A pair of E-2 Hawkeye airborne early warning craft took to the sky shortly after the debris from the Chinese planes kissed the water, and had scoured the skies for further threats ever since. The combat air patrol now surrounded the carrier group in concentric circles, creating a gauntlet around the Nimitz that even the most foolhardy enemy pilot would not dare to brave.

But still, Trapp questioned how the present situation was going to end. Though from his perspective, standing on the deck of the Nimitz, with blue ocean stretching to the horizon in every direction, he could see little—and what little he could suggested that the United States was heading for war with China.

"You're the OGA guy, right?"

Trapp turned around and appraised the sailor. He was young, barely more than a boy, and wore three chevrons on his shoulders. Trapp wasn't an expert on naval ranks, but the kid barely looked old enough to have graduated from diapers, let alone boot camp.

"You've been watching too many movies," Trapp replied.

OGA stood for 'other government agency,' a common enough shorthand for the CIA. But coming out of the young sailor's mouth, it sounded faintly ridiculous.

The kid blanched. "I'll...take that as a yes?" he ventured.

Trapp nodded curtly, chiding himself for biting at the green sailor. It wasn't his fault that he was pissed. "You're correct."

"The skipper wants to see you," the sailor replied, looking a little relieved at not having to spar with the grizzled special operator any longer. "Just follow me."

Trapp did as the man asked, marveling as he clambered up steep stairwells and cramped, airless gangways how someone could possibly live in a place like this for months at a time— and why anyone would choose to. Just as he had done on the USS Cheyenne, he thanked his lucky stars that he'd joined the army, not the navy. His powerful frame wasn't made for places like this.

Shortly afterwards, the young seaman brought him to the door of the captain's stateroom, where one of the commanding officer's aides was waiting for him, wearing blue fatigues topped with the gold oak leaf on his shoulders that designated his rank.

"I'll take it from here," the lieutenant commander said, dismissing the young sailor. The kid departed with conspicuous haste—clearly uncomfortable with venturing this deep into officer country.

"So you're our unexpected guest," the officer said, stretching out his hand. "Steve Hatch. Nice to meet you."

Trapp shook it firmly. "Jason," he replied, leaving out his surname. "Any chance you can bring me up to speed on what the hell happened while I was underwater?"

As he spoke, the door to the captain's stateroom opened, and a thin man with steely blue eyes and graying hair peeked out at the two men. "We were sort of hoping you could do the same for us." He jerked his thumb. "Come on in."

Trapp's eyes widened with surprise as he entered the luxuriously appointed room. He took his time looking around, taking in the floor-to-ceiling American flag mounted on the wall behind the captain's desk. It was torn in places, the edges burned, and the red and white stripes coated in a gray dust.

The captain caught him looking. "It's from Ground Zero," he said. "It was flying on the morning of 9/11. I bought it at a charity auction a few years ago, and brought it with me from command to command ever since."

He patted one of the enormous warship's thick steel walls

and grinned. "This old girl's the only one big enough to actually mount it on the wall."

Perhaps it was the exhaustion running through his bones,
or the thought of Eliza Ikeda, in the clutches of an unknown
enemy, but the sight of the battered American flag moved
Trapp.

"Captain," he said finally, after subduing the unexpected
wave of emotion, "I was wondering if I could trouble you for a
line to Washington. I've got"—he paused, wondering how to
phrase his request—"an urgent message to deliver."

The captain waved Trapp toward one of the dark brown
leather sofas that were arranged around a coffee table. The
only thing that separated this stateroom from a perfectly
pleasant Georgetown townhouse was the fact the furniture was
bolted to the floor, and the slightly lower ceilings.

He sat down himself, and grimaced. "I would if I could,
son," he said. "But voice comms have been down since yesterday. We're working on setting up a secure relay, but that won't
be ready for at least another twenty-four hours."

The captain and his aide were sitting on the sofa opposite
Trapp. Hatch leaned forward before the operative had a chance
to speak. "So what the hell happened out there? I'm guessing
your appearance on this boat is connected with World War III
kicking off out there?"

Trapp paused, considering what he could and could not say.
And then he threw caution to the wind. He knew little enough
as it was. Perhaps the navy officers could help him fill in the
gaps. It was worth a shot. "I presume we're speaking in confidence?" he asked.

The captain nodded, his aide echoing the action. "Naturally.
Just give me the big picture."

Trapp spread his hands apart. "Your guess is as good as
mine, sir," he said. "As you know from the tasking of the USS
Cheyenne, I was conducting a classified operation in the

Chinese city of Macau. It was supposed to be a simple snatch and grab. I was ordered to retrieve a piece of classified intel and get out without causing an international incident."

The captain snorted. "How'd that go?"

Trapp grimaced. "Not well. But it wasn't my doing."

The captain raised his eyebrow.

"Well—" Trapp grinned. "*I* didn't start it, anyway. It turns out we weren't the only people with eyes on my target. An unknown party kicked down the door, grabbed him along with one of my assets, and practically leveled the Ritz-Carlton in the process. I was in the process of tracking them down when my comms went out."

He glanced up unconsciously, as if looking for the satellites that had once orbited over this patch of the globe. "And that's when everything *really* went to shit."

"You think the two things are connected?" Lieutenant Commander Hatch asked.

Trapp shrugged. "I don't see how they can be," he admitted. "But then again, it seems like a hell of a coincidence, and...."

The carrier's captain finished the trite cliché. "You don't believe in coincidences."

Trapp shook his head. "Do you?"

The captain lapsed into silence for a second before responding. "Not when they endanger the safety of my crew," he grunted. "Or threaten to plunge this whole damn region into the next world war."

"You mind if I ask what happened out there?" Trapp said, filling the silence.

"The Chinese have been buzzing the battle group for the last twelve hours or so. We think they're probing our air defense systems. Finding out how close they can get."

"Pretty damn close," Trapp growled.

The captain ran his fingers through his hair, and Trapp noticed how tired the man looked. "The two jets that just went

down are modeled on the F-22. They stole the stealth technology from us. Their implementation isn't quite as good, but
even with the lookdown radars on our electronic warfare
planes, they're damn difficult to detect when they skim the
surface of the ocean. But it's not their airframes I'm worried
about."

"No?"

"They don't have enough of their fifth-generation planes to
do much damage. Maybe thirty operational, as far as we know.
Minus the two they just lost. Maybe half that will be combat-
ready. Between the hardware our escorts carry and our own
airpower, we can handle that number and stay in the fight."

"So what then?"

"Missiles," Hatch replied grimly. "Chinese naval doctrine is
built around area denial. They have enough short- and
medium-range ballistic missiles to turn the South China Sea
into an oil slick."

"Hell," Trapp said, his voice little more than a whisper as he
pictured the inferno.

"Hell is right," the captain agreed. He fixed Trapp with a
steely gaze that left the covert operative with no illusions about
the lengths to which the man would go to ensure the safety of
his crew. "And the Lord's not here right now to answer my
prayers. All I have is you, Jason. Things are about to heat up
pretty damn quick in this part of the world, and I need to know
if the Chinese are going to strike first."

Trapp didn't know how to reply. He had been asking
himself the same question ever since he lost touch with
Langley all those hours before. Something about the present
situation didn't make sense, and his mind kept drifting back to
the tattoo he had found on the corpse of one of his unknown
assailants.

He let out a deep sigh. "The truth is, sir, I'm flying blind. My
gut tells me that something else is going on here, that the

Chinese were just as surprised to find out they'd taken out all our satellites as we were. But that's all it is. A gut feeling."

The captain tousled his gray hair and sagged back into his sofa. "It might not matter anyway," he admitted. "They attack us, we fight back, they retaliate, and pretty soon you got yourself a good old-fashioned shooting war, even if neither side started out wanting one."

Trapp nodded. "Yes sir. That's why I need to get back in touch with Langley. I think we're being played. I just don't know why, or by who."

"If you're right, it's a hell of a game," the captain growled, his expression murderous. "I've got six thousand sailors under my command on this boat, not to mention those riding shotgun with our escorts. We are on the front line of this one. I don't like the idea of being a pawn to be sacrificed."

"Me neither," Trapp said, glancing around somewhat anxiously. He pictured a Chinese missile bearing down on the enormous ship, holing it beneath the water line, and the fizzing swell of the ocean sucking the Nimitz into its depths. He preferred fighting not just on land, or even face to face: but eye to eye, where you could see the man who planned to kill you. The idea of falling victim to a thunderbolt from the blue, of toiling in the bowels of the Nimitz and not even knowing you were in danger until the missile impact sickened him.

The captain clapped his hands together firmly, as though he had come to a decision, and stood. "Okay. I can't put you in touch with Washington, but maybe I can do one better..."

THE NEXT FEW minutes happened so quickly Trapp felt like he'd been strapped into a slingshot and fired out the other end. Hatch called up to flight operations, and put a two-seater F-18 naval jet on standby, with a pilot up front, and one Jason Trapp

—squeezed into a borrowed U.S. Navy flight suit—sitting in the back.

Their destination was Naval Base Guam. The base was connected by a deep-sea fiber-optic cable to the mainland, which meant that short of waiting for full communications to be restored, Trapp's best chance of finding out how the hell to help Eliza Ikeda was found in flying even further from wherever she'd been taken, riding at the speed of sound.

The pilot turned around, glancing at Trapp's hunched frame in the navigator's rear seat. His visor was down, as was Trapp's own, which made the pair of them resemble aliens more than humans. "You ever flown in one of these babies before?"

Trapp shook his head.

The pilot let out a sharp laugh. "You're in for a hell of a ride, sir. Just don't throw up. If you do, you'll be breathing it in for the next three hours."

"Great."

The pilot completed his final flight checks, the glass canopy closed and hissed into place, and Trapp concentrated on not touching anything that looked important. In fact, he didn't touch anything at all, just in case.

His powerful frame towered over six feet and carried over two hundred pounds of mostly muscle mass, and as the jet was maneuvered into position on the flight deck of the Nimitz, Trapp felt every last inch. He was crammed into the cockpit like a sardine into a can, and he wasn't exactly looking forward to the ride.

"How many hours have you got in this thing?" he asked weakly, feeling an unaccustomed wave of nerves wash over him like the wash of a swell against the aircraft carrier's bow.

Trapp hated being in a position where he was out of control —and this was about as out-of-control as it got. As soon as the F-18 galloped into the sky, he would be forced to sit on his hands until they touched down on the runway at Guam. Or worse still, if they ended up with a pair of Chinese fighter jets on their ass, he would be about as useful as an ice pick in the Sahara desert.

The pilot turned around. He smirked, and Trapp couldn't help but feel it was a macabre sight, as though the man was taking altogether too much pleasure in his passenger's obvious anxiety. He patted the panel in front of him. "What, this old girl? Must be at least twenty by now. I'm just a rookie. Needed to keep the hotshots on board in case the Chinese show back up, you know…"

"Asshole," Trapp grunted.

"That's what they call me," the pilot replied drily, flicking a switch in front of him by feel as he spoke. "By the way, I didn't introduce myself. Call me Chuckie."

"Jason," Trapp replied weakly.

What kind of name is Chuckie? he thought.

"Nice to meet you, Jason. Now, before we get going, did the crew chief show you how to bail out of this thing?"

Trapp shook his head quickly. "No. Am I going to need to?"

"With me flying?"

Trapp heard a *thunk* sound underneath the airframe, and felt the shock of a slight impact vibrate through his cramped knees. Before he got a chance to ask what it was, whether it was bad, or what he was supposed to do if the Chinese fired a heat seeking missile up their tailpipe, he heard a crackle emanating from inside Chuckie's headset.

It quickly became apparent that the sound was flight operations confirming they were clear to kick the tires and light the fires, because that's exactly what happened. Trapp glanced to his right, and saw one of the sailors on the flight deck delivering a complicated sequence of instructions through the medium of hand signals and flags. Chuckie registered his response, and before Trapp's brain was able to parse what the hell was going on, the high-pitched whine of the engine behind them drowned out his capacity for conscious thought.

The steam-powered catapult that ran down the center of the Nimitz's deck grabbed the F-18 Super Hornet and hauled it from a standing start to over 170 miles an hour in the blink of an eye. Trapp was yanked back into his flight seat, his light gray helmet colliding with the leather headrest.

And then the world ended.

Trapp felt like he was sitting on an exploding volcano as the Super Hornet fired off the end of the Nimitz's deck, hung in the air for a second as his vision compressed, as his eardrums threatened to explode, and then the F-18 kicked him in the back like an unbroken horse as Chuckie lit the afterburners and rode his airframe into the sky.

Minutes later, as they reached cruising altitude, and as the gray deck of the Nimitz and her escorts dwindled into the distance, indistinguishable against the steel of the endless ocean, Trapp finally allowed himself to relax.

Chuckie turned around. "Hey, buddy—you ever done a loop the loop?"

27

The F-18 kissed the runway at Naval Base Guam underneath a glorious blue sky.

The sun glinted off the waves surrounding the island, the glare bright enough to blind Trapp, had it not been for the visor built into his helmet. As he stepped out of the cramped cockpit, finally able to stretch his protesting limbs, and breathe fresh oxygen that wasn't pumped from a high-pressure canister, he thanked his lucky stars that he had joined the good old US Army all those years ago.

Trapp's arrival was not telegraphed, in case the Chinese were eavesdropping on US Navy communications. As a result, there was no Agency welcoming party waiting on the asphalt. Still, it didn't take him long to find the CIA station, hidden in a drab converted hangar in the depths of the base—unusual only as a result of the razor-wire topped steel fence that hemmed it in.

It needed no other security, since the only personnel on Guam were serving on US military contracts. He stood in front of it, still dressed in his flight suit, but no longer carrying the heavy helmet, the weight of which had pressed his dark hair into sweat-soaked strands.

Two men were slumped in a guard booth at the entrance to the small compound. Trapp made a beeline for them. "I need to speak to Langley," he said.

One of the men, a slight African-American wearing black wraparound sunglasses and dark fatigues, laughed. "Yeah, you and what army?"

Trapp didn't have time to play word games. He knew that every second he delayed was another in which Ikeda's life slowly but surely ticked away. The fact that she was gone was his fault, and his alone. And that meant it was his responsibility to get her back.

He glowered at the man, who immediately wilted, aware that he had more than met his match. "Run inside," he growled, "and find your boss. My authentication code is: Oscar, Mike, nine, nine, Delta. And while you're in there, get Deputy Director Mitchell on the line."

The two men glanced at each other nervously until Trapp clapped his hands together and made them jump in unison. "*Now*, gentlemen."

TRAPP WAITED, drinking in the glorious cool of the air-conditioning as a CIA technician with rust-red hair tied up in a ponytail established a video link with Mitchell's sub-basement in the bowels of Langley. His right knee thrummed up and down in an endless rhythm, the only outward sign that betrayed the tension that was rising in his body.

"That's it, sir," the technician said, tapping a key. "Just initialize when you're ready."

"Got it," Trapp grunted.

She cocked her head. "You need anything else?"

"Not right yet."

She made her exit, and the second the secure door shut behind her, Trapp started the call. The video blurred, then resolved, and the faces of Mike Mitchell and Kyle Partey appeared side-by-side from thousands of miles away on the immersive LCD screens opposite Trapp.

"What the hell happened out there, Jason?" Mitchell asked. The short, wiry Agency official looked strained, the crows' feet that decorated his eyes more pronounced than ever, and Trapp guessed he'd been working flat-out ever since the operation in Macau went sideways.

"Your guess is as good as mine," Trapp replied. "Listen, Mike, I need you to tell me you know where she is."

Mitchell grimaced. "No joy, Jason," he replied. "We're blind in the whole region, and honestly —"

"Honestly *what?*" Trapp growled. He had a very good sense of what his boss was about to say; he just wanted to hear the man say it.

The deputy director fixed him with a level stare. "Honestly, Jason, in my position I'm forced to make impossible decisions. And one of those is that I cannot put the life of one operative above the lives of millions of Americans."

Underneath the metal trestle table that was the only piece of furniture in the cramped communications room, Trapp gripped his dancing knee, digging his fingers in until his knuckles went white. He knew very well that for years, Mike Mitchell was one of the CIA's most trustworthy—and deadly— field operatives.

He wasn't some faceless Agency bureaucrat pushing pieces around a chessboard. He'd gotten his hands dirty perhaps more times than anyone alive, at least before Langley's seventh floor swallowed him whole.

"Do you have the drive?" Kyle interjected. As always, he was dressed like an Oxford don, the leather elbow patches on his tweed jacket occasionally visible through the video feed.

Trapp nodded. "I don't know if it's Alstyne's or the replica. I suspect the former. Ikeda wouldn't have bothered hiding the fake."

"She did good," Mitchell muttered, his expression pained. Trapp realized that the man was hurting just as badly as he was. He knew it wasn't easy to send men and women into combat, less still the endless gray zone that Trapp and his ilk operated within.

"She did," Trapp replied, his voice firm, expression unbroken as he gazed at the camera — and directly into Mitchell's eyes. "And I'm going to get her back."

Mitchell shook his head. "I can't let you do that, Jason. We're a hair's breadth away from an all-out war with the Chinese. President Nash has directed me to do whatever it takes to prevent that from happening."

Trapp laughed bitterly. "And how's that going?"

Mitchell slumped in his seat. "Not well."

"Who were those guys, Mike?" Trapp asked, leaning forward and placing his elbows on the metal table. "They were pros, I know that much. And they didn't give a fuck about cutting those MSS babysitters to shreds. They knew exactly who Alstyne was, and why they needed him. How the hell was that possible?"

Kyle glanced at his boss. "We don't know," he said. "We suspect that whoever they were, they had a source inside Chinese intelligence. We kept the circle tight on this one. Only about six people knew we were running this op."

Trapp thumped the surface of the table. The metallic sound clanged, reverberating around the small, dark room. "Dammit, Kyle. You're telling me you've got no idea who they were?"

The young analyst grimaced. "Maybe."

"What's that supposed to mean?" Trapp snapped, his

patience now tested almost to breaking point.

"It means," Mitchell replied, taking up the torch from his beleaguered subordinate, "that those guys are a myth. They aren't supposed to exist."

"Details," Trapp growled. "Now."

Technically, Mike Mitchell was one of the Central Intelligence Agency's most senior clandestine officers. He was running point on a covert mission of vengeance for the President of the United States himself. And yet he knew better than to take offense at Trapp's tone. He eyed the exasperated operative calmly and waited the tension out before speaking— asserting his authority without ever resorting to raising his voice.

Trapp nodded in silent acceptance.

Mitchell began. "What Kyle said was correct. We think we've identified the men who disrupted your operation in Macau. At least, one of them. The tattoo matches the description of a unit insignia from a North Korean special operations group."

"North Korean?" Trapp muttered, his mind moving fast. That didn't make any sense, and yet it also somehow fit. That was often the way with clandestine operations.

"We know very little about them. Just rumors passed to us by South Korea's National Intelligence Service from debriefings they've done with defectors.

"They call themselves Unit 61. From what we know, they were established along with several other similar organizations in order to generate hard currency for the North Korean regime. They control methamphetamine production and distribution, sex trafficking, even currency counterfeiting so good that even the Treasury can't tell the difference between legitimate notes and the ones they produce. You name the sordid pie, they've got a finger in it—even to the extent of hiring themselves out as mercenaries."

"You think that's what it was?" Trapp asked, his irritation forgotten and replaced with puzzlement. "You think someone contracted them to do a job?"

Mitchell spread his hands. "We have no idea. It's a theory we're kicking around, but like I said, we're flying blind over here. I need you to get back to Langley immediately. We'll arrange transport from Guam."

"No way," Trapp replied immediately.

"We need to analyze that drive, Jason," Mitchell said, his jaw set. "If the North Koreans have access to our nation's military secrets, we've got eighty thousand servicemen patrolling the DMZ whose lives are on the line. For all we know that drive contains information on how to bring down our air defense networks."

"Be my guest," Trapp snapped. "The drive's all yours. But I'm not babysitting a fucking thumb drive on a flight back to Andrews. Get the navy to fly it back. I'm sure some Marine staff sergeant will jump at the chance to get a week's leave just for chaining it to his wrist. But I'm not coming with it. I'm useless over there."

The tension between the two men was palpable, even through the fiber-optic cable. Kyle glanced from his boss, into the camera, and then back again, looking as jumpy as a field mouse.

"So what do you propose, Jason?"

"I'm going to Pyongyang," Trapp replied, the decision made at just about the moment the words escaped his mouth.

"You're going to Pyongyang?" Mitchell replied with an expression of stunned astonishment on his face. In truth, Trapp was just as surprised as he was by the words that had just escaped his lips.

"What, precisely, do you plan to do when you land? I don't know if you've noticed, but you're half a foot taller than me, and I'd tower over most North Koreans. Not to mention you're as white as the driven snow, and the locals most certainly are *not*. The second you land, the secret police will stick to you like shit on a stick."

Trapp grinned, encouraged by the fact that his boss hadn't immediately shut down the idea. The two men had worked together for long enough to know each other's strengths and weaknesses. Trapp knew that he could be foolhardy at times, putting himself into situations of danger that would make other men piss their pants—and doing so with frightening regularity. But he didn't risk his life for nothing, nor treat it as a game, as other men did. He wasn't an adrenaline chaser. He'd chosen this line of work because there were few men better at it alive.

"And there was me thinking I was working up a nice tan."

Mitchell kinked his eyebrow.

"Fine." Trapp shrugged. "I haven't gotten that far yet. But I figure doing something's got to be better than sitting around here waiting for the world to burn. I don't believe for a second that the Chinese are behind what happened the other night. But if we don't get ahead of this thing, then that won't matter a damn bit. This Unit 61, whoever they are, they are our only lead —right?"

A silence filled the line. Trapp waited it out.

"Right."

"Then I need to pull on that thread and see where it takes me. Because if I don't, in a week's time President Nash will be ordering an airstrike on Beijing, and you'll both be in a bunker somewhere under the Potomac as the nukes rain down out of the sky. It doesn't matter if I throw away my life, Mike. I'm used to it. But we can't let this thing escalate."

"Okay," Mitchell finally relented, his expression torn between pride and fear, like a father watching his favored son head to war. "But we do it my way."

28

T rapp entered China for the second time that week, this time traveling on a Canadian passport and hitching a ride on a commercial flight from South Korea.

He landed in Dandong, a city of over a million people, with several million more in the greater urban area. It was larger than all but five American cities, and yet it was a place that few outside of China had ever heard of.

Once again, Trapp couldn't help but contemplate the sheer size of this vast country—and the futility of ever going to war with her. America had the greatest military the world had ever seen. Trapp should know. He'd fought in it for years, receiving the best training any warfighter in history ever had.

That was how he knew that going to war here would be a disaster the likes of which his country had never tasted before. President Nash could send in the navy, the army, the Marines and the air force, and paste the Chinese coast with precision guided ordnance until the South China Sea ran red with blood. The first day of the war alone would cost billions just in spent cruise missiles and JDAM guidance kits.

Hundreds of thousands might die, maybe more.

And it would all be for nothing. As Trapp exited the gleaming surroundings of Dandong airport, tasting the thick, humid air of the Chinese summer, a stark contrast from the air-conditioned arrivals hall, and looked out on the endless buildings, he understood that if America picked a fight with this country, it would be like Germany invading the Soviet Union in 1941, or Napoleon doing the same a hundred and fifty years earlier. It would make the mire of Vietnam look like a cakewalk.

China had a hundred cities just like Dandong, with a population of more than a million. America had ten. It would take the American military months to replenish the weaponry expended in the first few weeks of the war, maybe years. But China was blessed with a population that stretched beyond a billion souls, and factories that had swallowed the American manufacturing sector whole.

If America lost an aircraft carrier to a Chinese missile attack, it would take more than a decade to replace it. No, as much as Trapp loved his country, he knew that anyone who believed this war was winnable was dead wrong. The only way for America to triumph would be to reduce China to a pile of smoldering rubble. It would make the aftermath of the Iraq war look like a kid's squabble.

Trapp's boss, Deputy Director Mike Mitchell, had impressed upon him the urgency of his mission. The hawks in Washington were beating the drums of a war they themselves wouldn't have to fight, the press was stirring up outrage, with wall-to-wall coverage of Chinese atrocities, both real and manufactured. Social media was alive with rumor and speculation.

President Nash needed a way out. He needed proof that the Chinese had nothing to do with what had happened to America's satellites—and he needed it fast. If events kept spiraling out of control, then the hows and whys of the situation wouldn't much matter. The Asia-Pacific region was simmering like Europe on the eve of the First World War. It wouldn't take much to spark a conflagration of apocalyptic proportions: just one more miscalculation, one miscommunication, and the world would descend into an orgy of fire.

And so Jason Trapp found himself in China with a simple brief: get his president the evidence he needed.

The city of Dandong sat just across the Yalu River from North Korea itself, connected with the reclusive country by the Sino-Korean Friendship Bridge, an iron structure built by the Imperial Japanese Army when they occupied the area during the Second World War. It was a stark reminder of the last time the world's great powers had gone to war. Trapp vowed to do everything in his power to prevent that outcome from happening again.

He hailed a cab, and after some difficulty owing to the language barrier, communicated the address of a nondescript business hotel downtown. His driver cut through traffic like a madman, swerving between trucks heading for the border with North Korean license plates which were as heavily laden as they were aged, and expensive SUVs with Chinese plates. The contrast between the wealth of the countries couldn't have been greater.

Trapp wondered as he drove, eyes swallowing every detail of the city around him, why the North Korean people didn't simply rise up and cast off their oppressors.

He knew the answer, of course.

It wasn't just that they were brainwashed into believing that their Supreme Leader, Chairman Song, was born at the summit of the most sacred Korean holy site, Mount Paektu; or that the volcanic mountain had spewed flame when the chairman's predecessor died, and he had somehow acquired supernatural properties. It was that the population was beaten and starved into submission, and any spark of resistance snuffed out before it had a chance to spread.

Trapp leaned forward and tapped the cab driver on his shoulder. "You speak any English?"

The man glanced back and grimaced apologetically, his head dancing from side to side. "Only a little."

The road ahead of them lead in a straight line to the glistening Yalu River. On the Chinese side, glass and steel buildings sprouted into the sky, and cranes almost too numerous to count swung their heavy payloads in graceful arcs as day by day, even hour by hour, Dandong grew larger.

By contrast, the North Korean side was flat, brown and agrarian.

Trapp jerked his head at the other side of the river. "Have you ever been over there?"

The driver shook his head, taking his eyes off the road as he pulled off a passing maneuver which would've had Trapp arrested back home. "What for? Nothing there."

Good question, Trapp thought. He was beginning to ask that question himself.

"Do they ever come over here? Refugees."

"Long time ago. Twenty years, during the famine."

"But not today?"

"No."

"Why not?" Trapp asked, frowning.

From this vantage point, the Yalu River seemed neither particularly wide, nor unusually fierce. River craft zipped up and down, paying no attention to the border, which nominally lay in the center of the river. It seemed an easy enough task to cross the body of water—and given the disparity of wealth between the two countries, Trapp had no idea why anyone would choose to stay on the other side of the border.

The cabbie gave Trapp a gap-toothed grin and made the sign

of a gun with his fingers. He cocked his thumb, placed it against Trapp's head, once again tearing his attention away from the road in a way that made his passenger's stomach churn, and fired.

"The border guards—they shoot?"

The driver shrugged. "Whole family. All punished. All die."

"Damn," Trapp whispered.

It was possible that the man was embellishing the situation for the sake of the impressionable foreign businessman. But he didn't think so. From what little he could see, North Korea was a grim, desolate place. One any sane person would be looking to escape, not enter.

So what did that make him?

As they pulled up in front of the hotel, a full ten minutes ahead of schedule—at least according to the estimate the maps application on Trapp's phone had suggested—he tipped the man double. Not for his efforts behind the wheel, which had endangered Trapp's life more than any enemy agent, but for the reminder of what he was going up against.

It might just save his life.

TRAPP WANDERED around the streets of Dandong as the sun began to set, uncomfortably aware that he was almost a foot taller than most of the population, and—it seemed—about the only Caucasian for a hundred miles. He stood out, and in his experience that was rarely a good thing. Especially in a country like China, and even more especially at a time of heightened tensions such as this.

Dandong was no Hong Kong, nor was it Macau. There was no way to simply blend in here, among the thousands of traveling businessmen and ex-pats who inhabited and visited each city, drawn to the lights and glamor like flies to honey. Trapp had no doubt that even now, he would be on the radar of the local branch of the secret police.

As his CIA briefer had informed him before he made the journey, China had more surveillance cameras per citizen than any country on earth. Combined with industry-leading facial recognition technology, it was entirely possible that every inhabitant of Dandong was tracked from morning to night, everywhere they went, and everything they did recorded in a database.

So Trapp took precautions.

He wore a black baseball cap, pulled down low over his face, a thin carbon fiber prosthetic worn underneath both his upper and lower lip to subtly thicken and change his features, and had slipped contact lenses into his eyes before leaving his hotel room, to disguise their unusual, divided nature. Unlike anyone else he had never met, while Trapp's left eye was gray, his right was as dark as the hull of the submarine that plucked him from the warm embrace of the South China Sea several days earlier.

He slipped into a dive bar not far from the river,in an area called Linjiang, about twenty minutes ahead of schedule, expelling a thin stream of saliva that had collected underneath the prosthetic before he entered. He selected a dark booth, and out of habit chose the section of leather seating that faced the entrance.

"I'll have a beer," he grunted when the waitress visited his table. He was careful to introduce a Canadian lilt to his accent, but judging by the look of sheer bewilderment that crossed the woman's face, it was spectacularly unnecessary.

Trapp groaned silently. He held up one finger, and enunciated carefully. "Be-er."

Still, no sign of comprehension was displayed on the women's face.

Trapp decided to take a different tack. He glanced around

the room, eyes itching beneath their contacts, and his gaze settled on an old drunk slumped over the bar, clutching a green bottle of beer. Perfect.

He pointed at the man and said, "I'll have what he's having."

If the words didn't convey his meeting, then the gesture certainly did. The waitress disappeared with an expression of relief on her face, and didn't linger when she set the beer down on the table in front of him, complete with a small paper receipt detailing the damage.

A shard of light into the gloomy bar at the door opened, from the streetlamps outside, and a man stepped into the bar, dressed in tailored slacks and expensive leather oxfords that hadn't seen very many miles. As the man's face came into view, Trapp realized it belonged to the contact he was here to meet.

Presumably since the dive bar presently only contained three patrons, two of whom were slumped over their drinks, and only one—himself—looked even faintly American, the man strode over confidently and stuck out his hand.

"Right on time," he said.

"You got a name?" Trapp asked, studying the man carefully. He looked fit, in a distance runner kind of way—not muscular, but lean. He wasn't sure what he made of the man.

"Call me Jack," the man said. His English was good, though unmistakably accented. Still, it was leagues better than Trapp's Mandarin, and the less said about the few words of Korean he'd learned on the plane ride over, the better.

Trapp kinked his eyebrow. "You don't look like a Jack."

"What am I supposed to look like?" the smuggler replied, a twinkle in his eye. He sat down, clicking his fingers to attract the waitress' attention, and ordered himself a bottle of the same beer Trapp was drinking.

"So," he said. "What brings you to Dandong?"

"What did the company tell you?" Trapp asked, choosing his words carefully.

The company meant *the Company*, complete with a capital C —the Agency, his current employer. But if someone was listening in, there was no sense in making it easy for them.

Jack shrugged. "Not much. That you were a VIP in town looking to"—he spread his hands wide and smiled—"do a deal."

"And that's your area of expertise, I take it?" Trapp asked. "You're the dealmaker."

"I dabble."

"Over the river?"

Jack nodded. "*Especially* over the river."

"I need you to take me there," Trapp said simply, deciding to trust Mitchell's judgment of the man. Every second he lingered this side of the border was another in which his country and China crept ever closer to war—and just as importantly, at least to him—was another second in which he didn't know whether Eliza Ikeda was alive or dead.

The man opposite him looked at Trapp appraisingly. He shook his head. "No chance."

"Why?"

"You need me to spell it out for you?" Jack said, tipping the neck of his beer back and drinking freely. Once he was finished, he dabbed the corners of his mouth with a cocktail napkin, then gently smoothed it against the table.

"Try me," Trapp growled.

Not for the first time, he wondered why Mitchell had been so insistent he take this meeting. If he'd done it his own way, he'd be in Pyongyang already, even if he had to cross the DMZ by foot. With his cultured manners and metropolitan taste in fashion, this mysterious Jack didn't exactly seem the secret agent type.

"Look around, my friend." Jack laughed quietly. "You don't look like us. You think those prosthetics will help you fit in across the border? My people would sell you out for a crust of bread."

Trapp's eyes narrowed. "Your people?"

Jack laughed. "What, you think I'm Chinese? In my line of work?"

Trapp paused before replying. He had indeed assumed that the man across the table from him was Chinese—perhaps fed an illusion by Jack's expensive attire. But now he thought about it, it made more sense for the man to be North Korean. Smuggling was a game where it paid not to stand out.

"I guess not," Trapp replied. "So tell me—what's your story?"

Jack leaned forward, placing his elbows on the table and looking Trapp directly in the eye. He had an air of fierce intensity about him now that was completely at odds with the relaxed personality he had presented just moments before. "You first. You want me to take you over that border, you have to tell me why."

"This is a business transaction," he said. "You don't need to know."

"That's where you're wrong," Jack replied. "Every time I cross the border, I take a risk. Right now, I pay the right people to look the wrong way, everything works out just fine. Maybe tomorrow my luck runs out. Or maybe you piss the right people off, and they take it out on me."

"You will be paid," Trapp said gruffly, waving away the man's objections. "Name your price."

Jack's nose wrinkled. "You Americans," he muttered. "It's not about the money."

He pointed at the unseen river outside the bar. "When I cross that bridge, I'm walking a tight rope. I've got good balance, so on my own, I'll probably make it across just fine..."

Trapp saw where this was going. "But when you add a two-hundred-pound American to your back —"

"Suddenly it's much easier to fall." Jack nodded. He paused before speaking. "Do you know why I do what I do?"

Trapp shook his head.

"I take goods across the border. Expensive wine. Whiskey, television sets. All of it goes to the elite in Pyongyang. To the very people who are bleeding my country dry." A look of disgust crossed his face.

"So why do it?"

"Because on the other way, my friend, I get people out. Maybe just one or two at a time. Maybe a whole family. They hide in my trucks, knowing that if they make a sound, they'll be sent to the labor camps in the mountains. And me alongside them. So if I take you, I'm not risking my business. I'm risking the lives of hundreds of people I can't bring back across the border."

Trapp stayed silent, gauging the man's expression for any sign that he was being played. He knew he had a decision to make. Back at Langley, the choice would have been an easy one —for the suits on the seventh floor, operational security was paramount.

But Trapp knew from long experience that it wasn't always so easy in the field.

His instructions were to tell no one where he was going, or why. But the man opposite him was no snitch, that much was clear. He was a true believer. And he was also Trapp's only route across the border—or at least, his only route that didn't involve stripping off and swimming across the river underneath the guns of the border guards, hoping desperately they didn't notice him. It wasn't an attractive prospect.

Trapp made his decision. "You watch the news?"

"I try not to. But nobody's perfect."

"Then you understand how delicate the present situation is."

"I do," Jack agreed with a slight nod.

"I don't believe the Chinese had anything to do with the attack on my country's satellites," Trapp said in a low tone. "And I intend to prove it."

Jack steepled his fingers, and a pensive expression played across his face. "If not the Chinese, then...."

He paused, lost in thought as he considered the import of what Trapp had said. His eyebrow kinked. "You think Pyongyang was behind it?"

Trapp studied his opposite number intently, watching for any sign of reservation. This was a delicate moment, he knew. He believed the smuggler when the man said he had no love for the North Korean regime. But if their mission was a success, and Trapp returned with evidence of the North Koreans' complicity, then it was entirely possible—likely, even—that many of his countrymen would die as the United States lashed out. "I do."

"And if you're correct, how will your country respond?"

Trapp shrugged. "That's up to the President. My job is to get him the proof he needs to stop this entire region going up in flames."

Jack took a beat to consider Trapp's point, nodded decisively, and reached his hand out. Trapp accepted the offer, and they shook firmly. "I understand. My friend, you have yourself a ride."

29

Eliza Ikeda was numb with exhaustion, though sadly for her, not numb enough to ignore the protestations of pain from her contorted body. She was nailed into a tiny wooden crate, hands bound behind her back, without space to turn, with barely enough air to breathe. The temperature outside was in the high 80s, which meant the atmosphere inside the box was hot and fetid, the air more suited to be chewed than breathed.

Her skin was scored with splinters from the rough wood. She hadn't been fed in what felt like days, and her parched tongue cried out for moisture. The only positive she was able to draw from her current state of agony was that it reminded her that at least she was alive.

Though perhaps, she thought, she might soon come to regret that fact. Maybe it would have been better to have died fighting, not broken at a torturer's hand.

Bile from her empty stomach chewed at her throat, and the salt from her tears, long dried, stung the lacerations and bruises on her face.

The crate jostled as, beneath her, the angry roar of a truck engine coughed and growled. The driver braked sharply, throwing Ikeda against its wall. She made no sound. Even in the depths of her despair, she remembered her training. She needed to stay alert, to drink in every detail in case it might become useful.

Still, it was difficult to lift her spirits out of the depths of her despair. During her initial interrogation, the North Korean soldiers had beaten her bloody, to a point at which she was clinging on to consciousness by only her fingernails, and then beyond, as she slid into a blessed darkness. They had locked her in this coffin-like prison without food, without water, without hope.

And yet her spirit was not broken.

She was a fighter. She had always been a fighter, even from her earliest days, coping first with the loss of her mother, then her father's descent into alcoholism and despair. Deep inside her, there was a reservoir of strength the likes of which most people would never know. It was that same strength that drove her on as her lithe body cut through the freezing water on yet another seemingly impossible swim.

So she listened.

She heard the telltale sound of a body of water somewhere close, the bubbling and gurgling of trapped eddies of water, the high-pitched whine of overtaxed speedboat engines. Was she near the sea?

Yes. She was in a port. They must have dosed her with something, then transported her unconscious body by boat to...

Wherever this was.

And Ikeda heard voices. Low, rumbling voices, the sound of men muttering as they waited in line. She recognized the language, too—Korean, as before. She caught her breath, ears straining and catching the caw of seagulls squawking angrily overhead.

Definitely the sea.

"Papers?"

"Let us through," another man growled, also in Korean, his voice laced with equal parts anger and arrogant power. "We're here under the authority of the Party."

Eliza attempted to make sense of her situation. Heavy machinery thrummed in the background, and the voices of workers and squeals of metal against metal combined with the sound of water crashing against the shore, far away.

She must be at a port. They must have taken her from China back to North Korea. She had failed. And her situation was now hopeless.

Tears pricked at the corners of her eyes, but she blinked them away angrily. She could not give up. She never had before. She reached for that reserve of inner strength that powered her through those frozen swims. It seemed so far away, shrunken and lost through a potion of fear, exhaustion, hunger and thirst.

And yet she vowed to survive. She bit down on her lip, finding in the pain that strength, and clung on to it with all her might. No matter where she was, no matter who had taken her and what they planned to do to her, she would survive it. And not just survive.

But *escape*.

Something jolted Eliza's wooden prison, spinning the crate and smashing her head against its rough-hewn planks. A crane, maybe. Or a forklift truck, picking the crate up and moving it, a gruff electric howl punctuating the action.

Not for the first time since her ordeal had started, and certainly not for the last, Eliza drifted into the clutches of unconsciousness.

∾

ELIZA WOKE AGAIN, with hot tears streaming down her face, stinging in the cuts and marks on her broken skin, washing her bloodied face clean.

No, not tears. Rain.

The raindrops fell in thick, heavy bursts, the water forcing its way with relentless efficiency through the cracks in Eliza's wooden prison. Her parched tongue cried out, and acting on pure instinct, like a wounded animal dragging itself to lap from the waters of a fast flowing river, she pressed her lips against the wood and greedily sucked droplets of water into her mouth.

As she drank, the crate vibrated and rocked, the growl of an engine cracking through the otherwise silent landscape. Eliza noticed none of it. She licked the filthy droplets of water until her thirst was, for a time at least, sated, a dull, throbbing hunger rearing its head in its wake.

She slumped back, once again forcing herself to take stock of her situation. The crate was on the back of an open truck, and Eliza was being thrown around with every pothole.

They were taking her somewhere.

It wasn't much.

But it was knowledge, and knowledge was hope. She would survive whatever they threw at her, wherever they were going. And somehow, she knew that as alone as she felt right now, someone was coming to get her. Not just any someone, but a man with the eyes of a wraith, and the hangman's scar across his neck.

She whispered his name. "*Jason.*"

Perhaps it was a vain hope, one destined to be dashed against the bitter rocks of experience. Few Americans had ever visited the hermit kingdom of North Korea, and certainly none had left the confines of strictly choreographed, guarded tour groups to wander freely around the country as though searching for a lost pet.

The idea that Jason Trapp would ride in on the back of a

white horse, slaying enemies left and right to rescue her was laughable. Ludicrous. And yet Eliza clung to it nonetheless. She couldn't do anything but, for the alternative was to give up, to allow despair and hopelessness to claim her, and drag her into the darkness with them.

Eliza Ikeda wasn't made that way. If Jason Trapp was coming, then she had to be ready. And whatever it took, she would be.

THE TRUCK'S engine growled for hours, whining as it climbed a steep mountain road. In that time Eliza had maneuvered her bound hands from behind her to the front, allowing her protesting shoulders some slight relief from the pain. With the newfound freedom, she enlarged a crack in the wooden planks that made up the crate with nothing more than her fingernails, whittling away until fat droplets of blood fell freely from her torn hands.

She pressed her head against the rough wall of the crate, closing one eye and peering out into the unknown with the other. A barren landscape flashed past, dark brown muddy hillsides, stunted green trees with gnarled boughs, impromptu waterfalls gushing off rocky outcroppings, painting the steel stone white with froth. The truck was following at least one other vehicle, and though Eliza could not see it from her vantage point, she guessed it was smaller, perhaps a Jeep.

"Where are you taking me?" she whispered.

It didn't take long before she was provided with an answer. The empty mountainsides gave way to a plateau, and for the first time, Eliza saw people. Most were wearing drab green army uniforms and polished black boots, but others looked like prisoners—trudging with their heads collapsed to their gaunt chests, clothed in lifeless gray overalls, and watched by men with guns.

The truck slowed, occasionally sounding its horn, and Eliza watched as the foot traffic scurried out of its way. To the side of the road was a fenced compound that reminded her of a Nazi concentration camp—low wooden huts, hemmed close in, with ragged prisoners collapsed on the edges, a few aimlessly searching for something edible on the bare dirt ground.

A chill ran through her body. She had heard tales of the atrocities carried out in North Korea's labor camps. Tales of beatings, of torture, of pregnant women forced to work in the fields even as their waters broke. And most pertinently, of prisoners so hungry they resorted to eating bugs straight out of the ground.

Was this her future? Branded as an enemy of the Korean revolution and forced to work here until the day she died?

Her train of thought was broken by the metallic screech of gates opening, then closing as the truck passed through. It screeched to a halt, and the engine died, matched shortly after by the first vehicle in the small convoy. For a second, silence reigned, and Eliza redoubled her efforts to get a sense of her bearings.

Was she in the prison camp?

No.

Wherever she was, it looked more like a military encampment. The truck had stopped on a paved parade ground, at the center of which stood a flagpole, crowned with two flags: the red star on a blue background that was the North Korean flag, and a rectangle of red cloth just below it, fluttering in the slight breeze.

Eliza was too far away to make out the yellow insignia that decorated the second flag, but she didn't need to. She knew exactly what it was: the hammer, sickle and ink brush logo of the Worker's Party of Korea.

Around the parade ground were buildings. Mostly just one or two stories tall, they were functional structures, constructed out of drab concrete. It could have been any military base anywhere, except for the flags.

The truck door creaked open, boots thudded against the ground, and it closed again. A harsh voice rang out, speaking in Korean. It belonged to one of her captors, and the memory of her beating made Eliza shiver. "Where is the colonel?"

She couldn't make out the indistinct reply.

But she didn't have long to wait to find out. A bell rang out, harsh and discordant against the otherwise quiet mountainside. Eliza's vision only extended a few inches to the left and right of the crack she had fashioned between the wooden planks, but even so she saw dozens, then hundreds of people streaming from the buildings that hemmed in the parade ground. Men, women—even children.

Why kids?

A crowd formed around the truck, not too close. All were dressed in military uniforms, even the children, who looked ridiculous in oversized fatigues that practically swallowed them whole. In the center of the crowd stood the five men she recognized—her captors. The men who had snatched her from the Ritz-Carlton in Macau days earlier, beaten her to within an inch of her life, and then taken her here, to experience fresh horrors that she could barely imagine.

A commanding voice rang out, immediately catching Eliza's attention. "You are late, Captain. I hope you come bearing good news."

The voice's owner strode into view, dressed the same as all the others, but wearing an air of unquestioned authority that was unmistakable. From her limited viewpoint, it was difficult to make out the finer details of his face, but it was impossible to miss the ugly scar that marked his cheek.

Eliza watched, attention hooked by the man's obvious confidence. He walked like he owned the place, like he was the king of all he surveyed. His voice was cold, dead, as though all emotion had been leached out of his soul.

Captain Jung's voice quavered. "The American is dead. But we didn't return empty-handed."

The colonel's eyes narrowed. He stood in front of his men, feet apart, toes pointing at ten and two. He held his hands clasped behind his back. His men—and the entire crowd—looked upon him with spellbound fascination, a fascination that was evidently laced with fear. Though she had never met the man, Eliza's chosen line of work had brought her into contact with many like him. In another place, at another time, he might have founded a cult or risen through the ranks of a gang of street thugs. From the cringing reaction of the crowd around him, he was clearly no stranger to violence. His emotionless voice suggested a sociopathic nature.

"That wasn't a yes," he spat.

The captain flinched. "He was dead by the time we arrived, sir. There was nothing we could —"

In the blink of an eye, the short, scarred North Korean colonel twisted his body and delivered a stinging slap that echoed around the silent parade ground. "You failed."

"We —"

The colonel switched his attention to one of the other men. They stood, ramrod straight, staring into the distance — plainly hoping that their boss would take the flak for the failed operation.

"You," he growled, pointing at one of the men. "Give me your side arm."

The soldier did as he was ordered, un-clipping his holster and handing his boss a small black pistol, the barrel reversed. He did not speak.

"All of you, on your knees," the colonel ordered.

Eliza could not tear her attention away from the macabre

sight. She had no doubt that she was about to witness a public execution—a punishment that had been retired decades if not centuries before in most civilized countries.

But North Korea was a country apart from the rest of human civilization. It did not obey the ordinary rules.

And this encampment, high in the mountains, seemed almost like a country within a country, ruled with an iron fist by this man with a scar on his face. His word was law. Eliza did not yet understand what he wanted, or why he had sent his men to retrieve Emmanuel Alstyne and his thumb drive full of American military secrets. But a tendril of fear coiled in her gut as she watched the scene play out in front of her—and not for her own safety. Whatever this colonel's ultimate goal truly was, she feared that if he was permitted to achieve it, it would come with an almost unimaginable cost.

The soldiers fell to their knees. Eliza had wondered if they would fight, or protest their innocence, but they did neither. They acted like beaten dogs—easily powerful enough to overcome their abuser, and yet unable to question the programming that had been beaten into them from birth.

A flash of insight struck Eliza in that moment. That was it—it explained why the kids were here. They were soldiers.

Child soldiers.

The realization sickened her, and for a brief moment she tore her attention away from the soldiers on their knees and looked at the blank faces of the young boys and girls in the crowd. They should be innocent, playing with their siblings, growing up in the homes of their mothers and fathers, and not in a place like this.

Instead they were torn as babies from their mothers' breasts and fashioned into instruments of death. Though Ikeda couldn't bring herself to simply forget the torments that Captain Jung and his men had inflicted upon her, she began to understand them, for the first time. Understand that they knew no other life than pain.

The colonel drew back the slide on the pistol, the metallic *snick* drawing Eliza's attention. She watched as he placed it on the trembling captain's forehead.

"Tell me, Captain Jung. Why should I allow you to live, now that you have failed me?"

The man's voice broke as he attempted to reply. He cleared his throat and tried again. "We have the drive."

"It's encrypted," the colonel snarled. "Without the American, it's useless."

"There was a woman..."

"What woman?" the colonel growled.

"The crate, in the bed of the truck."

The colonel snapped his fingers, and from outside her field of vision, Eliza heard the footsteps of attentive soldiers rushing toward her. Then thuds, as soldiers jumped into the truck, then her stomach swayed as hands lifted the crate. She fell backwards, and was once again blind in the darkness. Fear gripped her, her mind almost descending into panic.

No, she thought desperately. *Don't succumb.*

Hot tears filled her eyes, but she did not let them fall. As she had done before, she visualized herself in the water, buffeted by waves flecked with chunks of ice. A cold so piercing it stifled all conscious thought. A cold so all-encompassing it tempted her body to simply shut down, to give up. To conserve energy and heat around its major organs.

But just as she did on a long, Arctic swim, Eliza fought. She pictured her limbs cutting through the frigid water, concentrated on maintaining her steady breath.

In, one, two; out, three, four.

The panic faded. Eliza's chest stopped heaving, and her eyes blinked open in the darkness, no longer glistening with tears.

She would survive this. She didn't know how, but she would make it through.

Outside the crate, she heard men grunting, and then a shock rocked the wooden box as it was thrown unceremoniously against the ground. Once again, Eliza was tossed around like a child's doll in a tumble dryer.

"Open it," the colonel ordered coldly.

Eliza Ikeda had spent hours, perhaps days locked in the darkness of that box, with neither food nor water. Throughout all that time, all she had hoped for was to once again feel the heat of the sun on her face, to breathe air that wasn't infected with the acrid scent of her own piss and sweat. But as a crowbar splintered the wooden planks, she realized that at least in here, she knew what her problems were. But out there, she was about to face an entire ocean of unimaginable horror.

Remember, she urged herself, *you speak Mandarin. No English, no Korean. Just Mandarin.*

Eliza knew that the chances of her surviving this were limited at best. She needed every advantage she could get. Her captors thinking that she could not understand them was a slim one—but it was all she had.

The crate cracked open around her, and the light kissed her skin, almost blinding her. She huddled on the ground, unmoving, pretending to be unconscious—which in reality was not far from the case.

"Who is she?" The colonel said.

Eyes closed, Eliza listened.

"I believe she was sent to kill the American," the captain replied in a pleading tone. That was, after all, what he was doing—begging for his life.

"And you let her succeed," the man's commanding officer replied coldly. "You endangered the entire plan."

Eliza concentrated on maintaining a neutral expression,

knowing that to give any sign that she understood what was being discussed was tantamount to a death sentence. But battered as her body was, her intelligent mind went into overdrive.

She had assumed that acquiring Alstyne's secrets was the end goal—but that, apparently, was not the case. There was a greater strategy at play here—and if she got the chance, she needed to find out precisely what it was.

"Colonel," the captain whimpered. "You said yourself, the American was never part of the original plan. We only learned of him at the last —"

The colonel cut him off. "Plans change, Captain. And when they do, it is your responsibility to adapt to that change—not quail in the face of it. Does she have the encryption codes?"

"I —"

"You what?" the colonel sneered. "Do you know, or don't you?"

"I interrogated her personally, Colonel," the captain said. "She claimed not."

Eliza remained on the cold, hard ground, eyelids sealed shut. Though she could not see the scene unfolding around her, she could picture it—every actor in the *danse macabre* in their assigned positions. The five kneeling men. The sneering, vicious colonel. The entranced onlookers.

"Lieutenant Jin?"

"Yes, Colonel."

"Has the captain omitted any information that might later prove relevant?"

Jin replied haltingly, as though torn between the warring desires of self-preservation and not wanting to sell out his commanding officer. Eliza imagined the trembling of his jaw, his flickering eyes. "No, sir."

"Then stand up."

Jin's boots scraped on the ground. He moved with the excruciating slowness of a condemned man marching toward his own execution. A scrape, then a pause. Then a muffled grunt. Then a metallic sound, followed quickly by a sharp intake of breath.

"You know what to do, Lieutenant," the colonel said harshly.

Jin didn't reply. Eliza strained her ears, desperately trying to figure out what the hell was going on around her, though she dared not open her eyes. A moment later, a muffled, terrified groan rang out across the silent parade ground—the sound of a man understanding his fate.

And then a single gunshot cracked through the sky. A body slumped to the ground. For a few seconds, no one spoke. The wind did not blow. Eliza barely heard the sound of her own heartbeat, or the blood rushing in her eardrums.

Justice had been delivered. Of a sort.

An Old World sort of justice, where the aim was to strike fear in the hearts of those who were watching. And those who were listening.

It succeeded.

Eliza was left under no uncertain illusions as to her fate, if she allowed herself to meekly succumb to this sociopath's desires. She would have to find a way to survive, to escape this place. But how, she had no idea.

"Captain Jin," grated the colonel's emotionless voice, "congratulations on your promotion. I trust that you will not fail me like your predecessor."

"No, sir."

One of the surviving captors spoke up, his fearful tone indicating that he would rather not have to. "And the prisoner, Colonel? What are your orders?"

The reply was swift. ""Take her to Building 12. I will be with you shortly. I have some business to attend to first."

30

Almost exactly 24 hours after first meeting his North Korean contact, the enigmatic smuggler nicknamed "Jack," Jason Trapp arrived at the pre-agreed rendezvous point—a small warehouse and dock that sat at the edge of the Yalu River, the natural border between the People's Republic of China and the secretive communist state of North Korea.

Trapp was dressed in dark clothing and carried a waterproof bag on his shoulder which contained a small pistol, several magazines and ammunition, a compass and a foldable pair of field binoculars. Each of the items was wrapped in cloth, to minimize the chances of them emitting any sound that might get him caught.

He would need additional supplies once he was across the river, but for now he preferred to travel light. He also had a flat worker's cap pulled low over his forehead to obscure his face.

He could do little to hide his bulk. Few North Koreans could hope to measure up to his height—not even their tallest soldiers, who were assigned to face off with their South Korean and American counterparts at the DMZ, in a bizarre throwback to the Cold War. Like most of the rest of the North Korean population, the average army conscript stood at only a fraction over five and a half feet in height, a consequence of childhood malnutrition that was scarcely alleviated even once they received army rations.

Trapp, by contrast, was the perfect product of the system the North Korean regime so abhorred, towering almost a foot taller and eighty pounds heavier than anyone he was likely to encounter across the river. So, all in all, the cap hiding his face served little actual value. But old habits die hard.

As he entered the small, mostly empty parking lot outside the dilapidated warehouse, Trapp paused, eyes scanning the scene for anything that looked out of place. His contact was resting against the hood of the truck that hung low over its suspension, lit only by the glow of a single bulb on the exterior of the warehouse and the screen of the cell phone in his hands. Trapp didn't recognize the truck's logo, and presumed it had been manufactured either in China, or perhaps North Korea itself.

He hung back, his body pressed against the corrugated iron walls of the warehouse as he tasted the air, trusting his finely-honed instincts for danger to warn him if he was about to walk into a trap. He didn't expect to be double crossed, but then again, few people ever did.

But Trapp sensed nothing amiss. Just the smell of a cheap cigarette brand carried in the muggy evening breeze. He decided to chance it. He had already tarried in Dandong for far too long. Every second he waited was another in which Eliza languished in captivity, and in which the United States was carried ever closer to all-out war by a braying, salivating press eager for ratings and clicks, and the outrage of hundreds of millions of enraged citizens.

He strode toward the smuggler, still scanning his surroundings, just in case he had missed something lurking in the darkness. The man glanced up from his phone as he approached.

"Are you sure you wish to go ahead with this, my friend?" Jack asked, shaking Trapp's hand in greeting. "Because once we cross that border, there is no turning back."

"I'm committed, don't worry about that," Trapp replied. "Just make sure you meet me on the other side."

Jack's teeth flashed white against the evening gloom. "I'll do my part. Make sure you don't get caught."

"I'll try not to," Trapp said drily.

"I'm serious," Jack said, narrowing his eyes. "If you're in danger of being apprehended, then do not let them take you alive. Take the easy way out. I promise you, my friend, you will regret it for the rest of your life if you do not. I've seen the camps. I know what happens to those who enter them." He shivered. "Just don't let it happen to you."

Trapp grimaced, not at the prospect of his own capture and torture, which he knew was an occupational hazard, but at the reminder of what Ikeda was no doubt experiencing at this very moment.

Where was she, right now? He was on the verge of crossing into North Korea with only a vague idea of what he would do when he reached the other side of the border. Mitchell had supplied him with the location of the camp that was suspected to house Unit 61—but there was no guarantee the intelligence was correct, or that Eliza would be there even if it was.

But then—what other choice did he have?

"I'll take that under advisement," he replied, bouncing from foot to foot as a wave of nervous energy flooded through him, as it so often did before he entered harm's way. Trapp was no stranger to fear, but he did not hide from it, as so many other men tried to do. He knew that was a fool's errand. He embraced his fears. They were what kept him sharp; what kept him alive.

"I see you're anxious to get moving," Jack said, shaking his head in apparent amazement at the foolhardiness of his new American acquaintance.

"Indeed," Trapp replied. "But let's run through the plan one last time."

Jack nodded and removed a small, laminated satellite map of the area from his inside pocket, along with a thin pen light. He clicked the flashlight on and shone it onto the map. It was a commercial image, and lacked the resolution that Trapp was accustomed to after so many years of operating with the resources of the Agency at his disposal. But it didn't need to be perfect.

"We're here," he said, placing his index finger onto the map. He dragged it a couple of inches upward. "This is the Friendship Bridge, which links Dandong with the town of Sinuiju on the North Korean side of the border. I will cross it in about forty-five minutes, just before the guard post closes for the night."

Trapp nodded his understanding and gestured for the man to continue.

"A contact of mine is waiting on the river for you —"

"You trust him?" Trapp asked gruffly.

"Absolutely." Jack nodded. "If I didn't, I wouldn't be risking your life in his hands. He will take you up the Yalu, past Sinuiju, down a tributary of the river that passes east of Wihwa Island, here." He indicated a spot in a barren section of the map.

"What's there?" Trapp asked, scanning the map and committing the details to memory. "Guards? Fences? Dogs?"

Jack shook his head. "Nothing."

"What about defectors?" Trapp asked, confused. "How do the North Koreans stop them?"

Jack shrugged. "They don't need to. The Chinese catch them and send them back. My people know the price of being caught. It's a one-way ticket to the camps. There are a few guards, of course, but not as many as you would think. It's not in the army's interest to stop the smuggling across the border. They get their cut, so they don't care."

"Okay," Trapp said, taking the man's word for it. "What next?"

Jack shifted his position on the map, indicating a small conurbation next to a highway that seemed curiously free of traffic. "I will be waiting for you just north of this housing estate."

"That easy, huh?"

The smuggler smiled, though his expression was uneasy. "As long as you don't get caught."

THE SMALL WOODEN fishing boat that Jack had arranged cut through the water at scarcely more than a walking pace. Trapp spoke little Mandarin, and his pilot no English, so the two men sat in silence as the boat's aged engine spluttered loudly in the gloom, carrying across the still surface of the Yalu River.

Trapp hoped desperately that Jack was correct about the likelihood of him encountering any army patrols. His ride had to be bordering on half a century old, and it was making enough noise to wake the dead. He grimaced and waved for the fisherman's attention. He jerked his thumb at the engine, which was coughing enough black smoke to be visible even in the darkness, and drew his fingers across his throat.

The old fisherman smiled broadly, the half-moon overhead revealing chipped, yellow teeth. He waved away Trapp's protestations, clearly amused by the American's palpable anxiety. Realizing that he was making no headway, Trapp gave up and sank low into the wooden vessel's depths, the foul water sloshing in the bilges lacing his dark clothes with a fishy scent that he immediately knew would be impossible to remove.

"Guess it's your show," Trapp muttered. "You just better not get me killed."

The old man just grunted.

The motor growled for about twenty minutes as the boat traveled upstream. To keep his mind off the prospect of imminent discovery, Trapp studied the eastern bank of the river: North Korea. The contrast between the Chinese side and its nearest, strangest neighbor was impossible to ignore. North Korea was simply...

Dark.

While Dandong twinkled in the night sky, decorated by streetlights and neon advertising hoardings, North Korea was an enigma of empty blackness. Even the Yellow Sea to the south was illuminated, as giant cargo ships plied their trade across the empty ocean. Trapp knew that most of the country had little access to electricity. Like medieval peasants hundreds of years before, North Korean farmers toiled in the daylight and ended their labors as soon as the sun went down.

The sight gave Trapp a measure of comfort. Unless the North Koreans had guards dug into dark trenches, then just as Jack had promised, the border was unguarded. Even if they did, he was certain they wouldn't be equipped with night vision aids.

The fisherman cut the engine, and the boat began to slow, the flow of the river pushing it back in the opposite direction, out into the blackness of the ocean. Trapp glanced up, and the old man pressed his finger against his lips.

Great, now you decide to keep quiet.

Two wooden oars were clipped against the insides of the boat, and the fisherman lifted them up, then dipped them into the water. Trapp shot him a questioning glance, silently asking whether the man needed help, only to receive a shake of the head in response.

The slight old man was stronger than he looked. He pulled

the boat forward at a steady pace, one scarcely slower than the boat's antiquated engine had managed. After a few minutes traveling in that manner, he grabbed both oars with one hand and held up two fingers on the other.

Trapp's eyes narrowed. "Two minutes?" he mouthed.

The man nodded, apparently understanding the thrust of the CIA operative's hushed question.

Jason snapped into action.

He pulled his jacket and shirt over his head, then removed his pants, socks and boots. He placed all of the clothing into his waterproof rucksack and closed it tight, double-checking the seal. By the time he was done, the boat was no more than 30 yards from the opposite bank of the river. The border line between the two countries was flexible, and authorities from neither country bothered arresting the fisherman and traders who accidentally crossed over.

They had seen little traffic on the river, and certainly no evidence of military or police activity. It would have been easy enough for the old man to land his boat on the North Korean side and set Trapp down on terra firma. But there was no sense in courting danger if it could be avoided simply by getting his feet wet.

After grasping the old man's shoulder in silent thanks, Trapp lowered himself into the fast-flowing flow, clutching the strap of his waterproof bag. The water was surprisingly cold, for it gushed from thousands of mountainous streams, lakes and rivers, but Trapp knew that he would not be in it long.

He swam for the opposite bank, heading for the heart of darkness of a country that no American operative had entered since the end of the Korean War more than sixty years before, knowing that if he was caught, then he would surely die.

31

K im entered the stark concrete warehouse that had been converted into Savrasov's biohazard labora- tory. He wandered through the anodyne hallways, mind tussling with the problem his operatives had brought back from Macau.

Captain Jung had been right about one thing, though alluding to it hadn't saved the man's life. The Macau operation was never pivotal to the colonel's plan. Kim had learned of Alstyne's existence from a source in the Chinese Ministry of State Security, a man paid handsomely—and at no real cost to Kim. Every year, on this very site, Unit 61 produced hundreds of millions of dollars of counterfeit American currency, mostly hundred dollar bills, referred to by the US Treasury as "super-dollars."

The counterfeit banknotes were so perfect that unless a bank's scanner detected the same serial number on two notes at the same time, at opposite ends of the country, they blended into circulation undetectably. Kim had, in fact, funneled tens of millions of dollars into his own offshore bank accounts over the past decade—an insurance policy, in case he was ever forced to flee.

A smile crossed his twisted face. If everything went to plan, then before too much longer he would have no need of those accounts. A far greater prize was almost in his grasp: the resources of an entire nation.

Kim entered Savrasov's office without knocking, passing an armed guard stationed outside the doorway to act as a flesh-and-blood reminder to the Russian of who was in control. Not that the weak geneticist required any great encouragement. He was pathetically, desperately eager just to survive—all thoughts of personal enrichment long since forgotten. "Where is the girl?"

The frazzled scientist tore his eye away from the viewing scope of an electron microscope, a startled expression on his face. "What girl?" he stammered.

Kim grimaced, stuck his head into the hallway and barked a command. The guard nodded and turned on his heel—eager to escape the presence of his irritated CO. After all, only earlier that day he had seen the punishment for failure. Kim was pleased with the man's alacrity.

He returned to Savrasov's office. The man was anxiously kneading his lab coat between his fingers. "How is the virus progressing, Doctor?" he asked.

Boris' eyes glazed for a second, then refocused. He looked almost relieved to be asked a question about his area of exper-tise, as though it gave him a moment's respite from constantly questioning whether he was about to be executed.

Kim considered reassuring him, then decided against it. The threat of fear had, after all, worked magnificently so far. Why mess with something that wasn't broken?

Savrasov nodded. "Well. *Very* well. It's operating within the parameters I outlined. We infected them three days ago, and their bloodwork is already indicates a high viral load. They should be symptomatic in forty-eight hours, perhaps a little less."

Kim smiled, pleased. After the failure in Macau, it was nice to hear some positive news. He assured himself that Alstyne's death was nothing more than an outlier, rather than a portent of further failure. He should've sent a more experienced man in Captain Jung's place. He wouldn't make that mistake again.

"Good. And the delivery mechanism?"

Savrasov blanched. Kim understood the man's reaction—at least, in an intellectual capacity. The colonel had never experienced the wide range of emotions that other men took for granted. Like his height, his emotional development had also been stunted during childhood. He wouldn't shed a tear over the loss. If anything, it was an advantage. Emotions only served to blunt a man's decision-making, to obscure from him his true goal.

Kim wasn't weighed down by such petty concerns.

But Boris Savrasov was. Kim understood that when he confined himself to the realm of discussing viral loads and incubation periods, he was able to cloak his actions in the comforting obscurity of scientific jargon. It felt no different than discussing a case report back at Vektor Institute in Siberia.

There was no obscuring the true purpose of Kim's weapons, however. They were designed to kill—and not just to kill those in the immediate vicinity, but to bring down an entire superpower. A country whose boot had been on the neck of the Korean people for far too long. A country that Kim intended to humble.

"They will work." Savrasov coughed. "A little dated, but perfectly effective."

Kim smiled his rictus smile once more. He heard the sound of boots approaching in the hallway, rubber soles squeaking against the linoleum floor. "Good. As it happens, Boris, I have another candidate for your trial."

Before he was able to stop himself, the Russian shook his head. "I have enough data," he said quickly. "I don't need another."

"I wasn't asking, Doctor."

The battered female prisoner appeared in the doorway, flanked by two of Kim's men, who were practically holding her up by her shoulders, allowing her bloodied legs to dangle against the floor. Kim studied her for the first time. Underneath the bruises and cuts, and the ammonia stink of urine, she seemed a pretty woman. Taller than most Chinese, and with rosier skin. Her physique was impressive—like a gymnast's, her muscles contoured and defined.

"So," he said, speaking in perfect yet accented English. "You're the whore."

Kim watched carefully for a response, but none came. The woman simply dangled between her captors, her chest rising and falling, her breath occasionally catching as though in response to an unexpected lance of pain.

And yet, somehow, he believed that she understood exactly what he was saying. It was a result of nothing that the woman had said or done, just a sixth sense that Kim had honed over many hundreds of interrogations just like this one.

Well, not *precisely* the same, Kim thought. Today he had the opportunity to try something new. Something he had never done before. And though he had never felt shame, even after executing his own mother, nor sadness at the death of his family, the Korean colonel most certainly experienced his own twisted version of joy. The feeling overcame him, swelling in his breast.

"My men have the drive," Kim added. "We'll break our way into it before long. Your silence will achieve little."

The woman said nothing.

Kim shrugged. He pointed at Savrasov's office chair and ordered his two men to deposit the woman onto it. She slumped against it, still making no eye contact. Kim sensed that she was listening, however.

"Would you like to know what we're doing here?" he asked, opening up his body and gesturing around the Russian's messy office, at the electron microscope, the centrifuge, and various other pieces of equipment that Kim neither recognized, nor cared to ask about.

Still, no response.

"My dear, you should be excited. The whole world will soon learn what we have done." Kim grinned, looking toward Savrasov. "Or should I say, what my friend Boris has done."

The tubby scientist squeaked, though whether it was with approval or dismay, the colonel didn't much care. But yet again, the woman showed no sign that she had heard Kim, let alone understood his words.

Kim frowned. Perhaps, after all, she didn't speak English. Maybe she was exactly as she seemed—a pretty whore, in the wrong place at the wrong time. Perhaps Emmanuel Alstyne had died as a result of an unknown health condition: a brain aneurysm, or a heart attack.

Kim sneered.

He didn't believe that for a second. The bitch was neck deep in this. And he would discover the truth, one way or another. He studied her battered face, lip curling with disgust as he watched a thin strand of drool pool at the corner of her mouth then dangle with disgusting, infuriating slowness, before detaching and falling onto her leg. She made no move to wipe it off. No move, in fact, to indicate that she was anything more than a brain-dead vegetable.

But Kim knew better.

"You see, my dear, I think you understand every word I am saying. I think you are American. I think you were sent to murder your traitorous compatriot and retrieve the files he stole. And I think you are going to tell you everything you know, one way or another. So I will offer you a simple choice: come clean, and I'll allow you to die quickly. Lie to me, and you will choke on your own blood."

He waited for a response. When none came, he clicked his fingers.

"Very well then," he said. "It seems I shall have to show you."

In Korean, for the benefit of the guards, he added, "Take her to the observation room."

Kim walked behind his men as they dragged the prisoner down the hallway. "Boris," he growled, noticing the Russian scientist lingering behind, his expression pale with fear. "You too."

Inside the observation room, a curtain was drawn across the glass partition. Immediately, Kim knew that it was Savrasov's doing. The Russian detested what Kim was making him do. Even though the test subjects were not yet symptomatic, many soon would be. It was easy for Savrasov to hide from the consequences of his actions behind his microscope. Harder when he was confronted with men and women who would die as a result of his work. Kim enjoyed watching the man's self-loathing, the black hatred now twisting his face such a contrast to the impassive expressions on the faces of the two soldiers currently manhandling his prisoner.

"Open the curtain, Boris," Kim said. "Let us see your handiwork."

Boris blinked anxiously, gulped, then stepped forward, toward the glass partition. The curtain was drawn open and closed by a chain, and it rasped as he tugged at it with heavy fingers. The curtain opened, by inches at first, then feet, and finally the window was fully clear.

Immediately, the scientist turned away, hiding from the horrors he had unleashed into the world as a result of his greed.

But Kim was entranced. Inside the test facility, eight subjects lay on camp beds, secured by thin metallic chains that linked the cuffs around their legs to the bed underneath them, bolted to the floor. The eight: four Americans, and four Chinese, lay listlessly at first, but revived themselves when they saw activity on the other side of the glass.

Three of the four Americans started yelling, the fourth simply looked up hopelessly, tears streaking down her face. The sound was muted, so Kim walked to an intercom button set onto the wall, by the glass window, and pushed it.

"— us out, you motherfucker. What do you want with us?"

In the reflection on the glass, Kim watched as—just for a second—the girl's head jerked upward. Immediately she caught herself, and pressed her chin against her chest—but it was too late. Kim turned, with an expression of vicious joy stretched across his broken face.

"I thought so," he growled. He strode over to her, grabbed her chin roughly, and yanked it up so that he could stare into her slate gray eyes. Where before they were purposefully glazed over, now they were tinged with fear.

"The people in that room will die horribly," he snarled. "Burning up, drowning on their own blood as their very cells betray them. And now, girl, it's time you joined them."

32

Carl Erickson's passion was astronomy.

He had no scientific training, in fact had no quali-
fication of any kind higher than his high school GED,
and neither his appearance—a jovial face and thick white
beard that often prompted children to mistake him for Santa,
and a beer belly that sometimes peeked out from beneath his
shirt—nor his former profession as a plumber suggested that
he was a man who was fascinated with the night sky.

In fact, not just fascinated, but downright *obsessed*.

Carl didn't own a television, for he reasoned he had no
need for one, given the far greater delights that could be found
in the skies above. Why waste hours watching reality television,
he reasoned, when he could gaze into distant galaxies, studying
glimmers of light emitted by stars that might have died billions
of years ago? What wonders lay in the darkness, far beyond
humanity's reach?

Alien life? He was sure of it.

Other civilizations? How could there not be?

Carl's pride and joy was his Meade LX850 home telescope,
set on a GPS guided, computerized mount. It had cost him

almost $15,000 and taken him years to save up for, but in his opinion was worth every penny. His laptop's hard drive was filled with images of Saturn's rings, of dust storms blemishing the face of Mars, and a hundred other curiosities.

Delights could be found closer to home as well. He had whiled away more nights than he could count simply watching the International Space Station pass by overhead, or studying the sinking orbit of a defunct communications satellite.

The purchase of the telescope prompted other changes, too. His wife had died some years previously, shortly after he retired, and they had no children, which meant no grandchildren either. And so Carl decided to move deep into the Utah desert, where the night sky was not obscured by one of the few things that could raise the friendly old man's ire: light pollution.

So it was that Carl found himself that night in mid-summer, lying on a reclining chair on his deck with his laptop resting on his belly, connected by a cable to the only possession he truly cared about. A small cooler filled with ice and bottles of Budweiser sat by his side, and his dog Rex chased shadows as the sun faded beyond the horizon.

"Cut that out, boy," he growled fondly at the energetic Labrador.

As usual, Rex ignored him, disappearing into the darkness, but that was no problem. Carl's property was fenced, and he'd seen little sign of coyotes in the area recently. They were only usually an issue during the winter, when their natural food sources grew scarce and they were forced into scavenging near human settlements.

Carl shook his head and focused on his night's work. The LX850 outputted high definition video to Carl's computer, and a program running on it sent instructions the other way. He initiated a search program of his own design and settled back into his recliner, lifting the cool bottle of beer to his lips as the telescope's quiet motor whirred into action.

It wasn't long before the program had identified its first target: a French communications satellite operated by a private company. Carl dutifully made a check in his notebook against the satellite's designation, but while it was nice to be reacquainted with an old flame, the sight wasn't particularly interesting.

Ideally, Carl was hoping to see some signs of the debris field that was reportedly orbiting the planet at frightening speeds—a result of the destruction of a number of America's military satellites in the skies above Asia several days before. Unlike the explosion of a ship, or a plane coming down over the ocean, where wreckage might over the course of months be carried hundreds or thousands of miles on the tides, the destruction of the satellite could produce tens of thousands of pieces of debris —some only a fraction of an inch across.

And yet those tiny fragments were traveling at speeds of thousands of miles an hour, never slowing, for there was no atmosphere in space to hold them back. And until those fragments were pulled by the Earth's gravity into the atmosphere and burned up, they were a risk to all other spacecraft. Even a loose screw would, traveling at a high enough speed, be sufficient to kill every astronaut on board the ISS.

Of course, that was the last outcome that Carl hoped to see. But watching the space station firing its thrusters to move out of the path of the deadly debris would be quite a coup.

His laptop chimed, and Carl squinted at the screen. "What have you got for me, baby?"

The image in front of him was unusual. The telescope had fixed its view on a satellite, but not one that Carl recognized. He consulted his notes and ran a quick web search, which indicated that the object currently passing over his head was operated by the US military. And according to his notebook, this wasn't the first time he'd seen it. Perhaps not even the tenth.

But he'd never seen it like this.

The satellite appeared to have gained weight, bulging in the middle like a pregnant mother. He rubbed his eyes, wondering if he was seeing things, then consulted his hard drive for images he'd saved last time the satellite appeared ahead.

It looks completely different.

It was the same satellite, because it had to be. Satellites followed fairly predictable orbits, and their operators tended not to alter those flight paths dramatically, since the consequences of a crash could lead to costs of hundreds of millions, or even billions of dollars. And yet the satellite had quite undoubtedly altered its shape, almost doubling in size.

Which was impossible.

And then something altogether more impossible happened, with Carl watching on with open-mouthed astonishment, his heart beating faster than it had since an untimely heart attack almost two decades before. He blinked and double-checked that his laptop was recording video.

It was.

The satellite appeared to move. Not just move, but *separate* into two constituent parts, with one half remaining in the orbit normally followed by the military satellite, the other pausing, then quickly disappearing off screen. Carl quickly typed commands into the laptop's keyboard, attempting to follow it, but it was too late.

"What the hell?" he whispered.

Carl had no idea what he had seen. But as his mind cleared, he reached for his cell phone with trembling fingers. Whatever had just happened, he knew it had to be important. He needed to tell someone.

33

"How the hell did we miss it?" President Charles Nash whispered as he stared at the image displayed on the large screen that filled one wall of the White House situation room. "In fact, take it from the top. Tell me what I'm supposed to be looking at, and how worried I need to be."

An air force colonel, uniform slightly creased from the short drive over the Potomac from the Pentagon, cleared his throat uncomfortably, perhaps wondering whether the President had said *we* or *you*. The West Wing pass around his neck indicated his name was George Raven.

"Discovering it was a one in a million chance," the officer said, hands clasped behind his back and shifting his weight nervously from foot to foot in a way that made him look like he was swaying. "Our experts are telling us that, like our own reconnaissance satellites, this spacecraft is equipped with stealth capability."

"How *did* you detect it?" asked Ryan Stone, a diminutive African-American man in his 50s who had headed up the counterterrorism center before being promoted to his current role as national security adviser.

Raven looked pained. "We didn't, sir. An amateur astronomer picked it up last night and sent NASA the footage. NASA passed it along to us, and as soon as we realized what it was, we reported it up the chain."

"Elaborate, Colonel," Nash growled.

He wondered, yet again, why he ever wanted to become President. Why he had put himself through the grueling campaign, why he had cost himself any chance of reconnecting with his wife by throwing himself into his work. Better that some other man should be forced to bear the tremendous weight of the decisions he made in this room.

"Yes Mr. President," Raven said quickly. "We believe that the spacecraft detected last night is a semi-autonomous orbital drone, most likely of Chinese origin."

"Keep going..."

"Sir, two years ago, the Senate Committee on Armed Services authorized a two hundred-million-dollar black budget contract in closed session, set to be delivered by Lockheed Martin. The project was to build a satellite killer—a remotely controllable, autonomous spacecraft with stealth capabilities designed to close with enemy satellites without being detected."

"To what end?"

"Our device was designed to attach a limpet mine about the size of a baseball to a satellite, and then withdraw without being detected."

"And you think that's what's happening here?" Stone asked. "The Chinese are booby-trapping our satellites?"

"Yes sir." Colonel Raven nodded. "We believe this is an experimental device known as Project Songbird. The evidence suggests that the device is now operational."

"For what purpose?"

"As you know sir, our military relies on satellite technology like no other country on the planet. The People's Liberation Army wouldn't last a week in a standup fight with us. Not yet, anyway. But if they had a backstop—a way of leveling the playing field? A way of cutting off our eyes and ears, of severing our command and control networks... The stock market would crash on day one, our sea lines of communication would grind to a halt for weeks, and grocery stores would be empty in a matter of days."

He trailed off.

Nash pursed his lips before continuing. "Colonel, how bad could this thing be? I need your honest assessment. No bullshit."

Raven took a sharp intake of breath before replying. "Mr. President, Lockheed Martin's project is still in the drawing board phase. But according to the project team, our spacecraft was designed to be pre-positioned in space years ahead of any conflict, hiding in plain sight all that time. If and when tensions began to ramp up, it would be activated. Our version of the system is built to carry enough ordnance to take out approximately fifty satellites."

Expressions of shock immediately crossed the faces of the various members of Nash's war cabinet.

"How many satellites do we have?" Nash asked.

"One hundred ninety-three," the air force colonel replied, "between the air force and the National Reconnaissance Office. But..."

"But *what*, Colonel Raven?" NSA Stone asked in a tone that indicated he was sick of being drip fed information.

"Sir," the colonel replied, splitting his attention between the national security adviser and the President, "our doctrine called for the stationing of six satellite killers in various orbits around the planet."

The news hit the room with the force of a bomb going off. "Six," Nash whispered. "Dear God."

The President did the math in his head. It wasn't difficult. If the Chinese had followed the same development trajectory as the air force, then they currently possessed the capability of wiping out American military superiority—not just in the Asia-Pacific, but across the globe.

"Tell me," NSA Stone said, "that we have a way of eliminating these things."

Raven replied, but with a doubtful expression on his face that left no doubt as to his true feelings. "We're working on it, sir. But our antisatellite drones are mostly still in the testing phase—and even then, they are designed to take out spacecraft with limited maneuvering capabilities and predictable orbits. That will not be the case here."

"Do you at least know where the damn things are?" Stone growled.

Raven shook his head.

"Can we hack them?"

The colonel shrugged. "We're working on isolating its command-and-control frequencies as we speak. But without access to the ground terminal itself, it's unlikely we'll be able to seize control of the satellite killer or killers."

"And where is this terminal?" Nash asked.

"Our best guess," Raven replied, using a laser pointer to indicate a mostly empty, mountainous region of China on a map on the wall, "is that the development work was being done at Xishang Satellite Control Center, near to the city of Xinjiang."

"Excuse us, Colonel," Nash said, dismissing the hapless air force officer with a flick of his fingers. The man hastily took his leave of the situation room, clearly relieved to be out of the firing line.

"Where does this leave us?" Nash asked the team arrayed around the situation room table: Ryan Stone, his Chief of Staff Emma Martinez, General Myers and various other representatives of America's leading military and intelligence organizations.

Myers was the first to speak. His gruff, commanding voice echoed like a booming cannon in the surprisingly cramped conference room. "Mr. President, I believe the time has come to examine our first strike options."

A chill settled on the room. Everyone present knew exactly what that entailed. Especially President Nash, to whom the responsibility would fall to order an attack that might very well lead to the collapse of mankind itself. Unconsciously, Nash brought his hand up, where it brushed the breast pocket of his suit, which contained a card upon which was written a series of challenge codes.

Codes for the nuclear football.

"Walk me through them, General," Nash croaked, scarcely believing he was considering having this conversation. The challenge card felt like a lead weight in his pocket, compressing his chest, making it hard to breathe.

Myers stood, walking to the digital map glowing on the wall. He zoomed in, focusing on the Chinese coast and the South China Sea. "Mr. President, we have forward deployed five of our Ohio-class Trident nuclear submarines near the Chinese coast, with several more making best speed to the area. In addition, a squadron of B-2 bombers is currently en route to Guam."

The general paused, eyeing each person in the room in turn. "Once the strike order is given, the navy will make a VLF transmission to our submarines, containing targeting packages and launch authorization."

"How big an attack are we looking at?" Nash asked firmly.

Myers grimaced. "China's long-range nuclear arsenal primarily consists of multiple land-based ICBMs. We believe we know the locations of most of the launch facilities."

"Estimated casualties?" Stone asked.

"Sixty million within the first month."

The room went silent. You could have heard a feather drop, let alone a pin. President Nash's mouth was suddenly drier than he could remember, and he reached forward for a glass of water with trembling hands, hoping that no one had noticed.

It didn't seem they had. Every face had gone pale with shock as its owner attempted to process that unimaginable figure. More casualties than both world wars combined. And that was in the first month alone. Nash could only picture what would follow next; waves of radioactive dust contaminating a country of 1.4 billion souls, traveling across the rest of Asia, rendering both farmland and cities unlivable for generations to come.

Nash knew that if he gave the order, his name would go down in history as one of humanity's most evil tyrants. He would share a Hall of Fame inhabited by names like Hitler and Stalin. There had to be a better way. But if there was not, if it came to it, could he bring himself to give that order?

The truth was, he did not know.

"Sir," Martinez interjected quietly, breaking the stunned silence, "the Chinese ambassador is here to see you. He's waiting outside the Oval Office."

Nash closed his eyes, breathing deeply in an attempt to flush his brain with oxygen. The general's briefing had shocked him. It was more than shock, really. It was disgust: both that he had control of these weapons, and worse—that he was contemplating using them.

But perhaps there was still a way of giving peace a chance. Perhaps Jason Trapp would find a way of ending this before it was too late. Nash knew that he had to buy some time. For if he did not, then the alternative might well be the end of human civilization.

~

THE PRESIDENT briefly considered packing the Oval Office with decorated generals and senior members of the cabinet in a show of force, but decided against it. Ambassador Lam wasn't exactly a close personal friend, but they had met before on a number of occasions when Nash was still a freshman senator familiarizing himself with Washington's social scene, and were friendly.

Nash loved Szechuan food, and since the best Szechuan dishes in town were found at the Chinese embassy, he'd made the trip to Van Ness more than once, striking up a cordial relationship with a number of Chinese diplomats.

Today's meeting, however, could not be more different. There would be no waiters carrying silver trays of champagne, nor others whisking canapés around a luxurious ballroom. No small talk. Just the business of state—and one last chance of avoiding all-out war between the world's only two remaining superpowers.

But if he couldn't offer the man a glass of Californian sparkling wine, then President Nash could at least avoid getting the discussion off on a bad foot from the very get-go. As he well knew, the military option might well be inevitable. But he vowed to do everything he could to duck that outcome.

Nash pressed the button of the intercom on his desk and said, "Send the ambassador in."

He walked quickly toward the door and forced a friendly expression, hoping that his posture did not show the tension he still felt from processing General Myers' briefing just a few minutes earlier.

Ambassador Lam entered, a Secret Service agent closing the door behind him. He was a diminutive man, a head and a half shorter than Nash, and had a wiry cyclist's frame. In fact, if the President remembered correctly, the ambassador could be found on his bike most weekends, daring death on DC's congested roads.

"Ambassador." The President smiled. "Good of you to come."

Lam bowed his head. "I am pleased to see you again, Mr. President."

"Please," Nash said, indicating the two light-blue floral patterned sofas that sat opposite the Resolute desk. "Sit. Can I get you something to drink?"

"I'm fine without."

"Very well." Nash smiled, sitting opposite Lam and smoothing his suit pants to buy himself some time to think.

He knew that he had to play this encounter with exquisite delicacy. The US relationship with China had been heating up for years as America's long period of dominance as the world's only superpower saw its first real challenge in almost three decades.

By most metrics, China was exactly that: a superpower. It was a country with well over a billion citizens, more than two million active military personnel, hundreds of ships, dozens of submarines, and countless thousands of missiles. In a single three-year period at the start of the decade, China used more cement than the US had done in the entire twentieth century, building homes and cities, roads and hospitals for a population whose time on the world stage had come. It was an astonishing statistic, and one that chilled Nash's bones.

The twentieth century had been America's. But there was no divine guarantee that this would hold true forever. America's dominance had been paid for in the blood of her sons. Nash knew that it was his job to ensure that her decline was not soaked in it. To ensure it didn't happen at all.

The president cleared his throat and punctured a silence that he was uncomfortably aware had begun to build. "First of all, Mr. Ambassador, may I convey my deepest condolences for the loss of your country's aviators. I can assure you that we are doing everything possible to locate the bodies. If a retrieval is feasible, we will undertake it, and return your men for burial."

Lam inclined his head. "My thanks, Mr. President. Please pass along my condolences also, to the families of those lost today."

"Thank you, Ambassador. Now"—Nash grimaced—"perhaps we should attend to the equally pressing business of how we can step back from the precipice of conflict."

Lam remained quiet, displaying only an expression of mild interest on his face. Nash soldiered on regardless. In truth, he was angry, though he hid the rage bubbling inside him with the consummate skill of a trained politician. He was angry that the Chinese had so recklessly buzzed the Nimitz, when precisely this sort of escalation—accidental, yet deadly—was the obvious risk.

He was furious too, that the Chinese had so far said nothing about the loss of almost three dozen US satellites in orbit over the Asia-Pacific region—a loss that Nash's new director of central intelligence, George Lawrence, assured him was attributable to weapons controlled out of Xishang Satellite Control Center.

In private, just as in public, they were evasive not just about the precise details of what happened, but their own responsibility for it.

Nash had half a mind to scream and shout, to let loose the pent-up, acidic frustration boiling in his gut. But he did not. He exerted an iron force of will, controlling that desire. The American people had elected him to be a statesman, not a demagogue—and he intended to honor that trust.

When he spoke, his voice was calm, yet unmistakably firm. "Ambassador Lam. At this moment, in addition to the Nimitz carrier strike group, the US Navy is sending two additional strike groups to the region. Our naval and air force assets are on high alert."

Lam's reply was clipped. "We are aware."

"Then you must understand that our two countries find ourselves in a precarious situation. Another misstep like today, and it may not be so possible to pull back from the brink."

"I agree."

"Then, Ambassador, I propose a truce. A cooling-off period, if you will. I will instruct my military to conduct no operations within what you refer to as the first island chain. In return, however, I need something from you."

Lam inclined his head. "Pray tell?"

Nash stood, walked to his desk, and opened the first drawer. From it, he retrieved the image taken by the amateur astronomer several hours before. He walked back to the ambassador, and handed him the picture. "Do you know what this is?"

Lam squinted, and Nash was almost inclined to believe it wasn't an act. He handed the image back. "I'm afraid you have me at a disadvantage."

"This image was taken late last night. The air force tells me that your military refers to it as Project Songbird."

Nash studied the Chinese ambassador intently for any sign of recognition as he revealed that particular piece of information. There was none—but then again, that meant nothing. The job of the Chinese ambassador in Washington DC was a plum assignment, and given only to the best of the best. Lam was too good to be ensnared by a trap like that.

"I don't recognize the name," Lam replied calmly.

"The device is designed to destroy my nation's satellites in orbit. *All of them.* And we believe that it was activated in the past forty-eight hours. Mr. Ambassador, my country will not stand for the weaponization of space. If China does not deactivate this weapon immediately, then we will be forced to act."

"Is that a threat, Mr. President?"

"Not a threat," Nash said, biting back a wave of irritation that Lam was giving him nothing in return, and worse, that he was allowing himself to rise to the provocation. "A warning."

Lam stood, his expression inscrutable. "I took this meeting out of courtesy, Mr. President, and out of respect for you personally. However, I regret to inform you that my government has ordered the drawdown of all non-essential diplomatic personnel from our embassy and consulates across the United States."

For a second, the President was unable to respond. He stood and conspicuously did not offer to shake the man's hand. He replied with tight, pursed lips, "Be advised, Ambassador. If Songbird is used, I will treat it as an act of war. And it will be a war that you cannot win."

Lam shook his head sadly. "Unfortunately, Mr. President—neither can you."

34

The North Korean guards had hosed Eliza down before locking her into the laboratory ward with the other test subjects, the powerful jet of water washing away the blood and the urine, assaulting the scabs that had begun to form over her wounds, bruising already tender flesh. The chill of the water was a shock, but she welcomed it. It woke her up, the ice water flushing adrenaline through her system, making the pain fade away.

The two men took her into the ward wearing no more protection against whatever terrible virus was being tested on the eight innocent people inside than a thin blue facemask, of the kind you might see commuters wearing on any public transport system in Asia. Eliza had filed away the detail for future reference. She did not understand why they would be so casual about the threat of contracting a disease that could surely end their lives.

Were they vaccinated?

She pondered the question as the minutes ticked by, lying on a camp bed that had been added to the cramped room, chained to it by both her left ankle and right wrist. She was barely clothed, and as she stared up at a camera dome mounted on the ceiling, she wondered who was watching.

But Eliza felt no shame. Only a burning desire to get out of this hellhole, and to visit justice on the monsters who had incarcerated her within it.

The question was—how?

The restraints that held her to the camp bed were Eliza's lowest priority. Her free left hand dangled off the side of the mattress, out of sight of the overhead camera—and it was very busy indeed, working away at one of the thin links of metal which made up a latticework that supported the mattress.

"How long have you been in here?" Eliza asked softly, directing her question at a woman in the bed to the right of hers: a plump Chinese girl with short black hair and red-rimmed eyes. She spoke in Mandarin, assuming a Beijing accent.

She needed to understand what was taking place here before she could fashion a plan to stop it. It was plain that the eight—now nine—inhabitants of this ward were test subjects for a biological weapon. Eliza had been given a basic grounding in nuclear, biological and chemical warfare at the Farm, and while in the Russian's office she'd absorbed enough details to paint at least a narrow picture of what he was working on.

Yet the unknown answers to a barrage of questions frustrated her. Why had her guards seemed so lax about entering the laboratory—displaying no signs of fear?

Why were the test subjects divided as they were: a pair of Caucasian men and women, and matching pairs of ethnic Chinese?

What was the significance?

But most of all, Eliza needed to understand how much time she had to work with. As far as she could tell, none of the eight currently displayed any symptoms of disease. But how long would that last? And how long before the microbes that were doubtless breeding in her bloodstream at this very moment, burrowing into her cells and turning millions of them into bioreactors spewing poison into her veins, turned homicidal and finished her off too?

How long before, as the North Korean colonel had threatened, she was choking on her own blood, the immune system beaten, her cells disintegrating? Would she have enough time to get out of this place and warn Langley?

Because, Eliza realized, that was all that mattered. She didn't want to die, but if her death could serve some greater purpose, then at least it would not be in vain. She clenched her jaw and realized she was staring at the Chinese girl next to her with a fierce intensity. She blinked.

The girl returned Eliza's gaze blankly. The CIA operative took a different approach, speaking calmly, as if to a child. "Can you tell me your name?"

The sound of her voice prompted another of the captive women to begin weeping, as one or another of them had been doing on and off since Eliza had entered the anodyne laboratory ward. Though the girl next to her seemed to flinch at the sound, Eliza did not mind. She had no doubt that a listening device—or devices—accompanied the camera watching them at this very moment, and anything that could help disguise her intentions was fine by her.

The girl's cheeks were stained red, but she looked exhausted, as though she had cried herself out. "Chen," she finally whispered.

Eliza smiled. "That's a beautiful name, Chen," she whispered back, keeping her voice low. "How are you feeling?"

Chen's voice cracked as she replied, "Scared."

"Yeah," Eliza admitted honestly, "me too. But it's going to be okay, I promise."

Chen shook her head. "I don't think so," she replied in a beaten voice. "We're going to die here."

Eliza paused, not knowing how to reply. The truth was, Chen was probably right. They would both die here, never leaving this observation room again. Never knowing what had killed them, or why. But she couldn't think like that. She couldn't stop fighting. Not while there was still a chance. Not while she still had the strength to go on.

She smiled. "Maybe. Or maybe we can work together, Chen. Find a way out of here."

The Chinese girl stared back with the body language of a beaten, starved dog. She was on the verge of giving up, it was obvious. Whether or not the mysterious virus got her, something would—even just her body simply shutting down, giving up, unwilling to go on. But Eliza needed the girl to fight. She needed to fan the flames of hope inside her.

"Do you have a family, Chen?" she asked. "Someone outside of here who's waiting for you?"

Chen nodded, a single tear streaking down the path carved by many others. "A boyfriend," she whispered. "I'll never see him again."

On the opposite side of the narrow path between the two ranks of camp beds, the side of the observation room nearest the glass partition, one of the Chinese men got to his feet, fists clenched, and howled a bitter cry of defiance. The chain around his arm rattled as he shook his fist, a line of red sprouting around his wrist as the metal bit into the man's skin.

Chen's head turned to the unexpected sound.

"Stay with me," Eliza said quickly, needing to retain the young girl's attention. "Chen, I need you to tell me how you got here. Can you do that?"

The girl's head turned back, away from the tormented cries of pain from the man now sobbing on his knees, beating against the glass with his free hand. It was as though she was glad for the distraction—happy to have something to take her mind off the reminder of the peril she found herself in.

"I live in Dandong," she said. "With my boyfriend. We share a condo." Her eyes filled with tears at the memory.

Eliza wished she could reach over and grab the girl's hand, but the length of chain attached to her right wrist was too short to allow it. "It's okay," she crooned.

"I went to dinner with a friend," Chen added, biting back her tears. "And then —" Her face creased with confusion, as though searching her memory banks for a clue as to what had happened next."— I woke up in the back of a truck. I thought I had an accident, but..."

Chen had been kidnapped to order, Eliza realized. Snatched from the streets of her hometown and brought across the border from China. But the question of why her still rankled in the CIA operative's mind. If there was one thing the North Korean regime was not short of, it was political prisoners of their own, upon whom to test a biological weapon. Why run the risk of attracting attention?

Glad the girl was talking, Eliza followed up with another question. The one she truly needed an answer to. "How long have you been here?"

The question visibly stumped the Chinese captive. She shook her head anxiously, as though nervous about disappointing her newfound friend. "I don't know," she whispered. "How can I tell?"

Eliza grimaced, then softened her expression at Chen's reaction. It was a good point. She turned the problem over in her mind. "Tell me about the routine," she said. "How often do they feed us? Do they turn the lights out?"

Chen's expression was curious, almost hopeful. "It's always light. I try to sleep, but it's hard. Doctors come in every"—her face scrunched—"every few hours, maybe. They take our blood, check our temperature. Do you know what they are doing to us?"

Ikeda shook her head. She had a very good idea what was

happening in this place, but the last thing she needed was to terrify the young Chinese girl any more than was absolutely necessary. Especially now she had her talking. "And food?"

Chen's nose wrinkled. "Five meals, maybe six. It's disgusting," she confided. "I can't eat it."

Ikeda's face softened. "You need to. Keep your strength."

Chen nodded quickly. "Okay, I will."

The sound of weeping began to fade away, replaced by great long, snorting sobs, and then nothing at all. Eliza sat up, shielding her face from the camera overhead and the glass partition with a sweep of an arm, as though she was running her fingers through her hair, and pressed one finger from her restrained hand to her lips. Chen nodded softly.

Ikeda lay back, wondering what on earth to do. She let her left hand fall back to its earlier position and kept working at the thin metal wire. It was weakening, and she knew that before long she would be able to break away a short piece, which she could use to pick the lock on her cuffs.

But it was too soon.

If Chen was right about the number of meals, which was a stab in the dark itself, then that meant the test subjects had probably been here for several days already. Ikeda knew that viruses had varying incubation periods. If she remembered her classes at the Farm right, Ebola became symptomatic somewhere between eight and ten days after infection. Marburg was quicker, averaging only five.

She chewed her lip, breathing in the acrid disinfectant tang of the processed air in the sealed observation room through her nostrils. In truth, she was no closer to an answer now than she had been before.

Eliza knew only one thing for sure: that, for now at least, she only had one viable course of action. She needed to wait, to observe the patterns of activity inside this facility. Who entered the observation room, and how often. Whether the scientists were guarded when they entered—and if so, by how many, with what weapons. Until she knew, resistance was—as so often—futile. She needed to wait for the perfect moment to strike.

Overhead, the strip lighting buzzed, a constant backdrop to the sniffing of the prisoners, the squeaking of the beds and the rattling of their chains. The black camera dome stared down like an ominous, vengeful god. Always waiting, always watching.

And the longer she lay there, the more a creeping dread began to play in the shadow lands at the edges of her mind. She could picture the killer inside her, preying on her immune system, waiting for her to weaken.

It was a killer that Ikeda could do nothing to fight.

And a ticking clock, counting down to the moment where, like her freedom, even her will to survive would be taken from her.

35

D eputy Director Mike Mitchell was on edge.
As Trapp's scheduled check-in time drew closer, Mitchell took to wearing out his shoe leather, pacing up and down in the sub-basement beneath Langley that he had turned into a command post to support the efforts to hunt down those who had supported VP Jenkins' failed coup earlier that year. Now it was the nerve center for another effort entirely: one that was far more critical.

Occasionally, Kyle Partey glanced up from his computer screen and followed his boss' relentless, anxious movement with his eyes before returning to work. The third man in the room, Dr. Timothy Greaves, didn't once look away from his monitor.

Mitchell checked his watch. Five minutes to go. If Jason Trapp had survived his insertion into a country with which the United States was still—technically—at war, then he would shortly reach out to Langley, using an encrypted connection bounced off a Japanese communications satellite, since American assets over the region were still patchy.

But if Trapp had failed, if he'd been caught, and was at this very moment a prisoner of the communist regime, or worse, his body was riddled with bullets and floating in the Yalu River, then to put it bluntly, the Agency was fucked.

"What did we miss?" he muttered.

"You say something, boss?" Kyle said, glancing up from his screen.

"How are you guys getting along with the drive?" Mitchell asked instead.

Alstyne's flash drive had arrived stateside about twelve hours after Trapp landed in Guam. Since then, Partey and Greaves had been tag-teaming in their attempts to crack the encryption. So far, they'd had little success.

Partey glanced at Greaves' screen and grimaced. "Not well. The thing's a fortress. We might get lucky, but I'm not counting on it."

Mitchell formed a fist and punched his palm. A crack rang out in a cramped, stuffy basement. He was beyond frustrated. Mike Mitchell was a man who had always prided himself in being one step ahead of the curve. He was his country's fiercest defender, both as a young man with a pistol in his hand, and today, running the CIA's covert operations around the globe.

No occupant of his chair was supposed to be flying blind. And yet that's exactly how Mitchell felt. The operation in Macau had pulled the curtain back on an entirely new threat, one which was spiraling rapidly out of control, and yet they were still no clearer as to exactly what was going on than they had been when the situation blew up in their faces.

"There must be something on that drive," Mitchell mused. "Something the North Koreans needed so badly they were willing to piss off the Chinese to get it."

Kyle nodded.

It was the same problem they'd been tussling with for days, ever since identifying the tattoo on the body in Macau. China was North Korea's closest—and these days, pretty much only—

remaining ally. The Chinese supplied food, fuel and weapons to the isolated communist state, mostly out of fear of the consequences of the regime collapsing, causing millions of starving refugees to flood across the Chinese border.

So for a North Korean special forces unit to risk shooting up a Chinese hotel—particularly one with hundreds of foreign guests—was unprecedented. If the Chinese closed the border, the North Korean economy would collapse overnight, taking the regime and the military with it. Which meant that for some reason, the North Koreans were rolling the dice on the survival of their very way of life.

"It doesn't add up," Kyle agreed. "From everything we know about Chairman Song, all he cares about is his own survival. If the Chinese turn on him, he'll lose his grip on power. He's always played the odds. Why change now?"

"That's your job." Mitchell grinned weakly. "You're the analyst."

Kyle didn't smile. He merely chewed on his lip, his enormous brain turning the question over in his head. Mitchell had no doubt that if anyone could crack the problem, it would be Kyle. The young analyst was a prodigy, renowned in the Agency for drawing connections between seemingly disparate pieces of information that no other analyst could.

A satellite handset rang, the piercing electronic warble distracting the two men from their conversation. Greaves didn't move, his attention swallowed whole by the green lines dancing across his computer screen.

Mitchell started for the handset and answered the call, putting it on speaker. "Authenticate," he said.

"Good to hear your voice, Mike," Trapp replied, the encryption compressing his voice. "I read Oscar, Mike, Five, November, Yankee, X-ray."

"You too, Hangman," Mitchell said, glancing at the code sheet more out of habit than necessity. "What's your status?"

"I'm across the border," Trapp replied. Mitchell pumped his fist with relief. "It's about a hundred miles from here to the location you provided. But from what Jack's telling me, there's no way of getting close by road. Not unless I want half the North Korean army on my tail."

"What's your plan?"

"Jack will get me as close as he can without risking his life. I have to take the last part on foot. Maybe twenty, thirty miles through the mountains. It won't be quick."

Mitchell grimaced. "Things are heating up here, Hangman. Any chance you can speed up that timeline?"

There was a pause. Mitchell hated himself for asking the question. He had been in Trapp's shoes more times than he could count: deep behind enemy lines, surrounded by forces who wouldn't just capture an enemy agent, but torture and kill them to boot, and he'd always hated the rear echelon mother-fuckers who tried to hurry him along. Mitchell had always operated by the mantra: 'slow is smooth, and smooth is fast.'

"I'll see what I can do," Trapp replied guardedly. "But the terrain is a real bitch, and traveling by day will markedly increase my chances of being detected."

"Understood, Hangman," Mitchell said, wincing at what he was asking. "Do what you can."

"How are things on your end?" Trapp asked, wind whistling down the phone line and crackling in the speaker.

"Not good," Mitchell sighed. "The Chinese are pulling out all of their diplomatic staff, and we're about two minutes to midnight on the nuclear clock."

"Say again, Langley?"

"You heard me correctly, Hangman. If we don't find a way out of this mess, then might not be much of a planet left for us to fight over."

36

T rapp walked back to the truck. Over the course of a very long career, both with special forces, and then the Agency, he had been in more operations than he could remember, in more countries than he could count.

But he'd never been all that stood between two super-powers and all-out nuclear war. He wasn't sure he liked the added pressure on his shoulders.

"Wife and kids okay?" Jack joked. He flicked his cigarette onto the ground, where it sparked, a flaming ember caught by the wind.

"Not so much," Trapp replied. "We're going to have to move our timetable up."

"I was afraid you were going to say that," Jack said, reaching with trembling fingers for the cigarette packet stuffed into his breast pocket.

Trapp hadn't known the smuggler long, but he was beginning to like the man. Though he was putting on a brave face, he was clearly nervous about what he was doing. Which, Trapp reflected, was entirely sensible. Smuggling contraband for the North Korean elite was one thing—a dangerous business, but one for which the punishment was simply a creased billfold slipped into the right palm. But trafficking an American agent into the country?

That was the kind of treason for which a man would be punished slowly. And painfully.

Jack's truck had North Korean government plates—an investment that had set him back tens of thousands of dollars. And yet it was, he'd assured his passenger, the best money he'd ever spent. The plates allowed the vehicle to travel through most checkpoints without being stopped. The average North Korean soldier had no interest in mixing his nose up in government business.

On their journey already, the truck had been waved through several roadblocks, Jack scarcely slowing the vehicle as the barriers were pulled apart and they rumbled through.

"So, what's the hurry?" Jack asked after lighting another cigarette and taking a long drag.

The smell of the smoke reached Trapp's nostrils, and though he'd given the addictive death sticks up almost a decade earlier, the conversation he'd just had with Langley made him want to take the habit back up again.

Trapp gestured at the lit cigarette in Jack's fingers. "Any of those going spare?"

"I didn't know you smoked," Jack said with a kinked eyebrow, tapping one out of the packet and tossing it over.

"I quit," Trapp replied gruffly, catching a light from the smuggler's burning cigarette.

"Your call was that good, huh?"

"You don't miss much." Trapp grinned, inhaling a deep breath of the noxious smoke. It burned his lungs, and yet tasted like an old friend. He savored the familiar yet long-forgotten rush of nicotine, then tossed the cigarette onto the gravel road and extinguished it underneath his boot.

"It's how I stay alive," Jack quipped, while also matching

Trapp's gaze with an expression that demanded he be told the truth.

It was only right, Trapp thought, to share it. Both their lives, after all, were equally at risk—especially if the smuggler agreed to go beyond his original remit, and help Trapp still further. He filled the man in on his call with Mitchell, watching the man's face grow paler and paler as he appreciated the consequences.

"What do you need from me?" Jack asked when Trapp was finally finished.

"I need you to get me closer to the camp. Close enough that I can crawl the rest of the way. We're running out of time."

"Sounds dangerous."

"You in?"

Jack stubbed out his cigarette and returned to the cab of his truck. "Sure. Why not?"

37

Ikeda was losing track of time.

She watched everything that happened in the small, twisted ward with eagle-eyed attention, storing every detail away for future reference. And yet the longer she lay on that narrow camp bed, breathing in infected air, studying her fellow captives for any signs of symptoms, listening to their plaintive cries of fear, the less hope she had.

The facility maintained a simple, clockwork routine. At least, Ikeda thought it was like clockwork, but without access to a clock, or even the briefest sight of the sky overhead, it was hard to tell.

There seemed to be two shifts: Ikeda thought it likely that one worked through the day, the other at night, though it was entirely possible that they followed another schedule in this timeless prison.

By Ikeda's muddled count, she had been locked up in the laboratory ward for almost two days. She wondered what the North Korean colonel with the scarred face was waiting for. Why hadn't he interrogated her? Was he waiting for the prisoners to fall sick around her?

That would make sense, she thought. What better demonstration could there be of his power? Perhaps he thought that
the sight of the prisoners bleeding out around her would make
her crack.

Maybe it would.

Ikeda's stomach had been a bundle of nerves the entire time
she'd been stuck here. She wasn't good at waiting, she preferred
action—but in this place, it was impossible. The only option
left to her was to wait, to wait as her death marched onward
with every passing second, as the infection burrowed itself
deeper.

Perhaps the longer this slow torture lasted, the more Ikeda
feared for her life, the easier it would be for him to break her
when he finally came.

Or maybe he was out there right now, watching through
one of the cameras that whirred overhead, underneath the
thick black dome. Studying her half-clothed body with twisted
fascination.

Eliza blinked and shook off the thought. She needed to
distract herself. She ran through her mental notes once more,
examining the daily routine for patterns, for weaknesses, for
anything she could exploit.

Two North Korean scientists entered the ward, flanked by as
many guards. It unfolded the same way every time. The scientists were female, the guards male—and armed, with local
knockoffs of the AK-47. They wore no body armor, only dark
green fatigues loose around their waists, emphasizing their
gaunt frames.

Eliza forced herself to choke down the foul sustenance that
was delivered with each shift change: maggot-ridden white rice,
without even the barest hint of concession made to add flavor.
Twice, she noticed the guards stealing food from the prisoners'
trays.

She forced herself to eat because if it came to it, she knew, the two guards would prove no match for her training. They appeared to be conscripts, nervous at their current posting, not highly trained military personnel, and visibly weak and underfed. Every time they entered the room, Eliza pictured how she would take them down. Still, she needed to remain in fighting condition if she was to have a chance at success.

First, she would need to break the small piece of wire free from the underside of the camp bed. She had weakened it sufficiently already for that act to take just a matter of seconds. The bed had no sheets, no pillow, nothing to hide what she was doing from the camera overhead, or the observation deck, so she would need to act fast.

The cuffs around her wrist and ankle were similar to handcuffs back home. Ikeda had broken out of such restraints hundreds, perhaps thousands of times. But every time, it had been in training, with no consequences for failure.

When she finally chose to act, that would not be the case. One mistake, and the best-case scenario was finding the muzzle of an AK-47 pressed against the back of her head. The worst case would end up with her body fluids painting her plastic mattress red.

Which wouldn't be ideal.

Ikeda's mind traveled to the plight of the four American captives. Just like the Chinese prisoners, they were terrified— though perhaps more vocal about their anger. Twice one of the male Americans, a squat man who looked to be in his early 50s, with a linebacker's broad shoulders and the gut of a man who had allowed an athlete's body to go to seed, had confronted the scientists, demanding to know what was happening to him and his wife.

It hadn't ended well.

The man's wife was beautiful. Ikeda didn't know her name, but the dark-haired woman carried herself with a consummate grace, refusing to give up, even in these horrendous conditions.

Ikeda wished that she could say something to comfort her fellow countrymen. To assure them that she was on their side, that she would get them out of here, whatever it took. Then again, those immortal lines, "I'm with the government, and I'm here to help," had never seemed so apt.

Precisely what could she do to assist them? Revealing her true identity—and that of her employer—might only make their plight seem more hopeless. After all, if a CIA operative could be captured, what hope did they have?

So instead, she concentrated on figuring a way out.

Eliza knew that her only chance of escape lay in wrestling a weapon from one of the guards. It would give her options: either a way to force herself through the locked door that led to the laboratory, or the option to simply shoot through the observation window. She would have to move fast and hope that there would be few guards on duty.

She grimaced, scrunching her hand into a fist and biting her fingernails against her palm, until the pain drew a tear to her eye.

The electronic door lock snicked, and Eliza resisted the temptation to immediately snap her head to the left. Instead, she moved it slowly, lethargically, as though exhausted, or wallowing at the bottom of a pit of depression. It was the shift change. As before, two men strode through the door, weapons drawn, but not aimed at anything in particular.

"Hey, asshole," the squat American prisoner shouted. He stood up, the chain around his wrist rattling. All eyes in the room turned to his performance, but not Eliza's. She watched the guards intently. Their reaction was the only variable that counted.

"You better tell me what the hell is going on," the American growled. "I don't know what kind of game you sick bastards are playing, but believe me, you won't get away with this!"

Eliza couldn't help but think that, unless she was able to

pull a rabbit out of a hat, the North Koreans most certainly *would* get away with this kidnapping. Pulling her eyes away from the two guards for a second, she glanced at the American. His wife was stretching over, attempting to calm him down.

"Andy," the woman whispered. "Andy, honey, don't make them angry. You know what happened last time."

Eliza picked up a sound and her attention snapped back to the doorway. One of the guards, a short, thin man with yellowed, rotten, rearranged teeth, grimaced a twisted smile, waving his rifle languidly in the air. He began to shout, bellowing an unbroken stream of thickly accented Korean. Eliza had to concentrate hard to understand it. It sounded like a regional dialect—strangely formal compared to the language she'd grown up learning, taught by South Korean teachers, watching their shows, reading their books.

"Lie down!" the guard screamed. "Do what that bitch's says, or I'll put a bullet through your heart!"

Eliza's pulse began to race. The guard seemed unhinged, and she began to wonder if perhaps he was truly insane. She knew that methamphetamine use was common in North Korea, used to propel the human body to work the inhuman hours mandated by the government—and also to quell the population's hunger pains. Nothing comes without strings, however, and as America had long since learned, meth is linked to not just physical, but also severe *mental* degradation. The CIA operative was certain that was what was happening here.

To Eliza's right, she heard Chen cough. The Chinese girl made a thick, hacking sound, but the CIA operative thought nothing of it. She had more pressing business to attend to: the increasingly likely chance of the prisoner called Andy ending up with a line of lead piercing his chest.

And then Chen began to weep.

Eliza turned her head to look at the Chinese prisoner, not because the sound of the girl's crying was new to her, but because the tone of it was so different to the sound she'd heard before. Chen's chest heaved, desperately sucking in air through her teeth as panic overtook the young woman.

She was sitting cross-legged on her mattress, holding her hands to her mouth, dark-brown eyes wide and glistening with terror.

Eliza's stomach dropped out from beneath her. Not because of the fear and pain in the Chinese girl's eyes, or the likelihood that Andy was about to end up with a bullet between his, but because Chen's fingers were stained with sticky red blood.

Ikeda opened and closed her mouth silently, stunned by the sight. She knew immediately what had happened. All this time, she'd held on to the slim chance that all this was a charade, that there was no virus, that her imprisonment was just a trick being used to make her break.

But the blood on Chen's hands and the pain in her eyes made one thing immediately, absolutely clear.

The virus was real. And in just a couple of days, each of the prisoners in this room would succumb to its insidious power.

Including her.

Eliza acted on instinct, doing something she would regret for a very long time.

"I need some help. Please, help her!" she yelled at the top of her voice, briefly silencing the drama unfolding in the cramped laboratory prison ward, pointing desperately at Chen.

The guard stopped yelling, as if surprised to be confronted by another source.

And that moment, Eliza Ikeda realized her mistake. She'd spoken from the heart, desperate to get Chen some help. But she'd spoken in Korean, not Mandarin.

And if anyone was listening in the facility's unseen control room, that meant she'd just brought a whole world of trouble down on her head...

38

Eliza Ikeda's world had rapidly dwindled to a coughing, burning, hacking hell. Barely a few hours had passed since Chen started coughing up blood, just a blink of an eye.

But the virus moved fast, scything through the prisoners with rapacious intensity, turning strong, healthy individuals in the prime of their life into zombies sleepwalking to the cold embrace of death. Strangely, the four Americans were not yet symptomatic, and spent their time cringing at every hacking cough and pained moan. As far as she could tell, Ikeda wasn't yet infected either, but it was impossible for her to worry about her mistake when she was in the midst of a hurricane.

The electronic airlock door to the ward hissed open, and Ikeda immediately focused her attention on it.

This was unusual.

Ikeda had turned to her stomach in an attempt to tell the time. Back home, she was famous for her appetite. As a result of her training regimen, she could put away a five-inch stack of pancakes and bacon, smothered in maple syrup for breakfast, then four hours later complain of starvation—only to do it all over again.

What her stomach was telling her *now* was that it wasn't yet feeding time in this sick human zoo. She sat up, the chains connected to her ankle and wrist clinking against the bed's metal legs. Two guards entered, unarmed, followed by the two she'd seen before.

"What are you doing?" one of the Americans called out, her voice plaintive and broken. "Please, just let us go."

As usual, there was no reply. Ikeda had long ago given up on expecting one. The scientists and the guards did what they wanted, when they wanted, and there was nothing she or anyone else could do about it.

But usually, they stuck rigidly to the schedule. This was an aberration. A break with procedure. And to Ikeda's well-trained mind, it smelled of opportunity. Adrenaline flooded into her system, briefly hushing the anxiety that had begun to build inside her brain. Was this it?

Was this her moment to strike?

And then another flash of movement caught her eye. Someone was standing on the observation deck that over-looked the cramped laboratory hospital ward.

And not just anyone.

It was the North Korean colonel. The man with the horrific scar on his cheek and the cold, dead eyes of a sociopathic killer. And worse still, his attention was focused directly on her. Despite her best efforts, Eliza shivered.

In an instant, all thought of escape fled from the captured CIA operative's mind. She was outnumbered and outgunned. And although she had come to terms with that inevitability days earlier, the colonel's presence now changed everything. Her only chance of escape had rested on the element of surprise. Of somehow taking advantage of a break in procedure, or a guard's screwup, or an external emergency, and leveraging that opening to even the odds.

But that was no longer possible.

A scream broke her concentration—but for some strange reason, Ikeda couldn't tear her eyes away from the man's cold stare.

White-hot rage coursed through Eliza's veins, burning away the fear. She stared her vicious captor down, willing him to face her like a man, her gaze transmitting an implicit challenge.

Come down here and fight me like a man.

The colonel simply smiled a soulless sneer.

The strange spell broke, and immediately Ikeda turned to the source of the commotion. One by one, the American prisoners were being released from their chains and lined against the wall. She watched on in horror, wondering if this was the end—if they had all outlived their usefulness, whatever it was supposed to be. She couldn't stop herself from picturing the horrific scene that would take place if the guards took aim and fired.

In her mind's eye, her countrymen's bodies hung for a second in the air before their legs gave out, and they painted a trail of red down the wall.

"What are you doing?" a woman panted. "Where are you taking us?"

Eliza laid back, glancing up at the colonel to check if she was being observed. She was, but only for a second. The cruel, twisted officer gave her one last smile—a gesture that seemed to say, *I'll be seeing you soon*—before turning on his heel and leaving the room.

Finally, the last American was freed from the chains that had for so long held them helpless. Ikeda watched as the man lined up against the wall, her left hand creeping down the side of her bed, searching for the thin piece of wire she had worked on. In that instant, she was hit with a startling flash of insight.

She was already dead.

Ikeda could not see how she could possibly escape this camp alive. Even if she rode the odds and somehow made it out of this horrific room, she had no idea how many guards were on the other side of the door. If, by some miracle, she survived the initial fight, how could she possibly fight her way out of an entire military base?

It was impossible.

And so she returned to the conclusion that she was a dead woman already. In a way, it was freeing.

She might not be able to save herself, but she would be damned if she let her countrymen die without putting up a fight. Eliza Ikeda had already paid her debt to the CIA. She had done everything her training told her to, paid every price the country could possibly ask. The information she had held on to for so long was worthless.

So, perhaps, it was time to fight back.

"Please," a woman wept. "I'll do whatever you want. Just don't hurt us. Please..."

One of the guards' hands flashed up in an instant, delivering a hard slap that rocked the woman's head back against the wall. The stinging crack shocked Ikeda, though it shouldn't have. After all, their captors had unleashed a horrific disease on innocent people. Why wouldn't they also be capable of hitting a woman?

"Silence!" he snapped.

The American prisoners stiffened instantly. The low moan emanating from Chen's lips, her sightless eyes rolling in the back of her head as her body thrashed in the throes of a burning fever was all the reminder they needed of the penalty that came with disobeying their captors.

The guard nodded, apparently satisfied with the reaction. He clicked his fingers. "You four will come with me."

The American captives cast each other worried glances,

the husband-and-wife couple reaching to touch each other for the first time since their captivity in this room had begun. Each looked strained—the endless fears of the last few days, of wondering how long it would be before they too were struck down by the virus—now multiplied by this strange new occurrence. By this point, none of the captives could possibly believe that freedom awaited them at the end of this ordeal.

So why, Eliza wondered, were they being moved?

She was torn, and chewed indecisively on her lip, fingers caressing the thin strip of metal wire. She itched to break it off. She knew in an instant she would be able to free herself of the primitive cuffs that held her captive to this bed. A second later, she would be upon the guards, unleashing a week's worth of fear, anger and frustration like a banshee released from hell.

The conscripts wouldn't stand a chance. That wasn't arrogance, just justified confidence in her own abilities—and the amateurish appearance of her captors. They were weak, underfed men, with filthy weapons and little apparent training on how to *hold*, let alone fire them.

But what then?

The same fundamental constraints that had kept her from making a bid for freedom before still held true now. Action without a plan was no different from signing her own death warrant.

And while she would happily spend her own life to save those of her countrymen, in her heart of hearts she knew that now was not the time. Though they might well be walking to their deaths, that was not yet certain. A false move might well condemn them to a fate that was not set in stone.

And Ikeda wasn't willing to risk their lives. Not yet. Not until there was no other choice.

The Americans, flanked by their guards, shuffled slowly toward the door, the unlocked chains hanging loosely from their wrists. Eliza held her breath. If she was going to do something, it was now or never.

She chose never.

As the airlock door hissed shut, leaving Ikeda alone with the dying Chinese prisoners, a single tear streaked down her cheek. She closed her eyes and attempted to commit those four faces to memory. If this was indeed the last time she would ever see them alive, she wanted to remember them for who they had been. Perhaps, if she made it out of here and they did not, she could visit their families and give them some comfort.

After all, there was no one left to mourn for her. Just an anonymous star on the wall at Langley.

Only a man she barely knew, and who she would never see again.

39

J ason Trapp watched from the hills, binoculars pressed to his eyes, as a convoy of six commercial trucks was prepared in the military camp in the plateau beneath him. He lay prone on the ground, covered in a makeshift blanket of fallen branches and leaves that broke up his silhouette and blended his frame into the soil. Unless someone happened to step directly upon him, he was effectively invisible.

As he scanned the encampment, his thoughts drifted to the peril Eliza Ikeda was in. He wondered if she was even still alive, or whether—as he feared was more likely—the North Koreans had simply executed her the second she arrived in the country.

Trapp grimaced. He couldn't allow himself to think that way. As far as he was concerned, Ikeda was alive until he had positive, incontrovertible proof that she was not. And if she was alive, that meant his sense of honor committed him to attempting a rescue. And since he could not acquire such proof without entering the camp below him and discovering her body, whatever happened, he was going in.

But at this precise moment, Trapp's attention was focused

not on discovering a way to enter the camp without being seen by any of the guards—or dogs—who patrolled its borders with frightening regularity. Instead, it was drawn to the strange arrangement of trucks.

What are you doing down there?

The vehicles were arrayed in a straight line, unmoving, as a swarm of workers moved around them like ants around a nest. A low cloud hung over the mountainous valley, flattening the light and making it difficult to observe what was happening beneath him in any great detail. The activity below had commenced approximately sixty minutes earlier, when the trucks had rolled out of a large concrete warehouse with a corrugated iron roof, and the camp had sprung into life.

Trapp focused the binoculars on the trucks, studying them intently. The vehicles were marked with commercial slogans written in Mandarin hieroglyphics, which meant they were different from any of the North Korean trucks that Trapp had seen since leaving Dandong.

He knew, of course, that Unit 61's stated mission was to acquire hard currency for the North Korean regime by any and all means necessary. The shadowy organization was involved in extortion, counterfeiting, human trafficking and the manufacture of methamphetamines. Any and all of those nefarious activities might require access to disguised trucks capable of exiting North Korea's borders without suspicion.

But none, as far as Trapp could tell, necessitated this level of airtight security. He had spent the last sixty minutes trying to work out how to enter the camp without being detected, and every single plan he had contemplated, he'd immediately discarded. Whatever was going on down there, it had the North Koreans on high alert.

Until—and if—the trucks left, Trapp had to play the waiting game. There was no sense in going off half-cocked and getting himself caught.

So the question remained: what the hell was going on? What was in those trucks that was so damn important?

It was time to phone home. It was five in the evening in North Korea, which meant it was 4 a.m. back in Washington DC. If an international crisis hadn't been brewing, deputy director Mike Mitchell would undoubtedly have been tucked up in bed.

But the United States of America was on the brink of a nuclear war with the world's only other superpower, so Trapp had no doubt the man would be glued to his desk.

He pulled the bulky encrypted Japanese sat phone from a pocket of his combat pants, attached a wired headset, so that he could leave both hands on the binoculars, and powered the unit up. He'd left it switched off until now, both to reduce the chances of the signal being detected and to conserve power.

The phone only rang once before Mitchell answered, the relief in his voice evident. Trapp had no idea how the man managed it—sitting on his hands thousands of miles away from the action, waiting for his operatives to check in. Waiting for some who never would.

"Hangman, how you doing?"

"I'm hungry, thirsty, and I've got six inches of rock digging into my thigh. What about you?" Trapp said quietly.

"Staying alive," Mitchell replied. "Just about. What have you got?"

"I'm not exactly sure," Trapp said, pressing the binoculars to his face once again as a burst of activity took place on the plateau beneath him. "Hold on."

Mitchell knew better than to distract one of his operatives during an active mission, and though Trapp knew the pause would have driven his boss crazy, he didn't say a word.

Trapp watched through the high-power lenses as a lone ray of sunshine broke through the foreboding clouds overhead, lighting upon something metal that was being carried between two men in gray overalls. The process was being directed by two soldiers, their weapons ready, but not aimed.

He zeroed in on the glinting surface, focusing the binoculars on the payload between the two men. It looked like a canister of some description, almost like an old-fashioned milk urn. Trapp registered absently the way that the gray overalls the men were wearing were stained with filth, and the way they hung freely from the men's shoulders.

Trapp grimaced as he realized they were prisoners. And not just prisoners, but practically concentration camp victims. The idea that a practice so barbaric and archaic could exist in the modern world sickened him, but he pushed the thought from his mind.

Right now, it didn't matter who they were—it mattered what they were doing.

The two men paused, lowered the canister to the ground, and packed it into a wooden crate lined with straw, which they promptly nailed shut. Finally the crate was loaded into the rearmost truck, and the two prisoners returned to the warehouse.

"I've got something here," Trapp said. "How are you guys doing for overwatch?"

Mitchell hissed sharply. "NRO and NSA have re-tasked some surveillance satellites, but the coverage is patchy, and getting stick time is a bureaucratic cockfight."

"I'm sure," Trapp said drily. The bureaucrats back in the Beltway mostly seemed to forget their job was to keep America safe, not further their own careers. That habit was damaging enough when the world was at peace, but in Trapp's opinion, it was inexcusable when things were this close to boiling over into open conflict. "I need you to get an eye in the sky on my location, ASAP."

"Why?"

"I don't exactly know," Trapp admitted. "There's something going on here."

"Give me something to work with, Hangman," Mitchell said, stifling a groan. "The Joint Chiefs have got whatever sats we have left pointed squarely at the Chinese. Getting them to turn them the other way is going to take a little more than just telling them you think *there's something going on here.*"

"Call it a hunch, boss," Trapp said, watching as a second canister emerged from the mysterious warehouse, carried by the same two prisoners. The same sequence he'd seen before played out a second time. "But I think this is serious. Maybe chemical or biological."

"Shit," Mitchell muttered. "Can you follow them?"

"No can do," Trapp replied quickly. "I haven't got any transport, and if I move before dark, I'll be a sitting duck."

"Shit," Mitchell said for a second time. "Okay. I'll see what I can do."

"You need to do a damn sight more than that," Trapp growled, an iron sense of certainty clenching his stomach in a vise. "This is it, Mike. I know it is. This is the key to this whole mess. We can't lose sight of it now."

Mitchell didn't say a damn thing in reply. Trapp didn't mind. He wasn't worried about pissing off his boss. In this line of work, it was better to speak plainly than to let something go unspoken that might end up having devastating repercussions.

"Okay," Mitchell finally muttered. "I'll get it done. What's your plan?"

"I'm going in as soon as it gets dark," Trapp said, glancing at his wrist. "In about three hours if I can. If not, I'll wait until just before dawn. Either way, I'm getting in there."

"Understood," Mitchell replied, his voice catching as though he wanted to say something. "Just... Be careful, Jason. Okay?"

"Careful's my middle name." Trapp grinned.

"We both know that isn't true."

"Maybe," he allowed. "But going in all guns blazing isn't going to get Ikeda out alive."

"Ikeda isn't the priority," Mitchell said sharply. "She knew what she was signing up for. Those are the risks in this business."

Trapp's fist clenched, and a pang of anger shot through his body. He knew that Mitchell wasn't saying anything that he himself didn't believe. Hell, he'd said exactly the same to others many times.

But this, somehow, was different. It wasn't academic, or cut and dry. He had sent Eliza into that room and hadn't been able to protect her.

She might have known what she was signing up for. But she couldn't possibly have expected to have been failed in that way.

This was Trapp's mess. And he damn well intended to clean it up.

Still, he recognized the sense in what Mitchell was saying. This wasn't personal, and if he allowed himself to think that way, then he wouldn't just put the mission at risk, but endanger Eliza's life—the exact opposite of what he was attempting to achieve.

Consciously, with great difficulty, Trapp forced himself to relax. He mastered his breathing, pushing down on the rage that had spurted like burning lava inside him. It was the product of not enough sleep and too many days and nights spent worrying, he knew.

And if he wasn't careful, it might well get him killed.

"I'm getting her out, Mike," Trapp said. "But I hear what you're saying. I won't put the mission at risk."

"Okay," Mitchell replied, no doubt knowing that was the best he was going to get. "Stay frosty out there, Hangman."

This time, it was Trapp's turn not to reply. He appreciated the sentiment, but he didn't need it. His focus would not slip.

He would not allow it to slip. Not when the stakes were this high. Not with Ikeda's life on the line, not with the United States poised on the brink of war with China herself.

"I'll check in when it's done," he said simply. "Find out where those trucks are going, Mike. We can't afford to lose them. And get me some backup."

"For tonight?"

"No. At least, not directly. It stands to reason that whatever is in those canisters came from inside this camp. I intend to find out what it is. And when I do, we need to be ready to strike."

"Okay. You have anyone in mind?"

Trapp was about to fire back a quip along the lines of, *"I don't care who you get to do the job, just get it done,"* before he caught himself. An image of his rescuers floated into his mind from several nights earlier, bobbing on the waves of the South China Sea. "Lieutenant Mitchell Quinn and his team. They're good, and they're close."

"I'm on it."

Trapp glanced at the light now fading over the clouded mountains, the day departing more quickly at this latitude. He felt no fear at what the night held in store for him. Only a cool sense of determination to right his wrongs. "Good. I'm almost ready to go in. I'll check in when it's done."

40

Ikeda watched as Chen's sightless eyes scoured the ceiling, searching for a salvation that never came. Her golden skin glowed a bright red, evidence of the heat scouring her body of life. It would not be long now, and perhaps that was the only slight mercy she was ever likely to receive. Incoherent moans burst free of her lips, adding to the cacophony of similar sounds from the other four infected prisoners.

Eliza crooned a melody, tears stinging her eyes as she watched a woman she had never met slip remorselessly toward an unimaginably cruel death. She wished that there was something she could do to help, something more than singing half-remembered lullabies. She could not reach the dying prisoners. Could not touch them, wipe the sweat from their brow, or simply reassure them that she was there, and that someone cared.

In a way, her inability to help was a torment in itself.

Twice, the North Korean research assistants had entered the ward to take blood samples and temperature readings. Twice, Ikeda had begged them to do something, anything to help. To at least administer some painkillers, to allow their test subjects to slip away with a shred of dignity, to absorb at least some of their pain.

Twice she was ignored.

The assistants entered, never wearing protection, did their work, and left. Once, Eliza thought she detected an expression of dread, or else a paralyzed shame in one of the women's eyes. And then it was gone, its owner with it.

And Eliza was still there. In a room with the dying. Waiting to join them.

It had been hours since the Americans were taken. Ikeda couldn't stop wondering what was happening to them. Had they been taken for further tests—to determine why they hadn't yet fallen sick?

Or, more horrifying still, had their utility simply come to its end? Had they already been disposed of, a bullet to the back of the head, bodies buried in quicklime barrels, or else burned on a pyre to eliminate every last trace of the virus?

Had she failed them, just as she was now failing the dying Chinese, as she had failed her country?

The endless questions assailed Ikeda's mind. She had always been resolute, blessed with an iron sense of self-confidence, of belief in her own abilities, twinned with a gritty resolve that always got the job done. It was what carried her through those long, exhausting swims, what allowed her to push her body through challenges that would break most ordinary women.

But that resolve—naturally—was beginning to slip. The beatings, the exhaustion, the inadequate nutrition, and most desperately of all, the twisted waiting game she was forced to play—waiting for her own body to give way to an unseen, yet no less deadly enemy, each torment built upon the last, forming an impenetrable wall of fear that even Ikeda could not climb.

She coughed.

The action, which ordinarily she would have dismissed without a second thought, this time lit a spark of terror in the young operative's soul. Was it the first sign that she was infected, like all the rest?

She looked back over to Chen, at the thin trickle of blood oozing from the young girl's nostril, kept watching her back arch with pain as her body thrashed against the thin camp bed, its metal springs squeaking, the chain around her wrist jangling.

I don't want to die like this, Eliza whimpered in the safety of her own head.

And then she could not contain herself any longer. Like a damn bursting, Ikeda's resolve broke with it. She closed her eyes as burning tears forced their way out, as her own body matched Chen's, great wracking sobs standing in for fevered moans.

In a voice that was little more than a whisper, Ikeda admitted the truth to herself. "I don't want to die here."

The admission prompted a reaction—but not one she was expecting. For the first time in hours, the laboratory ward's airlock door slid open. With her body curled into the fetal position, tears running freely down her face, Ikeda did not notice the change. For the first time in days, she was on the verge of giving up—had, in fact given up—on monitoring the environment around her.

Rough hands grasped her shoulders, yanking her off the bed. The unexpected movement stunned Ikeda, and for once in her life her immediate reaction was to flinch. She fought the men, but not the way she had been trained to. Not with strength and guile, but sheer panic.

A blow connected with the back of Ikeda's head, immediately bringing an end to her resistance. As the two guards released her chains, a third man standing at a distance, rifle leveled at the CIA operative's chest, she simply retreated inside herself.

The two men led Ikeda through anodyne concrete hallways, their fingers digging into the tender flesh of her upper arms as they pulled her forward.

Neither spoke.

They led her to a small, windowless interrogation room. It could have been found in any police station in almost any country in the world. Except for the faded, rusty outline of a puddle of blood on the concrete floor. It was evidence, as though Ikeda needed any more, of the casual brutality of the men who ran this facility.

The guards shackled Ikeda's wrists to the table and pushed her down into a rusted metal chair. The coarse metal scraped against her bare skin.

And then they left.

How long she remained there, alone, the cool of the air conditioning biting against her skin, the iron stink of spilled blood assaulting her senses, Ikeda did not know. Seconds stretched into minutes stretched into what might have been hours.

Or might not have.

And all the while, the worries swirled in her mind. Was she infected? Was that cough the first sign that the virus was already ravaging her cells? How long would it be before she first coughed up blood, or the hot, polluted liquid trickled freely from her nostrils?

The fear was almost overwhelming. So too was the monotony, the silence and the quiet of the interrogation room. Over the past several days, Ikeda had grown used to constant company. Now, for the first time, she was alone.

And solitude bred fear.

Finally, a scraping sound echoed through the room, bouncing

off its hard concrete walls. The door opened, and Ikeda's chains rattled as she turned, eyes straining as she attempted to make out who had entered. As they grew accustomed to the halo of light around the doorway, her eyes flared with recognition.

The colonel walked slowly and deliberately into the room, his boots clicking against the hard floor. He was carrying a thin manila folder in his left hand and wore a pistol in a brown leather holster on his right hip. Eliza watched warily as he set the folder down on the interrogation table. It was closed, and the front jacket was blank. She said nothing, knowing there was no advantage to be found in breaking her silence.

He was the first to speak. In English. "Perhaps we should get acquainted with one another."

The colonel tipped back the chair on the opposite side of the table and pulled it back with measured calm. Its metal legs scraped against the concrete ground, making Eliza flinch internally. Still, she said nothing—did not in fact show any outward sign that she even recognized his presence.

"You see, my name is Colonel Kim," he said. He sat down with an accentuated swagger, reclining languidly, tipping the chair onto two legs. "And we haven't formally met. My apologies."

Ikeda studied the man intently, drinking in every last detail as a plan began to form in her mind. With her wrists in shackles, there was no chance she would be able to break free. But for the first time, her keen mind spied an opening.

There was no guarantee it would work. No guarantee, in fact, that it would even come to pass. But Ikeda vowed that she wasn't going down without a fight. Not this time. If the opportunity presented itself, she intended to attempt to take the colonel hostage. He was clearly the source of all power not just in this facility, but in the entire base. His word was law. And if he gave the order to free the hostages, his men would not dare disobey him.

But the inescapable fact remained that Ikeda was in chains, and her target was not. So to have any chance of success, she needed every advantage she could get. And that meant understanding her enemy.

Colonel Kim was a short man. Short, but wiry. Ikeda had no doubt that he possessed incredible reserves of strength. Though she was taller than him, and more powerfully built, if it came to a standup fight, she wasn't confident of success. Kim looked like a man who'd spent an entire lifetime fighting dirty.

No, she needed to get the drop on him. Somehow, she needed to take his weapon from him. It was the only way.

While her mind whirred, Kim flicked open the manila folder and made a show of studying its contents. Ikeda knew that it was all a game, a charade for her benefit. He knew exactly what that folder contained. But still, he let the silence stretch out.

Finally, he spoke. "And you, my dear," he said, "are Elizabeth Ikeda."

Kim's simple statement hit the captured CIA operative with the force of an atomic bomb. Despite herself, she looked up sharply, catching the North Korean's eye. She said nothing, but she didn't need to. The game was up.

A cold smile stretched across the colonel's face. "Finally," he said, "we agree on something. You do speak English, after all. According to this file, you're a businesswoman based in Hong Kong. But I think we both know that's not the entire truth, don't we?"

Eliza thought fast. She had a decision to make. Did she keep up the pretense that she couldn't speak English, when he clearly knew who she was? Or instead, should she beat a tactical retreat; accept the sacrifice of that pawn and move forward?

She chose the latter option. The question of *how* exactly

Kim knew the identity lingered. But she could deal with that later.

"You got me," she said, her voice rusty from disuse. "I won't ask you how you know."

Kim's eye twinkled, though the smile that creased his cheeks did not reach its depths. It was a chilling disparity. "What is it the British say? A gentleman never reveals his secrets."

Eliza fought the temptation to roll her eyes. Whoever this guy was, he enjoyed the moustache-twirling evil villain role a little bit too much. Then again, given the predilection for intense cruelty that he had already demonstrated, she saw no sense in sparring with him.

Instead she said, "What do you want?"

"You know what I want, Eliza. You were sent to eliminate a man. Sadly for me, you are somewhat competent at your job. Not competent enough to avoid getting captured, of course"— he grinned—"but you show promise nonetheless."

When it was plain that Eliza had no intention of responding to his jibe, Kim continued. "The dear departed Mr. Alstyne possessed something of great importance to me. Do you know what that is?"

"I can guess," Eliza replied.

Kim clapped his hands together sharply, an expression of happiness stretching across his face. The sound made Eliza jump, and the chains around her wrists rattle. "Wonderful! Then we are finally on the same page."

Eliza chose not to respond.

Kim clicked his fingers, causing her forehead to wrinkle with confusion. He reclined ever deeper into his chair, a malicious grin on his face.

Before more than thirty seconds had elapsed, the door to the interrogation room opened. Two guards stepped through, armed with AK-47 rifles. Eliza wondered what was about to happen. Another beating?

She could take more physical pain. It was the mental torture of being in that laboratory ward that had nearly broken her. That, she wasn't sure she could endure again.

The situation quickly clarified itself. Behind the two guards were the American captives, all four of them. They looked pale, terrified—and yet healthy.

How could that be? How was it possible that they were still alive—and not just alive, but showing no visible signs of the illness that had torn through the bodies of their Chinese prisoners?

The question broke free from Ikeda's lips before she could stop herself. "How —?"

Kim grinned, clearly delighted to be asked. "Fascinating, isn't it." He clapped his hands once more, and called out in a singsong voice, "Bo-ris..."

The chubby, now frail-looking Russian scientist sidled into the room. The collar of his lab coat was stained yellow with sweat, and he was nervously pulling his fingers, as if looking for something to occupy them.

"Good of you to join us, Boris," Kim said, smiling, yet speaking in a voice that was devoid of humor. Devoid of any emotion, in fact, except cold malevolence. "Why don't you walk this young lady through your marvelous creation?"

The scientist swallowed anxiously, regarding the North Korean colonel like a beaten dog would its master. In a way, Ikeda felt pity for the man.

But not much.

He cleared his throat and began to speak. "The virus is called Marburg. It's a viral hemorrhagic fever, first discovered —"

"Boris," Kim chided, his tone mocking. "Do it with *feeling*. You should be proud. Your name will go down in history. You will change the world. So don't bore my beautiful guest with a history lesson. Tell her what it can *do*."

Eliza's skin crawled at the sound of the Kim's voice, at the malevolent ease—and delight—with which he toyed with the Russian. She split her attention, half with Boris, and half with the four American captives, who had been lined up against the far wall of the interrogation room, silent tears streaming down their faces. Two of the guards stood in front of them, rifles half-raised in warning.

Boris nodded, and Eliza's gaze snapped back to focus on the scientist. "I'm sorry," he whispered, his voice breaking. "In non-laboratory outbreaks, the virus has a mortality rate of between twenty-five and eighty percent. In the wild, it's primarily transmitted by direct, person-to-person contact, but —"

He paused, wringing his hands.

Eliza's mouth went dry at the revelation. Though she had seen the effects of the virus, the rictus of pain on Chen's face, the blood spewing from the other victims, to hear the Russian scientist discuss the virus's features in such detached, clinical terms was nonetheless shocking.

Eighty percent mortality.

It was almost beyond comprehension, but Ikeda forced herself to concentrate. Her determination to get out of here was only mastered by her desire to somehow, someday, make the North Korean colonel pay for what he had done.

And warn the world of what is coming...

"— but," Kim stepped in, "what use is that? So slow, so *inefficient*. No, the good doctor has modified our little viral friend so that it can be transmitted by an airborne vector. Not just transmitted, but delivered."

Airborne.

The term hit Ikeda like a train. Her eyes widened with horror. She was no expert when it came to biological weapons, but she knew enough to get by. And she knew that for viruses like Ebola and Marburg, the only saving grace was that person-to-person transmission was a major hurdle, slowing down infection rates and allowing public health authorities to get ahead of a crisis. But if that same virus was aerosolized...

It would be genocide, on a scale never before contemplated.

Kim held his arms out. "How rude of me," he said. "I interrupted. Boris, do carry on. Tell the young lady the true extent of your genius."

Boris was trembling now. Ikeda had wondered why, unlike the man's research assistants, he had never entered the ward, nor even the observation deck that overlooked the horrific room. Now she had her answer.

Guilt.

"I —" he croaked. "At the Institute, at Vektor, my speciality was the genetic targeting of viruses. Isolating DNA markers carried only by specific subsets of human populations, and modifying viruses to target only those carriers. It was just proof of concept, mostly. We used the common cold. But —"

Kim cut in. "But it works just as well with Marburg." He smiled. "And Mr. Savrasov was kind enough to steal a sample from his former employers. He really is extraordinarily conscientious. I couldn't have done this without him."

The pieces slowly began to fall into place in Ikeda's mind. Why the Chinese prisoners were dying, and the Americans still alive. It was a test, to see whether Savrasov's tinkering had worked.

Patently, it had.

"But why?" she whispered. "What possible purpose could it serve?"

She stared, wide-eyed, at the manic expression that had appeared on Kim's face. Was he crazy? Did he simply want to watch the world burn—or was there a method to his madness, an underlying reason for his genocidal mania?

"Millions will die," the Russian moaned. "Tens of millions. More! You can't release it, Colonel."

Kim clicked his fingers, beckoning a guard over. "Do not test my patience, Savrasov," he growled. "And do not presume to tell me what I can and cannot do."

Boris cringed, as though waiting for a blow to rain down on his head. It didn't come. Instead, Kim directed the guard to lead the Russian out of the room. Once the door had clicked closed behind them, the North Korean turned to Eliza.

"A cowardly man." He smiled, as though they were friends, and she hadn't just witnessed his insanity. "And one whose usefulness is quickly drawing to an end, I fear."

Ikeda could barely comprehend the callous way that the man could dismiss a human life. But with the four American captives still lined up against the far wall, trembling with fear as they faced what looked for all the world like a firing squad, she did not dare anger him.

"What I need to know," Kim continued, "is whether you know the access codes to the flash drive that was in Mr. Alstyne's care when he died."

He fixed Ikeda with a piercing stare, as though probing her expression for an answer.

When it did not come—at least not instantly—Kim unbuttoned his leather holster, and withdrew the sleek black pistol contained inside it. He stared at it absently for a few seconds, and then, in one swift movement, raised it and fired.

The sound buffeted Ikeda's eardrums, almost deafening her in the cramped confines of the interrogation room. She jerked backwards, the chair falling away from behind her, only to be stopped by the cold metal of her cuffs digging into her wrists.

Next, a scream split the air.

Ikeda watched as a body slumped against the ground. The body of Andy, husband to a beautiful woman now crouching over his body, hands caressing her dead lover's face, smearing blood across his cheeks as tears fell freely from her eyes.

"What did you do?" Ikeda spat, attempting to pull her wrists free of the chains that bound them in place. "Why did you kill him?"

Kim replaced his pistol in its holster, completely unaffected by the death he had just caused. The guards had flinched at the unexpected sound, but they too seemed impassive, unmoved by the man's sudden death.

Not death, murder.

"My men will return you to the laboratory. You have twenty-four hours to supply me with the information I require. If you fail to do so by that point, I will give you the choice of executing your compatriots yourself, or forcing my men to do it."

He leered at Ikeda, true happiness seeming to cross his face for the first time since they had met. "And I assure you, if you choose the latter option, their deaths will be slow indeed."

Kim clicked his fingers one last time, summoning a guard. Ikeda was led out of the room, the colonel's macabre offer replaying over and over again inside her head. One question reared its ugly head.

If that was what he was willing to do when he thought she knew something, what would he do when he found out the flash drive was fake?

41

Trapp was equipped only with a suppressed pistol, a fighting knife, a slim night vision scope, and just shy of two decades of experience fighting in every conceivable environment.

In truth, few of his missions had ever worried him like this one. For the second time in under a year, he found himself fighting a war which he was woefully unprepared to win—except this time, he wasn't just faced with an implacable enemy, but an entire country of them. This side of the DMZ, he had to consider everyone an adversary.

Ordinarily, on an operation like this one, Trapp's primary role would be simple surveillance. He would have crawled to his observation spot high up in the mountains on his belly days before, built an undetectable hide, and kept watch.

Ordinarily, the fighting would have been someone else's job. A strike team would be sitting on stealth helicopters operated by the army's elite Nightstalker regiment, waiting for Trapp to give the order. And then all hell would break loose.

But not tonight.

Tonight, Trapp would have to go it alone. Ikeda's life—if she was still alive, that is—hung in the balance. As did so many others, cruelly and unwittingly caught up in a convoluted conspiracy beyond their ability to understand. One whose full breadth even Trapp did not yet grasp.

Though he was beginning to paint a picture.

For another man, the thought that so many lives hung on his next move might have been crippling. But not Trapp. For him, it was just another Sunday.

Moving with excruciating slowness, Trapp stood. Whatever moon might at that very moment have been crossing the heavens was obscured by thick cloud that now cloaked the mountainside. It was a double-edged sword. On the one hand, the thick fog meant that unless an enemy patrol quite literally walked into him, Trapp would remain perfectly concealed by the weather.

On the other, that same fog meant that he was operating blind, and since the thick blanket seemed to absorb all sound as well, he was also deaf.

Trapp took the time to dispose of all visible evidence of his presence. In the darkness, it was impossible to say whether he'd succeeded completely, but he did the best he could. By the time anyone discovered this spot, he hoped he would be long gone, with Eliza Ikeda in his arms and in possession of the information he'd been sent to acquire.

But the Hangman was a diligent professional.

Ninety-nine times out of a hundred, hell—nine hundred and ninety-nine times out of a thousand—sloppiness on a matter like this would have no negative repercussions. But Trapp was a percentages guy. And when the bet was his own life, he preferred not to test the odds. They wouldn't always be in his favor.

Once the job was done, he began to pick his way down the

mountainside, following an old goat track carved into the rock. The air was cooler now, the heat of the day long since dissipated this high in the mountains.

In a little less than an hour, Trapp made it most of the way to the valley floor. He paused several times to ensure he wasn't being followed, and used the time to study the army camp. Through the night vision scope, the world was lit up a ghostly green.

Not for the first time, Trapp marveled at how dark the world was north of the demilitarized zone. Unlike the rest of the Western world, North Korea was plunged into darkness the moment the sun disappeared below the horizon. Only the cities—and that mainly meant Pyongyang—received a consistent supply of electricity through the night.

Even the military installation below him did not entirely escape the curse of darkness. Most of the barracks buildings were unlit—especially those in the adjoining prison camp. The major administration buildings glowed with electric light, as did a searchlight that—very occasionally—danced across the perimeter fence.

The first time he spied the beam of light dancing across the scrubby patch of cleared land that surrounded both the prison camp and the military base, Trapp froze. It wasn't long after night had fallen, and he briefly wondered whether his best laid plans had already met their untimely demise.

Briefly.

Whoever was in charge of monitoring the camp's perimeter defense was either lazy, incompetent—or hopefully both. A two-man patrol circled the entire camp on the hour, every hour, and always traveling in a counter-clockwise direction. Other than that, and the searchlight occasionally firing up, briefly scanning the base's surroundings, there was little obvious security.

Trapp wondered whether he was missing something.

Perhaps the lack of guards and guns and dogs was a trick. But his gut told him not. The simplest explanation was often the best one, and in this case, the simplest explanation was that up here, in the mountains, in the depths of North Korea, they simply did not expect to be attacked.

After all, since the end of the Korean War in the 1950s, through all the fiery rhetoric, the nuclear tests, the missile launches and the sanctions, no one had come close to invading North Korea. Neither was the population a threat—starving and browbeaten, they were no more likely to rise up against their oppressors than animals rebel against farmers.

Trapp cleared his mind and concentrated, scanning the perimeter fence one last time.

The main entrance to the camp was lit up like the Hollywood sign, and even in the distance Trapp could make out enough bristling weaponry to take on an entire battalion. But he had no intention of knocking on the front door.

No, as he stopped for the final time, crouching low and bringing the scope to his eye, a mirthless smile stretched across his face. At the rear of the camp lay an enormous, open garbage pit. The noxious smell assaulted Trapp's nostrils even at this distance, and he hated to think how bad it would be when he got closer.

As he watched, a man exited a small gate that was watched by a single guard, sitting on a stool, with his rifle resting against the base's chain-link fence. He swayed a little—visibly drunk, then strode into the filth and undid his pants. Trapp couldn't see the stream of urine that emerged, but he knew exactly what the man was doing. He'd watched as a procession of half a dozen like-minded individuals—or perhaps the same guy, half a dozen times—had left the encampment to relieve themselves.

As the man returned, the guard at the gate barely registered his presence. Another notch in the plus column.

Trapp smiled one last time, the expression stretching across his face like a warning. He'd found his way in.

~

TRAPP HID AMIDST THE FILTH, smearing his body with thick mud and covering himself. He removed his fighting knife from its sheath and settled in to wait for a target to present itself.

It did not take long.

Within twenty minutes, a door swung open on the nearest barracks building to the camp's fence, and a uniformed soldier staggered out, followed by a blast of unfamiliar karaoke before the door thudded home once again. Trapp's gaze followed him every step of the way.

The soldier walked in an uneven S-pattern, swaying as he walked and clutching a bottle of beer. Scenes like this one played out in every army the world over. Trapp knew too well that if there was one thing soldiers were good at, it was drinking themselves stupid. Though he dreaded to wonder exactly what they were drinking. He didn't envy their hangovers the next morning.

If they lasted that long.

He followed the man's progress as he exited the camp by the same route his predecessors had followed, undoing his fly before he was even out of the gate, one hand pressed against the rifle slung over his shoulder. Once again, the gate guard did not look up. In fact, Trapp suspected he was asleep. He certainly wasn't moving.

The drunk soldier staggered into the garbage dump on the edge of the North Korean military base. He spread his legs wide, allowed his pants to drop fully around his ankles, and began to empty his bladder.

The second the urine began to fall, Trapp surged into action, exploding out of the darkness too quickly for the man to even register his presence. The knife's carbon-tempered steel entered the base of the soldier's neck, severing his brainstem immediately.

Trapp cushioned the man's fall, wincing as the bottle of beer that had occupied his hand smashed against the ground. The sound that ensued carried into the stillness of the night, and he froze, stilling even his own heartbeat as he waited to find out if anyone had heard it.

He waited sixty seconds, and then another minute just to be certain. Only then did he lay the man's corpse against the ground, leaving the knife in place to stem the flow of blood until his work was done. He took no pride in killing this man, who was no doubt a mere conscript, snatched from his family and forced to serve a murderous, evil regime.

It was men like this whose lives stained his conscience. It was deaths like this one that kept Jason Trapp up at night. He saw the faces of all those he had killed before he slipped into unconsciousness. He knew he would see them until the day he died.

But right now, he forced himself to squash his conscience. On a night like this, it would only get him killed.

Quickly and efficiently, he stripped the dead guard naked. A small trickle of blood had leaked from the man's open wound, soaking the collar of his uniform, but unlike its former owner, Trapp could live with it. He took off his own clothes and shrugged on the uniform. It was tight around the chest— thankfully absurdly oversized for the starving conscript—and the pants rode up above his ankle, but from a distance it would do.

If they get close enough to see me, Trapp thought wryly, *I'm already dead.*

The disguise didn't need to be perfect. In truth, the CIA operative's enormous size would set him apart from most, if not all, of the North Koreans he'd watched operating inside the base's fences the second someone set eyes on him.

But for just an instant, it might give Trapp the advantage he needed to survive. He would take it.

He slung the man's weapon across his chest, leaving the strap over his shoulder. The rifle was dirty, probably hadn't been cleaned in months, but Trapp knew that it would fire. The Russians knew a few things about war, and they knew a few more about how to equip a poorly trained conscript army.

The AK-47 was a masterful piece of engineering. It would fire wet, dry, with mud in the breach or sand in the barrel. The one in his hands was a North Korean version, the Type 58, and produced locally, but it would get the job done.

Then again, it would also wake the living dead. Trapp kept it, just in case, but knew that if he was forced to fire it then all hope of making it out of the North Korean army camp without being detected had just gone up in smoke.

He hid the man's body as best he could, disguising it among a pile of garbage. In the cold light of day, the trick would be quickly discovered. Trapp hoped that by then, he would be long gone. He quickly surveyed his work and decided that it would do. Then he turned and began to stagger toward the camp's side entrance, matching the gait of the previous owner —whose uniform he was currently wearing.

In his right hand, held reversed, was his fighting knife, blade now wiped clean of the dead soldier's blood. He didn't want to kill the guard, too. But if it came to it, Trapp knew that he would not flinch.

He thanked the fact that the darkness was almost all-consuming on this side of the North Korean military base. He kept the helmet so that it hung low over his face, disguising the color of his skin—even his weathered complexion was lighter than that of the man he had just killed.

But in the end, it was unnecessary. As he closed on the gate,

Trapp heard the guard's light snoring and breathed a sigh of relief. The man would never know how close he had come to a brush with destiny.

Casting one last look at the man's closed eyelids, Trapp slipped into the military base, cushioning the action of the gate closing behind him.

He was in.

42

M ike Mitchell paced the sub-basement beneath the CIA's New Headquarters Building in Langley, Virginia. It was an action with which he was becoming uncomfortably familiar. At this very moment, he knew, Jason Trapp would have begun his insertion into the North Korean military encampment.

"How long?" he growled.

Dr. Timothy Greaves tapped his keyboard and briefly glanced down at his screen. "Five minutes until the keyhole satellite begins its pass. We'll have about forty minutes time over target, and then we're blind again until ten this evening."

"Will that be enough?"

The two analysts—Kyle Partey and Timothy Greaves— looked at each other with discomfort before Greaves replied, shrugging, "It's a big, mountainous country. Plenty of places to hide."

Mitchell briefly closed his eyes, but found no peace in the darkness. Instead, images of a biological weapon loose in the streets of America flashed on the back of his eyelids. Pictures of sick and dying children, of mothers, fathers, grandparents weeping over what they had lost. Images of riots at grocery stores, fighting breaking out at the fuel pumps.

It was everything he had spent his entire career trying to prevent.

But in all those years, at least since the fall of the Berlin Wall, the real threat had come from terrorists, not nation states. After 9/11, the United States military and intelligence communities became extremely proficient at identifying terrorist networks and hunting them down before they could commit atrocities in the homeland.

That new skill had come at a cost.

Analysts had been taken away from their traditional desks and forced to watch over Middle Eastern goat herders, causing once finely-honed proficiencies and prized local knowledge to wither away. And now the consequences of those decisions were coming home to roost. Once again, America faced mortal peril at the hands of an old enemy—an enemy, in fact, with which it was still technically at war.

And she was woefully unprepared to survive it.

"Boss?"

Mitchell's eyes flicked open, and he saw Kyle staring back at him, the bookish analyst's face contorted with worry. The director of the CIA's Special Activities division forced himself to snap out of his train of thought. "Okay—tell me what you can do in forty minutes."

Greaves cleared his throat. "The plan is to take low-resolution shots of every likely route from the target base to any port, airport or air force base north of the DMZ. We'll feed those images into a search algorithm, and...hope we get lucky."

Mitchell frowned at the man's sheepish expression. He had hoped for something a little more scientific than *getting lucky*.

"Let's go back to basics," he said. "What the hell do these guys want?"

The question hung in the thick atmosphere of the basement without answer. The various pieces of the puzzle had bounced around in Mitchell's brain for days, coming further into focus with each new discovery, each revelation of a new threat, but never seeming to fit together.

"We can assume that they were behind our satellites being knocked off-line. Somehow they gained access to China's anti-satellite capability—including this new satellite-killer—and deployed it. They tried to steal the secrets on Alstyne's thumb drive. But to what end?"

"I think I have an answer to that," Greaves said.

The large man ran his fingers through his dyed hair, attempting to tame the long locks, but inevitably failing. He grabbed a laptop and set it down in front of Mitchell. "I cracked the encryption on the thumb drive."

"When?" Mitchell growled.

Greaves shot his adopted boss an anxious glance. "Um, about forty seconds ago..."

Mitchell waved his fingers in apology. "Fine, spill."

"Okay, so they wanted to blind us, right? To take out our biggest advantage over the Chinese."

"Right."

"And our working theory is that Unit 61 is behind everything, correct?"

"Doc—I suggest you get to the point. We're running out of time."

Greaves cleared his throat anxiously. "Well, what if their goal was to turn China's weapons against us, and ours against them? To provoke a war between the two countries."

Mitchell's eyes gleamed with intrigue. "Go on..."

"The first attack against our satellites got me thinking. It was a false flag—the North Koreans did it knowing we would blame the Chinese. Same with the sat-killer, Project Songbird. The Chinese are the only ones with the capability, ergo we were always going to blame them."

"So how does the drive fit in?" Kyle asked.

"I cross-checked it with anything to do with biological weapons. It was just a hunch. But I got a hit."

"Doc..." Mitchell growled. "Sometime this week would be great."

"I found a reference to a DOD research project from back in the '80s, codenamed AFTERMATH. It was carried out by a company that Atlas later acquired, that's how it ended up on the drive. The idea was to create a biological weapon that could be used in the event of all-out war with the Russkies. It was only to be released in the event that we were losing."

"What did it do?"

"They wanted to create a smart bioweapon, one that would wipe out only the Russians and leave us unaffected. It didn't work, of course. Back then the technology wasn't advanced enough. They shut it down in '86."

Mitchell's forehead wrinkled. "I don't get it."

Greaves shrugged. "I might be wrong. But I think the North Koreans found a way to build that weapon. I think they are about to release it. And I think they want to blame it on us."

The pieces clicked into place in Mitchell's mind. It was a stretch, but it just about fit. The North Koreans were trying to provoke a war between China and America, by attacking each country and blaming it on the other. Two simultaneous false flag operations, using technology that only the other could have created, to make the finger of blame unmissable.

But that means...

The US wasn't the target of the bioweapon at all. China was. And right now, a worldwide conflagration hung in the balance. If that bioweapon got released, or the sat-killer was activated— or worse—if both happened at the same time, then war would be unavoidable.

Across the basement, a computer pinged. "What the hell is

that?" Mitchell grunted, his mind roiling as he tried to assimilate this new piece of information.

Greaves stood up and lumbered over to the computer. He frowned, tapped a key, then turned to face his boss. "The keyhole satellite just picked up the location of the control terminal for the Chinese sat-killer."

"Xishang?"

The data scientist shook his head. "No. North Korea."

43

Trapp prowled the shadowed streets of the North Korean military base, thankful for the fact that even the armed forces appeared to be affected by the shortages of electricity that afflicted the reclusive country.

He was hunched over in a vain attempt to hide his true size, but knew that if anyone got close, the ruse would quickly be discovered. The stolen uniform couldn't decide whether to be tighter around his chest or his thighs.

He glanced down at himself, briefly examining the uniform in the glow of a ray of moonlight. It was plain, patched in places, and threadbare in others. Its former owner must have been an enlisted man, he figured, which meant that he would have to be careful. It would have been better to have stolen an officer's uniform, to give overzealous guards a second thought before they approached him, but beggars could not be choosers.

It appeared that the vast majority of the camp's inhabitants were asleep, a fact for which Trapp was thankful. A light breeze bit at his exposed face, carrying the yowling sound of tussling cats—perhaps picking over the garbage pile to the rear of the base.

He absently wondered if they had found the body he had left in his wake.

The sound of a match striking exploded in the still mountain air, and Trapp pressed himself against the wall of the nearest barracks building, a one-story concrete structure with no windows on his side. In the darkness, he was almost invisible.

A man walked into view, pausing briefly to light a cigarette held gently between his lips. It flared, and then he tossed the lit match against the ground. It arced through the darkness like a firework, and Trapp followed its progress all the way. It exploded in a flurry of sparks, and then disappeared.

The man resumed his progress, wandering ever closer toward Trapp's position. By now, the CIA operative's vision was perfectly accustomed to the darkness. He left the night vision scope in his pocket, knowing that his opposite number's night vision would have been wiped out by the act of striking the match and lighting his cigarette—and thus that he had the advantage.

In a way, the ease of the operation so far disgusted Trapp.

He welcomed it, of course, but if his unit had been this lax with perimeter security when he was in the army, they would have been chewed out six ways to Sunday. But the men of Unit 61—as fearsome a reputation as they had in the field—were arrogant on home turf. They believed they were untouchable in their mountain fortress.

They were complacent.

Still, Trapp's heartbeat thundered in his chest—the blood rushing in his ears so loudly it was almost impossible to believe that the soldier now only a few feet distant from him could not hear the ruckus.

But, patently, he could not.

The man hummed an unfamiliar tune, and took one last, fateful step in Trapp's direction. The experienced operator did not hesitate. He exploded out of the darkness, the blade of his knife invisible. His boots scraped against the ground, but otherwise he moved silently.

His target's head turned, startled by the sound, but too late. Before his eyes could focus on the newfound threat, Trapp was upon him, hand clamped over his mouth, blade pressed against his throat, and hot breath caressing the skin of his cheek. Trapp smiled malevolently. "Don't you dare fucking move."

The man froze, trembling, but did precisely as Trapp ordered. The CIA operative smiled coldly and released his grasp on his prisoner just a touch. He brought one finger to his mouth and made a shushing motion, and waited until his captive acknowledged the request.

"You speak English?" Trapp growled.

The North Korean officer looked up to the assailant with terrified, uncomprehending eyes. Trapp grimaced. The limits of his plan had come immediately into focus.

He tried again, reaching for his Mandarin. "What about Chinese?"

His captive's eyes flared in understanding. The man's head bobbed up and down anxiously. "Yes," he whispered. "A little."

Trapp's own command of the language was rusty—and that was putting it kindly, but it would have to do.

"Good," he whispered in broken Mandarin. "Tell me where you're keeping the American."

The North Korean officer practically whimpered at Trapp's demand, shaking his head in protest. "I cannot."

At least, that's what Trapp thought he said. He couldn't be exactly sure.

Trapp pressed the blade of his knife against his prisoner's throat. It was razor-sharp. He'd honed it himself, and now he tested the blade against the man's skin, drawing a single bead of blood.

"Try that again," he said. "And this time, give me the answer I'm looking for."

He caressed the man's throat with the blade, pressing his palm against his captive's mouth to stifle his terrified whimpers. He leaned forward, pressing his lips right up against the man's left ear, and whispered, "Where is the American?"

The North Korean said nothing for the longest time. Trapp was preparing to repeat himself when he finally spoke. "I tell you," he stammered in broken Mandarin, "I die."

Trapp shrugged. That wasn't his problem. "You don't," he enunciated slowly, "you still die."

He punctuated his statement by tapping the blade of his knife against the officer's throat. The man got the message.

"They are in the north side of the camp. The big warehouse, Building 12."

Trapp frowned. Either Unit 61 was holding an entire menagerie of American prisoners, or—more likely—he needed to work on his Mandarin pronouns. Either way, he could figure out the details later. Right now, the clock was ticking. Every moment he lingered was another in which the alarm could be raised. And once that happened, this operation would get very hairy indeed.

He tapped the satellite phone in his right pocket for luck. If Mike had done his job, then the Navy SEAL known to his men as Nero would be standing by, along with his entire platoon, ready to save Trapp's bacon.

If he hadn't, then that same bacon was going to end up extra crispy.

"Take me to her," he ordered.

Trapp released the blade of the knife from the North Korean's throat, but made a show of flashing his pistol. The threat was plain as day, even if he would have struggled to deliver it in Mandarin.

You screw me, the weapon said, *it'll be the last thing you do*.

If it came to it, of course, Trapp would dispatch the man with the knife, not the gun. It would be messier, but quieter. And the last thing he could afford to do was arouse an entire camp full of enemies.

He allowed the officer—a lieutenant, if he read the shoulder patches right—to walk a couple of paces ahead of him. It was better that way, the lieutenant providing cover in case they encountered any other travelers out for a midnight stroll.

But as the man led Trapp to an enormous, stark concrete warehouse, they encountered no one else. They did not, in fact, see another soul until the lieutenant pointed out a guard standing at a nondescript side entrance to the concrete building.

"They in there," the man stammered as they sheltered in the darkness cast by a grandiose administrative building. "All of them."

What does that mean? Trapp wondered.

The lieutenant looked as though he wanted to slip away, his work done. Trapp shook his head and smiled, disabusing his new friend of that notion. "How do I get in?"

The man shook his head, almost as though pleading with his captor. "I don't know. No have authorization."

"Then you better think fast," Trapp growled, the unfamiliar, sibilant language coming to him more easily now as his brain unlocked long-forgotten language lessons. "Because either you get me in there, or you die."

"They kill me either way," the lieutenant whimpered.

"Not my problem," Trapp replied callously. "You screw me, you die right here and now. Understood?"

The man nodded jerkily, clearly unhappy at his predicament. But what choice did he have? Trapp had him between a rock and a hard place, and he wasn't letting go. "Okay," he muttered. "I help. But you hit me. Hard. Better you knock me out and leave me on the ground."

Trapp frowned. What the hell was the man talking about? And then he understood. Just like the Chinese official a few nights before, the lieutenant wanted him to leave a mark— proof that he'd been assaulted. Hell, he was more than happy to oblige.

"Fine," he grunted, gesturing at the enormous warehouse with his pistol. "Now let's go."

They trudged across the hardpacked dirt that separated the two buildings, Trapp a pace behind his captive, his presence an unspoken threat.

The CIA operative held his breath as they closed on the entrance to the warehouse. He tilted the stolen steel helmet over his forehead in an attempt to disguise his appearance, but in truth there was only so much he could do. The next few seconds would go one of two ways—and he had a suspicion about which of those it would be.

The lieutenant waved at the sentry standing by the warehouse door. He said something in the unfamiliar, tonal language that sounded like a cousin to the Mandarin that Trapp was reacquainting himself with, without being similar enough to understand.

Trapp could not comprehend the sentry's reply, but the tone was clear enough—unsure, laced with distrust. The sentry raised his weapon, jerking it in Trapp's direction, and called out a challenge.

Fuck.

Trapp burst into action. He couldn't take the chance that the lieutenant would be able to smooth this over. One stray shot from the Type 58, and the whole camp would be swarming with enemy combatants.

In an instant, Trapp closed the distance between them, ducking under the man's rifle and ripping it bodily from his arms. The young conscript blanched with terror, and for the second time that night Trapp found himself with the blade of a knife pressed against the man's throat.

He fixed the lieutenant with a glare, the man's movement toward the fallen rifle had not escaped him. "Don't try it," he growled. "Translate for me."

The officer nodded, his expression displaying the abject terror running through his veins like an open book.

"You let me in," Trapp said, "I let you live. Understood?"

He glanced back at the lieutenant, who relayed the offer in Korean. The sentry knew better than to bargain. He nodded quickly, but said nothing.

"Tell him if he triggers an alarm, he dies. If he so much as looks at me wrong, he dies. You get that?"

"Yes," the lieutenant whispered.

"Good. What are you waiting for?"

Again, the officer relayed Trapp's instructions. Trapp marveled at the speed at which the man spoke. Even allowing for the discreet, hushed tone of voice, it was impossible to make out where one word ended and the next began.

The sentry nodded energetically for a second time, and Trapp relaxed his grip on the man. He took a pace back, knowing that if he had judged the sentry wrong, then the next few seconds would determine not just whether he lived or died, but the fate of his entire country.

He held his breath as the sentry turned and began to punch a code into a keypad by the door, fingers trembling. At any second, Trapp expected to hear alarms, barking dogs, boots thudding against the ground.

And then the door clicked open.

44

Trapp hadn't known what to expect upon entering the warehouse. On the outside, the building was stark and brutalist, and even in the darkness it was impossible to miss the streaks of rust that flooded down from its corrugated iron roof, staining the concrete walls.

Worse still, there could have been anything on the other side of the door. He hadn't known what he was stumbling into —a situation he had always tried to avoid over the course of years spent in this messy line of work. Trapp preferred to prepare to the nth degree, studying the blueprints of a target building until they were imprinted on his memory as irreversibly as if they were written in indelible ink.

But that wasn't always possible. This was one of those times.

And right now, Eliza Ikeda's life rested on him leaving his comfort zone and entering the unknown. He crossed the warehouse's threshold with his pistol drawn, ready to throw himself into battle with yet more unknown enemies.

As it turned out, all that lay on the other side was an empty hallway.

Unlike the rest of the camp, the linoleum-floored warehouse was ablaze with electric light, which flooded out the doorway before Trapp quickly kicked it closed behind his small party. He had a feeling that most ordinary soldiers on this base wouldn't come anywhere near the warehouse without receiving a direct order—and even then they would feel uncomfortable.

Hell, he felt that way himself.

"Ask him about cameras," Trapp said to the lieutenant in a hushed voice, scanning the empty hallway for any sign of a threat.

"What about them?" the lieutenant said dumbly.

Trapp shot the man an irritated look. "Are there any? If so —where?"

He scanned the hallway as the North Korean army officer translated his request. It stank of disinfectant, and the light was almost blinding after spending the last few hours swallowed by the darkness. After leaving—if he got out of this alive—he would need to use the scope in his pocket. His natural ability to navigate the darkness would be fried.

He focused his attention back on the lieutenant, who was shifting his weight anxiously from foot to foot. "Well?"

"No cameras," the man said. "At least, not that he knows of."

Trapp surveyed the two terrified-looking North Korean soldiers briefly, wondering if he had any more use for them, or whether they would simply get in his way. He realized that by pressing them into service, he might well have signed their death warrants—at best.

And yet, he had no other choice. There was simply too much at stake. He chewed his lip, then made his decision. If the two men paid the ultimate price, he would have to bear their lives on his conscience too. But right now, he needed to operate with complete freedom—and he couldn't do that with the pair of them tagging along.

There was a door about ten yards further down the hallway. He pointed at it. "What's in there?"

The lieutenant relayed his question, and turned back with the answer, a questioning look on his face. "Just a storage closet. Why?"

"Perfect," Trapp grinned. He gestured with the barrel of his pistol. "Move."

The two men did as instructed, shuffling slowly down the anodyne hallway. The closet was tiny, barely large enough to fit the three of them standing. Cleaning and maintenance supplies with unfamiliar, Korean labels were stacked on shelves that ran around the closet's walls. Trapp rifled through several boxes until he found what he was looking for —a long line of electrical cord. He sliced several long lengths of it, and gestured toward the ground. "Both of you, on your asses."

The prisoners did as they were ordered, but the lieutenant's hand glanced out and grasped Trapp's wrist, looking up at his captor with a pleading expression. It was the only thing that saved him from Trapp's immediate instinct to strike back—and hard. Although it turned out that was exactly what he wanted.

"Hit me," he moaned. "You promised."

Trapp winced.

He had no desire to beat a helpless man.

It went against everything he stood for—a thumb in the eye of the moral compass that had guided him for so long. But, he realized, it was the only way. He might very well be condemning these two men to a horrible, painful death. The least he could do was give them a fighting chance. He grimaced, and handed each of them a cleaning rag.

As they stuffed them into their mouths, Trapp bound the two men efficiently, back to back. Unless either of his prisoners was a cousin of Harry Houdini, there would be no escaping these restraints.

Finally, he gagged the two men, aware that every second he lingered, his chances of detection increased measurably. He stood, took a deep breath, then wound his arm back and broke the lieutenant's nose.

The stifled sound of the man's cries of pain pulled him up short. But Trapp bit back on his disgust and hit the man again, not with the full power his enormous bulk could have generated, but enough to leave a mark on his eye that would last weeks.

Eventually, the lieutenant fell silent. Through it all, the sentry looked up at Trapp with an impassive expression—the look of a man who had seen, and lived, a life of such deprivation that even Trapp could scarcely imagine such horror.

The act of brutalizing the young man too physically sickened Trapp. But he had to do it. It was the only way. When he was done, the gaunt conscript slumped over, but not before casting Trapp one last look. In a way, the emotion it conveyed was almost worse.

Gratitude.

The door to the closet had no lock, but as Trapp closed it behind him, he figured it was unlikely that anyone would succumb to the desire to do some cleaning at this time of night. It was more likely that an alarm would be raised by the discovery of the body he'd left in his wake, or the absence of the sentry outside the warehouse.

Either way, it was as good a shot as he was going to get.

He prowled the hallway, pressing himself against the walls as he rounded corners. There was little signage, as far as he could tell, though what there was, he could not read anyway. In the end, it was more by luck than design that he stumbled across the observation deck.

The door was open—the first he'd come across like that, and it naturally drew his attention. Once he entered the room, leading with his pistol, he wished he hadn't.

The scene in the room below was carnage.

Nine beds, like the ones he'd slept on back in boot camp all those years before, were squashed into a room which would best fit half that number. Five of the beds were occupied, three by women, two by men—all Asian.

There was blood everywhere, and Trapp was pretty sure that the occupants of at least two of the camp beds were already dead.

Dear Lord.

Trapp wasn't as religious as he had once been. In his line of work, and after the horrific nature of his early childhood, it was sometimes hard for him to see God's hand at work. But in that moment, he offered up a prayer for the souls of the poor individuals in the room below him.

He could not see how those that were still alive could possibly remain that way for long, and judging by the grisly sight in front of him, the two that had already perished must have died in excruciating pain.

Trapp stood, slack-jawed, in front of the polished observation window, almost losing track of time as his brain attempted to process the sight in front of him. It looked like something out of a Nazi death camp—a twisted tribute act to Dr. Mengele's foul experiments.

He almost didn't want to move, in case those poor individuals dying beneath him might look up and think that he was responsible for their pain.

And then he saw something altogether more shocking.

One of the patients moved, uncoiling from her fetal position. Her dark hair fell away from her face, and she looked directly up at the observation deck. Her slate-gray eyes met his gaze. And Trapp's mouth fell open with horror.

It was Ikeda.

45

Ikeda's eyes widened with shock, the scale of which seemed to match Trapp's mounting revulsion. She blinked several times, as though she could not understand how he could possibly be on the other side of that glass, as though she was second-guessing her own sanity.

Trapp pressed his palm against the polished barrier, and in that moment he felt a tenderness that he had rarely experienced before. He knew that he would do whatever it took to free Ikeda from her tormented prison, even if it cost him his life.

He glanced to the left and saw a speaker box against the wall. A feeling of joy danced inside him as he realized that he would be able to talk to this woman who he barely knew—and yet who he had grown to care for so deeply. Trapp started toward it, catching himself at the last moment, his finger hovering over the button, as he saw the stifled shaking of Eliza's head, and the silent dismay in her eyes.

What the hell?

And then he realized. His eyes danced upward, and he saw

the camera dome that decorated the ceiling of Eliza's prison. She had stopped him just in time.

He dropped his hand and Ikeda sagged with relief. She nodded her head forward slightly, as if to say, *thank you.*

He felt sick that she would think of something like that, when she was in there, infected with a deadly, malevolent disease, and he was safe. She had just saved *his* life, and yet she was the one that was grateful.

Trapp grimaced, his mind desperately searching for a way out of this predicament. He had come so far only to find Ikeda, her face cut and bruised—a reminder of the unimaginable suffering she must have been through, in a state that even at his worst, Trapp could not have imagined.

He had been prepared to find her broken body, and had long ago resolved that whatever it took, he would return her home. He had been prepared to find her battered, broken, and clinging to life.

But he hadn't been prepared for this.

A surge of anger plodded through his body, hot rage flushing his cheeks, his fingers curling into white-knuckled fists. Through his childhood, Jason Trapp had seen his father lose control hundreds of times, giving in to the drink and the rage that swelled within his breast, and he had vowed he would never become that man. His entire life, he had forced himself to live within a tight bound of emotional control.

But right then, he wanted to find whoever had put Ikeda into that box and beat him into a bloodied pulp.

Seconds later, Trapp realized that his eyes were closed. He opened them to find Ikeda looking up at him imploringly and bit down on the rage, feeling only shame that she was handling this so well, and he was not. He bowed his head with apology, but—with little more than a flicker of her eyes—she batted it away.

She began to tap against her breastbone, causing Trapp's forehead to wrinkle in a frown.

Light, light, hard, light.

Light, light.

Hard, light.

Hard, light, light.

And then it struck him, a flash of lightning burning away the confusion. Hiding her actions from the camera above, looking like she was simply trembling, Ikeda was signaling to him in Morse code. Trapp kept watching, and she kept tapping, until her message was complete.

And her message was simple: *Find the scientist.*

46

Trapp stormed into Boris Savrasov's office with ice in his veins and fire in his heart. He led with his pistol, opening and closing the door silently behind him.

His respect for Eliza Ikeda had only grown as he'd watched the impressive operative signal the correct directions painstakingly against her breastbone. Even after all she had been through, horrors that Trapp could not even bring himself to imagine, she had remained strong. And not just strong, but prepared.

Even if she could not execute it herself, she had a plan. And it was time to go to work.

Trapp didn't know who the scientist was, or what role he had played in this foul business. But he intended to find out.

The man, it turned out, was chubby and balding, and presently curled up on a narrow cot in the corner of the office. He was asleep.

At least, he was until Trapp pressed the barrel of his pistol against the man's temple and growled in his ear. "Wakey wakey, motherfucker."

It was a corny movie line, but Trapp didn't care. He was in

no mood to be messed around with, and he wanted the man scared to all hell. He placed the full weight of one knee on the scientist's chest, preventing him from rising, from even properly filling his lungs.

The scientist jerked awake, eyes opening and staring directly up at Trapp's own, wide with shock. "Who —?"

Trapp moved the muzzle of his pistol, pushing it into the man's mouth and through his teeth until the barrel was half way down his throat. The scientist gagged, tears stinging his eyes and leaking down his cheeks, a retching sound filling the air.

"I ask the questions," Trapp spat with disgust.

He did not know how the individual beneath him had become involved in the plot that had reached out and ensnared Ikeda in its web. But he knew one thing: anyone with a moral compass skewed enough to stand idly by and watch the things that were happening in that room didn't deserve to be treated with kid gloves. "You speak English?"

By now, that much was evident. But the scientist nodded anyway.

"Good," Trapp said. "If you make a fucking sound, you die. Understood?"

Another nod.

Trapp withdrew the barrel of his pistol from the scientist's mouth and wiped the saliva on his chest. The man trembled with fear as he stared up at the CIA operative's impassive expression. He was right to. In that moment, Trapp did not care whether the scientist lived or died. He was here to get answers, and he had no intention of leaving without them.

Whatever it took.

"What's your name?"

"Boris," the scientist replied, his accented voice trembling as he spoke. "Boris Savrasov."

"Okay, Boris. Why don't you start by telling me the good news?"

"What good news?" Boris ventured, his face knotted with confusion.

"That you have a cure for whatever sick fucking virus you're testing on those poor people."

Boris's eyes flickered closed, and for a second it appeared as though he was communing with a higher power. When he spoke, his voice cracked with fear. "There — there is no cure."

Trapp's heart plummeted fifty stories in an instant. He pictured Ikeda's tired smile as she looked up from inside that bloodied room. How could he face her again, knowing that she was destined to suffer a fate more painful than anyone should have to endure?

He pressed the barrel of the pistol against Savrasov's forehead, ramming the weapon forward until the Russian's head could not move against the cot beneath him. "That's not the answer I was looking for, Boris," he growled. "So why don't you try that again?"

For a second time, tears bloomed in Savrasov's eyes. He sagged back against the bed, the life draining from his eyes. "Please," he whimpered. "Just kill me. I deserve it. Either you do it, or I will."

Trapp's finger tightened on the trigger. Another half ounce of pressure is all it would take for a round to exit the barrel and blow Savrasov's brains out. The man's gray matter would spatter the stained white sheets beneath him, and the sound would warn anyone within hearing range that someone had breached the camp's defenses.

But it would be worth it.

This man had sentenced Ikeda to die.

Shouldn't he meet the same fate?

The two men remained locked in that dark embrace, the silence punctuated only by Savrasov's heavy breathing, and

Trapp's teeth slowly grinding against each other as his frustration grew.

Finally, Trapp relinquished the pressure and staggered backward. He kept the weapon trained on Savrasov, but there was little need—the man was patently broken. He posed no threat. He just lay there, shivering, silent tears streaming down his exhausted face.

"I can't let you die, Boris," Trapp finally croaked. "At least, not yet."

It took all of his self-control to resist the temptation to end the Russian's life right there and then, but Jason Trapp knew that there was more at stake here than just Ikeda's life. Even as he spoke the words, he pictured the bullet tearing through Boris' skull. And yet he knew he would not pull the trigger.

"You've killed her," he stated simply. "And I promise you, you will pay for that crime. But there are other lives on the line here. You can still save them."

Savrasov's reaction was not the one that Trapp expected. He frowned as he spoke. "Killed who?"

Trapp didn't want to humor the man with conversation. When he looked at Savrasov, he saw a murderer. And yet, at the same time, speaking Ikeda's name felt like the right thing to do. Almost as though he was paying homage to one of the best people he had ever met.

"Eliza Ikeda," he growled. "She's still alive. But for how long, Boris?"

Savrasov shook his head violently. "No," he croaked, his tongue tripping over the words in his eagerness to talk. "No—you don't understand."

"Understand *what?*"

"She's immune. The colonel put her in that room to torture her, so that she was forced to listen to those men and women die. He wouldn't give them painkillers, wouldn't let me end their lives in peace, just so that she was forced to hear them scream. He wanted to break her!"

Savrasov's words barely registered in Trapp's mind. He heard them, but the meaning did not compute. "What are you talking about?"

"The virus," Savrasov almost shouted, his expression manic. "It's genetic. It only targets a specific genetic sequence, and the woman you call Ikeda, she is not a carrier. I promise you. She is not susceptible to the strain of Marburg that I created."

Marburg.

Again, Savrasov's words—or at least, one of them—hit Trapp like a sledgehammer. He knew that virus. It was one of the deadliest ever categorized by the Centers for Disease Control. So contagious, so deadly, that very few researchers were even authorized to study it. It was a word that carried so much weight that once uttered, Trapp barely registered the rest of Boris's sentence.

And that was what Ikeda had.

Even now, the virus cells were dwelling in her cells, turning them into breeding grounds, from where they would surge, infecting the rest of her body, liquefying her organs and flooding out of her from every pore, her every blood cell turned into a vector for further transmission. An age old horror, playing out yet again to scar yet another generation.

But finally, Savrasov's meaning became clear.

Trapp almost stumbled with shock. "Not...susceptible," he repeated. "You're saying she'll live?"

Savrasov nodded, a sheen of sweat now visible on his forehead. "Exactly. She's not sick, because she could never *get* sick."

"But..." Trapp trailed off, picturing the charnel house of horrors Ikeda was currently lying in. "If she's not the target, then who is?"

And at that moment, it became patently, horrifyingly clear.

America's citizens were not the objective for the North Korean bioweapon. China's were.

"Why?" Trapp mouthed, stunned by the potential consequences of the virus getting loose. "It could kill millions..."

"Hundreds of millions," Savrasov moaned. "More. It could wipe out the entire country. You need to stop it!"

Trapp thought fast. He didn't yet see how all the pieces fit together. What game were the North Koreans playing? Why wipe out America's satellites, blinding her, then release a weapon of mass murder into China's cities, towns, schools and homes?

And then it hit him. The North Koreans weren't trying to humble either America *or* China, at least not directly. Their goal was to pit the two superpowers against one another, to weaken and exhaust the two countries, like two heavyweights in a ring.

And the plan was horrifyingly close to working already. If this virus was released, it would be the final straw.

"Boris," he growled, wanting to reel from the shock of his discovery, but not allowing himself the time, "tell me what was in those canisters. Where are they going?"

Boris' eyes flickered, not daring to meet Trapp's own gaze. He bore a heavy weight of shame, but Trapp didn't have time to humor the man.

Trapp laced his tone with warning. "Boris..."

"The virus. I aerosolized it. The canisters are the delivery mechanism. They're taking them across the border, but I don't know the target."

Aerosolized.

"Fuck," Trapp growled.

He was torn between two competing motives: first, to save Ikeda from that hellhole. But he knew there was more at stake here than just one life, even one he had come to care for so deeply.

So he chose the second option.

He pulled the satellite phone from his pocket, powered it on, and held down the call button. It defaulted to the last number dialled. Mitchell didn't hesitate before answering.

"Hangman," he said urgently, pre-empting Trapp's own revelation, "we've got a problem, and you're smack dab in the fucking middle of it."

"You can say that again," Trapp replied, the strain of his newfound discovery evident in his tone. "Tell me you know where those canisters are, Mike?"

"Not yet, but—"

Trapp filled Langley in on his suspicion that everything that had happened over the past week was simply a shell game designed to bring America and China to the brink of war, entangle them in a death lock—and then shove them over the precipice.

Only to find that Mitchell was way ahead of him. "So Greaves was right," he groaned. "Shit."

"You knew?"

"It was just a theory. Not anymore."

"We have to inform the Chinese, Mike. They can't let this crap across the border. We're not responsible for this cluster-fuck, but no one's gonna believe that. They'll see a billion dying Chinese and point the finger directly at us."

"I know it," Mitchell said softly.

The phone went quiet for a few seconds.

"Find me those canisters, Mike. I'm on the ground. If I can, I'll stop this without the whole world finding out. But I don't have long."

"Got it," Mitchell replied quickly, not second-guessing his operative. That was what Trapp liked about the man. He knew that there were some operations that simply could not be quarterbacked from Washington. This was one of them.

"And Mike?"

"Yeah?"

"Get a team to my location. *Stat*. Full protective gear. I found Ikeda, but she's been exposed, so I can't extract her without releasing this thing. In about no fucking time at all, the locals are going to wake up and find out I've disturbed the whole nest of hornets. I need backup by then. We need to take this position, sweep it for intel, and hold it till we can figure out how to extract her."

Trapp listened as Mitchell covered the mouthpiece and barked a command in the background. A second later, the director's voice crackled down the line.

"We're way ahead of you, Hangman. I've already got a team holding just off the coast, Lieutenant Quinn's SEALs supported by a company of Marines from the USS America."

"Damn," Trapp muttered, impressed. "You don't do things by half."

"They were gassed up in case we found the control terminal. And we just did. It's right on top of you. I'm sending you an image of the building now."

"ETA?" Trapp asked urgently, the stress of the situation dissipating only momentarily with the news that help was on its way.

The lightness of Mitchell's tone was evidence that—for once in this whole sorry mess—his news was going to be good. "Oh, about twenty minutes."

Trapp pumped his fist. "Good job. I'll hold the fort till then. Oh—and one last thing..."

"Yeah?"

"You reckon you can speak to President Nash and get him to hold off on World War III until I get a chance to fix this little snafu?"

"I'll see what I can do."

47

President Charles Nash watched the display on the wall of the situation room in a state of numbed exhaustion. He had long ago forgotten what most of the icons indicated. Aircraft carriers, frigates, destroyers and submarines.

It was like a video game, a young boy's dream—and his waking nightmare: a game of battleships, except one wrong move would bathe the world in flames.

Harried fragments of conversation drifted over his head. They were all operating on too much coffee and too little sleep. It was no way to run a bagel shop, let alone a country. But what other option was there?

"— the Nimitz strike group will be on station in six hours —"

Nash wondered why the hell he had ever wanted to become President in the first place. He'd only been in the job for six months, and already the gray hairs were multiplying on his head like weeds. He had survived—literally—the Bloody Monday crisis by the skin of his teeth. And now it was happening again. Except this time, the target wasn't just him, or even the entire US government, but the American way of life itself.

He idly wondered whether he would run again. And then a chilling thought struck him. If he handled this crisis wrong, would there even be a presidency left to run for? Or would America simply be a charred wasteland? He might emerge from the White House bunker only to be president of the cockroaches.

"Sir, I've got Adm. Nielsen on the line," a uniformed aide said, snapping Nash back to the present. "It's audio only, sir. Shall I put him on?"

It took the President a second to place the man's name.

Nielsen. Head of the Pacific Command. They'd met at a drinks reception several months earlier. Big guy, barrel chest. Booming laugh.

Nash nodded, though he felt like a giant hand had reached out and was even now squeezing his stomach in its grasp until it was no larger than an acorn. What he had come to realize was that when an admiral came calling, they were never bearing good news.

"Mr. President?"

"I'm right here, Bill," Nash said, remembering the man's first name and projecting an air of confidence that he certainly did not feel. "How are things going over there?"

"It's ninety above and sunny here on Pearl Harbor, Mr. President. But that's not why I'm calling."

"I thought not. What's the fire?"

"Sir, a drone operated from the USS Nimitz sighted a Chinese carrier strike group approximately two hours ago. We have since confirmed the fleet's vector, and it confirmed that it is on a direct intercept course with the Nimitz."

"Where's the carrier group now, Admiral?" Nash asked, his voice audibly strained. He looked up at the wall mounted display, a map of the Chinese coast and the broader region, and watched as a new set of icons blinked into existence—red, against US navy blue.

A Chinese fleet.

"About five hundred nautical miles off the coast of China, Mr. President. On your orders, we pulled both our strike groups back out of range of the majority of China's shore missile batteries."

"What are their intentions, Bill—do you know?"

Nielsen paused before replying, and in the background, over the speaker, Nash could hear frantic activity. "That's unclear, sir. But my staff is concerned that they are setting a trap."

"Explain, Admiral," Nash said, a chill creeping down the back of his neck that had nothing to do with the air conditioning.

"We've detected signs that Chinese submarines are operating in the waters to the south of the Nimitz' current position. If they sail north, they put themselves at risk of shore bombardment. If they hold position, then the Chinese fleet itself will be within effective striking range inside of twelve hours."

"Give it to me straight, Admiral Nielsen. What is your recommendation?"

Nielsen allowed a silence to brew for several seconds before replying. "Speaking plainly, sir, we're out of good ones. You know as well as I do that if the Nimitz is attacked, that is as good as a declaration of war. And right now, the Chinese have the upper hand. We are surging additional units into the region, but it's going to take time."

Nash bit the inside of his lip, holding on to the wave of pain the action generated. It helped him to clarify his thinking, pushing aside the unimportant, extraneous information and allowing him to focus on what mattered. He knew one thing with absolute, striking clarity. The American people had not elected him to, like Neville Chamberlain on the brink of the second world war, stumble into a global conflagration by accident.

He knew his countrymen well—as well as any leader could. Fresh-faced country boys and hard-nosed urban folk alike, they would both line up in droves at the recruiting stations the second war broke out. He could picture it now. Excitement coupled with anxiety on a million lips. Tears in mothers' eyes, and suppressed pride on fathers' faces.

As one, they would march to their deaths in a war that simply could not be won; an endless stalemate thousands of miles from home. Nash knew that it was his duty to do whatever he could to stop that from happening. If he failed, at least he would meet his maker knowing that he had given his all.

The President clicked his fingers, attracting his chief of staff's attention. She leaned toward him and he spoke in hushed tones, for her benefit alone. "Emma—get Ambassador Lam in my office as soon as possible."

Martinez nodded silently and disappeared out of the situation room, clutching an encrypted cell phone to her ear.

"Admiral Nielsen, your orders are to pull the Nimitz back as quickly as possible without exposing the carrier or her escorts to needless harm. Buy me as much time as you can to make one last push on the diplomatic front."

"Understood, Mr. President." Then came a pause. "I have to warn you, sir, that if those Chinese subs are lying in wait, we may not get a warning before we lose a ship, or worse."

Nash frowned, his forehead creasing and eyes closing as a wave of exhaustion washed over him. He pictured the Nimitz sinking beneath the waves of the South China Sea, thousands of sailors trapped inside her steel hull as it plummeted toward the bottom of the ocean. And then he stiffened his resolve. "Your concern is noted, Admiral. It's the only way. Please advise me the second the situation changes."

"Yes sir." The line clicked dead.

As Nash leaned back, aware of a dozen pairs of eyes focused on his own, Martinez re-entered the room. She leaned close to him.

"Sir, the Chinese won't put me through to the ambassador. They're loading up at Dulles Airport. Their ride out of the country is scheduled to leave inside the hour."

Nash grimaced. He hadn't truly expected this one to come easy—so little did—but just once, he wished it would. He made his decision. It wasn't a good look for the American President to go begging at the airport like a jilted lover, but he would do it in the name of preventing a nuclear holocaust.

"If the mountain won't come to Mohammed..." he muttered quietly. "I guess we better get going. Inform the tower at Dulles that they are not to clear the ambassador's plane for departure until I arrive. Understood?"

Martinez nodded, quickly hiding the doubts that shone in her eyes. But not before Nash noticed them. He did not mind. He didn't see how a Hail Mary play could work either. But it was all he had.

"I'm on it, sir. When do you want to leave?"

Nash rose to his feet, followed quickly by the rest of the room. "Yesterday."

48

Deputy Director Mike Mitchell drove as though he had the metaphorical flames of hell chasing him, and knowing that if he failed, their very real counterparts would soon follow.

He entered the fenced compound that surrounded Washington DC's Dulles Airport chasing the blue and red lights of a hastily commandeered cop car that ordinarily sat outside Langley's main guard post. Mitchell drummed his fingers anxiously against the steering wheel gripped in the white knuckled fingers of his opposite hand.

In a matter of minutes, he saw one of two People's Liberation Army Air Force Y-20 transport aircraft appear on the runway ahead of him, surrounded by frantic activity, the colossal dark gray planes decorated with a red and gold starred insignia.

Closing from the opposite side, he saw President Nash's convoy, a mix of unmarked black Suburbans, heavily armored limousines and police cars complete with flashing lights. He breathed a sigh of relief. He'd made it to the President before his impromptu meeting with the Chinese ambassador.

To get this close, he'd been forced to contact the head of the President's Secret Service detail himself and assure the man that the information in his possession was vital not just for national security, but the preservation of the very planet itself. Even that almost hadn't been enough to grant him access. The Secret Service was operating on a hair trigger right now, seeing threats around every corner.

Mitchell followed his escort vehicle in completing a wide semicircle around the two Chinese transport planes, followed the whole way by watchful diplomatic security personnel. The CIA official didn't notice any visible weaponry, but he knew that it wouldn't be far away. He pulled to a stop, watching as President Nash walked toward the Chinese ambassador, hand outstretched.

Mitchell grabbed his case, flew out of his car and rushed toward the two men. The President's detail knew he was coming, but still frisked him, just to be sure.

The CIA executive breathed a sigh of relief as the firm but efficient agent cleared him. He'd made it, and in the nick of time.

"Mr. President," Mitchell said, shooting his boss a meaningful look. "Might I have a word?"

"Can it wait, Mike?" Nash replied, flashing Mitchell a withering look of irritation.

"No, sir. It can't."

Nash sighed, scratched the side of his cheek, and then turned to the Chinese ambassador. "Ambassador Lam," he said. "My apologies. Let me deal with this first, and then we can talk."

Lam, a short man with graying hair whom Mitchell had never met, nodded tightly. "As you wish, Mr. President. However, I cannot delay my departure too long. My orders from Beijing are clear, you understand."

Nash bowed his head. "I do."

Then he flicked two fingers toward Mitchell. "Mike, over here."

Mitchell followed the president dutifully, wondering how exactly he was supposed to pitch the intelligence he had just acquired. Before he had a chance to arrive at a conclusion, Nash stopped dead, about twenty feet from Lam, and spun on his heel.

"Deputy Director," Nash growled acidly. "This had better be good. I'm not sure if you're aware, but this country is two skips and a jump away from nuclear war—and this might be my last opportunity to stop that from happening."

Mitchell briefly reflected that it was never good to be referred to by one's title, as opposed to their name. It indicated Nash's mood, which was far from genial.

"I do, sir," he replied soothingly. "And that's why I'm here. I have an asset at the location at which we have identified the control unit for the Chinese anti-satellite system."

Nash's attention snapped quickly on to his subordinate, irritation at least momentarily forgotten. He glanced around quickly, checking that his Secret Service detail was far enough away for the two men not to be overheard. "Hangman?"

Mitchell nodded tightly. "Yes sir. And that's not all."

Nash grinned, a wave of relief rolling across his face like clouds scuttling across a windy sky. He clapped one hand on Mitchell's shoulder. "Good man." Then his visage darkened. "You said there was more? Good news or bad?"

Mitchell winced. "Bad. Very bad."

"Fill me in."

The deputy director did as instructed. He informed the President that at that very moment, a quick reaction force composed of Navy SEALs and US Marines was somewhere low over North Korea, about to assault a military installation above the 39th parallel for the first time since the end of the Korean War.

And, even as Nash was processing that momentous revelation—one which under any other circumstances would have required a congressional investigation at the very least, Mitchell filled the President in on the far more chilling news of the discovery of weaponized, genetically-targeted Marburg.

When he was done, Nash stood silently for more than a minute, his eyes closed, head tipped slightly back.

"Mike, come with me."

"What's the plan, Mr. President?" Mitchell replied, just about keeping pace with the much taller man.

He glanced nervously at the Chinese ambassador, who was standing with his hands in his pockets, studiously inspecting the asphalt runway. He had a feeling that Nash was about to share some highly confidential information with a man who was not just a foreign national, but a diplomatic representative of America's foremost competitor. And, more to the point, a country with which America might well soon be at war.

As they reached Ambassador Lam's earshot, Nash smiled confidently. "Mike, the plan is that you are going to tell the ambassador what you just told me."

Mitchell cleared his throat anxiously and forgot his manners entirely. "Say again?"

Nash fixed him with a stern glare. "Everything, Mike. Don't hold back."

He took a second to compose himself, and then bowed deferentially to the Chinese ambassador, a man of about his height, who was now glancing quizzically between his two American counterparts. "Mr. Ambassador, I am —"

"Deputy Director Michael Mitchell, of the Central Intelligence Agency's famed Special Activities Division. I know who you are."

Mitchell was a little taken aback by Lam's demonstration. He recognized it for what it was: a warning that the ambassador was a man who did not like to be messed with. He took the message on board. It reminded him of why he hated politics.

"Yes, sir," he said, acting unruffled. "Mr. Ambassador, I will be blunt, because we don't have much time."

Lam gestured at him to continue.

"Sir, the Agency has reason to believe that a genetically targeted biological weapon is at this moment in or near your borders."

Lam's eyes narrowed sharply. "What is this—another threat?"

Mitchell shook his head and looked to the President for a lead. Nash motioned for him to continue. The deputy director grimaced. The President knew the stakes as well as anyone, and had apparently given Mitchell his full confidence. Mike only wished he felt the same way.

"No sir," he continued, fishing his agency-issued cell phone from his pocket, and bringing up an image. "A warning. We have reason to believe that the events of the last few days were orchestrated by this man—a North Korean colonel now running a group known as Unit 61."

Mitchell studied Kim's reaction closely. For years, in the field, that skill had saved his life on more occasions than he could count. Now, though, hundreds of millions of lives hung in the balance. He watched as Lam's pupils flared, as a muscle on his left temple twitched. Was it a tell—a sign of recognition?

Or, with so much on the line, was he describing meaning to something that deserved none? It was impossible to say.

"Do you recognize him, Mr. Ambassador?"

Lam did not immediately reply. When he did, his tone was guarded. "I've heard of the unit, but not the man."

"We think his goal is to engineer a conflict between our two countries."

Lam frowned. "For what purpose?"

Mitchell grimaced. "That, unfortunately, I cannot answer. It is no secret that tensions in our relationship with the DPRK are running high. But why they would involve you in the matter, we do not know."

Again, Lam held his response, as though buying himself thinking time. Mitchell knew better than to cut in. He had showed his cards. Now it was time for the ambassador to do the same.

Or not.

"North Korea is not my brief, you understand," Lam began. "But I read the diplomatic cables. I like to stay abreast of what is happening so close to home."

Mitchell glanced at Nash, then nodded, not wanting to interrupt. The President was clearly nervous, his expression strained, yet he did the same.

"Over the past eighteen months, we have seen signs of a struggle for power within the regime. Executions of high-ranking officials. Troop movements. Increased security at the Chairman's residences. And whilst it is by no means certain, I have seen intelligence that this Unit 61 is behind these moves against Chairman Song."

"So you believe us?" Nash interjected.

The Chinese ambassador smoothed his suit jacket formally, and directed his attention at the president. "President Nash. *Charles.* We have known each other for a long time, as you say. But you will understand that I cannot present these accusations to the Politburo without proof. It would do more harm than good."

Mitchell bit the inside of his lip. He wished he could consult with the President about what he was thinking of doing, but knew the situation was too delicate. He knew that for the Chinese leadership, losing face was akin to announcing one's weakness. And announcing weakness—especially in the face of the Americans—was impossible.

"Ambassador Lam," he said. "We know what happened in Xichang."

Nash shot his subordinate a furious look, but Mitchell barreled on regardless. "We know that China had nothing to do with taking down our satellites. We also know that you lost control of a weapon codenamed Project Songbird. Mr. Ambassador, you need to come clean. *China* needs to come clean, and we're running out of time. If you do not, then our two countries will end up at war, and millions of deaths will rest on your conscience —"

"Michael," Nash growled. "Enough!"

Mitchell's mouth opened and closed several times silently, like a captive fish, before he clamped his jaw shut.

"Ambassador Lam," the President muttered, his cheeks crimson with embarrassment. "I apologize."

The Chinese ambassador did not respond, his head bowed, lost in thought. When he spoke, his voice was quiet. "I will see what I can do. But I make no promises. I will need evidence to present to my superiors. And a show of good faith."

"We'll get it to you," Nash said, relief washing over his face, chased closely by tendrils of hope. "Whatever you need."

Mitchell gambled again, his quick mind as always half a dozen moves ahead of everyone else. He figured that he was happy for Nash to fire him, if it meant preventing a world war. "Mr. Ambassador. If you can, close the border with North Korea. We are working on tracing the delivery mechanism, but I don't know if we'll get there in time."

Lam dipped his head. "I will do what I can."

He glanced over his shoulder, where a gaggle of Chinese diplomats and security personnel had gathered, milling anxiously near the transport planes, whose engines had begun to whine ominously. "But for now, my orders are clear. I must return to Beijing."

Nash cut in. "I understand. Do what you can, Ambassador."

"I will."

Nash and Mitchell watched in silence, flanked by the president's Secret Service guards, as the Chinese finished loading up the two Y-20 transport aircraft. It wasn't long before the high-pitched whine of the idling jet engines turned into a roar, and the two planes, ushered through Dulles' ordinary air tower congestion, leapt into the sky.

As the two aircraft disappeared into the steel sky, Nash finally spoke—without turning to face his counterpart. "I hope you know what you're doing, Mike."

Mitchell winced. The President's tone wasn't accusatory, but neutral—and yet he knew he had overstepped his bounds. His job was to advise, not to direct America's foreign policy. And yet he had seen no other choice.

"Yes sir," he muttered. "Me too."

Nash turned to leave, signaling his detail, who closed in around him. He looked exhausted, shoulders slumped, the weight of the world pressing them down.

"Mr. President —" Mitchell ventured. "There's one last thing."

"There always is," Nash sighed.

Figuring that was about as good as an opportunity as he was going to get, Mitchell continued, after glancing at his wristwatch. "We are about to hit Unit 61's camp. Any moment now. But our boys are going to be mightily outnumbered, and I've got an operative down there who's been through hell—and more to the point, exposed to this virus. I want to buy them time."

Nash's reply was succinct. "How?"

"Air support."

The President's eyebrow kinked. "Deputy Director Mitchell —are you asking me to authorize the invasion of North Korea?"

49

Jason Trapp turned back to the Russian scientist, Boris Savrasov. In truth, he was fuming—both at what the Russian had told him and from the evidence he had seen in front of his own eyes. The sight of Eliza Ikeda, behind glass, imprisoned with the dead and dying.

"I have some friends on their way, Boris," he growled. "So the decisions you make in the next few seconds will guide how they are disposed to treat you. Do you understand?"

Savrasov nodded slavishly, his eyes wide with fear and red with tears.

"Good," Trapp grunted. "Because the alternative is me putting two pieces of lead in the back of your skull."

"I will help you," Savrasov whined. "I promise. I didn't know what they were going to make me do. I —"

"*I* don't care," Trapp replied, a mocking scowl tearing his face. "You sold your country out, Boris. But worse, you sold out your fellow man. You knew exactly what this virus could be used for. You just didn't care."

Savrasov's head slumped against his chest. He knew better

than to argue with Trapp's righteous fury. Or perhaps he'd just given up.

"The cameras. Are they monitored?" Trapp said. "The ones in the laboratory ward."

"In the control room? Only by my assistants. The colonel detailed one of his men to stand watch, but he left earlier this evening and no one replaced him."

"Good. Then Boris, I have a task for you."

"What?"

Trapp tapped the North Korean Type 58 rifle by his side meaningfully. "I need you to take this to a friend."

JASON WISHED that he could do more for Ikeda at that moment, as he passed the supply closet in which he had stashed the two captured soldiers and exited the warehouse. He was torn. A large part of him wanted to turn back, to stay by her side until help arrived.

But he knew that he could not.

And moreover, he knew that Ikeda would not *want* him to babysit her like a helpless damsel in distress. She was a tough cookie, there was no doubt about that. And once Boris smuggled in the assault rifle, she would be well-equipped to resist any attempt to surprise her—at least until help arrived.

Right now, though, as Trapp crossed the empty, dark courtyard between the warehouse and the administrative buildings there was another task that deserved his attention. He had a rough approximation of the location of the Project Songbird control terminal, and before he left the Russian scientist he'd grilled him for every piece of information he could remember about the North Korean base.

It wasn't a lot. Savrasov had been confined to the laboratory facility for most of his stay. But what little he knew, he told.

And so Jason Trapp strode through the darkness with fire in his blood. The signal emitted by the control unit lined up with Colonel Kim's headquarters building. The CIA operative suspected that a man with the delusions of grandeur that the North Korean displayed would want to keep the device by him at all times.

The unit itself, according to Lockheed scientists quizzed back at Langley, was probably only the size of a small suitcase. It would have its own power supply, encrypted communications link, and worst of all, a dead man's switch. If it was destroyed while the weapons it had deployed were active, then the munitions in the sky would attempt to re-establish communication three times.

Upon failing the third interrogation, they would detonate.

Taking every last one of America's eyes in the skies with them.

Trapp knew that this outcome could not be allowed to happen. And since preventing it most likely meant coming into contact with the man behind imprisoning and torturing Eliza Ikeda, it was a task he was more than happy to undertake. He grinned as he pictured beating the man into a bloody pulp with nothing more than his fists.

Merry Christmas, jackass.

The colonel's office building was a squat concrete block, distinguished only from a dozen identical units by a number stenciled on its side. Trapp mentally cross-checked the identification with the directions Savrasov had provided him with.

Jackpot.

Trapp quickly cased the building. It consisted of only two stories, and all of the windows on the first floor were shuttered. There was another exit at the rear. He grimaced. The tactical layout was far from ideal. He had no idea how many enemies might be inside, how they were armed, or where they might be situated.

He contemplated waiting until the cavalry arrived, but quickly discounted the option. With luck, the North Koreans would assume that the helicopters belonged to them, at least for a few critical seconds as the SEALs descended, rifle barrels spitting fire.

But he quickly decided that it was a risk he could not take. It would be the work of seconds to trigger the munitions that were attached to America's satellites, rendering her immediately blind, deaf and dumb, and potentially triggering the outbreak of a third world war.

Not an option.

That only left one move: to go in fast, hard, and quiet—and to take no prisoners. In truth, that was the way Jason Trapp liked it best. He devised a simple plan: enter the building, neutralize any enemy combatants inside, and protect the control unit from all assailants until backup arrived.

It wasn't exactly a strategic masterpiece. Especially since the second he fired his pistol, the locals would wake up, and boy would they be pissed.

Trapp crouched in front of the main entrance, pistol drawn, and his knife clenched in his left hand. In the darkness, he hoped, the outline of his helmet, combined with the cut of his uniform, would make him indistinguishable from the locals.

It might buy him the seconds he needed.

Trapp tested the door knob. It turned, creakily protesting its lack of maintenance. He sent up a prayer, not to protect his life, but to the god of getting the job done.

And then he charged through the door.

50

Colonel Kim slept with a woman in his bed and a gun by his head.

He didn't screw the girl, he was not that crude. She was there for the same reason as the weapon. To calm his fevered dreams. They were always the same. Full of death and pain and violence. Memories of his own childhood, and dreams containing the anguished faces of those he had stolen.

The room was dark but his sleep was light. The second he heard the squeal of the door, he shot upright, knocking the girl who slumbered anxiously on his chest aside. In an instant, the pistol was in his hand, and he was crouching by the side of his bed, tasting the air for danger.

The girl moaned, and his hand shot out, covering her mouth. He could barely see her in the darkness, but he radiated threat by sheer force of will. Before long, he withdrew his covering palm, but the bitch remained silent, as he knew she would. Everyone on this base knew the consequences of disobeying their commander.

Inside that fence, his word was law. He was their god, for it was he who gave the gift of life and death.

Kim's head was at first foggy with sleep. But the surge of adrenaline now running through his veins instantly cleared his mind.

Someone had entered his sanctum. That much was immediately clear. There were only two culprits, and he quickly discounted the first, for none of his underlings would dare wake him unless the fires of a revived Mount Paektu were at that very moment swallowing the base whole.

Since Kim could not hear the groan of the earth cracking open, nor the spitting of lava, he knew that somehow an intruder had dared to test him.

An invader.

Kim crept naked and barefoot through the darkness. He analyzed his tactical position. There was only one explanation for the presence of a trespasser in this building. Someone, likely either the Chinese or the Americans, had discovered the location of the control unit and had sent a team to secure and destroy it. He dismissed a third option instantly—that Chairman Song, the weak, fat Supreme Leader of the Democratic People's Republic of Korea, had discovered his plan and had sent a loyalist to eliminate him.

There were no loyalists. Not in North Korea. Not anymore. One by one, Colonel Kim had rolled them up. Offered them the carrot and shown them the stick.

Kim grinned, his yellowed teeth flashing in the darkness, more resembling a snarl than a smile. He knew what the man on the other side of that door did not—could not—know. A Korean might have learned that the colonel slept where he worked.

But not the Chinese. And certainly not the hated Americans. They had no sources beyond the demilitarized zone. And with their satellites destroyed, they were blind.

Which meant that he had the advantage. His opponent could not possibly know he was there. The door that led to

Kim's sleeping quarters was nondescript, resembling the entrance to a supply closet more than a bedroom, nothing that would raise the slightest suspicion. He'd left nothing to chance. And Kim had one last card up his sleeve: a trap door, specially built, that led to a tunnel whose exit lay beyond the camp's outer fence. He'd constructed it in secret, and had every prisoner who worked on it both isolated during construction, then executed immediately after completion.

But the colonel left that option in reserve. He had the upper hand—and, more importantly, the control unit lay in the office, not his sleeping quarters. Besides, a vicious rage was burning inside him now. Someone had dared to test his power. Someone had dared think him *weak*.

Someone had dared to disrupt plans that were years in the making.

And now that someone would pay.

Kim crept forward at an angle, pistol leveled at the door, but his body shielded from any projectiles that might be fired through its frame. He froze, listening for every hint of movement, picturing the office that lay on the other side of the door, and attempting to locate his opponent within its layout.

A tiny scrape sealed the man's fate. An adversary less practiced in the dark arts of death than Kim would not have heard it, let alone instantly formed a targeting solution in his mind. The colonel stopped dead, and for a second time a snarl stretched across his scarred face.

The intruder was on the other side of the door.

Kim leveled his pistol and fired three times. The shots ripped through the door. As the echoing roar of the weapon died away, he heard a grunt, then a thud. A vicious wave of satisfaction flared in his mind, almost orgasmic in its intensity.

The intruder was a dead man.

51

T rapp threw himself backward, acting on pure instinct. His conscious brain never processed the inputs that saved his life: the whisper of sound as the North Korean threw back his bed covers, the racking of the pistol's slide.

But his subconscious did.

The experienced CIA operative knew better than to doubt his instincts. He did not this time, as chunks of wood blew free from the door, splinters missing his torso by mere inches.

Trapp's life did not flash before his eyes. He did not vomit from fear, or freeze in the face of onrushing danger. But as he pressed his back against the wall, forcing his chest to stop heaving, and regaining mastery over the adrenaline-induced tremors in his fingers, he knew instantly that he was in for a fight.

Worse still, the pistol's report had put paid to any notion that he could carry out this operation with stealth on his side. If the North Koreans had assigned even a halfway competent watch, then it wouldn't be long before the camp was swarming with pissed-off soldiers.

He was in for a whole world of hell. His only option was to hold them off for long enough for Lieutenant Quinn to rain down fire on his assailants. It would be like the Alamo, except with only one of him, and the bad guys equipped with automatic weapons.

Trapp took stock of his position. Barely half a dozen seconds had passed since the two gunshots had ripped through the wooden door. Judging by the sound the weapon had made, it was a 9 mm pistol. Plenty powerful enough to rip through blood, flesh, even timber—but the half foot of concrete protecting Trapp's back would be impenetrable.

As long as his opponent wasn't packing anything heavier...

Trapp heard a woman's murmur, then a harsh retort. The woman's voice cut off immediately.

Colonel Kim, he thought. It had to be.

The man who had caused so much torment was on the other side of the wall that separated the office space from what Trapp now realized were sleeping quarters. It was an oversight that had almost killed the CIA operative. He should have known that the man would have stayed close to his prize.

The question was, was the control unit on his side of the wall, or Trapp's?

Trapp had barely completed an initial scan of the darkened office before the shooting started. He was looking for threats, not computers. But he knew he had to make a decision, and fast. If the North Korean colonel had access to the control unit, then Trapp only had a matter of seconds to spare.

In a situation like this, it was use it or lose it—and that was what Trapp feared.

He rose smoothly to his feet and began backing silently away from the doorway, closing the angle so that any further shots fired through the door could not hit him. As he did, his eyes scanned the room for any sign of the control unit.

Shapes began to emerge in the gloom around him, and

Trapp dismissed them one after another, keeping enough of his attention focused on the movements of his opponent to ensure that he would not be surprised. He kept his weapon trained on the closed doorway, finger stroking the trigger, ready to fire with only the briefest half second's notice.

The North Korean was making noise now. His movements might not have been audible to an amateur, but to Trapp they were as clear as day. Perhaps he thought that Trapp himself was dead. Perhaps he simply didn't care either way—believing himself to be invincible. It fit the profile. Childhood trauma— as the CIA operative knew well—can change a man. Molding him for good, or evil.

In Trapp's case, it was both.

But having seen the prison camp attached to the North Korean base, and the callous disregard for human life evidenced by the dying Chinese test subjects, there wasn't much debate about which path Kim had taken.

A voice called out. The accent was unmistakable. The tone cold, harsh, mocking. "Did I hurt you, American?"

Trapp did not respond. There was no sense in being dragged into a slanging match—unless he stood to gain something from it. At that present moment, he did not. Speaking up would only give away his position, giving his opponent vital information.

Kim tried again. "Lay down your weapon. We can—how do your people say it?—talk this out."

Trapp's eyes never stopped roving. One after another, he discounted items that might be found in any office across the globe. Computers, filing closets, staplers, even a *typewriter*.

And then Trapp saw it. A squat case, a bit like a large ammunition box. It was split open by hinges, and connected by a thin wire to a closed laptop. A second wire emanated from the box, this one running to the nearest window and out. Trapp suspected it led to a satellite dish on the roof of the office building.

Relief flooded through him like the breaking of a dam, unblocking at least a fraction of the tension that had ridden with him all this way. The control unit was on his side of the wall, and that put Trapp in the driver's seat. Possession was nine tenths of the law, and if the North Korean wanted to wrestle back control of the device, he was going to have to come get it.

And that meant exposing himself.

"I don't think so," Trapp growled, breaking his self-imposed silence. "I'm fine right here."

He knew that he had to keep Kim talking. He quickly glanced at his watch. The ETA of the cavalry was under five minutes—but that was a best case scenario. The naval helicopters would have to fly low, across unfamiliar, poorly mapped terrain, in order to avoid North Korean air defenses.

It was five minutes if he got lucky. And given the events of the last week, he wasn't counting on lady luck being on his side.

"So you *are* American," Kim replied, a note of triumph in his voice. "I thought so."

Trapp heard movement outside—the thud of boots against concrete, muffled cries, confusion, barked orders. Moving silently, he checked that the window shutters were bolted tight shut and locked the main entrance, dragging a desk in front of it to provide extra reinforcement. Throughout, he kept low, with his weapon trained unerringly on the offending doorway, knowing that any moment his enemy might seize on his distraction to strike.

"You can't win, you know," Kim said, almost conversationally. "My men will wear you down eventually."

Trapp knew that much was certainly true. But what Kim didn't know—couldn't possibly know—was that Lieutenant Quinn, his Navy SEALs, and the best part of a company of pissed-off leathernecks would shortly surge from the skies and rain down lead on anyone who stood in their way.

He didn't have to last forever. Only until help arrived. It was a waiting game, all right. Only to Kim's eventual surprise, the odds were stacked firmly in Trapp's favor.

As a droplet of sweat trailed down his forehead, then tickled the bridge of his nose, Trapp readjusted his aim. His mouth was dry, muscles exhausted from the efforts of the past few days. From fighting in Macau, from diving into the depths of the South China Sea with the Cheyenne, from crawling through mud and rock in the North Korean mountains to get to this very point.

His thoughts drifted to Ikeda, to that filthy, cramped laboratory. A pang of regret gnawed at his stomach. He had left her alone and surrounded by reminders of a fate she did not yet know wasn't to be hers. And yet he wrestled himself back from the brink. A single mantra echoed in Trapp's mind.

Keep him talking.

"What's your endgame, asshole?" Trapp growled, crouching low and shielding his body behind a thick metal desk. "You're picking a fight with the two biggest countries on earth. This can't possibly end well for you."

Outside, the maelstrom only grew in intensity. Floodlights clicked on, and thin shafts of light broke free of the shutters. Truck engines coughed and growled, and the shouts grew closer. Trapp's heartrate redoubled its intensity and sweat winked into existence on his palms. He shifted the pistol into his left, then wiped the right dry before switching back.

Trapp licked his desert-like lips. He hoped he was right about this. He glanced anxiously at the control unit, knowing that one stray bullet could send the whole world up in flames. The device was no doubt set up like a dead man's switch. If it was put out of action in the midst of a battle, then pre-positioned munitions on dozens of satellites circling the globe would detonate at the same time.

And catastrophe would ensue.

"That's where you're wrong," Kim replied confidently, his voice muffled by the door—yet sounding closer than it had before. "It matters not whether we win, only that *you* lose."

Jason attempted to fix the North Korean's position, but gave up. It was impossible. Two well aimed bullets could scythe through the wood and cut the colonel down. He could stop a war.

Or start one.

If he fired his weapon, the soldiers now circling the office building outside could easily open up with everything they had. The walls were thick, but they could only withstand so much. Trapp realized that if he was going to take Kim down, he needed to do it without firing a shot. The integrity of the control unit was paramount.

"Come in here," he yelled. "We can settle this like men."

It was a corny line, but then again Trapp didn't believe that Kim would go for the invitation. It was just another delaying tactic.

"Don't take me for a fool," Kim replied, voice dripping with cold derision. "I know better than to trust an American. Your country has had its boot on the neck of mine for generations. In a week, you will be dead, and that boot will be gone—China will do the dirty work for us."

Trapp's ghostly eyes flared with understanding as the final chess piece fell into place. Kim wanted to provoke the Chinese into doing what his own country could not: clear the DMZ of American troops and leave the road to Seoul clear.

Astonishingly, he was willing to plunge the world into nuclear war to achieve his goal. It was scarcely comprehensible.

Outside, a voice called out.

It sounded like it was being amplified through a megaphone—compressed, metallic and impossibly loud. It was in
Korean, and Trapp did not understand a word. He threw an
anxious glance at the doorway, checking for movement. But
there was none.

"Can you understand him?" Kim called out.

"No."

The North Korean chuckled. "I thought not. Korean is a
beautiful language, don't you think?"

Trapp fought the temptation to roll his eyes, not that Kim
could see. They were in the midst of a standoff as deadly as any
from the old Wild West, and this sociopath wanted to talk
semantics?

"I couldn't say."

"Strange, isn't it?" Kim replied. "That you cannot understand my people, when your colleague does so well..."

Hot rage bubbled in Trapp's gut as he processed Kim's
words like lava spewing from a tectonic volcano. He saw Ikeda
then, as she'd appeared before she recognized his face. Marked
with bruises, and the blood of the dying around her. Tortured
like no one—let alone a woman—should ever be.

He took a step forward, knuckles blanching from the
tension he was applying to his pistol. His knee thudded against
the metal desk, which made a sound like a stone dropping into
the depths of a well.

Don't do it, jackass.

Jason Trapp had only survived this long by acting at all
times with cold precision. Perhaps it was a result of his horrific
childhood, but he could master his emotions like few others in
the world. It certainly wasn't healthy, but it was damn effective.
And yet in that moment it took everything he had not to burst
forward, kick down the door, and tackle Kim to the ground.

"She is your colleague, is she not?" Kim gloated. "Or
perhaps more than that? A friend? A *lover*?"

The man's words curdled like soured milk. Trapp's fingers stroked the trigger. It would take so little to put an end to this. A fraction of an inch.

And then a sound broke in the skies overhead that changed everything...

52

In the mountainous terrain the heavy rotorcraft were inaudible until they were almost on top of the North Korean camp. It was as though they were ghosts emerging from the fog. One moment the world was silent.

The next it exploded into life.

Trapp barely had a second to process this new piece of information before a naked demon burst through the doorway, a pistol in his hand. In the darkness, it was impossible to make out details, but as the banshee passed through a grate of light thrown from the shutters, he saw a deranged grin on the man's scarred face.

Involuntarily, the CIA operative took a step back. His finger began to retract on the trigger, but he stopped himself at the last moment. All hell might be about to break loose, but it hadn't happened yet. He couldn't risk firing a shot.

"Stay back!" Trapp yelled.

He pictured the room in his mind. It was rectangular, with a door at either end. One was the exit, the other led to Kim's sleeping quarters. The exit was nearest Trapp's current location, and the control unit. Between Kim and the end of the world lay half a dozen desks.

But a fraction of a second later, Trapp realized that the North Korean colonel was not aiming for the device. The man's target was...

Me.

In one fluid movement, Jason holstered his pistol and retrieved his fighting knife. He kept his body low so that Kim could not target him. Though he could not risk firing a shot, the North Korean was under no such restrictions. It was far from a fair fight.

Kim hurled a desk, his genitalia briefly lit up by a shaft of light. Trapp absently wondered if this was all just a dream. If he'd wake up and shake his head and blame too many drinks the night before.

But he knew that was not the case. And even as his mind wandered, he was already moving. He could not stay where he was, or Kim would be on him within seconds. He crawled low, using the desk for cover, and rolled behind the next in the row. He kept his body between Kim and the control unit at all times. If it came to it, he knew he would take a shot for that thing. He would have to.

Thunder crackled outside.

But Trapp knew that it was not the weather. It was an M-230 chain gun, capable of spewing six hundred rounds a minute out to a maximum range of over three miles.

"Come out!" Kim yelled. "Show yourself!"

His voice had taken on a manic edge. Trapp knew it well. It was the sound of a narcissist whose view of the world was meeting cold, hard reality. He clenched his free fist with satisfaction.

Trapp let out a low chuckle. Before it was done, he crawled to a fresh spot, briefly peeking out around the side of the desk covering his position. Kim was standing about ten yards distant, his feet shoulder width apart, arms trembling under the weight of a small pistol of a model which Trapp did not recognize.

"You brought them here," Kim said, his voice low and desperate. "You!"

No kidding, asshole.

Trapp did not mouth his response. Some things were better left unspoken. And this was one of them. The North Korean was working himself up into a frenzy that was clouding his judgment. And Jason Trapp was happy to take advantage. As the colonel smoldered, he moved.

He did so silently, like a jungle predator, his spectral eyes glinting as they passed through a ray of light shattered into pieces by the window shutters. And then he was on Kim, bursting upward, the darkened blade of his knife slicing the man's thigh from the crease of his hip to the top of his knee.

Blood started out. Hot, steaming, slippery, coating Trapp's hands.

He expected Kim to take a step backward, to collapse from the pain, but the man did nothing of the sort. He snarled, anger made more animal than human, and whipped the butt of his pistol round so fast Trapp had no time to duck.

The weapon collided with the CIA man's stolen helmet. The steel bucket wasn't padded, so while it absorbed the worst of the blow, Trapp's skull took the rest. He staggered back, half-stunned, as the weapon skittered harmlessly away, scraping against the concrete floor.

"Fuck," he groaned.

Trapp grimaced, setting his jaw and blinking as he attempted to regain control of his thoughts. Slowly, they came back. But the knife in his hand was gone, and in the darkness he could not see where it had fallen.

This would be old-fashioned, hand-to-hand combat.

And amazingly, the North Korean colonel was already limping toward him, blood dripping freely from the savage wound on his leg.

"My lucky day," Trapp muttered. Somehow he was going face-to-face with a psychopathic killer who looked like he was on bath salts.

He unclipped the helmet from his head, grasped it by the rim, and hefted it like a weapon. It was ungainly, round, but if it hit someone hard enough, it would do real damage. And since it was all Trapp had, he was prepared to make do.

"Come on then, you prick," he growled. "What are you waiting for?"

Kim's brown eyes were black in the darkness. His teeth flashed yellow as he dived for Trapp, bronzed skin stained dark with blood, a kaleidoscope of muted color. It was like a scene from a horror film.

Reactions still dulled by the blow to his head, Trapp was a second slow to respond. He swung the helmet, but it was still rising as Kim's fingers clutched his throat.

It hit the man.

But too late.

The North Korean's forward momentum collided with Trapp. Though the man was far shorter, and wiry—almost emaciated—his size was a poor guide to his strength. His fingers were locked around Trapp's throat in a death grip, and even as the CIA operative toppled backward, colliding with the desk and rolling to the side, Kim continued to rain down a relentless series of blows from his knees and legs.

Trapp was winded, but the fall dislodged Kim's grip on his neck for the briefest second. Enough to snatch a breath, to fill his lungs with badly needed oxygen, and to come up with a plan.

It didn't need to be complex.

Fight back.

Like the knife before it, Trapp's helmet was now gone. Kim's naked body lay against Trapp's chest, and the man attempted to lock him in a wrestling grip. But Trapp lashed out with an angry fist that collided with the colonel's temple, stunning him for long enough for the operative to scramble backward.

His heart was thundering, breath stolen from his impossibly fit body in the way that only combat can. Adrenaline flared through his veins, soothing his aches and pains and pushing him on. Trapp made enough room to stand up and pulled himself to his feet, adopting a crouched position. He could scarcely believe what he was seeing. Kim was like a rabid animal, his mouth snarling in a deranged grimace, anger burning in his eyes.

But Trapp knew that he had the advantage. Strong as his opponent was, he had eighty pounds on the man. Hand-to-hand combat has a remorseless logic.

Weight wins out.

Kim charged, and Trapp waited until the man was almost upon him before he lashed out once again, this time connecting with his stomach. The Korean barely seemed to feel the blow, firing a series of his own into Trapp's midsection.

The operative absorbed the strikes, but barely.

He started to reassess his original assessment.

The two combatants traded attacks for what felt like hours, but might only have been seconds. Kim struck, then Trapp fought back. Though the CIA man had power on his side, Kim fought with an intensity the likes of which Trapp had never seen. He seemed to be driven by a mad fury that blocked out pain and exhaustion and the ability to know when he was beaten.

Trapp knew he had to end this, fast, or the decision would be out of his hands.

Kim chopped out with his elbow, striking Trapp on the nose. It crunched, and broke. It wasn't for the first time, and probably wouldn't be the last.

But it was a shock nonetheless.

Trapp staggered backward, clutching his face with one hand. He wiped the blood, and resumed a fighting stance.

"Give up, American," Kim crowed. "You can't win."

The North Korean bobbed forward, bouncing from toe to toe on a wave of energy that Trapp certainly did not share. He thought he had won. Trapp stumbled backward, allowing the man to make ground on him.

Too much ground.

At least, for Kim.

The wiry predator burst forward, believing his prey was exhausted. He was wrong. Trapp exploded forward, his shoulder packed, leading with his fist in a blow powerful enough to stun an ox.

The diminutive Kim went down like a sack of potatoes, out cold.

"Says who?" Trapp grunted. He collapsed onto the ground, exhausted, knowing that if the fight had gone on another second, he would have lost.

Between his raised heartrate, the blood rushing in his ears, the sound of Kim's panting and the adrenaline foaming like beer in his veins, Trapp had no idea what was happening outside. The cavalry had arrived, but that did not mean they were winning.

An explosion ripped through the camp. It was so bright that for half a second, Trapp wondered if he had failed, and the nukes had started falling. The floodlights were knocked off-line, and even the computers around him stopped whirring— those that were not already shattered.

The sound of gunfire outside faded away.

Only to be replaced by another, even more worrying sound. A thudding, crunching noise that was close.

Too close.

Trapp swallowed, dragging his broken body backward. Someone was outside, and they were coming in — invitation or not. He attempted to grab his pistol, but the holster was empty. Somehow, it had been dislodged in the fight.

"Fuck."

Trapp glanced around. With the floodlights dead, it was almost impossible to see inside the office. But his eyes passed across the familiar shape. It was only a few feet away.

In the darkness, Trapp's fingers groped for the fallen pistol. Stretching, stretching, he found it. The model was unfamiliar—it must've been Kim's, dropped as he struck Trapp—but he did not care. He rolled over, his finger on the trigger, and raised the weapon with trembling fingers, too exhausted to even take cover.

The door shattered from the outside, splintered wood giving way in the face of an irresistible force. Barely a second later, with shards of timber still falling, and clouds of dust dancing in the rush of light from outside, the barrel of a weapon poked through.

Trapp made ready to fire.

This was it.

He knew that he could not last long. But he intended to go out in a blaze of glory.

And then he froze.

He recognized that weapon. It wasn't an AK-47, nor even the Type 58 knockoff. It was *American*.

Its owner leapt on to the desk that Trapp had left pushed against the door, face hidden by the scope of a pair of NVGs. When he spoke, the voice was familiar, like a stack of pancakes on a Sunday morning. Trapp let his aching head fall against the ground, and the pistol to his belly.

"Hey, Hangman." Nero grinned. "Heard you could use a little help."

53

Trapp staggered out of the North Korean office building, fell to his knees and splattered the concrete with a thin stream of vomit. It had been almost 24 hours since he'd last eaten, so the explosion had little substance. That didn't stop it from burning his throat as it rose.

"Nice to see you, too." Nero grinned, his teeth flashing in the darkness.

The Navy SEAL lieutenant held his weapon casually, as if entirely unconcerned by the battle raging all around. As Trapp glanced up, he could see it was just for show. The man's eyes never stopped moving, roving around the camp, taking in every possible threat.

Trapp knew that if one presented itself, the rifle would be up and at the man's shoulder before he could blink, the target eliminated before the soldier could consciously process the risk to his life. That's just the way the SEALs were made.

"Sorry," Trapp muttered, wiping his mouth clean. "Long day."

"I bet," Nero replied, slightly raising his voice to be heard over the sound of the fifty cal machine gun fire spewing from the tail ramp of one of the MV-22 Ospreys that was hovering overhead, laying down suppressive fire.

He jerked his thumb at the still unconscious body of Kim, whose feet were dragging against the ground, ankles and wrists cuffed together, being frog marched by a pair of pissed-off looking Marines. "What do you want us to do with him?"

Trapp's exhausted, befuddled mind took longer than he wanted to respond. Right now, all he wanted to do was throw in the towel, to return to Ikeda's side, and not leave until he'd sprung her from this hellhole.

But a higher power called: duty cutting through the tiredness. The satellite-killer control unit was now under the protection of the US Marines, and a technician from the *America* was even now working feverishly to disable the munitions in the skies overhead. That threat had been eliminated.

But a far larger one remained. The genetically targeted Marburg virus could not be allowed to be deployed. Once it began spreading in China, it would not stop. Hundreds of millions would die.

And then the missiles would start flying, as surely as night follows day.

Trapp wiped his face clean as rifle fire crackled all around him, the Marines making it patently clear that they did not intend to give up their beachhead. "Keep him alive, we need answers. Did anyone brief you on the virus?"

Nero nodded, indicating his protective hazmat suit, and the mask hanging loose around his neck. "Why do you think I'm wearing this piece of shit?"

The CIA operative sympathized. The protective suits were thick, heavy, and hot as hell. "Good." He glanced up at one of the navy helicopters circling overhead, occasionally laying down a burst of machine gun fire. "I need to borrow one of those, and a few of your men."

"Where you going?"

Trapp replied grimly, "I don't know yet."

"We got incoming!"

Trapp could not make out the source of the yelled warning, but he didn't need to. The cry was one that would chill the blood of anyone who'd ever spent time in the infantry. Like death, taxes and gonorrhea, the threat of airpower haunted every soldier's waking dreams.

"Fuck," he growled, glancing toward Lieutenant Quinn. "Nero—you bring any Stingers?"

The lieutenant crouched behind the limited cover provided by the nearest concrete wall. "On it," he muttered before murmuring instructions into his throat mic.

Trapp pressed his back against the same wall and beat the ground with frustration. He didn't have time for this. He needed to get moving. Every second he lingered was another those canisters got closer to China.

And then a second sense of creeping dread began to gnaw at his stomach. Five aircraft were circling overhead, low to the ground: three Ospreys, two helicopters. To the incoming North Korean fast movers, whose dull roar he could already hear rolling over the mountains, it would be like shooting fish in a barrel.

But the aviators' deaths were not what worried him. They knew what they had signed up for when they joined this mission. Their lives were forfeit the moment they crossed the border, just as his was. But he also knew that an op like this was the adrenaline rush of a lifetime. None of them would have willingly missed out.

No, Trapp's worry stemmed from the fact that if they lost those aircraft, his only way of making up ground on the canisters would go with them. So right now, the fate of the region—perhaps the entire world—rested in the hands of a couple of Navy SEALs equipped with Stinger surface-to-air missiles.

Nero pressed two fingers against his headset, listening intently. Then he yelled into his mic, "Boys—get down!"

Trapp followed the man's lead as he threw himself to the ground. His conscious mind wondered what the hell was going on, but he knew better than to question orders in a moment like that. A second's hesitation could cost him his life.

The roar overhead grew until it was like standing on the rim of a volcano. Trapp looked desperately up into the night sky, but saw nothing.

Almost nothing.

Four pinpricks of light exploded into the darkness, winking into existence side-by-side.

Missiles.

Trapp waited for the North Korean ordnance to rocket down to the ground, blowing him and every last one of the Marines into smithereens, and taking their rides out in the process.

But that's not what happened.

The missiles moved laterally, not vertically. They streaked through the darkness, burning a line onto Trapp's retinas like a long-exposure photograph.

And then it struck him. They were air-to-air missiles, not air-to-ground.

He pressed his palms against his ears, ready for the night sky to explode overhead, and rain down burning shards of American aircraft, detached rotors spinning through the sky and sending death where they landed.

But that's not what happened either.

Because when the missiles found their targets, four detonations blossomed in the dark skies overhead, briefly creating a second sun, and bathing the military encampment with light. Briefly, the ground fire stopped chattering as combatants on either side stared to the skies with awe.

The jet engine roar did not fade away. If anything, it only grew in intensity.

And when Trapp could almost not bear the sound any longer, a pair of F-35 fighter jets rocketed overhead, waggling their wings over the camp, moving almost too fast to be seen.

One of the SEALs, Homer, was the one who actually yelled it, but Trapp could not disagree. "Yee-haw!"

54

The blades of the MH-60 Knighthawk helicopter that had carried Lieutenant Quinn and his men into battle cut through the humid air over the Korean Peninsula. Inside was Jason Trapp and half a dozen of Nero's SEALs. The lieutenant himself had remained at the initial insertion site, entrusted by Trapp with two equally critical tasks: first, to secure Eliza Ikeda's safety; and second, to get the location of the Marburg canisters out of Kim by any means necessary.

Nero's men, their faces darkened by camouflage paint, barrels already warmed up by the assault on Unit 61's camp, wore grimly determined expressions. They knew how critical their task was. They knew, too, that their chances of success were low. A pair of F-35 Lightning fighter jets out of Osan Air Base were providing top cover overhead, protecting them from any further gun runs by the North Korean Air Force, but that was it.

Otherwise, they were on their own.

Trapp was dressed in an eclectic combination of North Korean battle fatigues, a US Marine helmet and radio system still stained with its former owner's blood, and the man's M4 carbine. The helmet was sitting on his lap, and over his ears he wore a headset that allowed him to communicate with the helicopter's crew.

"How we doing for fuel?" he inquired.

The copilot replied without turning around to face him. "A couple of hundred kilometers. We're riding heavy, and flying this low ain't doing shit for our fuel economy. The air's too thick."

Trapp detected a hint of strain in the man's voice. It didn't surprise him. What they were doing was crazy in anyone's book. If the lone Knighthawk suffered any form of mechanical failure, or encountered incoming ground fire, then they would be a hundred miles up shit creek without a paddle, with a million angry North Korean soldiers chasing after them like fire ants defending their nest.

Worse still, they had no idea where exactly they were heading. Trapp had given the pilots only the vaguest of directions—the North Korea/China border. They were less than thirty minutes' flight time out, and were still none the wiser as to the precise location of the canisters—or even whether all six were still at the same location.

"Understood. We gotta do what we gotta do, Lieutenant. If we have to ditch the bird, we will."

The prospect of escaping the country on foot wasn't exactly a promising one. Especially as North Korea's nearest neighbour was China, a country with whom, if this mission failed, they would most likely be at war.

Trapp's headset crackled. He recognized the sound of an external radio transmission, rather than the helicopter's crew intercom. "Spartan One-Niner, this is Osan Tower. How copy?"

"Lima Charles, Osan Tower," the pilot replied in a tone of absolute insouciance, meaning 'loud and clear.' His voice seemed entirely unaffected by the stress of the low-level night flight behind enemy lines.

"Spartan One-Niner, sorry to be the bearer of bad news, but we just picked up a hell of a lot of activity on the Chinese side of the border. Six J-20 jets are in the air, on a vector that has them crossing the border in under ninety seconds."

"Copy that, Osan Tower," the pilot replied, tone still unruffled. "Keep us in the loop."

"Will do, Spartan One-Niner. Good luck out there. Osan, out."

Trapp had listened to the exchange with growing unease which now blossomed into full-fledged anxiety. If those Chinese jets crossed the border, then this mission was about to get a whole lot more interesting. Hell, the J-20 Falcon Hawk jets were similar to American stealth fighters. They could sit well beyond visual range and fire off their loadout of air-to-air missiles, without their target even needing to be in sight.

And unfortunately for Trapp, the MH-60 Knighthawk made for one hell of an inviting target. The F-35s overhead would put up a fight, but they were heavily outnumbered, and by equivalent aircraft. There would be the only one outcome to this fight.

"What's the plan, boss?" the pilot asked.

Trapp thumbed his mic, glancing around at the SEALs, wondering what they were thinking. None betrayed a hint of emotion on their faces, but that didn't mean they weren't piss-scared. Did they regret joining him on a suicide run? It was impossible to say. And it didn't matter anyway. So he gave the only response he could. "We keep going. We don't have a choice."

"You got a location yet?"

Trapp grimaced. "Still working on it."

55

President Nash had returned to the White House situation room. The real-time visual display on the wall was now trained on the Korean Peninsula. Red icons representing several Chinese fighter jets had just crossed a dotted line that indicated the Chinese border with South Korea.

And they were headed directly for a trio of blue icons—three American aircraft. Two fighter jets and a helicopter.

This was it.

The moment of truth. If the Chinese opened fire, then it was all over. And worst of all, Nash knew that there was nothing he could do about it. He had played his cards. Done everything possible to avoid the outbreak of war. But would it be enough? It was impossible to say.

Nash's stomach fizzed with acid, making him glad he hadn't finished the rest of the cup of coffee that now sat sadly on the table in front of him, its porcelain walls dark with use. He gestured to the man who had accompanied him back from Dulles. "Mike—any update?"

Mike Mitchell looked up from a laptop that was balanced

precariously on a stack of open folders. His face was grim. "Nothing yet, sir. The Marines have secured the camp, and we have air superiority in the immediate area, so there's limited prospect of a North Korean counterattack. But the prisoner is not being cooperative."

Nash lashed the table with his open palm. "Dammit," he growled. "So those boys are flying to their deaths for nothing?"

Mitchell said nothing for a second, a look of sorrow flashing in his dark eyes. Nash remembered that he knew Trapp well. For him this wasn't just business, it was also deeply personal. "That's what they signed up for, sir. They knew the risks. And if there's a chance we can discover the location of those canisters, we'll need boots on the ground to take them down."

Nash ground his teeth together. He cast his mind back six months, to when he had met Jason Trapp for the first time, in a basement not all that far from this very room. He looked into the man's eyes then, thanked him for saving his life, and had seen nothing but cold resolve staring back. He knew that Trapp would have it no other way.

But the President also knew that it was in his power to save him. He could order that helicopter to change course, to head for safety. His was a unique power. A crippling burden.

A US Air Force technician spoke up, her voice cracking. "Mr. President, I've, uh, I've got Ambassador Lam on an encrypted line."

"Put him on, dammit," Nash growled.

He stared at the small black Cisco speaker on the center of the situation room's polished mahogany conference table, as though by doing so he might reveal some detail that would help him clean up this whole mess. It was at least better than staring at the map of North Korea, at the red and blue icons drawing inexorably closer together, presaging a crisis from which there would be no turning back.

The speaker crackled. "Mr. President—can you hear me?"

The audio quality was poor. Nash could instantly tell that the ambassador was speaking from inside the Chinese military transport plane—the roar of the jet engines in the background was unmistakable. "Crystal-clear, Ambassador," he said, attempting to keep the tension out of his voice. "We have a situation here—"

The Chinese ambassador's tone was urgent. He cut Nash off. "Sir, we verified the source of your information. We have the location of the biological weapon."

The President's heart stopped beating. His mouth went dry and he reached out for the stone-cold cup of coffee, swinging it down regardless of the taste. "Say again, Ambassador?"

"The canisters are sitting in a vehicle park, approximately 6 miles inside North Korea, over the border with the city of Dandong. We have a high-altitude drone circling the area now, and the trucks exactly match the images your CIA provided us with."

Nash glanced up at the screen. The Chinese jets had now crossed the border, and the blue icons, marking out the American aircraft, blinked ever closer. The image focused his mind. "That's fantastic news, Ambassador. What are your intentions?"

"Mr. President, I'm calling to request your help. My country is deploying its own special forces units as we speak, but they were"—he broke off—"positioned for a conflict on a different frontier."

President Nash knew what the man was talking about instantly, no matter how hard he had attempted to couch it in diplomatic language. 'A different frontier' was code for 'war with America.' A war, he hoped, that they might narrowly avoid.

"Ambassador Lam, your request is granted," he said. "We have a unit en route, ETA —" He looked up.

Mitchell mouthed, "*Nineteen minutes.*"

"— ETA under twenty minutes. If you can provide us with

the exact coordinates of those vehicles, I assure you that my country will do whatever it takes to prevent this threat to your people."

There was a long pause before the ambassador replied, punctuated only by the dull roar of the transport plane's heavy engines. "Thank you, Charles," Lam said softly. "I appreciate it. We are sending you the coordinates now."

Nash sagged with relief, but he knew his job was not yet done. "One last thing, Ambassador. Your Air Force —"

"Is there to support this operation," Lam interjected. "They have strict instructions not to harm your people."

"Thank you, Ambassador."

"No, Mr. President. Thank you."

As the call clicked off, Mitchell pumped his fist with satisfaction. "Mr. President—we got 'em."

56

The Knighthawk's crew was clearly uncomfortable with the presence of the Chinese fighter jets in the skies around them. Fifteen minutes had passed since Osan Tower first communicated the presence of this new force, and Spartan One-Niner was still flying, so Trapp considered that a fairly good outcome, all things considered.

In truth, he was shit scared.

He always was in the hours, minutes and seconds before going into battle. Perhaps other men felt no fear. Perhaps they managed to subsume that part of themselves, bury it deep within their consciousness.

Perhaps they were simply born different.

But Jason Trapp was not. His skills were not born of nature, but nurture. He didn't enjoy his fear, but he nonetheless welcomed it. It meant he was still alive.

It meant he hadn't yet screwed up.

That day would most likely come, Trapp knew. Special operators were a breed apart from ordinary fighters. But no one can put themselves into harm's way day after day, year after year and expect not to suffer the consequences.

So Trapp was scared. His senses were on high alert. The fear kept him sharp.

And perhaps it would keep him alive for one more day.

His headset crackled. "ETA four minutes," the pilot said. "We'll go in low and fast. Good luck, gentlemen."

The operation was shaping up to be a shit show. Modern military doctrine typically pushes leaders to hit a target hard without giving any defenders the opportunity to shoot back.

That would not be possible today. It was for a simple reason: like the control unit, the canisters could not be punctured. This close to the Chinese border, even an accidental release of the genetically-targeted Marburg virus would be disastrous.

Each of the men with Trapp knew that the night's operation had one simple commandment: that they were to only fire their weapon if they could be absolutely certain they would not hit a canister.

"See you all in hell," one of the SEALs drawled over the roar of the rotors, a sardonic grin on his face. If Trapp recalled correctly, his callsign was Homer. "You reckon the bad guys won't fire back neither?"

"It's *either*, ya dumb fuck," Santa muttered, shooting his buddy a wink.

"Guess we'll find out," one of his comrades muttered back, compulsively checking and rechecking his weaponry.

Each man had his own ritual in the face of combat. Trapp focused on his own. He mastered his breath, dragging in great soothing gulps of air, taking back control from the fear that threatened to paralyze him.

Before he knew it, the pilot was back on the intercom. "Sixty seconds."

In what seemed like an instant, they were there.

The helicopter burst over a line of trees and hovered over the target—a military vehicle park that was little more than a dirt parking lot with a gaggle of one-story wooden buildings at the northernmost end. The six trucks, immediately visible by their commercial livery, were parked in rows of two at the opposite end of the lot, and several more military open-topped six-ton trucks sat between the buildings and Trapp's target.

The thick black ropes dropped out of the sides of the Knighthawk, and before they even hit the ground, the first SEAL had jumped out after them.

"Go, go, go!"

The instruction was superfluous. Trapp barely heard it. He fast-roped to the ground, borrowed gloves saving his palms. His stomach had barely fallen out beneath him before his boots hit the deck and the stock of his M4 was pressed to his shoulder. The night vision goggles over his eyes bathed the world in a ghostly green glow.

Trapp came up in Delta, but he'd worked alongside SEALs many times before. He wouldn't say it out loud, but in the privacy of his own head he could admit they were at least up there with the best of the best. They moved through the night like jungle predators, practically sprinting toward their targets. A pair of them charged toward the row of military trucks, from where they intended to draw any fire that might emerge from the darkened buildings.

The CIA operative went straight for the nearest truck. Its canvas sides were tied down, fixed that way with rope.

The first gunshot split the night. The flash from the barrel of the SEALs' carbine lit the cab of another of the trucks and a strangled cry rose up from its inhabitant, audible even over the roar of the Knighthawk overhead.

Another trigger pull, and the cry winked out.

His headset crackled. "Tango down."

Trapp glanced up, and watched as the Knighthawk helicopter settled into position over the small collection of barracks buildings. He doubted that the North Koreans would be

equipped with any shoulder launched missiles, but an RPG
certainly wasn't out of the question. The chopper's crew were
taking a hell of a risk.

Another gunshot cracked into the night, and Trapp focused
on his mission. He pulled a knife from the holster on his thigh,
closed the distance to the truck in front of him, and slashed the
canvas. He took a pace back, returning the M4 to his shoulder,
and poked his head inside.

He saw a man looking back at him.

Shit.

"They're in the back of the trucks," he said urgently into his
throat mic. "I repeat, they've got men in the back of the trucks."

Trapp dared not use the carbine, not this close to the canister. The steel cylinder wasn't big, but still it dominated his
thoughts. But his opponent had no such compunctions. A
pistol flashed up, and barked twice, the lead rounds missing
Trapp's center mass by mere inches for the second time in one
night.

"Crap."

He threw himself left, dropping his M4 entirely and
switching the knife to his dominant right hand. The old line of
not bringing a knife to a gunfight ran through his head, but he
didn't have a choice. He rolled back to his feet and settled into a
crouching position, body pressed up against the truck's rearmost wheel.

His opponent's pistol revealed itself, poking through the
canvas. Trapp knew that he had one advantage that the other
man did not: night vision. Scuttling clouds obscured a half
moon overhead, and even this close to China there was little
light pollution. Trapp had the upper hand.

And he intended to use it.

He exploded upward, slashing at an exposed inch of wrist
with the wicked blade of his knife. The steel bit in, sending a
spray of arterial blood flying, and the pistol skittered harm-

lessly to the ground. Trapp winced, wondering if this would be his unlucky day, but the mechanism hit the dirt without loosing off a round.

Trapp never stopped moving.

With his free hand, he reached out and grabbed his opponent's bloodied wrist. The man's flesh was slick with hot fluid, but Trapp's gloves provided him the grip he needed. He yanked his arm back, pulling the man out of the truck and onto the ground. As his opponent hit the deck, he let out a bloodcurdling squeal of pain.

Trapp dived on to him, stabbing the knife down hard into the base of the man's throat, and driving the blade upward. The handle lodged in his chin, bouncing off bone. Blood spurted upward, soaking Trapp. He yanked the knife free, not needing to check whether the man was dead. That much was evident.

He wiped the blade against the fabric of his leg and returned to his crouching position, scanning the environment for targets.

But the world was quiet.

"Truck One, clear," his headset crackled, slightly quiet, since the speaker had dislodged from his ear in the scuffle.

"Two, ditto," came another calm voice.

Trapp unclipped his pistol from its holster and returned to the fray, clearing the last two trucks alongside a barrel-chested gunnery sergeant. The men inside the cabs had been taken out instantly, but only two of the freight compartments had contained enemy combatants: the one Trapp had taken down, and one other.

Both were equally dead.

"Santa," the gunnery sergeant growled into his radio, "how them buildings looking?"

"All clear, gunny," Santa replied, his voice accented with a melodious Hispanic twang. "I've got movement, but no one dumb enough to risk putting their head up."

"Roger," gunny replied. "Don't hesitate to light them up if you be needing to, now."

"You got it, boss," came the reply.

Trapp circled the trucks one last time, double-checking that no North Koreans had slipped through the net. As he did, his headset buzzed once again. "Ground team, this is Spartan One-Niner. We're picking up incoming. Choppers, looks like six of them."

Trapp keyed his mic. "Friendly?"

"Unclear."

"Great," he grumbled to himself. "Won't this day ever end?"

The helicopters came in fast and low, just as the Knighthawk had done on its own assault, their rotors beating an unfamiliar sound. They weren't American, that much was plain.

"Okay, ladies," Trapp said into his radio. "Tighten up on the trucks. We cannot allow these canisters to fall into enemy hands, understood?"

The question didn't really need asking. The looks of grim acceptance on the faces of the men around him said everything he needed to know. Whoever this new enemy was, they would meet the same deadly resistance as all those who had come before them.

Six helicopters broke into view and circled the lot.

Floodlights clicked on beneath the two choppers leading the formation, instantly blinding Trapp through the scope of his night vision goggles. He knocked them aside, fingers massaging the butt of his pistol.

A voice sounded over the radio in his ear. "We, uh, got a plan here?"

Trapp was almost ready to give the order to open fire when one of the helicopters did something unusual. It began to land. It didn't set down fast, as Trapp would have expected if this was an assault, ready to disgorge men onto the ground. It moved gracefully through the air, and when it landed it simply stayed there for a few seconds, as though waiting for a reaction.

"Hold fire," Trapp growled. "They might be friendly."

A man jumped out of the side of the helicopter. He was wearing dark green camouflage fatigues in an unfamiliar pattern and did not appear to be armed.

"I've got a shot," another voice informed him, before adding disdainfully, "Holding fire."

The man strode toward the small collection of trucks, a broad grin on his face. Trapp's forehead wrinkled. What the hell was going on?

"I think they're Chinese," one of the SEALs said, gazing up at the circling helicopters, with a hand shielding his eyes from the floodlights. "They're friendly."

The SEALs allowed the new arrival to approach, although their barrels never dipped, even as he closed on them. Trapp walked forward, careful not to block his men's fields of fire. He squinted at the guy, who had three silver stars on his shoulders, which Trapp thought he remembered meant he was a captain. "Can I help you?"

"We watch," the Chinese officer said in thickly accented English, a broad smile creasing his face. He gestured to the dark skies overhead. "From drone."

"You did, huh?" Trapp said, exhaustion beginning to settle in—along with a sense of appreciation for what they had accomplished. All he wanted right now was a beer. And a hot bath. And to get the hell out of this country with Ikeda in his arms, and never come back.

The Chinese army captain reached out with his hand, in a gesture that was familiar the world over. "Thank you," he said. "You protect my country."

Trapp shook the man's hand. It seemed like the right thing to do. "Any time."

57

President Nash sat behind the Resolute desk, toying with the Mont Blanc fountain pen that had been a tenth wedding anniversary gift from his wife. The high-stakes drama of the past week had driven the thought of what was facing him from his mind, but as the military situation pulled back from the brink, the weight on his mind returned.

It was a very different kind of burden—an ache of the soul, not a matter of state. And yet it was no less difficult for that. He'd spent twenty years of his life with one woman, and now that life was over. In truth, their marriage had been over for a couple of years, even if they were only formalizing it now. But that didn't make it any easier to come to terms with the fact that he was now alone. And for at least the next three and a half long years he was destined to remain that way.

After all, while the office of the presidency was one hell of a powerful aphrodisiac—perhaps the best icebreaker any man could ask for—it would also attract precisely the wrong kind of woman.

Nash tore open the envelope and pulled out a small stack of

papers. They were marked where he was supposed to initial and sign. He didn't bother reading them—they'd already been reviewed by his lawyers. He uncorked the pen, and the nib hovered over the desk for a few seconds before he scrawled his name freely wherever it was indicated. Strangely, a wave of relief washed over him as he did so.

When it was done, he buzzed Emma Martinez in. He needed to get rid of the papers before he had second thoughts.

"Mr. President?"

Nash sealed the papers in a fresh brown envelope and pushed it across his desk. "Emma—get this couriered over to my wife, will ya?"

Martinez picked up the envelope, holding it as though it contained a bomb. She knew exactly what was inside—her boss's divorce papers, and the obvious implication was that they were now signed.

"Yes, sir." She grimaced. "Do you... want to talk about it?"

Nash raised his eyebrow. In truth, he felt more relaxed now than he had in months. The knowledge of what he had to do had hovered over him all that time like a dark cloud, and now it was gone.

"Let's not go there, Emma." He grinned.

"No, Mr. President," Martinez said, shaking her head with obvious relief. "And sir—you've got Mike Mitchell on the secure line."

"Thank you, Emma," Nash said.

He waited for his chief of staff to leave the room before glancing at the secure telephone handset on his desk. A red light blinked over the button that indicated line one. He punched it and picked up the phone. "Mike," he said in a tone of genuine satisfaction. "How you doing?"

"Very well, Mr. President. And yourself?"

"Slept like a baby," Nash chuckled. "I spoke to Premier Wang this morning, and he expressed his gratitude for our role in cleaning up this mess. I wanted to pass those congratulations on to you. You did good, Mike. And so did Jason."

"Thank you, sir."

Nash paused, and his tone grew colder as he thought of the man who had caused him so much stress—and far more importantly, cost the lives of innocent Americans. "Tell me Mike, how is our friend?"

Mitchell cleared his throat. "Mr. President, I think this is one of those situations —"

"Mike," Nash chided. "If you're about to try and keep me insulated from the political fallout, then I'll advise you to hold your tongue. I want to know what you're doing with him, and I want to know now."

"Yes sir. As we speak, Colonel Kim is on an Agency jet heading for a black site in the Philippines. We have interrogators standing by to squeeze him until his pips squeak."

Nash squeezed his fist tight, grinding the base into his desk. Later that day, he was due at Andrews Air Force Base to receive the bodies—what little had been recovered—of the naval helicopter crew that had died when the Chinese jets buzzed the USS Nimitz. He would console widows and parents, see the grief on the faces of children who did not yet know what they had lost. They might well blame him, and that would be fine. It came with the job. But he wanted to be able to look them in the eye and tell them that the man responsible for their pain had paid with his life.

The President made his decision, and spoke with cold determination. "He died in the assault on Camp 61, Mike. Is that clear?"

Mitchell paused to take on board his President's instruction. Nash wondered if the man would push back. After all, killing a prisoner—no matter how vile an individual—without a trial was far from legal. But in the president's view, it was justice of an old-fashioned kind, and the only kind that Kim deserved.

And Mitchell agreed. His tone was laced with quiet approval. "Understood, Mr. President. I'll make the arrangements when my men are finished with him."

"Thank you Mike," Nash said. "That will be all." He put down the phone.

President Nash leaned back in his chair and contemplated what he had just ordered—a cold-blooded execution. It went against everything he had once believed in. But six months in the job had taught him that while sometimes, as with Ambassador Lam, diplomacy was necessary, there were other times when might was the only thing that sufficed.

This was one of those times.

And if he ordered men and women like Jason Trapp and Eliza Ikeda into harm's way, then the least he could do was share the hard decisions that had to be taken to keep the country safe. Nash settled back and decided that on this occasion, he wouldn't lose any sleep over it.

EPILOGUE

3
6 hours later
USS America
Sea of Japan

JASON TRAPP STOOD on the deck of the USS America, hands resting gently on his hips, and gazed out into the horizon. He wore borrowed combat pants with a desert camouflage print, tan boots, and an olive T-shirt with US MARINES stenciled in black over his breast.

Trapp was a product of the Green Machine. He wasn't a Marine. Never had been, never would be. But the fine men of Charlie Company had pulled his bacon out of the fire and helped pull the world's only two superpowers back from the brink of war. So he figured it wouldn't do any harm to play dress-up.

But only this once.

The Sea of Japan was still, and a red glow hugged the horizon, heralding fine weather in store the next day. But though

Trapp's eyes were fixed on to the middle distance, he wasn't admiring the view. He was searching for something.

Some*one*.

The smell of aviation gas carried on a light breeze, tickling Trapp's nostrils. He barely noticed it as his eyes flickered, his mind working overtime to determine whether the smudged speck on the horizon was what he was looking for. He never blinked as the aircraft hove into view.

The Chinook flew low over the surface of the ocean, flanked on either side by a pair of Viper attack helicopters. The Bell AH-1Z choppers looked like gnats, but they packed a hell of a punch. Trapp was glad of it. The cargo in the belly of the hulking great Chinook transport helicopter was special.

After what Eliza Ikeda had been through, that protection was the least her country could offer. If Trapp was any judge, it would take her a long time to recover. Not just from her physical wounds, but the mental scars, too. She'd survived the kind of horrors that few could contemplate, let alone live through.

Ikeda was as hard as any operative he'd ever worked with. But only time would tell if she'd come out of the cauldron of hell stronger for her experience. There would be no shame in throwing in the towel after what she'd been through. Trapp sure as hell wouldn't blame her.

A small group of Marines and sailors had gathered on the flight deck, near Trapp, matching his silent vigil. One of them, a young man with tousled ginger hair, turned to him. "You need any help, sir?"

Trapp shook his head absently. "I'm good."

"Thanks. For what you did out there."

Trapp turned and noticed for the first time that the eyes of the assembled group were on him, rather than the middle distance. He didn't know how long that had been the case, but it made him uncomfortable. He was used to blending into the shadows, not becoming the center of attention. He cleared his throat, somewhat self-consciously. "Forget about it."

The kid who had spoken up, a Marine who didn't look much older than twenty, fixed him with the kind of serious gaze that only the young can pull off without embarrassment. "I mean it, sir. We all do."

The Marine, a lance corporal, took a half step back and peeled up a crisp salute. He held Trapp's gaze with a fierce intensity that took the CIA operative aback. That emotion was doubled when, in turn, like a flock of gulls bursting into flight, the small gaggle of military personnel behind the Marine joined suit.

Trapp didn't know how to respond. He had a decade on most of them, almost two on some. But each shared an expression of powerful honesty—an admiration that left him feeling as uncomfortable as it did proud. An unaccustomed choking sensation made its presence known in his throat, rendering speech almost impossible.

But he had to say something. "Thank you, Corporal. I mean it."

Thankfully, the spell was broken by the Chinook's heavy blades tearing the air asunder. Trapp's gaze snapped instantly back to the ocean, where he saw the two Vipers hanging back and the huge transport chopper coming in to land.

Half a dozen navy corpsmen appeared on deck, wearing high-visibility neon vests that warned of their presence like a fire engine klaxon. They hung back in a tight group, waiting to pounce the second the Chinook had touched down.

The second the enormous helicopter's wheels hit the deck, its ramp began to lower. Trapp knew that he should let the corpsmen do their job, but he couldn't help himself. His legs propelled him without any conscious thought, and he found himself waiting at the foot of the ramp, hanging back as the corpsmen jogged up it, their boots tramping against the heavy metal.

As the rotors were still turning, the Chinook began to disgorge its cargo. A single individual, Eliza Ikeda, wrapped in a device that looked like it had arrived straight off the set of a science-fiction film. It was a hazmat gurney, a fully self-contained unit with its own air supply, designed to transport individuals exposed to biological or chemical contaminants.

Ikeda certainly qualified. Though the modified Marburg virus, now beginning to be referred to as MAR-G, or Marburg Genetic, was not targeting her cells, she was still a carrier. She would be in isolation until the doctors completely cleared her of infection. That might take weeks. Ikeda, the distance-swimming, triathlon-competing health nut would almost certainly be driven half-mad by her confinement.

But the alternative was far worse. Trapp knew she would understand, as much as she might rail against the decision. The risk of transmission was simply too great. That was why she was out here, on the *America*, in the middle of the ocean, on a vessel that was already steaming away from the Asia-Pacific, the other three American hostages already safely aboard, and receiving treatment in the decks below.

It was a firewall made of water.

As the gurney made its way to the bottom of the ramp, carried by four Marines, it stopped in front of Trapp. He was in the way, but no one was about to steal him of his moment. He grinned, placing his hand on the plastic shell of Ikeda's gurney. "How you doin'?"

The hardy operative's pupils were dilated when they met his, evidence of a mild sedation that was about as far as the navy corpsmen had managed to get in their efforts to give her medical attention, given the hazmat restrictions. She would be treated on board. The best doctors in the navy were already on their way. Trapp had made sure of it.

"Joey," Ikeda said, her voice barely over a whisper, but a smile crossing her dazed face. Her slate gray eyes flashed up at him, hungry with recognition. "You made it."

Trapp's forehead wrinkled with confusion. "Huh?"

"It's from Friends, dummy."

The weathered CIA operative cracked a grin, a real one this time, a look of unadulterated relief crossing his tanned face, handsome even with his nose still swollen from the impact it had taken a couple of days prior. He didn't know why he cared for this woman so deeply. In truth, he scarcely knew her: just a swim in the bathtub sea off the coast of Hong Kong, then a mission blown to all hell.

But Trapp had invested so much in getting her back, he felt bound to her. Like he knew her on a deeper level than seemed possible, given the brief time they'd shared. Like soldiers in a foxhole, the pair of them had lived through a trauma, and come out whole on the other side.

"Never watched it," he admitted.

Ikeda pouted, her hand haltingly, jerkily rising to meet his. She was weighed down by exhaustion, but fought through it. "That'll cost you."

"How much?"

"Ten points."

"How do I pay?"

She grinned, but even as she did so, her eyes began to close, lids drooping heavily. "You'll have to wait to find out..."

Like a child, Ikeda fell asleep mid-conversation, her arm dropping gently to her side. One of the navy corpsmen cleared his throat half-heartedly, clearly not wanting to interrupt, but knowing it was his duty. "Um, sir—the doc's waiting..."

Trapp glanced up and saw four Marines doing anything and everything possible to avoid meeting his eye, a pale pink decorating their tanned cheeks, and a pair of navy corpsmen chewing their cheeks as they fought competing desires: on the one hand, to avoid offending a man they considered a true blue American hero, on the other their duty to their patient.

And as it should, the latter won out.

"You got it," he muttered, patting Ikeda's gurney one last time. For luck. "Take care of her, now."

"We will, sir."

Trapp watched as the procession went on without him. He felt at a loss as the flight deck scurried into action around him, preparing to land the two Vipers. Everyone had a duty, a role to play.

Everyone except him.

For once, he was useless. And for now, at least, Trapp realized he didn't mind it that way. He could use the rest. It had been a long time since he'd had any. Maybe once this was all over, the debriefs done, the medals handed out, Eliza Ikeda given a clean bill of health, they could go somewhere quiet and forget that any of this had ever happened.

Trapp grinned ruefully. Maybe he was getting ahead of himself.

But he hoped not.

ALSO BY JACK SLATER

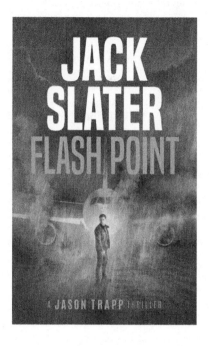

A Russian S-400 surface-to-air missile system takes down a passenger jetliner in the skies over Belarus, showering the fields below in burning scrap.

As the world begins to mourn the horrific accident, one man—new CIA director, George Lawrence—knows it is anything but. Three hundred innocents were sacrificed in order to snuff out the life of one man: Professor Alexey Sokolov, a senior adviser to the Russian government. As well as a CIA asset recruited by a ghost known as the Hangman... Trapp doesn't know any of this. He's hundreds of miles away in rural Tuscany with Eliza Ikeda, and on a mission of his own: recovery. Both are hurting, but this is their chance at a real life. Together.

But it doesn't take long for trouble to arrive at their door. He should have known that his past wouldn't let go that easily. The question is: why did Sokolov run? How did the Russians discover who he truly was—and what secret could possibly justify the murder of three hundred innocent men, women and children to cover up?

Trapp doesn't want to know. But he sure as hell intends to find out...

Head to Amazon to read Flash Point, book three in the *Jason Trapp* thriller series.

FALSE FLAG AUDIOBOOK

False Flag audiobook is out now! Scan the code above to go
straight to Audible.

FOR ALL THE LATEST NEWS

I hope you enjoyed False Flag. If you did, and don't fancy sifting through thousands of books on Amazon and leaving your next great read to chance, then sign up to my mailing list and be the first to hear when I release a new book.

Visit - www.jack-slater.com/updates

And keep reading if you want to learn more about the real-life inspiration that led me to write *False Flag*...

Thanks so much for reading!

Jack.

AUTHOR'S NOTE

Thanks for making it to the end of my second Jason Trapp novel! If you've got this far, then I guess I must be doing something right...

I think the further I explore Jason's character, the more complicated his life gets! At the beginning of *Dark State*, he was hurting, but he had a simple mission: make things right with his former partner's brother, Joshua Price, and then inflict revenge on the man that Trapp thought was responsible for his best friend's death. Obviously things didn't work out that way—and in that characteristic way he seems to, Trapp stumbled into a pretty cataclysmic plot to bring down the democratic system of government of the United States of America.

By the end of the book, he discovers that the world wasn't quite the way he thought it was. He changes, but he gets revenge on the man ultimately responsible for Ryan's death—the vice president, Robert Jenkins.

This bleeds into the beginning of *False Flag*, a little bit: Jason is on a mission to tie up the last loose ends left at the end of *Dark State*. But throughout the start of the book, he's wondering whether he even wants to live this life anymore.

He's given his country some of the best years of his life—perhaps it's time to retire. Let someone else take up the fight. And besides, previously it was always him and his partner against the world. Now, it's not so easy. Without someone he trusts by his side, Trapp begins to question who he's fighting for.

I guess that's where Eliza Ikeda steps in. She had a tough time of it in this book, but I'm looking forward to seeing her flourish as I continue the series.

So—how real are the scenarios I talk about in *False Flag*?

As far as the North Korean angle goes, I've actually stolen more from real life than you might believe. Unit 61 doesn't exist —at least, as far as I know, and to my knowledge, there aren't any evil recruiters going around labor camps in the mountains north of Pyongyang, and making children execute their own parents...

But much of what I described as occurring in that camp does, in fact, happen in real life. North Korea's labor camps are probably the closest facsimile of a Nazi concentration camp we have in the modern world. In the West, our awareness of these horrific places is somewhat limited—we can see them from above, with satellites (thankfully not blown up!), and we have accounts from former prisoners who have managed to escape, or who were released and then defected into South Korea or China.

Prisoners live in 500 ft.² huts, with thirty or forty individuals crammed into that tiny space. The barracks are not heated in winter, during which temperatures go below -4°F (-20°C) outside. As a result, most prisoners get frostbite, along with a variety of other diseases for which they do not receive treatment. When they finally succumb to their illnesses, they are buried naked, the very clothes from their back stripped by their desperate comrades. They are fed two hundred grams of corn gruel three times daily. No meat, no vegetables, nothing of any substance, and on these meager rations they are expected to work sixteen hour shifts every day.

Many drop dead from sheer exhaustion.

It is believed that 40% of all political prisoners in these camps die from malnutrition. One defector estimated in the late 1990s that 20% of prisoners in his camp, Daesuk-ri, died in any given year from starvation.

In 1987, there was a riot in Camp 12 that was brutally suppressed, leaving over five thousand dead. In North Korea, if you commit a crime against the government, or are even seen as "undesirable", it's not just you who is sent to the camps. It's two entire generations of your family. Just imagine that. I hope I managed to convey some of the horror of these terrible places, without descending into gratuitous descriptions of violence. It's a difficult balance to strike, and I try and stay on the right side of that line. As always, I'm happy for you to get in touch and tell me if you think I managed to strike it correctly.

As far as the broader plot, much of this is taken from real life. That holds true from even very small points, such as Trapp not wanting to contact Langley using a non-secure computer connection. It is in fact believed to be the case that from 2010 onward, over a period of two years, the Chinese Ministry of State Security killed or imprisoned more than a dozen CIA sources and assets within China, hamstringing US intelligence gathering in the region to this day. A New York Times report described the intelligence breach as "one of the worst in decades", and also described how "according to three officials, one [source] was shot in front of his colleagues in the courtyard of the government building—a message to others who might have been working for the CIA."

Brutal.

For a long time, the Agency had no idea how the Chinese managed to roll up their network of spies within China. It is now believed that the MSS managed to penetrate the covert dead drop system the CIA used to communicate with its assets, just as I wrote in *False Flag*.

As far as the military balance between China and America goes, it's definitely fair to say that China remains a long way behind the US—but the gap is closing, and closing fast. In 2018, the Chinese defense budget was around $250 billion, compared with US spending of $639 billion.

Now, there are a couple of issues that make a straight-up comparison between the two numbers difficult to make. First of all, a dollar spent in China goes a lot further than that same dollar would in the US. Labor is cheaper, land is cheaper, and there's a massive industrial base. So the Chinese defense budget, while significantly smaller, is probably much closer to parity than you would imagine just from looking at the numbers.

The Chinese Communist Party derives much of its legitimacy from something known as the "century of humiliation". Few Americans know this, but starting in the nineteenth century, America and other Western powers began to significantly exploit China. In 1900, a secret Chinese organization marvelously known as the Society of the Righteous and Harmonious Fists, lead an uprising against the Western and Japanese influence efforts. It was known as the Boxer rebellion —and was eventually put down by a force of international troops, including American soldiers. Chinese forts were sacked, and the rebels were executed.

(Forgive the history lesson!)

The Chinese, understandably, don't remember this time too fondly. It's linked in their minds with the later Japanese invasion which was extremely sadistic and brutal, and in popular memory it's kind of a nadir, from which modern China's meteoric rise is even more astonishing.

All this is a long-winded way of explaining China's current military doctrine. It's built around denying America (and everyone else) freedom of access to the seas around China, and thus protect their homeland from any further such humiliation. They have focused huge amounts of money on "asymmetric" weapons, including anti-satellite weaponry very similar to the types I described in the novel, as well as a huge investment in missile tech.

Both of those work hand-in-hand with each other. The American military advantage is that we can put an aircraft carrier—basically a chunk of sovereign US territory—a couple of hundred miles off the coast of any country in the world, and bomb them back into the Stone Age. Combine that with the massive US edge in satellite surveillance and guidance, there's nowhere for an enemy to hide, and a GPS-guided bomb or cruise missile can be dropped directly on their position.

But what the Chinese have done is build up a missile force that is more than capable of "area denial". If it came to conflict, I think the U.S. Navy would be extremely wary of actually deploying any ships anywhere close to China, because it only takes one missile to get through to send a hull to the bottom of the ocean, and the Chinese have thousands.

If the US military lost their surveillance advantage as well—and it's relatively difficult to create defensive countermeasures for an orbital satellite—then any military response becomes much more difficult, especially since China would be operating in their own backyard, and America thousands of miles from home.

Finally—because I realize I'm droning on—ethnic bioweapons. Do they, or could they, really exist?

In short, yes. A 2004 report by the British Medical Association suggested that "hundreds, possibly thousands, of target sequences for ethnic specific weapons do exist. It appears that ethnic specific biological weapons may indeed become possible in the near future."

Now, it's very unlikely that any individual weapon would be

a hundred percent accurate, since there is no 100% correlation between race and genes. But what would certainly be possible is creating a virus that preferentially targeted ethnic Chinese, as opposed to Caucasians, for example. Caucasians would still die, but at lower rates than the target population. I took a little bit of artistic license making it more accurate in fiction than it might be in real life.

But who knows what the future holds...

Anyway, as always I would love to hear from you about whether you liked the book whether that's in the form of a review (shameless plug—if there's one thing that will help me write the next book faster, it's getting a gleaming five-star review on my sales page), or via email.

You can get in touch with me at Jack@Jack-Slater.com. I do my best to answer every email that comes in, and I love hearing from you guys!

Specifically, I'd love to know whether these author's notes are worth doing. I enjoy writing them—usually when I'm floundering through a stretch of writer's block—but I have no idea if anyone actually reads them... So if anyone *has* read this far, then shoot me a message to let me know I'm not shouting into the void!

Finally, if you haven't joined already, then why not head to www.Jack-Slater.com/updates to sign up to my mailing list. I won't be emailing you every other day, or even every other week, only when I have a new release—mainly because I'm too lazy and introverted to want to bother doing it any more frequently than that!

I'm about half way through a novella that delves into Trapp's early days with the Central Intelligence Agency, fighting alongside his dead partner, Ryan Price. I'll be emailing it for free to every subscriber once it's finished and edited, but it won't be available in the Kindle store — so the only way to get your hands on it is to sign up...